THE
BELLE AND
THE
BLACKBIRD

THE BOOK OF ALL THINGS

USA TODAY BESTSELLING AUTHOR
SARAH M. CRADIT

ISBN: 978-1-958744-35-2

Cover and Interior Design by The Illustrated Author Design Services
Map by The Illustrated Author Design Services
Hardcover Art ("The Observatory") by Alexandra Curte
Anastazja and Tyreste Portraits by Ivy Gwendolline
"What You Do To Me" by Nora Adamszki of Adamszki Art
Editing by Novel Nurse Editing

Publisher Contact:
sarah@sarahmcradit.com
www.sarahmcradit.com

SARAH M CRADIT

WEAVER of WORLDS

For all those who have gone up the mountain
to return better, stronger.

PRAISE FOR
THE BELLE AND THE BLACKBIRD

"Wow! Cradit has done it again!! Ana's journey is dark, twisted, and full of surprises. And Tyr is a tortured hero who is both delicious and compelling. What an unbelievable ride!"
~Elle Madison, USA Today Bestselling Author of The Lochlann Feuds

"The Belle and the Blackbird is a gorgeous unraveling of a fantasy romance with dire twists and a love worth bursting into flames to defend!"
~Casey L. Bond, author of Where Oceans Burn

"I am in love with this retelling and literally adore each and every character here. A must, must-read book."
~Anshul (@stories.buddy)

"The way Sarah brought so many of the different storylines from The Book of All Things series together. Tied them all together so beautifully to further along a bigger plot that unites them all, all characters & all journeys. This was a perfect addition to the series and I cannot wait to see what other incredible stories Sarah will continue to create!"
~Pia (pias_bookshelf)

"When two worlds collide you don't expect the implosion that these two provide. Sarah really blew me away with the enticing love story of people who just need something to go right."
~@BearkodaReads

INTRODUCTION

There exists a kingdom set upon an isle, surrounded by a sea no one has ever traveled beyond. The Kingdom of the White Sea it is called, or simply the kingdom, for they have no other name for it.

The individual Reaches—Northerlands, Southerlands, Westerlands, and Easterlands—once ruled themselves. Two centuries past, the Rhiagains washed upon their shores, claiming to be gods. From gods, they became kings.

Carrow, the first king of the White Kingdom, built his reign on the false promise of respect for the culture his people usurped. Within ten years he'd already broken this promise, raising arms to quash all opposition to his increasingly totalitarian reign. Among the worst of his crimes became known to the broader kingdom as the Great Massacre. To those left behind in the wake of his cruel genocide, the Vjestik of Witchwood Cross, it would forevermore be *Nok Mora*.

The Nightmare.

But terrible endings spawn unforeseen beginnings. A decade after Nok Mora, Drazhan Wynter, the grieving heir of the Vjestik, traveled to Duncarrow in a bid for revenge, intent on crushing Carrow and the crown, and instead fell dangerously in love with the young princess, Imryll of Glaisgain. This love began a new era for the Vjestik, mingling powerful bloodlines and rare magic and birthing a resilient dynasty.

Over two hundred years later, Anastazja Wynter is the current heir of the Vjestik. She was born second, but a tragedy made her first. This inheritance is about more than who rules Fanghelm

Keep; it comes with rare magic so coveted, she can't safely travel beyond the borders of Witchwood Cross.

The biggest danger, however, comes from within. When Ana was still a little girl, a cunning woman came to Fanghelm. Magda proved herself an invaluable counselor to the steward, who was soon after unexpectedly widowed, and bewitched him into marriage with a solemn vow to look after his three children. One child in particular.

Magda has had designs on Ana since long before she was born. She's been patient, biding her time, waiting for Ana to come into the powers she was destined to have—powers Magda needs for her disturbingly dark dealings with the raven priests and priestesses of the mountains, the Ravenwoods.

Ana, isolated from her beloved father and twin brother, carries a terrible burden. To confide in the one person she trusts enough to tell—a pubkeep named Tyreste Penhallow—would all but assure his death. Their lustful escapes were never meant to become love, for everyone Ana loves becomes another tool for Magda to wield against her. No one who loves Ana, least of all the boy she unintentionally gave her whole heart to, is safe.

Tyreste knows none of the horrors Ana faces when she returns home at the end of the day. For two years, he's studied every curve and valley of Ana's body, desperate to know the curves and valleys of her soul as well, but her life beyond the four walls of his bedchamber is a void she's not let him enter. Her highborn blood makes her unattainable, but her secrets are the real chasm between them.

He has his own secrets, a dark past that haunts him. Translating rare documents by moonlight should be an escape, but it only pulls him further into the dark enigmas of the kingdom, ones intended to be and stay buried.

Soon a stack of letters will enter his life. The depravity within them will rock him to his core. The desperate correspondence reveals a truth so terrible, he'll break his own vow of neutrality, racing time and fear to find a way to stop the malevolence spreading across the icy mountains in the far north of the kingdom.

A malevolence that lives in Ana's home, twisting the minds and hearts of her loved ones and playing a game of gods and monsters with the ravens in the mountains.

A malevolence that began thousands of years ago, in a world beyond their own.

Within her, Anastazja has the power to defeat this evil, but she lacks the knowledge to harness it.

Through the letters that will consume his life, Tyreste has the knowledge, but it's useless without the power.

Only together can Anastazja and Tyreste end the terror that has gripped the Vjestik and the Ravenwoods for centuries.

Fear, heartbreak, and a helping of dark magic has torn these lovers apart.

Fate demands a foe more formidable, more powerful than all of it combined to unite them once more.

Forgiveness.

FANGHELM KEEP

Village
Witchwood Cross, Northerlands

Steward & Stewardess
Arkhady & Magda Wynter
Ksana Arsenyev (first wife, deceased)

Steward's Children
Stepan (deceased), 24
Anastazja "Ana" (twin), 20
Nikolaj "Niko" (twin), 20

Others at Fanghelm
Grigor Arsenyev (younger brother of Ksana)
Ludya (vedhma)
Lenik (vodzhae)
Feyhan (vodzhae)

The Kyschun
Mishka Petrovash (head kyschun)
Olek Petrovash (brother of Mishka)
Raisa Petrovash (daughter of Mishka)

Notable Wynters and Glaisgains of the Past
Steward Drazhan Wynter and Stewardess Imryll of Glaisgain
Steward Aleksy Wynter (son of Drazhan and Imryll)
Lady Zofia "Zo" Wynter & Lord Torrin Dereham (daughter and
son-in-law of Aleksy)
Duke Octavyen of Glaisgain and Duchess Aloysha of Dhovaeys
(brother and sister-in-law of Imryll)
Paeris "Par" of Glaisgain (grandson of Octavyen and Aloysha)

TAVERN AT THE TOP OF THE WORLD

Village
Witchwood Cross, Northerlands

Proprietors
Olov and Fransiska Penhallow

Penhallows
Pernilla, 26 & husband Drago Barynov
Tyreste "Tyr," 24
Agnes, 23 & fiancé Francisz Stojan
Rikard, 19 & wife Faustina Belzykh
Evert, 18
Adeline, 15

& Rikard the Mouser

MIDNIGHT CREST

Keep
The Rookery

High Priestess
Elyria Ravenwood

Other Ravenwoods
Raelyria Ravenwood, 14
Varradyn Ravenwood, 18

VJESTIK TRANSLATIONS

ahen vodah: "fire water" / hot springs

dobranok: Goodnight

dobryzen: Good morning

frata: Brother

grimizhna tea: contraceptive drink

hej: (greeting) hello

hejka: (parting) good-bye

hvala: thanks/gratitude

kahk si: (greeting) How are you?

koldyna: pejorative term meaning "evil witch who communes with demons"

kyschuna/kyschun: archivists, keepers of histories and storytelling

nien: no/negative

Nok Mora: The Nightmare, referring to the massacre on their people led by Carrow Rhiagain

oma: mother

onkel: uncle

opros: sorry

ota: father

pjika: (term of endearment) bird

pros: please

stranjak: (friendly term) outsider / anyone who doesn't have Vjestik heritage

tak: yes/affirmative

uljez: (pejorative term) outsiders who are not friendly

vedhma/veduhn: shaman/diviner

Vjestik: traveler community of witches who immigrated to Witchwood Cross hundreds of years ago

Vjestikaan: old language of the Vjestik

volemthe: love / I love you

vozhdae: spiritualists assigned to male leaders
vozhd: assembly of the vozhdae
Vuk od Varem: Season of the Wulf
zolvha: spiritual adviser
zydolny: "the touch"

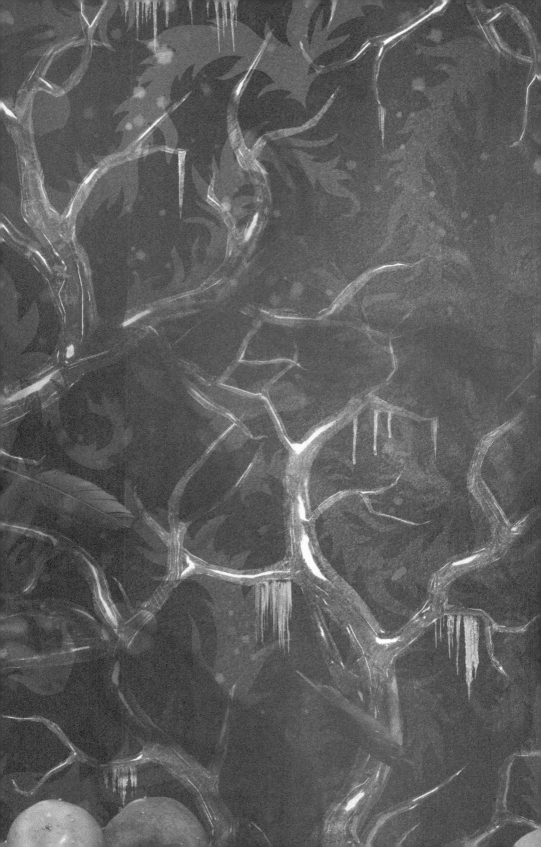

DEMONS DEAL IN DARKER DENOUEMENTS

ONE

ONLY BLACKBIRDS SING ALONE

Tyreste Penhallow's face buried between her legs as he voraciously devoured her, body and soul, was Anastazja's favorite escape.

His skilled tongue was a virtuoso, conducting its masterpiece.

The symphony of desserts was designed to leave her dangling along the narrow precipice between joy and agony.

Though his greatest ability—his *true* power—was the way he made her forget.

Tyreste hooked his thumbs inside her, spreading her until she felt the sharp tug of flesh, the first whisper of pain. His modest cabin at the forest's edge had always had an icy nip in the air, which he claimed heightened her need. She couldn't say if it made a difference or not, because around Tyreste, she lived in a constant, relentless state of need.

Rising moans hummed against her tender core, sending her clawing farther up the table, her toes and fingers curling against the wood. She never wanted to come down. To *crash*. Those moments were the only ones when she still felt alive. When her ragged, strained breaths were evidence she was real and her pleasures were hers to take and give. When none of the rest had ever happened, or ever would.

A sudden, delicious shock of pleasure caught Anastazja off guard. She pitched forward on the table, her head thrown back in ecstasy, earning a splinter in her ass for her excitement. She didn't muffle her screams; Tyreste loved the sound of her coming undone. He'd more than earned every desperate moan and whimper.

Just as she was cresting, he freed his thumbs and thrust three fingers inside her, right as her muscles clamped hard, fighting his intrusion. His shoulders strained as he bore down, his fingers dug deep, clashing against the tumultuous waves of her release. Every one lasted longer than the one before but never, ever long enough.

When Tyreste withdrew his hand—an agonizing retreat she could hear as much as feel—Anastazja collapsed onto the wood. She slowed her labored breaths, resisting the inexorable return to reality.

Tyreste came up from where he'd been crouched, his eyes dancing with devilry, and before she could breathe out, he'd come over her like a ravenous predator and filled her full with his cock.

"You're so fucking beautiful when you come." He grunted, slamming into her and driving more splinters into her flesh, drawing blood. She relished each stab of pain. Only the living bled, and it meant she was still alive.

Tyreste looped an arm under one of her legs and fastened it beside her head. He slowly pushed all the way in, mischief dazzling his gaze as he watched her react to how hard and swollen he was after hours of play—how deep he could go. The first time he'd done it, she'd walked away with bruises—ones she could see, and ones she could not—but she craved the pain the way she needed air to breathe.

Pain was living too.

Tyreste's wet hand circled her ankle. His fingers slid with every thrust, unable to hold on for more than a few strokes at a time, but Anastazja was flexible enough to lock the pose herself. Besides, she had another idea, a gift that would drive him unthinkably wild.

It was their last time together. Might as well make it memorable.

Anastazja peeled his hand from her ankle and, with her eyes sealed to his and her teeth dragging her bottom lip, she brought his fingers, moist with her cum, into her mouth. His eyes rolled back, a hard, guttural groan vibrating from the depths of his throat as she sucked his fingers until they were tickling the back curve of her tongue.

With his hand still in her mouth, Anastazja moaned, garbled but clear enough to make his eyes widen. *"Harder."*

Soon enough, Tyreste would hate her. He'd rue the day they met, avoid her on the narrow village roads of Witchwood Cross, and retreat to the back room of his family's tavern when she passed by.

But in that moment, he was entirely hers.

And she was his.

His mouth hung, lips glistening and sweat rolling in industrious drops down his temples. They'd fucked for hours, but he always denied his own finish until the very end. *My parting gift,* he called it, sweet, seductive. *Evidence of what you do to me.*

He always left enough "evidence" that Anastazja single-handedly kept her vedhma busy making grimizhna tea.

She secured one leg around his hip, the other pinned above her head in obedience. And then he said it, the words she'd been starving for and dreading in equal measure: "Only you, Ana." She could hardly make them out through the jarring rhythm of his impaling, but she knew them by heart. "No one but you."

Flesh slammed flesh, the savage song mingling with debauched cries. She knew his tells by heart—could feel, well before it happened, his balls draw up and tighten against her ass, and the explosion of hours' worth of pent-up release. But she was still breathless with shock when the flood hit. Every inch of her tingled with hypnotic warmth, drowning her from the inside out.

Tyreste went stumbling as though he'd been punched by a man twice his size. He gaped down at his cock, shaking his head with a wonder-filled exhale. "I wasn't ready for it to end, but it would take the Guardians themselves to rouse him again."

"*Him.* Have you named the poor dear too?" Anastazja laughed, despite what was coming. Sweet Tyreste was just as enticing to her as Wild Tyreste. She would miss them both equally.

He glanced up with a stymied look. "What should I call him? Not Poor Dear, surely?"

"I was only teasing." Anastazja searched for the many layers of her dress, strewn in careless heaps across the room. They told the story of the afternoon, of Tyreste's hungered, wordless answering of the door. Of her tripping and stumbling over the back of one of his chairs when she'd tried to shimmy out of her overdress, only for him to join her on the floor and take her before she could finish disrobing.

"If anyone should decide, it's you." Tyreste went on, clearly still pondering the merits of naming his cock. "He is yours, after all."

Anastazja froze as she retrieved her slip dress. *Only you, Ana. No one but you.* Her eyes burned to a soft blur, but there was little danger of spilling tears. Years at Magda's mercy had trained her to keep her emotions safely contained, unless she wanted them weaponized against her.

"Ana?"

She wasn't ready. She hadn't been ready when she'd left Fanghelm Keep before dawn. She hadn't been ready when she'd raised her fist, hesitating before rapping on Tyreste's door. She wasn't ready still, when everything inside her screamed to turn and fold herself into his arms, her only safe place.

A stretched tightness in her chest—the pricks of lightheadedness swimming up to greet her—reminded her she'd *never* be ready.

It has to be now. Magda knows I haven't been going where I say I'm going. If she ever finds me here...

Anastazja shimmied into her slip and then her underskirts before answering. She lifted her gown to have something to hold on to for strength. Her words finally came as she stepped into it and worked it carefully up her body and over her arms. "This has been so fun." She scrunched her face. Those weren't the words she'd practiced. Neither was the fractured mess of rambling that followed. "Ah, what we've been doing, you and I, I mean. I've thoroughly enjoyed our trysts."

"Trysts."

She was purposefully turned away, like a coward, but she felt the precise moment the joy left the room.

"Is that, uh... what this is, Ana? What we've been doing for almost two years?"

"What else could it be?" She bit down hard on her lip, but it was no match for the sorrow rolling forward. *I must do this. I must do this for him.* "You're a *pubkeep.* It was never going to be more than secret afternoons." Her thoughtless shrug was a gross betrayal of her heart. "Most distractions last half as long."

Tyreste's silence was brimming with everything she was thinking too. "I see." He cleared his throat and laughed. "No. Actually, Ana, I *don't* see. I don't understand this at all... Are you..."

"Tired. What I am is *tired.* Of this, of you." She released the bold words in an outpouring of determination. Her gown sat unlaced, because like a fool, she'd embarked on the punishing task of breaking Tyreste's heart before she could ask for his help. No, she was a fool for wearing a dress at all. She'd known her intent from the moment she'd awoken that morning. "I really do ca—" *No, you can leave no room for hope. Only cruelty will protect him.* "I've enjoyed the pleasures you give me."

"The... pleasures I give you? What is this?" He moved closer.

She felt the warmth of him radiating when he drew near, the heady essence of sex and sweat.

"You sound like you're repeating something you've rehearsed. Badly."

"So I cannot speak my mind unless it's what you want to hear? I'm not allowed to end an arrangement that no longer suits me?" She cringed at the false note of anger in her voice, but it was better than him hearing the heartbreak creep in. "It's not like... not like we're in love."

The lie sent an invisible fist crashing into her gut.

"You..." Tyreste's breaths came in a series of awkward, confused starts with premature ends. "I *know* you. You're not yourself. Something happened, didn't it?"

"You know how I like to come." Her feet curled into the soft fur rug. "You know how I taste. How I feel. But what do you know about *me*, Tyreste Penhallow? What do you know about Anastazja Wynter when she leaves your little cabin and returns home to Fanghelm?"

"I've *tried* so hard to know your world." Tyreste started forward, shifting the energy once more. "I have, for *years*, tried to be a part of it. Our differences don't scare me, Anastazja. They never have. And until now, I would have said they didn't scare you either."

"My father has begun marriage negotiations," she blurted. It was the first thing that had come into her mind, and though it should have been true, it wasn't. At twenty, she should have been betrothed two years ago, but the north had fallen into three consecutive perilous winter seasons, and travel beyond or to Witchwood Cross was impossible for most of the year. Or, at least, that was the now-rote refrain her father repeated to those who asked. He couldn't very well tell people he was under the thrall of an evil koldyna, the true authority of Witchwood Cross these days.

"Oh yeah? When?"

"He's waiting for Vuk od Varem to pass, and then... then I'll be matched with a man of my station."

"The Season of the Wulf." Tyreste scoffed. "You turn your nose at my honest profession, when the Vjestik have been sacrificing their sons to the wulves of the north for *generations*. Your own *brother*, Ana."

"Sometimes they prevail." Hot defense rose into her cheeks, but it was better than thinking of the way Stepan had left two years ago to face off against the wulf and never come home. "And our sacrifices keep this entire town safe. Your family included."

"Safe from wulves we could take down with arrows and swords. Right."

"You don't understand the wulves of these forests! Stranjak don't have any idea how hard my Vjestik ancestors fought, for generations, before any of you showed up." Ana's shoulders rolled forward in a defeated slump. "Doesn't matter."

Tyreste came up behind her before she could retreat. His fingers spread along the nape of her neck in a gentle trail. His hands slid down her shoulders, slowing when they reached the stays of her dress. With a wordless sigh, he laced her up. "Ana."

All she could do was shake her head. If she spoke, he'd hear the regret, the weakness she couldn't completely hide.

"I know something happened. You can *talk* to me." His hand rolled back over her shoulders. He leaned in close, burning her with the fire of every word. "Whatever it is, I can help you. I... There's nothing I wouldn't do for you."

Anastazja had been wrong about her ability to hold back tears. They streamed down her rosy face like a flash flood. She shook her head again, because if she turned to look at him, it would be over. She'd cave and tell him everything, and then he'd insist on sharing the burden.

But that could never, *ever* happen.

Magda would kill him.

"*Please* talk to me. I know there's more than what you're saying."

Anastazja inhaled a quaking gasp, then swallowed it in a hard gulp that steadied her. "I mean it, Tyr. This..." She closed her eyes and tried again, but all she could think about was how soft and wonderful the weight of his hands felt on her shoulders. Her tender, protective lover. "This went on far longer than it should have." *Say it. Leave no room for doubt. Leave no opening for him to walk through. You must wound him to save him.* "I didn't expect you to get attached to me, and I can't have you hanging on like a stray kitten when I'm trying to make a good marriage for myself and my family."

Tyreste's scruffy tomcat, Rikard the Mouser, curdled a deep, throaty meow. *I didn't mean you, Riki. Sorry, boy.*

"It would almost be easier if I believed you. You've never been much of a liar though."

She felt his rebuttals echo in his hands, in the light shake in them.

"You're afraid. I understand. I even understand pushing me away, because that's what I did for years, before I met you. But you know, no matter what we might call this, it's more than that. You're afraid of saying the words we both hold in every time we're together, hoarding them like... like we're waiting for the perfect moment. But what is the perfect moment if not now, when you're pushing me away out of fear?"

"I don't love you, Tyreste, you fool. How could I? How could someone like me ever *love* someone like you?" She wrung her hands through the cruelty that was cutting herself almost as deep as she knew it was cutting him. "You're just an... an amusement I enjoyed longer than I should have. A toy I didn't tire of quickly enough. A... a tavern boy with a talented tongue and a generous cock." She sucked in her lip. "Fortunately for me, there are many men who can fill those needs when you're gone."

Tyreste's breathing tapered. His hands slid away, and the air cooled with distance between them. "I'm going to give you an opportunity to take that back. To tell me *why* you're so afraid, so I can help you. If you—" A muffled, gravelly tremor threaded his solemn tone. "If you tell me what's going on, I can help you. I can forget how hurtful what you just said to me was because I know all too well how fear can hold us in its grip, convince us... convince us we don't deserve happiness. But if you walk out that door, Ana, then you and I... We're done. Forever done. I'll never want to see your face again. Because there's no room in my life..." His voice clogged with emotion. "For someone who thinks so little of me."

Anastazja's heart had broken before she'd even said a word, but finally it shattered altogether, the remnants diffusing through her like shrapnel from an incendiary. How easy it would be to speak the truth of her heart and say the words. *Let's run away together, where we can be whomever we want to be.* But leaving wasn't an option. Tyreste had told her enough of his past for her to know he craved the foundations he'd built in Witchwood Cross over the past five years. And she could never abandon her father and brother to the mercy of Magda.

Ancestors, give me strength.

By the wings of this life or the bones of the next.

"I don't need your opportunities. Your concern. Your *understanding*. Any of it," Anastazja hissed. She raised the skirts of her half-laced dress and marched for the door, careful to keep her face—her truth—hidden. "And I definitely don't need *you*, Tyreste. So please, make good on your threats. Don't follow me. Don't meet my eyes on the village roads. Don't fear me coming into your lowly *tavern*." She dug her toes into her boots and said it, the thing she knew would add the finality required. The final serrated dagger. "Your services are no longer required, publican."

Anastazja flung the door wide and slammed it behind her without stopping. She raced down the snowy path and into the comforting arms of a fresh storm, not stopping until she reached the towering gates of Fanghelm Keep.

Tyreste trudged straight from his cabin, marching across the snow-covered field and down the rocky path leading into the narrow passage behind the Tavern at the Top of the World. He hadn't bothered with his cloak or furs, wearing only the same long-sleeved shirt, rolled to the elbows, that he'd had on when Ana had shown up with that languid smile in her eyes that always turned him into a puddle. After he'd watched her leave in a storm of confusion, he'd hardly managed a shirt and trousers, unbuckled, before his desperation for fresh air had sent him hurtling out into the storm.

Neither the fresh snow nor the chill wind rolling down off of a sinister-looking Icebolt did a thing to douse the fire burning him from the inside out. His flesh was scorched with fury and grief and frustration, with no viable means of release. She'd always known how to turn his foul emotions into fairer ones. The right words... the right touch. On his worst days, when he'd first come to Witchwood Cross after fleeing deep trauma in the Westerlands, she'd saved his life with those words, and that touch.

He slammed the heels of his palms against the back doors of the tavern and flung them wide with his entrance. Agnes glanced up with a liberal eyebrow raise and returned to scrubbing dishes at the steaming basin. Evert stepped out from the distillery, his lip curled at the edge, and shook his head before dipping back in to finish his work. Only little Adeline—who at fifteen wasn't so little anymore—came over to see if he was all right. She couldn't voice the words, instead spelling her concern with her hands, a skill she'd had to learn after losing her hearing in the terrible fire that had transformed the Penhallow family forevermore.

Her sweet, guileless face dulled his angst long enough for him to smile and assure her he was fine, but as soon as she was behind him, his smile departed. He strode past all of them and slipped into the office.

"Tyr." His father dipped his quill, squinting at the ledger he was notating. The eyeglasses Tyreste had purchased him in the market last year sat across his desk, defiantly untouched. He never had to wonder where his own stubborn pride had come from. "You're not scheduled until this evening. You're covering nights for Rik until the baby is born, remember?"

"I need to work *now*," Tyreste said. He gripped the back of the unstable chair and leaned over his father's broad desk. "Where do you need me?"

Olov re-inked his quill and continued scribing, his bushy eyebrows curling in concentration. "Ah, well, seeing as we're in between the morning and evening rush, I *don't* really need you. Not yet. The others are on prep, but they'll be nearly done by now."

Tyreste sliced his tongue along the back of his teeth. "Surely there's ale to be tended." His death grip rattled the chair, which finally made his father look up.

Olov set the quill neatly beside his logbook and watched his son with a shrewd look. "Did something happen?"

"Didn't sleep well," Tyreste said. He hated lying. The lies of others had ruined his life. But both Olov and Fransiska had cautioned Tyreste about his dalliance with Anastazja, the "pretty highborn beyond his reach." The only thing that could make him feel worse would be their sympathetic, knowing smiles when they realized they'd been right.

"Just waking up?" Olov mimed looking out a window, despite that the office had none. "It's nearly dusk."

"Is there work for me, Father?"

Olov stretched his arms to the sides with a long sigh. He'd probably been hunched in the same position for hours. "Sit."

"I just want—"

"*Sit*, Tyr. I'm not asking."

Tyreste grumbled words he would never actually say clearly and plopped onto the rickety chair with an affronted glare at the desk.

"Where's your mother?"

"I don't know, why?"

"She wasn't in the back when you came in?"

Tyreste shook his head.

Olov's cheeky grin almost went unnoticed as he lifted the pipe from his inside vest pocket and nodded toward the door. "Never mind sitting. Let's go outside."

Tyreste narrowed one eye in amusement. "You told Mother you quit."

"We all need our corruptions. Go on."

On the way out, Olov dipped his pipe inside the kitchen hearth to light it, making a shushing gesture with his finger toward Adeline. The delightful sound of her giggles trailed them outside.

Olov climbed the small, forested hill behind the tavern and dipped behind a broad-trunked pine tree. He pulled a deep, productive puff from his pipe, released the smoke, and leaned against the bark. "You're not going to tell me, are you?"

Tyreste debated playing the fool, but his father was sharper than that. If he'd seen through his first protestation, he'd see through another. "Doesn't matter. I just... just want to work. I want to feel needed."

"You're always needed," Olov said and took another puff. "Always *wanted*. The best gift the Guardians ever gave me was when you showed up here in the Cross, after we'd spent years believing we'd lost you. Isn't a day goes by I don't pay my respects for that gift."

Tyreste kicked at the packed snow at his feet. They'd never spoken of those years. "I mean no disrespect, Father, but I can't talk about that."

"Fair enough." Olov leaned his head back and exhaled. "Twenty-four. You're a proper man now, Tyr. Long been. Are you not itching to settle down and make a family of your own?"

Anastazja's bright-eyed giggle infiltrated his thoughts, followed by a licentious shiver he once would have welcomed. "I have everything I need here."

"Do you?"

"I get to help you and Mother with the tavern, and I have my scribing. There's little room for anything else."

"Pern and Rik have families and work. Stojan and Agnes aren't even married yet and they make time. You don't have to choose." Olov chuckled with a short shake of his head at the frozen ground. "But you already know that."

Tyreste looked out over the small valley that divided the town from the Howling Sea. It was visible even through the fog of snow, the hazy sunset burning against the horizon.

"Only blackbirds sing alone, son."

Tyr pulled a waft of cold air through his nose.

"That's not why I brought you out here though." Olov's pipe burned red with his inhale. "You'll have a visitor in the morning," he said through his exhale. "At the end of your shift."

"A visitor?" Tyreste frowned. His father wouldn't have worded it that way, *a visitor,* if it were someone local. But no one traveled to Witchwood Cross if they didn't have to. The small village consisted primarily of Vjestik families like the Wynters, who were only grudgingly tolerant of outsiders. And no one traveled that far north in wintertide if the reason wasn't essential. "I don't... follow."

"So he didn't tell you. I assumed as much." Olov chuckled and swiped his tongue along his lips. "He always was a secretive man, our Asterin."

Tyreste took an unintentional step back. "*Asterin?* Asterin is coming *here?*"

"Mm. He's already here, actually, but I sent him to an inn for the evening because I wasn't expecting you until later. I figured you'd be more comfortable talking when your work was done. He brought the other one with him... the eunuch from the Reliquary."

"Sesto," Tyreste muttered absentmindedly. Asterin, there. In Witchwood Cross. Without so much as a message sent ahead. Whatever his impulse was for the secrecy, it could be no light matter. In the five years Tyreste had lived in Witchwood Cross, Asterin Edevane—or any of Tyreste's friends from his old life—had never ventured north. "It's... It's not Rhiain or one of the children, is it?"

"No, no," Olov said quickly. "Rhiain is doing wonderfully, from what Asterin says, convalescing comfortably in Riverchapel. You remember the birth announcement. Their *fourth.* No, he's come on business. What business, he declined to say." He lifted his arms out to his sides. "I don't have to tell you to be cautious. Whatever he wants to say, he didn't feel safe saying via a raven. If what work he has for you promises danger—"

13

"I know." Tyreste was still mulling the possibilities. Asterin and Sesto must have been traveling for weeks in the current weather. Had they even found a guide willing to provide an escort through the less-traveled paths, with the Compass Road closed north of Wulfsgate? And he'd brought Sesto, the second-best scribe working for their little group of translators, which meant there was no one translating at all until they returned.

"Well." Olov pushed himself away from the tree with a forlorn glance at his pipe. "I've said what I needed. He'll return to the tavern at dawn, and you can decide whether his trip was wasted or well spent. If nothing else, there's never harm in reminiscing with an old friend, is there?" He tapped the debris off of his pipe and tucked it back into his vest. "You can help Evert with the still. The backup hasn't stopped putting out that putrid swill, and we can't afford to be down a single vat when the weather is acting up... and with the Cider Festival just around the corner. Guardians know the Cross has nothing better to do in the cold than drink themselves silly." He wiped his mouth. "Don't forget to lock the doors during the service pause. You always forget."

Tyreste watched his father shimmy back down the hill. Olov was slower than he'd used to be, and for the first time, Tyr saw the signs of aging. The extra second his father afforded himself when standing. The minor hitch in his left leg. How lately he'd spent more time in the office than in the tavern room.

But Tyreste's mother seemed to love her husband more with every passing year. Theirs was a true love, the rare kind. Like Asterin and Rhiain's. Tyr had never hoped for anything so meaningful for himself, until...

He bunched his face, blinked hard, and shook his head, clearing it.

Work.

He needed to work.

Only in purposeful action could he dull the abhorrent misery.

14

Tyreste brainstormed fresh ways to attack the problem of the still as he jogged down the hill toward his family's tavern.

How would a stronger person handle knowing the exact day they were going to die? Would they live their life differently? What choices would fire their days and haunt their nights if they knew they were not long for the world?

Anastazja pondered those questions every day. While she bathed, while she rode her mare, Enzi, while she moved through the village of Witchwood Cross with her basket and her favorite disguise... Even when she was flying and her troubles seemed small, the void beckoned.

Blissfully oblivious was how she'd have described the first ten years of her life, before she'd been confronted with the terrible fate awaiting her. She'd given no care to the food she ate or the clothes she wore. She'd been perilous with her words, careless with her choices, and more than a little petulant to the people she loved. Her curated world of snow and crackling fires had been free of consequence, of pain.

And then Magda had crashed into their lives. She of implausible beauty and no family name. With magic that was too helpful, too convenient. Suspiciously soon after, Ana's mother was dead, and Magda the cunning woman became Magda the adviser to Anastazja's grieving father, the steward of Witchwood Cross. It shouldn't have been surprising when he'd married her, but it was. Anastazja had hoped her sweet, lonely father would remarry and find happiness again, but not like that.

Not to a koldyna, who had everyone fooled except Anastazja.

Anastazja had seen Magda for what she was the moment she'd shown up at Fanghelm Keep, feigning a beggar, her eyes glistening with yearning malevolence.

The Wynters, like all Vjestik, hailed from witches, but Magda was no mere witch. She communed with the demon world, a place most didn't even believe existed. But no one at Fanghelm saw this

15

side of her, except Ana. Even Anastazja's twin brother, Nikolaj, didn't believe Magda was that powerful—or that dangerous.

It was dusk when Ana reached the towering gates of Fanghelm Keep, which meant everyone would be gathered for supper in the dining hall. They'd be wondering where she was, but they wouldn't hold the meal up for her. They would have *before* Magda, but...

Anastazja often thought of her life as before Magda and after Magda. Blissful ignorance shattering into painful clarity.

She quietly slipped into the central hall and shimmied out of her boots to avoid the clicking drawing attention to her entrance. Pausing, she listened, but heard no one nearby. If she had the backbone to slink down the corridor toward the dining hall, she'd be able to hear if everyone was accounted for at supper, but there was nothing she craved more than the fleeting peace of solitude.

Anastazja skittered across the stones in her stockings. She caught a slick spot and slid to the wall next to the inner staircase, then righted herself and darted into the narrow passage to climb to the third floor, where the family apartments were housed.

When she reached the top, she verified she was still alone. The hall was completely vacant to the left and the right. Not even the staff were milling about, which was uncommon but fortuitous. There wasn't a single one she trusted not to report her actions to Magda, except her vedhma, Ludya, but she wasn't expecting a visit from Ludya until tomorrow.

Ana closed her eyes and allowed herself a deep breath before starting toward her apartments. Glances back confirmed she hadn't been followed, and her anxiety melted away, offering space for grief to return.

She turned the handle of her door, but it was already open. Someone was inside. It was probably an attendant, or maybe Ludya had come unannounced to deliver more grimizhna tea.

But that was not what her instincts were telling her.

Anastazja debated backing away and returning down the staircase to join her family after all. Magda would be there, but she'd rather face the koldyna when there were others around.

16

Except she was certain it was Magda inside her room.

"Are you evaluating whether to converse with me or run from me? No, don't answer. I can practically *feel* your insipid thoughts from here."

Anastazja violently shivered at the funereal intonation of the crone's voice. Around others, Magda affected the soft, unassuming lilt of the jewel who had entranced the steward of Witchwood Cross. When it was only the two of them, she dropped the pretense and revealed her true self.

If only others could see her as Anastazja could.

Ana held her head high and entered. There was nothing to fear except giving power to fear. Magda wasn't going to kill her. There were still six months before her death as foretold by the koldyna, and until then, the evil bitch still needed her.

"You're not at supper," Anastazja said, enjoying the flippant turn in her voice. She didn't sound as scared as she felt. For once.

"Nor are you, girl." Magda's voice traveled from the other side of the room, enveloped in darkness. None of the candles had been lit for the evening. More likely they had been, and the crone had snuffed them out, like everything else she touched. "I can smell the sex on you. It gets stronger every time you return home." She pulled in a hard, animalistic sniff. "Same boy. Or is it a man? You think I won't find out?"

"I don't owe you an explanation of who I spend my time with."

"Anything you said would be a lie anyway, wouldn't it?" Magda laughed, but it sounded more like she was coughing up a wad of hair. The rocking chair creaked, signaling her advance. "For a young woman who has but two seasons left to her life, one would think you would use that time in a more meaningful way."

"As I said—"

"You waste too many words, Ana. Always have. You were never wise enough to keep your own counsel. I suppose that's what happens when a girl loses her mother and rejects the gifts of another."

17

"You are no one's *oma*." Anastazja snorted. She wanted a drink. Something. Anything. She could navigate to the beverage cart in the dark, but not subtly. Not in a way that wouldn't reveal the fray in her nerves.

"Tick. Tick. Tick. Tick." Magda's creaking steps drew nearer, but she was still obscured by the room's darkness. "The sound of your life slipping away. Can you hear it, Anastazja? Can you *feel* it?"

"What do you *want*?" She ripped off her cloak and threw it. She didn't see where it had landed.

"What a question. You can't know all the many ways I could answer!"

"If you have something to say to me... say it in front of my father," Anastazja answered boldly.

Magda laughed again. "If I did, he would hear the words so much differently, wouldn't he? Just as he sees me differently."

"They all do. But I know who you are. *What* you are," Anastazja charged. Spittle flew from her mouth. "I see you, witch. *Koldyna*."

"More wasted words," the crone chided. Her next step brought her into view. Though Anastazja had seen her stepmother's true form many times, she was never quite prepared for the startling asymmetry of her ghoulish features. The degree of crook in her nose... the uneven trail of a mouth that seemed to house an eternity of evil. Deep trenches of wrinkles were on every inch of exposed flesh, and where hair should be was only a sprig of orange fuzz. Her precipitous grin revealed blackened teeth, some sharpened to points and others overlapping the ones beside them, a cramped collage of terror. "I came to tell you that we're going up the mountain tomorrow."

Anastazja's breath held. It choked her. *Nien. Nien, not again. Not anymore. I can never, ever...* Dizziness swept down from behind her eyes, and she sidestepped into a nearby chair, gripping the soft leather. "But..."

"But the weather is foul? But it's too soon since our last venture? But... But what?" Magda sputtered into a contemptuous imitation of Anastazja. "Save your rebuttals for someone who cares, girl. Your life will end soon and then Niko will take your place when you're gone. Unless, of course, we find success before your time is ended. An outcome that's entirely up to you."

Anastazja's shoulders clenched at the painful but unnecessary reminder. It was never *not* on her mind that if she couldn't find a way to either satisfy Magda or stop her, Niko would inherit her pain.

"And this time, you'll do more than lure them for me. I have something a bit more *vigorous* in mind for you."

Anastazja's tongue dried up. It kept her from asking the terrible question Magda seemed to be waiting for, but she wouldn't give the crone a win when she'd already accumulated too many. Their trips up the mountain had been more than Ana's conscience could carry. The thought of being asked to do more...

"Tick. Tick." Magda grinned, a rotted black line of teeth and death. "Dawn. Meet me at the well north of the stables. Do not even think of standing me up, girl. Not unless you want me to eat your brother for breakfast."

Magda charged forward and brushed against Anastazja hard enough to send her tripping toward the wall. The crone's cackles contorted into sinister echoes as she thundered down the hall, claiming every sconce and stone with each malignant step. Anastazja heard them even as the koldyna descended, but she could no longer trust her senses to be certain if it was her ears or her tortured mind. It was the same sound she heard in every nightmare.

At her feet, a shiny red apple spun in a perfect circle, brushing just above the stones in the center of the doorframe. A gift from Magda.

A promise.

Anastazja, shaking, slammed the bolt closed on her door. She stared at it in horror until a soundless scream rolled up from her chest and forced her mouth wide, and that was how she stayed until exhaustion introduced her to another bout of tortured slumber.

TWO
RARE RED ROSE

Tyreste worked his shift in a daze. It was a hectic night for the tavern, but that was true of most nights in the land of eternal winter. There was little else to do when the sun dipped behind the Northern Range in midday, the infernal cold rolling off Icebolt Mountain like plumes of smoke stepping forward to claim the night.

The Tavern at the Top of the World was one of a dozen pubs in Witchwood Cross but the only one owned by outsiders—or what the Vjestik called *stranjak*. The Penhallows weren't from the Cross, or even the Northerlands, and the tale of how they'd become exiles was one, even five years later, he couldn't allow himself to think about.

The tavern was even busier than the one they'd run in the Westerlands, and it was precisely that bliss of perpetual motion and blurred reality he'd needed to clear his head of Anastazja Wynter.

His rare red rose.

No. Not *his*. She'd never been his. She'd made it excruciatingly clear.

21

Holding on to the truth and not the dream was the only way forward.

Dawn broke, and the only customers remaining were the stalwart patrons who had never left. They were always halfway to the Guardians, intentionally divorced of any reality beyond the Tavern at the Top of the World's wooden walls, and so Tyreste didn't bother expelling them when the time neared for his meeting with Asterin and Sesto.

Asterin. And Sesto. They were *there*, in the Cross.

"I can give them the boot," Olov said as he finished stacking the washed mugs behind the bar.

Tyreste waved the rag in his hand. "Nah. They'd be lucky to remember their way home, let alone have the capacity for nosiness. Wouldn't want them freezing in a ditch."

"Could send a raven to their families to collect them."

"I have a feeling that call would go unanswered."

Olov chuckled. "Aye. That's true." He wiped down the bar in long, aggressive strokes. "Drago is already here doing prep, and Pern and Evert will be along shortly, but they know to stay in the back, to give you space. You know, I can brew a pot of strong coffee and wait with—"

"No, Father. Go on to bed. I won't be far behind."

Olov watched him closely. "You don't want to spend time with your friends? They've come a long way to see you."

Tyreste nearly corrected that word, *friends*, but it would have been an old instinct, one he hadn't felt in years. The Edevanes and Sesto were his friends, then and now. His only close friends in the world, beyond his family.

But a quick visit north was only a tease of what he could have if they all lived closer. Tyreste's heart was already raw, and their unannounced arrival only reminded him of all he'd lost.

"Everything all right, Son?"

"Yes. Course." Tyreste lifted the last two chairs and stacked them atop the last table he'd cleaned. The rest were done, except the corner one he'd reserved for his visitors.

Olov didn't look convinced, but he nodded anyway. "I've bolted the entrance for the service pause, so you don't need to concern yourself with it. Your friends know to enter through the back. Drago, Pern, and Evert can hold everything down, and Faustina is coming in for a few hours as well. All I'm saying is we have more than enough help. There's no reason to stay any longer than you want to."

Tyreste shook his head. "Faustina, huh? It's only been a month since Rik wed her, and you're already putting her to work?"

Olov grinned. "She's a Penhallow now. And nobody does more or less than they want to do here. You know that." He tapped the bar. "See you tonight?"

Tyreste nodded and watched his father leave through the back. The two holdouts, sitting at opposite ends of the bar, both pointed hollow gazes at their ales. He wondered if they even knew where they were anymore.

He glanced around, searching for any work still needing done, but he'd already finished it. The bar was shined, and the floors and tables as washed as they'd ever be.

A low, raspy meow sounded from the other side of the room. Rikard the Mouser had finally made his way to the tavern, on his own time. He'd been a feral stray when Tyreste had "adopted" him all those years ago in the Reliquary dungeon, and not much had changed, except that the tomcat wasn't locked away from leaving anymore. He chose to stay, every day and night, and the choice made him family.

"Over here, Riki," he said, and Rikard padded over with a jaunty twitch in his striped tail.

With nothing else to do but wait, Tyreste pulled out a chair and sat.

Anastazja slunk down the stairwell with the same hushed, shameful energy of the carefree little girl who used to sneak in and out of Fanghelm to explore the village. Back then, there'd been no

23

real risk, no consequences. The few times she'd been caught, all she'd earned was a sound but soft scolding, and by the following evening, her father would be back to reading to her from his vast library, her mother humming old Vjestik songs as she plaited her only daughter's hair.

Now, the risk was real. The consequences were real. And there were no comforts to be found at the end.

Demons dealt in darker denouements.

Porridge wafted into the hall, greeting her at the bottom of the steps. When her mother had been alive, they'd had elaborate breakfasts, with meat and quail eggs and freshly picked vegetables from the stewardess's garden—one of the few in the far north to produce anything but root plants. Ksenia Arsenyev Wynter was said to have had zydolny, or "the touch," a Vjestik way of describing the unique symbiosis some of their people had with flora and fauna.

Anastazja hadn't inherited her mother's zydolny. Like most of her people, she had magic of her own, but it was useless against Magda, who could cut through her illusions, her healing, or anything she tried. The one thing she'd inherited the koldyna *couldn't* silence—her phoenix form—was the very reason Magda needed her.

Only the Wynter heirs could shift. Anastazja's older brother, Stepan, had had to die for her to gain her wings. Every time she was forced to shift, to fly up the mountain, she missed Stepan all the more. Nothing made her feel closer to him, yet also further away.

She braced, plastering a smile for her father and Nikolaj, and entered the noisy dining hall.

Niko brightened when he saw her, though he looked surprised she'd shown up at all. Her father offered both scruffy cheeks for her to kiss. Her heart briefly soared at the way his cheeks pulled up in a quick smile, just for her.

Anastazja greeted them without looking at Magda, though she was persistently aware of the witch's hard stare drilling her from the side.

"Dobryzen, Ota," she said as she took her seat.

"Dobryzen, Pjika. We missed you last night," Arkhady said before spooning porridge into his mouth. "Magda said you were unwell."

That's one way of putting it. Anastazja waited for the attendant to fill her bowl before speaking. "Opros, Ota. I had supper in town."

"What did you have, Ana?" Niko asked. He wiped his mouth on his sleeve, something he'd only started doing again recently. It was one of many little tells that he was regressing back into boyhood, a tragedy made worse by the slow breakdown of their once-unshakable twin bond. "We had roast pork last night. The skin was so crisp and delectable!" Niko's entire face erupted into a tableau of joy.

"Such a good boy, aren't you, Niko? Always eating everything on your plate. Doing as you're told. Your father's perfect little gentleman. Could there be a better son?" Magda clucked her tongue in approval. Her spoon scraped the bowl in grating passes. "I've asked the kitchens to make it again tonight for our perfect little gentleman."

Niko's mouth parted in overdone wonder. "Really? For me?"

"For you, sweet boy."

"Hvala, Magda!"

"Oma, Nikolaj," Magda stated, correcting him.

"Oma." Niko grinned wide.

Anastazja wanted to hurl and scream. At the same time.

"Feeling better this morning, then?" Arkhady asked. Though he was looking at Anastazja, his eyes were as glazed, as they always were lately. She thought of them as a window to his trapped soul. But the framing was made of solid stone, and she had no tools to chip it away. "If you're still unwell, Pjika, perhaps you can help Magda tomorrow instead."

"No," Magda barked, revealing—too quickly for most to notice—a hairline crack in her curated facade. "Ana is fine, aren't you, love? You *want* to come help me in the observatory. Isn't that what you said last night when I came to your room to nurse you? Practically begged me not to count you out."

Anastazja stabbed her porridge with her spoon. "I couldn't possibly refuse."

"She's never shied away from work," Arkhady said. He dabbed at his mouth with his usual faraway look. Tears pooled under his lids. "Takes after her oma."

"Magda is our *oma* now," Niko said brightly. He held the handle of his spoon in his fist, like a toddler. "How fortunate we are."

"That's right, love. And I would do anything for my dear children, wouldn't I?" Magda folded her hand atop Niko's forearm. Anastazja glimpsed the bony, gnarled fingers she hid through illusions. "One day, when Ana has... moved on... It will be your turn to help me in the observatory."

Anastazja's spoon dropped into her bowl with a clang, loud enough everyone should have looked her way, but no one did.

Niko puffed up with an exuberant breath in. "Really? You promise?"

"*Promise*, darling boy." Magda squeezed his arm before withdrawing hers. She slithered it back to her lap.

Arkhady stared at the fire crackling in the hearth, his spoon frozen midway to his mouth. He seemed to be somewhere else. Wherever it was, he went there often.

Anastazja liked to think it was the one place he was safe from Magda.

Unfortunately, she knew better.

"Did you hear, dearest? The Vuk od Varem has ended," Magda said. "The Castel boy didn't make it."

Magda's spirited delivery of *didn't make it* did nothing to lighten the horror of her revelation. Another son of Witchwood Cross lost to the wulves, like Stepan. Another springtide when their people would be forced to pay huge markups on imported meat because the local forests weren't theirs for hunting—those who could afford to pay extra anyway. The others would ration their storage of dried boar and elk-kind and pray for a better year.

"I'm very sorry to hear it," Arkhady said with a low nod. "We'll dig into our coffers. There's enough for us to purchase rations for the entire Cross, for a season at least."

"Waste of gold," Magda muttered. No one but Anastazja seemed to hear.

"I'll see that it's done, Ota," Anastazja said with a cool sideways glance at her stepmother.

"It would put my soul at ease, Pjika. Tak. Ah, Grigor," Arkhady said, looking more lively than she'd seen him in months. "How fared your trip to Wulfsgate?"

Anastazja only realized her uncle was seated at the far end of the table when her father addressed him. Grigor was the irregular shadow of Fanghelm—rarely there, and when he was, he blended in so seamlessly, they often forgot he was. He was her mother's younger brother, the solemn protector of the Cross, more mercenary than man. Though he was only a decade her senior, he wore the grim pall of one who'd had the misfortune to live a dozen lifetimes.

"We'll speak later, Arkhady," Grigor growled with a quick, hard look pointed at Magda. He returned his focus to his oversized bowl of porridge.

"Are marriage contracts not the business of women?" Magda snorted. "Oh, you think I didn't know what you sent our bear south to do?"

"Marriage contract? For whom?" Anastazja couldn't help asking.

"Niko," Arkhady answered. A tremor started in one hand and then traveled to the other. He tried to look at Magda, but some unseen force was keeping his gaze fixed forward. "To Lord Dereham's youngest daughter. The poor girl's betrothed died of the sweating sickness, and now your brother is a serious contender for her hand."

"*No.*" Magda's low hiss silenced the table. "There will be no marriages for the twins until they're ready."

"Ready." Anastazja shook her head, laughing. "We're *twenty*. Niko should be running his own keep by now. By the standards of this kingdom, I'm already an old maid."

"We make our own standards," Magda said. "And we do not go behind each other's backs to broker betrothals we have not agreed need brokering."

"As you say, dear," Arkhady said, monotone, and went back to his food.

"That's... That's it?" Anastazja shoved her bowl so hard, it tipped. Gelatinous porridge slowly crept across the porous wood. "Niko has the opportunity to make the finest marriage he could..." *To break free of this wretched woman and her curse.* "And you want to wait? For what? There will be no better match for him than a Dereham! *Ota*, he'd be a *lord*!"

"Ana." Arkhady's sharp warning had the tremor of a rare moment of clarity.

Anastazja looked to Grigor for help, but he was leaning back in his chair, mired in his own thoughts, his arms crossed. He'd never treated Magda with anything but cold regard, but he'd never spoken against her either.

"We've sufficiently broken our fast," Magda said with a decisive shove back from the table. She towered over Ana. "Get dressed. Meet me outside. If you still have questions, little bird, you can ask them of *me*."

Asterin greeted him with a hug so fierce, Tyreste sputtered through an awkward laugh. He clapped his hands on his old friend's back, prepared to break the embrace, but Asterin wasn't letting go.

"Tyreste." Asterin released him with a sigh, shaking his head as he drank him in. Tyr's old commander looked as dashing as always, groomed and garbed for a meeting with a lord, not a reunion with an old friend at dawn. "I daresay you've grown."

"I daresay as well," Sesto said with an appraising look. His brows shot upward, creasing his bald head. "Been hauling timber, have you? Sacks of bricks?" His mouth curved in bemused consideration.

Tyreste inspected himself, frowning. "Ahh..."

"It was a compliment," Sesto whispered, winking, and pulled him in for a quick embrace. "It is good to see you, Scribe."

Tyreste's mouth hitched in a half grin at the old moniker. "You too, Abbot."

"Rhiain wanted to come along—tried to come along—and you know I'm not in the business of telling my wife what she can and cannot do, but... not that I *could*, even if I wanted to. We are, after all, talking about Rhiainach." Asterin blew out a breath. "It took some persuading..."

Sesto curved a hand on his face and mouthed *whipped*.

Tyreste chuckled, whisked back to a far different time in his life, one as awful as it was wonderful. "Reckless as ever then?"

"Less so now that we have children," Asterin said. With a half-hidden smile, he continued. "And we thank the Guardians for it every day. Needless to say, she couldn't be here, but she was insistent I come for both of us." He gestured toward the table, and they made their way to their seats. "It's been far too long, Tyreste. I meant to come see you sooner. Guardians know Rhiain has been wanting to... but with the little ones and the business, time gets away from you."

"Perhaps if you'd quell your libido long enough to let the woman *breathe*, we might have more opportunities to travel," Sesto quipped.

Asterin flushed and shrugged, a small smile playing at his mouth. "I'm a lucky man. I know it today as well as I knew it the last." He accepted the ale Tyreste had poured him from the pitcher he'd readied while waiting. Asterin took a long swallow. "Penhallow ale is as fair as I remember it. Was good to see Olov again. He seems well."

"He is," Tyreste said, an edge of wariness creeping into his words. "He likes it up here. We all do. It's... different."

29

"That it is," Asterin agreed. He gave the tavern floor another sweeping look. "The tavern alone is bigger. What is it, twice the size as the one in Parth?"

"Three times," Tyr said, "according to my father, who is quite precise with his accountings in other areas, so I'll assume he's accurate about this as well."

"Does it ever fill up?" Sesto asked. "Like the other one?"

"There are nights when we have to turn people away," Tyr answered, glancing from one to the other nervously, wondering when they were going to explain why they were thousands of miles from home without so much as a raven to announce they were coming. "And others when we're washing the same mugs ten times over for the want of something to pass the time."

"And you, Tyreste?" Asterin asked. "How are *you*? Life in the north seems to suit you."

Tyreste pursed his mouth and nodded. "Sometimes I miss the Westerlands. Even that cursed dungeon in the Reliquary held a certain charm..." He laughed to clear the remembrance of those years. "But my family has never been happier. The tavern isn't in the red from all the taxes anymore. Pern and her family are moving in the springtide. Rik was just wed last month. Agnes is next. All of them wed to a Vjestik, if you can believe it. I don't think the Cross quite can. They're wary of us stranjak." He rambled on without taking a breath. "Evert has an apprenticeship waiting for him in Whitechurch, and we're all so proud of him. And Addy..." Tyreste smiled at his hands. "She's doing really well. A quick learner. She'll be handling as many translations as me in no time, so I'll be asking for more work soon. I think she may be leaning toward joining the company when she's older, if you're open to it. Oh, and can't forget Riki, the most resilient cat in the realm. Still as cantankerous as ever."

Rikard the Mouser purred under the table.

Asterin nodded with a glance at Sesto, who lifted a brow. "It warms my heart to hear your family is doing so well. They deserve all that and more. But Olov already ran down the same list of accomplishments with me. I asked about *you*."

Tyreste shrugged, conscious of the flush rising from his neck. "I have everything I need."

"Rhiain would never let me hear the end of it if I didn't make sure that was true, Tyreste."

"We both know what Rhiainach is like when she isn't *happy*," Sesto said.

Asterin rolled his eyes with a bracing look, which had Tyr imagining how their journey north must have been.

Tyreste stared at his threaded hands. "What is happiness, if not the absence of worry? Of fear? The knowledge you'll never want for anything, and your loved ones will never either?"

"You describe security," Sesto said. He folded his arms over his dark-brown cloak. Though he'd stopped wearing the abbot's dress when he'd left the Reliquary, his style was still reminiscent of those days. "Which we all need. But it isn't the same as happiness." He rapped the table. "Have you a lady friend, Scribe?"

Asterin smirked at him. "A lady friend, Sesto? Really?"

Sesto laughed and tilted his hands outward. "Is that not what you were really asking?"

"If I wanted to know if Tyreste had a *lady friend*, I'd have asked him if he had a *lady friend*."

"Oh, because you've never been vague and cagey about anything, have you, As? Not ever?"

Asterin's nose scrunched in mock annoyance. "I should have left you and your smart mouth at home."

"A smart mouth?" Sesto pressed his hands to his chest and fluttered his eyes. "How you flatter me, my liege!"

Asterin pivoted so Sesto was behind him. He forged a smile at Tyreste, as if to say, *you see what I have to deal with*? "Forgive us. It's been a rather long journey."

Tyreste couldn't help but smile. They were both just as he remembered them, yet also changed for the better, a product of time and circumstance. Asterin was as serious and stoic as ever, but with a playful side he seemed more comfortable indulging. Sesto's sharp wit was tempered by a maturing confidence, no doubt born of Asterin's confidence in him. They were business partners but also friends. *His* friends. The only thing that would have made the reunion better was if Rhiain had come.

Straddling two worlds, Tyreste wondered—for the first time in a long time—if he belonged in either.

His smile faded.

Asterin took another sip from his ale and pushed the mug to the side. "You're wondering why we're here. Why I didn't send word. Why I left my newborn son, three rambunctious toddlers, and a recovering wife, for weeks, to deliver a message I could have sent via raven or courier."

Tyreste held out his hands in agreement. "I am. Yes." He glanced at them both. Rikard stuttered a meow. "Happy as I am to see you, I can't help feeling like this is an ambush."

Asterin and Sesto shared a look and then Asterin reached under his cloak and pulled out a leather pouch. He set it on the table. Tyreste reached for it, but Asterin clamped a hand over the top and nodded at the drunkards. "They going to be a problem?"

"No, they're not a problem to anyone except themselves. I picked this table because it was closest to the hearth."

"Learned that from you, he did," Sesto said. "But do we not wonder why our Asterin is so versed in the cloaking qualities of a blazing fire?"

Asterin flicked his eyes at Sesto with a grim smile and removed his hand from the pouch. "Tyreste, I've asked you before if you speak Vjestikaan."

Tyreste eyed the unopened pouch. "Yes, and I told you then that I didn't. I still only know the same few words." He cleared his throat. "The Vjestik don't really speak it either. Maybe at home, with each other. But never in here." He gestured around. "Or around outsiders."

"Mm." Asterin dragged his thumb and forefinger along the edge of his chin. "What about the young woman you were spending time with? Ana?"

"You can ask about a lady friend, but I cannot?" Sesto snorted.

"That's done." Tyreste's voice broke. He downed more ale. "She can't help."

"Sorry to hear that, Tyreste," Asterin said slowly, watching him. Eventually his gaze traveled back to the pouch. "Is there no one for hire? No local you trust, who would keep your secrets?"

"If there was, is it safe to show them whatever is inside?"

Asterin nodded to himself, thinking. "It's not safe to show anyone until we know what the letters say, and once we do, it may be even less safe."

"Letters? Between whom?" Tyreste asked.

"A young woman and a young man," Sesto answered. "The letters are two hundred years old, or more. My Old Ilynglass is still rather spotty, but my rough translation tells me the letter writer from Duncarrow was a young man writing to his cousin here in Witchwood Cross. As for her identity, well, she was a Wynter. That much I *could* read."

Even the name, Wynter, was a blow. Tyreste squinted, to expel the way Anastazja's blonde waves felt sifting through his fingers. She'd raced out of his life with a quickness, but there was no escaping her. "What's the connection between Duncarrow and Witchwood Cross?"

"Two hundred and fifty years ago, Drazhan Wynter traveled to Duncarrow to guard one of their princesses, Imryll of Glaisgain. Instead, he fell in love with her and brought her home to Witchwood Cross. All Wynters since descend from these two." Sesto shrugged. "I'm surprised you haven't heard the tale, living here. Drazhan and Imryll are legends in the north, as I hear it."

"It's starting to sound familiar." Now he remembered. Though the account was chronicled in *The Book of All Things* chapter for the Northerlands, the matter of the runaway princess had been erased entirely from the Rhiagain chapters. A proper royal embarrassment. "Why do we care about letters between cousins?"

With a cautious glance at the half-gone men on the other side of the tavern floor, Asterin leaned in. "Has there been any trouble with the Ravenwoods?"

Tyreste flinched. "The Ravenwoods? What kind of trouble?"

"You tell us," Sesto said.

"I wouldn't know if there was. It isn't as if the ravens eat in our taverns or buy from our markets." Tyreste scratched through the stubble on his cheek. When he'd moved to Witchwood Cross, he'd harbored an elaborate fantasy about the Ravenwoods being completely integrated into society with men. The opposite had proven true, and as far as he knew, they never came down from their mountain keep at all. "Can't say I've ever seen one beyond the skies. If I have, I didn't know it."

"No rumors of problems? Nothing out of the ordinary?" Asterin probed.

"Like I said, I wouldn't know. No one here would. They don't come down from their little mountain fiefdom unless they have to." As he'd said it, *no one here would,* he realized there were some who might. One in particular… whose family had a long-standing alliance with the Ravenwoods, and whose ancestor was one of the letter writers.

Always fucking Ana.

"Could be nothing," Asterin said, sitting back. "These letters are two hundred years old, after all, and whatever troubles were bothering the cousins might belong in the past with them."

Tyreste tilted his head. "And yet you wouldn't have traveled for weeks, in treacherous conditions, if you believed that. So why? Why do these letters matter to you now?"

"Because I *can* read some of the Duncarrow lad Paeris's words, enough to wonder…" Sesto glanced to the side. "If there isn't some nefarious business between Duncarrow and the ravens. The kind that transcends time."

"Transcends time? What does that even mean, Sesto?"

"The Meduwyn," he whispered. "The Rhiagain sorcerers."

Tyreste folded his arms and flopped back with a laugh. "Sorcerer is a colorful way of saying they have magic, just like a third of the kingdom does. They're not the immortal, all-powerful beings people like to whisper about, you know."

Asterin wasn't smiling, nor laughing. "Mortain. Oldwin. Recognize those names?"

Tyreste didn't answer. Of course he recognized them. They were known throughout the kingdom as the king's henchmen. His *sorcerers*, used to shock and subdue crown enemies.

"Their names, Tyreste, are *in these letters*." Asterin poked the stack with his finger. "Two-hundred-year-old letters."

"If they're not immortal, they certainly have some sort of arrangement, don't they?" Sesto said more than asked.

Tyreste cleared his expression. His thoughts he left tucked away, not wanting them to interfere with whatever Asterin and Sesto were about to say next. "All right. I agree, that's strange."

Sesto rolled his eyes toward Asterin. "Strange."

"There are probably other sorcerers with the same names. A lot of men are named after their fathers and grandfathers."

"There are always explanations, if we're determined enough to believe only what's convenient," Asterin said slowly. "Sesto couldn't decipher much, but he read enough to be concerned. Enough to realize..." His voice lowered to a whisper again. "Something terrible was going on then, and if the same perpetrators are around, having outlived those who knew what foul business they were up to, why would it not be happening now?"

Tyreste squinted, shaking his head. "What, you think... You think the Rhiagain sorcerers are plotting against the Ravenwoods?"

"Plotting infers ideas. Plans. Whatever the Meduwyn have against the Ravenwoods, they're *far* past plotting, Scribe." Sesto stared at the stack. "The letters stop, rather abruptly. The last one is from the Wynter girl, Zo. That's how she signs her letters, Zo. And the last one, it's not to the boy, Paeris, but to a woman named

35

Annelyse. Of course, like all of Zo's letters, I can't read more than a word or three."

"Two hundred and fifty *years* though, Sesto," Tyreste replied. "That was a long time ago."

"Then let's rule it out," Asterin said sensibly. "Let's just do what we can to decipher the message, and if we determine the past is the past, I'll happily sell the letters to the Reliquary."

It was evident Asterin was only pretending to consider that the relevance of the letters was purely historical, but his stubbornness was stoking Tyreste's concerns. Asterin Edevane was a man of reason, not an inciter of fear. "But why... Why would Zo write her letters to Duncarrow in Vjestikaan? No one in Duncarrow speaks the language."

"If you want to be sophistic, they don't speak Old Ilynglass either," Sesto replied. "They're both dead languages. One forbidden by the king, the other lost to time. So if you ask, why Vjestikaan, you must also ask, why Old Ilynglass?" He nodded at the letters. "They chose to communicate in languages few know for a reason. Don't have to be a sleuth to deduce it was to keep others from reading their words. How they learned each other's dead languages, well, that must be part of the mystery. As far as we can tell, the letters made it to the mainland by accident, found in a trunk belonging to a Rhiagain who'd settled in the Easterlands. Perhaps there was a cipher that was lost along the way."

"*All* of this is supposition until we know the contents," Asterin said, sounding closer to the man of learning Tyreste remembered. The scholar fingered the leather on his gloves, tracing it in nervous passes. He blotted his temple on his sleeve. "And until we know the contents, I can't ethically sell these to anyone. Certainly not the Reliquary, who are funded by the same crown who controls these creatures."

Tyreste gripped the edge of the table with a long look at Asterin. His mouth parted, but it was another moment before he knew what to say. "You're scared. You've never been scared by anything we've translated before."

"A reaction, I hope, is proven embarrassingly unwarranted," Asterin replied. "But my instincts are all I have. And they're *screaming* at me to beware of the hands these might fall into."

Tyreste reached a palm down, for Rikard to rub his head against. Both men watched him, waiting. Could they see the plume of dread rising from his chest? Did they sense his simplistic questions were a ploy, to cover his apprehension?

For there *had* been whispers about the Ravenwoods. He hadn't remembered at first. Exhaustion wasn't just calling, it was hollering, and his memory wasn't to be trusted when he was so tired. He'd never been one to concern himself with the doings of others who came in and out of the Tavern at the Top of the World. It was the way, the creed, of a taverner to never engage, never share. Within their walls was a promise so sacred, it never needed to be said. What happened in the tavern stayed there.

But as his old friends shared their concerns, little wisps of conversation returned to Tyreste. The high priestess of Midnight Crest had purportedly paid an unexpected visit to Steward Wynter several months past, in the dead of night. No one knew why. Those who might weren't saying.

Yet what business was any of it of his? Of Asterin's and Sesto's? If there was trouble in the mountains, it had nothing to do with them. If that trouble involved the king and his sorcerers, it was cause for more caution, not less.

Tyreste Penhallow had already borne enough trouble for an entire lifetime.

No. I sound as paranoid as they do. If I mention what I heard, they'll stay, and if they stay, they'll be stuck here for weeks.

"I don't speak Vjestikaan. I can't help with this one." Tyreste pushed the letters across the table. He couldn't meet either man's eyes. "I'm sorry you came all this way for nothing."

Asterin pushed them back. "If you can't translate them, we can't sell them. Keep them. Maybe you'll find another way."

"You don't care about the money. You never have." Tyreste scoffed.

"No." Asterin finished his ale, pushed his chair back, and stood. "It's my conscience that bade me leave my wife in her convalescence when there was nowhere else I'd rather be than at her side. Fear has me farther and longer away from my children than I've ever been. I hope it's unfounded. But I don't think it is." He nodded sideways at Sesto. "I figure we have until noontide before we need to be on the road, to stay ahead of the storm. We'd love to catch up, Tyreste, if you're not too tired."

"No," Tyrese said quickly, stifling a yawn. "No, I'd love that."

"Good." Asterin lifted the letters from the table and thrust them at Tyreste's chest. "And if you can't find a way in the end... burn them. It would be a shame to lose such historical relics, but we'll all sleep fairer at night knowing we weren't complicit in something terrible."

THREE
THE ROTTING CENTER OF IT ALL

Anastazja, her head hunkered and swallowed by her double hood of furs, trudged behind Magda. *Deliver us, springtide* was the saying around the village, more of a jest than a prayer. Every season was winter in Witchwood Cross.

The snow was deepest in the valley between Fanghelm and the forested foothills of Icebolt Mountain. Hunters had been forbidden from the forests for the past five years, a consequence of continuously failing the Vuk od Varem, so the paths were overgrown and packed with seasons of snow and ice. The eerie silence, blanketed by the towering pine-needled sentries, was another reminder they didn't belong.

There'd been a heavy storm since her last visit, but Anastazja could just make out the divots from when she and Magda had trekked through a fortnight ago, for Magda's last "endeavor." That was what she called her terrible experiments, *endeavoring*, as though she was merely dabbling in evil and not existing at the rotting center of it all.

It took an hour to reach the cave by foot. Horseback wouldn't have been much faster without a true path, and it might have been deadly for the horses with the way hidden beneath the shifting banks. Anastazja loved Enzi so much, she'd stopped riding her altogether, terrified of one day finding her throat cut in her stall as punishment. Magda had already taken everyone else Ana loved.

Not everyone. You can still keep him safe.

Ana winced. It was a colossal effort keeping Tyreste from her thoughts, a necessity born not only of fear of Magda potentially reading her mind but of addressing a heartbreak so tender, it left her retching anytime she remembered the awful lies she'd said to push him away. She wondered what he was doing, *how* he was doing, but that was too far. She had to stop. She *had* to forget him. Magda would afford him no mercy if she knew he wasn't just an amusement.

Though, Ana had never had amusements. Tyreste had been her first and, though she hadn't realized it back then, her last.

Better for Magda and others to believe her loose with her associations than careless with her heart.

"Plan to stand there all day, do you?" Magda's shingly snarl returned her to the present.

Holding her tongue was sometimes the only form of power Anastazja had in the otherwise excruciatingly lopsided association. She instead stepped inside the small cave and shrugged off her layers of cloaks, piling them neatly in a corner as she always did.

She returned in her gown and boots, but Magda extended an arm toward the corner and shook her head. "All of it this time."

Anastazja's eyes narrowed. "What do you mean 'all of it'?"

Magda snapped her fingers. "Gown. Undergarments. Boots. Off."

Ana's flesh tingled, the first part of her to awaken to the meaning of Magda's request. "But I've been shifting just fine in my clothing."

"You won't be needing your clothing when you return." Magda's outstretched arm was a solid monolith, unyielding. "Now."

"It's far too cold for that!" Ana exclaimed, though her reply was only a cover for the dread creeping around her heart like fingers of ice. Naked. Magda wanted her to lure a raven *naked*, and every plausible explanation for the demand was worse than the last. Ana glanced toward the cave entrance like a cornered animal readying for encroaching danger, but Magda didn't bother trying to block her escape. They both knew it wasn't herself Ana was afraid for.

"You're a Wynter. You carry the blood of the wulf. Of the Vjestik. The cold won't kill you, but if you don't take the rest of your clothes off, you can be certain I will." Magda's boots creaked on the patches of ice as she came closer. "Will be no bother to me. A tad ahead of schedule, you dying, but Niko will make a fine replacement for our endeavoring, until I tire of him as well."

The threat worked. It always worked. Dangling her brother's fate was the real power Magda held. It wasn't her dark magic, nor her calculated, ancient evil. It was Ana's unwavering belief that once she was gone, Nikolaj would first take her place and then be disposed of when his purpose had been served.

Heavy with trepidation, Ana moved slowly toward where she'd left her furs. Her hands trembled as she pulled at the stays of her gown, releasing them one by one. As always, her mind spun around ways out of the hold Magda had over her, but as always, she found none.

Shivering, with one arm crossed over her chest and the other covering her nethers, Ana shuffled back to the crone.

Magda nodded approvingly. "Yes. That'll do." She clapped her hands twice. "Splendid. Tell me the rules."

Ana's teeth clacked. "Inspect... isolate... lure. No..." She fought violent shivers. "No high priestesses. No heirs. No spares. Find... Find one who won't be missed." That last rule was the worst, the most foreboding, because she didn't understand what it meant.

41

After she lured them for the koldyna, her part was over. And Magda always released the ravens when her endeavoring was done.

Can I be certain about that?

"Yes." Magda's empty amber eyes were lifeless pools. "No women this time. You don't return until you have a suitable raven male, and Guardians help you if you're still flying around at nightfall."

"Why no women this time?" Ana was stalling. She already knew the answer. She just wasn't ready to acknowledge it.

Magda sneered. "Questions are not a part of this arrangement. You know that." She stepped closer and tipped a gnarled finger under Ana's chin, lifting it. Her chiseled nail dug into the soft flesh. "You won't be returning to the cave. You remember your way to the observatory, from the sky?"

Ana nodded. *Why the observatory,* she almost asked but didn't.

Questions were unwelcome. The less she understood, the better. Her ignorance to the specifics of Magda's endeavoring was the mortar holding together the loose bricks of her steadily crumbling life.

"Observatory," Ana repeated with a protracted exhale. She squinted into the dense squall forming outside the cave. She'd warm up once she shifted, but what about when she landed again?

You won't be needing your clothing when you return.

Don't think about it. Don't you dare let your thoughts wander down that path. There's no coming back.

Tyreste's crooked grin appeared in her mind. She heard his giggles—rare but so real, so pure, and so wonderful—and felt his calloused hands running along the curve of her lower back, then settling on her ass with a claiming squeeze. Tasted the lingering sweat and cider at the edge of his jaw as she trailed kisses. Saw the deep pools of care reflecting in his eyes as he listened to her share things she'd never shared with anyone, but never all she wanted to share.

Whoever married Tyreste Penhallow would be a fortunate woman indeed.

She only knew it would not be her.

Marriage—*life*—was no longer a future she had any claim to. All she could do was use the time left to her to keep her loved ones safe.

"Ana. Forgetting something?"

Ana's shoulders lifted in tension. She closed her eyes, braced herself, and turned to accept what she knew Magda would be holding in her palm.

A charmed apple.

She took it without looking at the crone and pivoted away, tucking the apple under her chin to keep it from falling when she shifted. She wasn't sure it would work. Usually anything she wore or had stowed into her clothing was safely included in the magic, but she'd never shifted—or shifted back—in the nude before.

Ana lowered her hands to her sides, broke into a sprint, and launched herself into the open. As she caught air, her face elongated into a beak, her feet drawing up and tight into talons. Feathers coated her cold flesh, restoring her sense of warmth—and safety.

A phoenix was, after all, born of fire.

Anastazja soared through the storm, aimed for the peaks of Icebolt.

It was past noontide by the time Tyreste said his good-byes to Asterin and Sesto. Asterin wore his concern for his wife in every tic and frown, and Tyr felt terrible the man had come at all. In the end, it was the only reason he'd agreed to try the translations. Whatever Asterin really believed was in the letters, it was serious enough for him to leave the one person he couldn't bear to be parted from.

Tyr had once loved Rhiainach Skylark too, but it had taken many years for him to realize she'd never belonged with any man except Asterin Edevane. The love between them was the realest he'd ever seen, and he'd thought with Ana...

No.

That time in his life reminded him too much of his present heartbreak. Would he have been happier to see his old friends if they'd arrived before Ana had walked out on him? It wasn't their fault the confrontation had brought all his old, buried traumas spilling forth. He didn't love them less, but he'd felt the Tyr of the past slipping back in, trying to reclaim his place, and that could never, *ever* happen.

We could stay another night, catch up...

No, no, another storm is expected, and you'll want to be south of Wulfsgate when it hits. We can catch up another time. Maybe... Maybe I'll make my way to Riverchapel soon. Springtide is just over the horizon.

A lie, but a kind one. He wanted to mean it. But he knew in his heart there was no going back.

Tyr stretched and cracked his knuckles over the fire. He glanced at the table and the stack of letters half spread along the surface. A candle sat nearby, perhaps too close, and he thought, briefly, what if there were to be an accident...

But then his entire cabin would be lost with it. He'd built the place with his own hands and stubborn determination.

He was swallowing a sip of ale from his mug on the hearth when a soft knock sounded. Adeline never knocked hard because she didn't know what her knocks sounded like. Not anymore. Not since the fire in Parth.

If it had been anyone but Addy, he'd have ignored it, but she was the one person he'd never slight.

Tyr opened the door, and his little sister smiled at him. She signed on her chest, *Can I come in?*

He signed back, *Of course. I have cider brewing.*

Addy beamed at that and flounced in. She glanced around as she always did, like it was her first time, though she was his most frequent visitor. Aside from Rikard—his brother, not the wayward cat jittering at his feet, casually attempting to trip him with every step—and, until recently, Ana, she was his only visitor.

Her shrewd eyes zeroed in on the letters right away. She turned to sign, *From Steward Edevane and Abbot Sesto?*

Tyr chuckled to himself. *Another translation.*

Her brows crinkled. *Why didn't they send them by courier?*

Because they wanted to see me, obviously. Tyr tousled her hair, pulling a grin from her, but she wasn't satisfied with the answer.

Will you not tell me the truth?

Tyr sighed and glanced at the stack. *The truth is I don't know. I haven't translated them yet.*

Can I help?

He'd been teaching Adeline the old languages for the past two years. She'd caught on well, enough that he could confidently funnel work her way, so she could pocket some coin of her own. On his way out of town, Asterin had promised a place for her in the company, when she was ready.

But Tyr's sinking dread returned when he thought of her coming anywhere near whatever was in those letters.

Not today, he signed with a smile he hoped was enough to make her drop it.

Addy scrunched her face into a pout. With a devious grin, she bolted for the table and snatched the letters up before Tyr could stop her.

She moved to the window and the light, to read, but her face registered her confusion. Clutching the letters to her chest with one hand, she turned and signed with the other, *Is this Vjestikaan?*

Some of it.

She shifted the letters under one arm to free up her other hand. *How are you going to translate a language you cannot read, silly?*

They're not all in Vjestikaan.

Addy squinted and turned her focus back to the stack. She held the letters close as she sifted through, shooting wary looks at Tyr every few seconds. *Some are in Old Ilynglass.*

Indeed.

From a boy named... Her eyes narrowed. *Paeris of Glaisgain? Is he related to Imryll of Glaisgain?*

How do you know about that?

My scholar from Books of All Things teaches us the histories of Witchwood Cross.

Don't suppose he taught you some Vjestikaan?

Addy laughed. *No more than the few words you know.*

Her knowledge of the Wynters might prove useful, but until he grasped the seriousness of the correspondence, he didn't want his little sister anywhere near them.

Can I stay? I won't be in your way. Promise.

Tyr crossed his arms and fought the low groan brewing in his throat. He always tried not to make sounds that made her feel more excluded. *If you mean that promise.*

That's what a promise is, brother.

Wouldn't be the first time you broke one when mischief called.

She grinned. *Can I pick a book from your library?*

"Library" was generous. His collection consisted of a small shelf with a couple dozen books, all gifts from Asterin and Rhiain. Even with the coin he made from translations, he couldn't afford to buy his own—and even if he *could* afford it, there were far more practical things to spend coin on.

Go on.

Addy scampered off and disappeared into the back room.

Tyr went back for his ale and settled into a chair. The uneven legs knocked along the floor. Rikard the Mouser sounded a long, grating meow before dropping in for another nap.

The letters were in chronological order, all dated. He studied the first, written by Zofia Wynter in Vjestikaan, decided he was no better at reading the language today than he had been the day before, and set it aside for the one underneath, from Paeris.

He went for his quill and ink but changed his mind. He'd read first, then transcribe everything later.

Tyr twisted in his chair, trying to get comfortable, and read.

Dearest Zo,

I know I should not complain about the precariousness of midwinter to you, living in your ice fortress, but this has been an especially vexing season. Ships cannot reach Duncarrow when the tide is so fickle, and so we've been subsisting on a ration of dried meats and fruits for the past month. I've forgotten the taste of fresh meat.

Tyr's eyes, heavy from the long night, started to close. Translating in his mind was taxing, and he was nearly spent. He blinked hard and pushed through, determined to finish at least one letter.

Mother has been unwell. Medicine offers little relief. I don't understand why Mortain or Oldwin cannot heal her. They say it's not in their charge, but I know they heal. I've seen it! I suspect they enjoy lording their power over us. Lest we ever forget they're immortal, their sallow skin and soulless eyes are there to remind us.

Grandfather tells me never to say a foul word against either of them. More of a warning, really. He's terrified of them both, but especially Mortain. He won't say why. He thinks they can read his mind, and he's likely right.

What does your grandmother say about the Meduwyn? Does she speak of her time in Duncarrow, when she was a princess? Or does she keep those thoughts to herself as well?

Ah, well. The hour grows late, and I'm told any ravens must leave tonight, or it will be weeks before they can fly again. I have more to say, but it can wait for my next letter.

I'm intrigued, if not a little afraid, of what you shared about the Ravenwoods. How many have disappeared? Has the trouble worsened since you wrote? Are you any closer to understanding the cause? Whatever it is, be careful, Zo. It takes power to bring down power, and the Ravenwoods are not weak. Do not find yourself in the path of whoever—whatever—has them in their sights.

I know you'll never come to Duncarrow, but I'm working to persuade Grandfather to make a trip to Witchwood Cross before he's too aged for travel. He often speaks of his sister... of wanting to see Grand Aunt Imryll one last time. It's hard to watch him grow old. I will very much miss him when he's gone.

Your cipher is near perfect, but you occasionally use words I don't understand. I just wanted you to know that, in case I fail to respond to something you mention.

With heart,
Par

"It takes power to bring down power," Tyreste said, gently tracing the words with his finger. He slumped back, ruminating on what he'd read. So far, it all matched Asterin and Sesto's limited assessment. Nothing unexpected. Nothing indicating the missing Ravenwoods were anything but an unfortunate one-off occurrence, or even a mere rumor.

There were still dozens of letters in the stack. But no matter how far he got, he'd still only be getting half the story.

With a sigh, he pushed back from the table. He checked to make sure Addy was still in the library and then tucked the letters away in a place only he would think to look—in the stone cubby he'd built for precisely this purpose, on the underside of the second hearth, the one in the cozy sitting room he almost never used.

When they were secured, he turned and saw the discarded wine glasses on the table. A rim of red rouge lined the top edge of one, and he saw Ana again taking a slow sip, with her drawn-out blink and easy grin. He reached out to grab hold of a nearby chair when air left his lungs, which turned into a choking sob he slammed his mouth shut to keep down.

Ana was in trouble. He *knew* it in his heart, in his bones. She hadn't meant a word she'd said, and if she'd just turned so he could see her eyes, he could have confirmed it.

My soft heart is my downfall. It nearly ended me once before. Witchwood Cross was supposed to be a fresh start, not more of the same. I was given a second chance, when most men are only given one.
Forget her.

He heard the words in the voice of old Tyr, embittered and sequestered in the Reliquary dungeon. He never wanted to be that Tyr again, but even less did he want the heartbreak indiscriminately spreading an incomparable ache from limb to limb.

Forget her.

Tyr scooped the glasses up, dropped them into the basin without another thought, and went to check on Addy.

He found her curled up on the floor, sleeping, a book cradled in her arms.

Smiling, he knelt and lifted his sister into his arms. She stirred only slightly as he carried her to the modest bed in the corner of his study. He'd built it just for her, for times like this.

Tyr leaned down, kissed her forehead, and closed the curtains to give her some darkness.

Sleep well, he signed.

FØUR
ENDEAVORING

Anastazja settled on a peak northeast of Midnight Crest. She'd been dancing along the jagged edges of Icebolt Mountain for hours, using the cloud cover as a shield from the Ravenwood scouts gathered along the ramparts. There wasn't anything else that could hide her bright plumage, at least until night fell.

Ancestors help her if she was still out in the dark. Stepan had once told her a story of how a past Wynter had been chased from the night sky by furious Ravenwoods... how they'd swallowed the boy from all sides in an invisible blanket of terror and driven him into a cave where he'd stayed for days, afraid to fly, until a search party found him and brought him home.

She thought of that story often when endeavoring. But what interested her most was the part of the tale that remained untold. What had sent her ancestor into the skies that night, that had angered the Ravenwoods enough to nearly murder him?

As always, the answers were close enough to reach out and grab, but she couldn't. Wouldn't.

51

The Rookery was an inconceivably large keep, carved into the peaks of Icebolt itself. There were no roads, no paths, and no means of reaching the dark stone fortress save one: flying. Every Ravenwood could fly, but Ana was the only non-Ravenwood with the ability, only cursed with the heir's gift because Stepan had fallen to the Vuk od Varem. When Magda disposed of Ana, that curse would fall to Niko. If Niko died, the designation would return to their father. If *Father* died...

Both of Arkhady's parents were long gone, and his only sister was a scholar with the Reliquary, in the heart of the Easterlands. She'd never been back to the Cross, even for a visit. There were cousins, aunts, uncles... all so far removed from what had been happening at Fanghelm that they'd be the perfect pawns.

There was a little comfort in realizing Magda couldn't annihilate the *entire* Wynter line, because then she'd never get what she wanted from the Ravenwoods.

But though Ana had been unwillingly assisting her since Stepan had died, she still didn't know what Magda really wanted from the elusive coven of ravens at the mountain's top. *I want to study them. Understand them,* the koldyna had said, and Ana had no choice but to believe it was that simple, because she already carried the unthinkable burden of keeping her father and brother alive. She had no space left in her brutalized heart for the fate of strangers.

Ravenwoods walked along the battlements, oblivious to the phoenix stalking them from a nearby peak. They milled about, some alone, others in small packs. They looked no different from the people Ana had grown up with. Almost every Ravenwood had pitch-dark hair, except the one or two who had rare silver manes. And they were all, every one of them, related to each other. The priestesses ruled the skies, mating with brothers, uncles, and cousins. It was a bizarre custom made necessary by their isolation, which was essential to their survival. Magda was living proof that the threats against them were very real, and their secluded hideaway, unreachable by foot, was the only thing keeping them safe.

Some of them anyway.

One male in particular caught Ana's eye. While the other Ravenwoods moved with solemn ease, this one wore his grim purpose in his creased brows and decisive stride. His cheeks blazed with... something. Endeavoring aside, she couldn't deny her curiosity.

He disappeared into a curved spire, one of the many stairwells in the Rookery. Her eyes followed the perimeter of the stone structure, which stretched all the way to the uppermost battlements. In all her flights to Midnight Crest, she'd never seen anyone go up there. She imagined a wind fierce enough to send even the strongest flier hurtling to their death. It must be why he was taking the stairs instead of shifting.

Once the clouds passed into place, Ana returned to the skies, bracing against a sharp attack of sleet. The shift in temperature clawed at her bones as she was knocked around the sky by the push and pull of the building squall. Visibility diminished the higher she climbed, hail pelting her wings, knocking her off course. Everything inside her screamed to turn back, but the faces of Niko, her father, and Tyreste all flashed before her, so she pushed on, shaking but determined.

The clouds cleared, leaving both her and the Ravenwood exposed. She was shocked to find him completely nude, standing in the direct center of the drenched battlements. One hand stroked his cock while his head lolled back in blissful surrender. Sleet hammered his body, creating frozen pools between the stones at his feet, but he didn't seem to notice or care.

Ana held her position, unable to draw closer or turn back. The Ravenwood continued his ministrations, his bare feet planted, his toes dug against the flooding mortar, and his tongue clamped between his teeth.

Then his face came downward, and his eyes locked onto hers. He released his cock and charged forward, his head tilted in dawning horror as he struggled to make sense of the situation.

She quickly weighed her options. If she took off, he'd alert his people, and they'd know the Wynter heir was in their skies without authorization. They'd send an emissary to her father, demanding to know why he'd violated their long-held alliance. Violence would follow. Any illusion of trust would disintegrate, and, with it, any use the koldyna still had for Ana and the people she loved most in the world.

Or she could do what Magda had sent her to do.

Ana angled her nose downward and dipped close. She unfurled, her feet catching a sprint as they landed, slapping the wet stones. She caught the apple when it dropped from the underside of her chin, and she held it aloft for the Ravenwood, quaking with a fusion of exhilaration and terror.

I only need to lure him. She never asked me to do anything except lure him.

Then why did she send you without your clothing?

The Ravenwood pulled to a halt, his mouth and eyes dilating as the seconds ticked by.

"I brought you something." Ana moved closer, holding out the apple. She angled her body away, as though it did any good when she had nothing to cover herself. Her heart was pounding so hard, her eyes widened with each wild beat.

"Who the... Are you..." His head shook in slow passes as his eyes scanned her. His lips parted when his examination continued south. "You're not a Ravenwood."

"Is it the hair?" She didn't know why she said it.

"The hair?" The Ravenwood didn't seem to know where to go with that. He gawped at her and then the apple.

In the end, they always went for the apple.

He stretched a hand forward, then coiled it back as though stung. He lifted his gaze. "Who *are* you?"

"A dream," she said. Her words were enveloped by the roaring storm, so she said them again. A fierce wind rattled her sideways, and her mind caught up to the terrible chill racking her body. She couldn't dally. She had to get him to follow her before they both froze to death.

"Why are you naked?" he asked.

"Why are *you* naked?"

"It's the only place I can be alone here." It was a half answer, but she wondered what his life was like, that he had to climb to the top of their remote castle for privacy. "A dream, you say?"

"Mhm." Ana closed her fist over the apple and shook her hand for him to accept it. Nothing so vibrant, so juicy, grew in the Ravenwoods' icy kingdom. Apples were a genuine delight, a treat none could easily refuse. Even men relished them. The village of Witchwood Cross held an entire damn festival celebrating their love for the succulent food.

With a tentative step closer, the Ravenwood bent his hand forward and accepted the apple. He held it up to the sky, turning his hand. "Some dream. I couldn't have conjured this in my greatest imaginings."

"Try it."

The glamour faded. His eyes narrowed. "Why?"

Ana clenched, steeling and switching on a side of her she loathed almost as much as she loathed the koldyna. Her grin was slow, full of dark purpose. "Because what joys are there in life without taking what has been forbidden to us?"

The Ravenwood's face brightened, then darkened again, his eyes turning to slits. Now it was hunger she read in him. Primal. Feral. He dug his teeth in for a generous bite, his eyes rolling back as the juices slid down his chin. "Fuck." He took another bite, a groan echoing in his throat. "Do you have more?"

"So much more. As many as you want." Ana's voice warbled.

She didn't have to wait long for the charm to take effect. He finished the apple and tossed it into the distance before charging toward her with long, violent strides.

The Ravenwood thrust his hands behind Ana and took her hair in his fists, forcing her head back. With a hard sniff, he traced his tongue along the hollow of her neck, sweeping upward until he reached her chin. His teeth clamped onto the edge, enough to make her wince. She felt his cock throb against her belly, swollen with intent, and if she wasn't fast enough, Magda's charm would outmatch her own magic.

Ana tore away and skittered back. Her flesh was nearly frozen, her bones blocks of ice. "The rest of the apples are elsewhere, raven."

He licked his lips. A menacing air surrounded the roll of his shoulders and the quick sneer as he sized her up. Something was different this time—something about the charm. It wasn't the apples he wanted.

It was her.

Magda had changed the intent, and if Ana didn't shift *immediately*, the raven would overpower her, and there'd be nothing she could do except scream into a void of nothing.

"Where then?" He strained his words through a gruff moan, his hand back on his cock.

"Follow—" Ana shifted before she could finish, fright shooting her into the skies for the race of her life.

Steam snaked along the surface of Tyreste's mug. He preferred taking his cider outside, even in the springtide. There were perhaps a dozen days each year in the Cross warm enough for him to leave the furs inside, and he relished every one of them.

The first night he'd spent with Anastazja had been like that. The Cider Festival had been in full swing, and she'd come into the tavern and taken a seat near the window, alone, impishness coloring her gaze. *Can you join me out there, or are you too busy?*

You don't have someone else you'd rather, ah, go with?

If I did, I'd have asked them. Though… I hope you didn't have your heart set on the festival.

What do you mean?

Eighteen years I've watched the men crush apples beneath their feet like barbarians, and I just don't think they can add anything new to the sport, do you?

Can't say I fancy watching men do drunken dances on a field of apples, either. But there's not much else to do in Witchwood Cross, is there?

We'll think of something. She'd whispered the words, and he'd been delightfully caught by her roguish grin, her plump red lips pursed and inviting.

Tyr's father, with a knowing half smile, had nodded for him to go with her. So he had. Ana had taken him up into the foothills, climbing nearly as high as the Shrine of the Ancestors. She'd insisted she went there all the time, but she had been so winded by the hike, he doubted it. It was only later he learned she usually flew.

Flew. A phoenix. An actual, honest-to-Guardians shifter. How ironic it was that Tyr's mother had called *him* one, after he'd risen from the ashes of the old tavern in Parth and made it north to his family, back from the dead.

But his father's assessment seemed far more apt. A blackbird. Solitary by nature.

He and Ana had talked for hours, about the most wonderfully inconsequential things, and then they'd made love by a fire, spinning magic under the stars.

He'd never been the same since.

Acrimony creeped into his bones. He could almost feel the wall rebuilding itself brick by brick, blocking out both the darkness and the light. Slowly, the soft perfume of apples, of *her*, faded, and there was only his bitter root coffee and the gently swirling snow. A storm between storms.

Tyr started to turn and go back in when he spotted bright orange streaking through the sky. He started forward, squinting as the phoenix tilted sideways, angling downward into the foothills, in the direction of the observatory and the shrine.

Directly behind her was another bird. A raven. Close enough to give the impression of a chase.

She's not your problem anymore, he told himself, his eyes still pinned on the sky as he retreated inside.

Anastazja's heart stayed in her throat when she shifted back. She hadn't slowed her momentum when she'd landed, rushing for the blazing lights under the dome of glass, despite there being just as much danger ahead as behind.

She burst through the door and whipped her head around, searching for something to drape over her. There were no cloaks on the rack. Her clothing was nowhere to be seen. The cavernous room had always been light on furnishings, but it seemed garishly empty now. The bearskin rug near the single hearth was the only thing resembling relief, so she raced over and huddled near the flames.

Strong hands gripped her hips from behind and tugged. She lost her footing and went sprawling, slamming her hand against the mantle on the way to the ground. She tried to grab hold as she fell but instead went tumbling to the rug with a strangled cry.

The raven rolled her onto her back and loomed over her. Lit by flames and stars, his expression flickered between menacing and peaceful. She swallowed hard, knowing which was true yet wishing she was wrong. He'd eaten the apple. Until the effects wore off, he would be in thrall to Magda's command.

A much, *much* different command than any endeavor that had come before.

"Caught you, phoenix." He grappled for her hands and pinned them on either side of her head. She tried to move, but entire sections of curls were stuck under their joined hands, pinched and burning with every tug. Her legs were equally incapacitated, locked wide by his muscled thighs. "I do like it here better. Good choice."

Magda! Instinct produced the cry for help and killed it in the same breath. Nothing defined her relationship with her stepmother more clearly than knowing her worst troubles started and ended with the koldyna.

She shifted sideways with a desperate groan, but he was stronger. The effort sapped her burst of energy. "What's your name?" she asked through gritted teeth, hoping to keep him talking long enough to find a way to escape.

"Varradyn." His tongue lashed his bottom lip after he sounded the *n*. He bucked his hips.

She dug upward along the rug in retreat.

Where was Magda? She'd always been waiting when Ana landed with a raven. Always dismissed her as soon as she delivered them, leaving her ignorant to whatever happened next. Everything about this round of endeavoring was different. Until that moment, Ana hadn't fully believed Magda was not just dangling her as bait but offering her up as the prize.

She's not my friend. Not my mother. She will watch from the shadows as this spelled raven does something so terrible, it will destroy both him and me.

"Varradyn," she said, voice shaking. His hands were pinched so tight around her wrists, she'd started to lose feeling in her fingers. She'd never outlast the magic. Her only chance was to break through to the man inside. "Listen to me. I don't know you... I don't..." She twisted again. "But I know you're not yourself. And I know this because—" Her breath arrested in the wake of his intense glare. "Because it's the *apple*. The apple that... that turned you into... into this." She clamped her legs against his outer thighs in an attempt to move him enough to regain ground. "Varradyn. *Please*. Let me go."

Varradyn dragged his nose along her neck and up to her chin, opening her mouth with his tongue. She clenched her jaw, expelling him, and he coiled back in offense.

"You said there were more apples." His mouth contorted into a petulant snarl. "I want them."

Fresh hope filled Ana. "More apples. Yes! Yes, I can get you more apples. If you move... If you let me go, I'll get you as many as you want."

"After," Varradyn growled and ground against her thigh again in vacant, mindless movements.

She wiggled enough to lift one of her legs over her pelvis and used it to block him from advancing any further.

Ana turned her face to the side to dodge another drugged kiss. *Think, Ana. Think!* If he released even one of her wrists, she was within reach of the poker. One hit was all it would take. It might be more than enough.

But she realized she didn't want to hurt Varradyn. He wasn't a predator. He was just a Ravenwood, who had been minding his business, lured away from his home to do Magda's bidding. If he survived the ordeal and had any memory of it, he might never forgive himself.

It wasn't his fault.

This is what Magda wants. She's here, hiding. Watching. Waiting for it to be over. For me to be hurt, humiliated, and humbled.

Varradyn grunted and tried to force her leg back down, but in the struggle, she freed the other and used both to push him off. He went sprawling backward, but he didn't stay down. He was already crawling over her again by the time she pulled herself up. "This is what you wanted, phoenix. You're the one who came to me." He shuffled forward, and she clambered back. "Now *I* want what you promised."

If I disobey her, she'll take it out on Father. On Niko.

Maybe. But if I allow this raven to assault me, who knows where he'll stop? What the magic has bid him to do? What if he kills me?

"Varradyn," Ana said. Her scratchy throat buried half of the word. She cleared it. "Varradyn! I *don't* want this. Neither do you. It's the magic... It's the apple. The apple made you like this, and when it wears off, and you realize what you've done, you'll never look at yourself the same again."

"Too late," he murmured, empty-eyed, and lurched forward. He would have landed atop her had she not leaped to her feet just in time.

Ana stumbled sideways into the hearth. He caught on to what she was doing, but she swung down to grab the poker before he could. She clutched it in her hands, against her chest. "I don't want to hurt you. I really, *really* don't."

"How strange." Varradyn pushed to his feet. He looked down at his hands, then back at her with a vacant stare. "I desperately want to hurt you."

"No," she said, shaking her head. "No, you don't. It isn't *you* that wants this. It's the foul magic you consumed. It will wear off. This will pass. I promise."

"But you gave me the apple."

"I should not have! I didn't know—" Ana's shivers cut off the rest of her words.

"It's as though I have no will of my own," he said, a musing smile playing at his mouth. He moved closer, and she shook the poker, gripping it with both hands. "Or perhaps I'm just waking up to who I truly am. What I truly want."

"Varradyn, not a step closer!"

"You brought me here, witch."

"I'm not a—" But she was. All Vjestik were. Magda, while not a Vjestik, was undoubtedly a witch, albeit of a much darker persuasion, and it was her magic that had turned him into an animal. Magic *Ana* had fed him. *I didn't know. I didn't know.* "Please. Just... Sit down for a moment. We can talk."

The corner of his upper lip peeled back. "I didn't come here to talk."

"I know," Ana said, trying to keep calm, which was damn near impossible when she was standing naked, wielding a poker to keep a naked Ravenwood from jumping her bones. "I know, Varradyn. But it's what we need to do right now. If you come closer, I'll have no choice but to take you out with this." She nudged the poker. "If you stay put, we can have a conversation. A

61

proper one. And I'll tell you everything. How I found you. How we got here. Who sent—"

"That's quite enough!" Magda's shrill voice radiated off the glass, settling into the stones. "You've made a proper mess of this situation, girl, and it's time to end it. Kill him."

"*What?*" Ana turned around, toward the direction of the words, but she couldn't see the koldyna anywhere.

Even Varradyn stumbled out of his stupor momentarily, cocking his head in befuddlement.

"Kill him. I'd have preferred you fucked him first, but I should have known you'd need more warming up to the idea."

"Warming up to *what* idea? I would never, ever have done it. No matter what threats you hold over me. You may as well kill *me* if you think I'll ever do *anything* like this again!"

"We'll see." The words creaked like boots on wooden steps. "Underneath the hearth you will find a dagger strapped. It's yours. Take his heart."

"I will not." Ana backed away from Varradyn, from the fire, and from the dagger supposedly waiting for her. "Varradyn, *go. Run.* Fly away from here *now* before it's too late!"

"No, Varradyn," Magda said, placid as a lake. "You will not go. You will not run. You will not fly anywhere."

"I will not go. I will not run. I will not fly anywhere," Varradyn repeated, monotone.

Ana whipped her focus between the raven and the traveling sound of Magda's threats. "You're completely mad. This is *not* what we agreed to. This is not simple *endeavoring.*"

"And how would you know? You always leave before the good part begins." Magda's shadow appeared first, then she stepped out from behind the large pulpit at the head of the dome. She flashed her blackened teeth. "Take his heart, Ana, or I take yours."

Tears ran down Ana's face as she spread her arms wide, poker held aloft. "Take it then! You have already taken my mother! You're slowly taking my father, my brother! What else is there? *What else is there, koldyna?*"

Varradyn watched them both, shivering.

"What else..." Magda glided forward. Her thin orange hair was matted in small clumps around her face, almost as if she'd styled it that way. "You think I don't know you gave your heart away? That I cannot see the signs of love in your eyes? In the way you choose your words? That I cannot read the flush in your cheeks when you've returned from town?" Her cackle sent a chilling bolt through Ana. "Oh, girl. Little stupid pjika. Of course I know. And now that you've angered me, I'll find out *who* has distracted you so, and I'll tear his heart from his chest, still beating. You'll find it one night on your dinner plate, instead of supper. And unless you want me to slit your father's throat in front of you and precious little Niko, you'll *devour* it. Every last bite. Every last drop of blood he spilled, for loving *you*. A fitting end. And then no one will ever make that mistake again."

Ana ambled sideways until she slammed into the hearth again. The room was spinning so fast, she no longer knew right from left from up from down. Varradyn. Magda. Glass. Fire. In her mind, she saw herself hurl the poker into the glass and run. Run *hard* until she reached the entrance and then lift, shifting, and flying away from all the pain, sorrow, grief, and regret. From *her*. From all of it.

It was only when the first bolts of hail peppered her wings that Ana realized her escape hadn't been in her head at all.

She swooped around, catching a breeze that carried her sideways until she was facing the way she'd come.

Magda stood outside the observatory.

Watching.

Waiting.

Glowering.

Ana locked it all away for later and raced across the sky toward home.

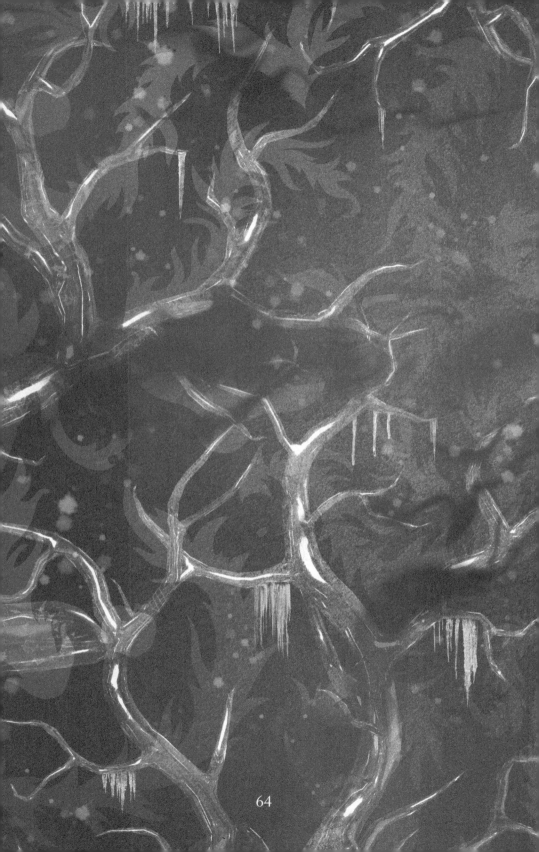

FIVE
USE YOUR ILLUSIONS

Ana flew around until nightfall. On her descent into the snowy courtyard of Fanghelm, she heard the mournful notes of a funeral dirge floating up from the bottom of the hill.

The song may as well have been for her. She wasn't dead yet, but she would be. Soon. A part of her had died in the observatory.

Drained, she searched for a place to land, but the dark keep was still too lively for her to use any of the common entrances. She'd chanced a return to the cave to see if Magda had left her clothing behind, but it wasn't there. There was no way she was flying back to the observatory to do another search. But she couldn't waltz into the keep naked either.

There was *one* thing she could do, but she was so exhausted...

She settled her phoenix between some crenulations of the north battlement. Once she'd verified no one was watching, she soared past a dozing sentry and unfurled just as she reached the top of a long stairwell used only by guards coming to and from their posts. When she was sure he wasn't going to look her way, she pressed her hands to her chest, closed her eyes, and focused on how she *wanted* to look.

Dark, wavy hair. Big blue eyes, like a doe. Skin fresh as snow. A touch of red in the pout. A gown stitched with all those colors but also the bright yellow of the sun.

A soft shimmer passed through the cold air, prickling her flesh. She drew in a shaky inhale, and upon breathing out, she glanced down to find herself much changed.

Ana was too tired to hold the illusion for long, so she darted down the circular staircase. Sweat streamed down her temples. She missed several steps and went inelegantly stumbling down to the nearest landing, twisting her ankle. Dark stars splattered behind her eyes, but she couldn't stop. She couldn't stop until she reached her room, and even *then* it might not be safe, if Magda was there waiting for her.

She rounded the hall, made sure it was clear, and ran, shivering, the rest of the way to her apartments. The illusion of clothing was not the same thing as clothing itself, and she couldn't wait to wrap herself in something warm.

With a hard shove, she flung the doors inward and turned with a huff allowing the trickery to fade away. She grabbed one of her cloaks off the rack and wrap it around her before sinking onto the closest chair.

"Ana?"

She whipped her head up and scrambled to her feet. Niko was perched on the edge of her bed with a heavy, indecipherable look that killed her tears instantly.

"Were you *naked* when you came in here?"

"It's a..." She wiped her eyes and pulled her shoulders back. Forced a smile. "Long story, Niko. You know me. Can't help getting myself into strange binds."

Niko's hands were folded in his lap, his eyes aimed her way but fixed on the door behind her. His soft blond hair fell in waves over his shoulders, the longest it had ever been because the koldyna liked it that way. "Would it have something to do with the way you sabotaged Magda's work today?"

"The way I—" Ana's laugh stuck in her throat. "Is that what she told you?"

"She tells me everything."

Ana tightened her cloak. "Tells you lies, you mean. They're *all* she knows, Niko. She—"

"She said you'd say that." He shook his head as he lowered it. The angle and darkness of the room obscured his face.

"And you believe her over your own sister? Your twin?"

"She's not... not *wrong*, Ana. You haven't been yourself since she arrived. I know you're angry she's replaced Oma—"

Ana laughed so hard, it turned into unintelligible sputters. "She could *never* replace Oma! She has no warmth, no nurturing, no kindness in her. All she does is take and take—"

"And what do you do? You leave Fanghelm all day, return every night. Where are you when Father needs you? When I need you?"

"That's not fair." Ana balked, standing taller. "I don't go skipping around town without a care in the world. Most of the time, I'm doing *her* bidding. Doing things I could never tell you, and even if I did, you'd never believe me, would you? She's gotten her claws into you, and now you'll do or say or believe anything she tells you. I'm curious, what does *she* say we're doing in the foothills?"

Niko sighed, an exhausted sound. "Her workshop is where she mixes her ointments and tinctures. Where she does good, healing work. If you would listen to yourself, you're implying saving lives is a mortal sin."

"Saving lives." Ana snorted. She stepped closer, the stones like ice against her aching soles. "Have you ever *been* to her workshop, Niko?"

"Nien. Of course not." His chin tucked downward in offense. "I would never go unless she invited me."

"Not even a little curious?"

"I have no reason to doubt anything she tells me," Niko said evenly. He sighed and shook his head.

Ana's eyes welled with tears. She looked away. "It's only me you don't trust, right? *Me*, your confidant. Your closest friend. The other half of your soul. The one who has never, ever betrayed you, and never would." *The one who would, and will, die for you.*

"Ana." Niko pushed to his feet. He continued staring past her as he approached. She couldn't think too hard about the way his eyes used to light up with vibrancy and life... the infectious, bombastic laugh that lightened her heart no matter how foul her mood. That young man was gone. What remained was a husk, a creature who looked like her brother but wasn't. "Apologize to Magda, or you and I have nothing more to say to one another."

He never met her eyes as he yanked open the doors and walked away.

Ana sat alone in the darkness, waiting for the keep to settle into the slumber hours. She hadn't slept, eaten, or drank, beyond finishing the grimizhna tea Ludya had left for her.

The defiant smile Ana wore as she stepped into her trousers lacked the fire she usually felt when engaging in disobedient acts. For years, she'd been wearing Niko's clothes on the sly. There was something so energizing, so freeing, about pants—about flaunting her disdain for what had always been a stupid rule made by stupid men.

Though she'd regret it later when her room turned to ice, she opened the window and took flight from there. She didn't have the heart for another illusion, not until she had time to catch up on sleep, and she couldn't count on her luck in subterfuge to continue.

Ana soared back toward the foothills, flying over the sleepy village. The row of taverns made her heart hurt. Even from the sky, she knew which one was his. She still remembered the day he'd shown up, a few years after his family had opened the Tavern at the Top of the World. He'd worn the world's burdens in his haunted eyes, and her soul recognized kin. She'd been drawn to him from the start, watching him bat snow from his hair as he stood outside his modest cabin, staring at the stars like they held all the answers.

Maybe that had been the beginning of her falling for him. Maybe it had come later. All she knew was it had happened along the thread of thousands of tiny moments, and there were no shears sharp enough to sever the resulting knot.

And now Magda knew. She *knew*. It didn't matter that she didn't have Tyreste's name yet. She would. The Cross was a small village, and it would take so little to find out who Ana had been spending her afternoons with.

Soaring past the observatory, she tried to grab a glimpse of either the Ravenwood or Magda. But the recently fallen snow blanketed the glass dome, obscuring her view of everything inside.

Ana hadn't stopped thinking about Varradyn either. She wanted to believe he'd escaped, but if he wasn't already dead, he would be. Desperately she wanted to help him, but the cost would be higher than she could bear. She had no defense against Magda. Not yet.

Ana climbed higher, all the way to the hidden outcropping near the top of the peak. It was small, easy to miss, and challenging to reach from the ground. The Shrine of the Ancestors had been built for the heirs to pay homage to all who had come before, and entreat them for strength and wisdom. Sometimes she made the climb the traditional way, a sort of pilgrimage of penance, but tonight she'd have collapsed on the first switchback if she'd even tried to hike the path on foot.

When she reached the ledge, she shifted back and dusted her clothes before heading into the cave. From the outside, the door was deceiving; it seemed little more than a nook. But stepping beneath the arches revealed an entire world of wonder. The ceiling stretched stories high, all the way into the slope of the peak itself. Along the sides were statues of the heirs past, including her brother, Stepan, whose likeness had been completed that past springtide. The other Wynters were buried in the crypts, but not the heirs of Darek Summerton. They were brought to the shrine upon their deaths, for their descendants to preserve their immortality through the gift of memory.

The tall, deep cave glittered with crystals crowning the stalactites and stalagmites the shrines had been built around. Some grew up and around the statues, but others were in the way altogether. But the Vjestik Wynters respected the land they'd chosen, and they had never cut down a single protrusion more than was needed.

Echoes from Ana's boots as she started down the long approach to the back kept her grounded. She was still there. Still real. There was yet fight in her, though she didn't know where or how to excavate it.

At the end of the cavern were three shrines so large, they stretched nearly to the ceiling. As a girl, she'd tried climbing one and had fallen, breaking her arm. Niko was the better climber, though he'd never liked visiting the shrines. Stepan had always been willing to go, until he got older and spent all his time training for the Vuk od Varem.

On the left was Darek Summerton himself, the one who had communed with the wulves and fashioned the arrangement that had allowed the nomadic Vjestik to settle in Witchwood Cross. Next was Drazhan Wynter, and beside him, his wife, Imryll of Glaisgain, the rogue princess from Duncarrow. Darek was considered the father of the Vjestik, but most of their people revered Drazhan and Imryll more. They'd rebuilt the town after the Nok Mora and had restored hope when it had been believed irreparably lost. Imryll, the mother behind Books of All Things, had reinvigorated learning and education. Children of the Cross learned to read and to appreciate the world they lived in beyond the town walls.

Their phoenix form had also come from Imryll, who, it was said, carried inside her the blood of the otherworldly sorcerers of Duncarrow, the Meduwyn.

"Imryll, give me strength. Show me how to find the way, as you found yours all those years ago when you came into your wings. Show me how to save Father and Niko. Tyreste. I accept my own demise if it means preventing theirs. I've been waiting to die for years, and my only regret would be doing so before I find the means to save them." Tears flooded Ana's eyes, dropping onto the dusty cave floor in dark spots. She pressed her hands along Imryll's intricately carved boots. "I don't know where the koldyna came from. I don't know what she wants... why she's chosen *us* for her evildoing. All I do know is if she cannot be stopped, it will be the end of us. And perhaps the Ravenwoods as well."

Ana sank to her knees. Her shaking hands cupped the toes of Imryll's boots as she sobbed. "Show me how to stop her. I will do *anything*."

A dense shadow slowly slithered up the lower half of Imryll's stone gown. Ana shot to her feet, wiping at her eyes, and turned to face the koldyna with the last of her bravery.

But it wasn't Magda. It was her uncle, Grigor.

The man who had always seemed like a giant to her was perfectly at home among the shrines. He'd always been all muscle and grit, and every time he returned from wherever it was he went, he seemed a little harder, a little tougher. He was made for his role of overseeing the Wynter guards, even though he was an Arsenyev and not a Wynter.

"Onkel. Hej." Ana bowed her head in deference to her elder. "Why are you here?"

He shifted his eyes toward the side and scoffed. His hand passed across his mouth as he looked around and then back at her. "You're troubled," he said simply. "I followed you."

"I'm fine," she lied, squinting her remaining tears away. She dusted her dress at the knees, marveling at how he'd scaled the mountain so quickly. "Sometimes I just need to be in the presence of the Ancestors. To feel grounded in their wisdom."

Grigor studied her, stone-faced. He looked up at Imryll, then back at her. "You're troubled, Ana," he said again.

Something in his voice—it wasn't quite kindness, not the way others would define it, but it was the closest thing he could offer—made her heart constrict, and her tears returned. She tried to hide them, but he pinned his hawklike eyes onto her, offering her no pardon. "I..." The lie didn't come so easily this time. The deceptions of the past years were coming together to suffocate her, so she decided upon the truth instead. "I feel like I'm... like I'm drowning, Onkel."

Grigor considered this. He crossed his arms. Nodded. "Then start swimming."

"It's not that simple." With a stilted laugh, she turned her head toward the cave ceiling. "How I wish it were."

"Soldiers drown. Warriors rise. Strike. Defend."

Ana couldn't help but laugh again. "I'm no warrior, Onkel. I'm hardly..." She didn't know how to finish the thought.

"You *are* a warrior." He set his jaw and swept his gaze over the three shrines. "You descend from warriors."

"I wasn't supposed to be the heir," she said weakly.

"You are, or you wouldn't be." Grigor tightened his crossed arms. A sinewy outline shaped his shirt along his forearm, a reminder he was more beast than man. "You have the blood of every powerful people in this realm. Vjestik. Meduwyn. Medvedev. And yes, even Ravenwood." He lifted his shoulders, and his bulky furs crowded his angular face. "*You* are what others envision when they dream of becoming a warrior."

Ana had never heard her uncle say so much at one time. They'd always had a bond, but it had been more about fondness than closeness. But he would never say something he didn't mean. "If that's true, then how do I become one?"

Grigor twitched his nose. "I cannot answer that for you."

Ana lowered her eyes with a grim sigh. It was tempting to share her concerns about Magda, but if anyone had the power to slow the koldyna, it was Grigor Arsenyev, and he'd done nothing.

"You are not helpless. Your problems are solvable. Your victories are plausible." Grigor clapped a hand on her shoulder, so quick she almost wondered if she'd imagined it. He cleared his throat. "Your tavern boy is safe."

Ana stopped breathing. "What?"

"I'll check in on him. But *you* cannot be seen there." Grigor shrugged his furs higher onto his shoulders and started to leave. "Use your illusions, Anastazja. Dobranok."

"Dobranok," she answered distantly.

Grigor marched away, his heavy steps an echoing gong as they bounced along the cavern walls.

Ana inched back until she was almost sitting on Imryll's boot. *Use your illusions, Anastazja.*

Her eyes widened, a flurry of thoughts catching up and threading together. Her mouth dropped open as an idea—an insane, laughable, imperfect idea—took shape.

Use your illusions.

Grigor Arsenyev walked into the Tavern at the Top of the World right as Tyr was about to lock the doors for the daily service pause. Anyone still in the tavern when the time arrived could stay but wouldn't get served again until the Penhallows had finished their morning preparations.

Tyr looked up from the bar and started to tell his newest patron to come back in an hour when he realized who it was.

Grigor was what Tyr thought of as "old Vjestik." He was built like a bear, solid and rugged, but his face was all angular lines, a beast both beautiful and terrible. Tyr knew from Ana that her uncle wasn't in the Cross often, and when he was, he didn't squander time frequenting taverns—least of all in the middle of the night.

Tyr spread his hands along the bar and watched the man, to see what he'd do or say next. He forged an aloof expression to hide the unease spreading through his limbs like wildfire.

Grigor approached the bar with a stern, lineless countenance. "Two."

Objections formed but died. Tyr fumbled his next words. "Two mugs of ale, you mean? Will, uh, someone be joining you?"

"No." Grigor crossed his bulky arms and waited to be served.

"Very well." Tyreste's nod was so feverish, he wondered how it looked to the stoic mercenary waiting, irritably, for him to pull himself together. With a harried head shake, he turned and poured two ales from the mugs he'd just cleaned for the morning rush. He had to start over twice when his hands forgot how to work.

What the fuck is wrong with me?

Ana. Always cursed Ana.

Even when she wasn't there, he couldn't escape her.

Had she sent her ox of an uncle to spy on him?

With a foreboding swallow, he considered another possibility.

Is she all right?

Tyr remembered the phoenix streaking across the sky... a raven in hot pursuit. His pulse raced, thinking also of the clandestine midnight visit between the high priestess of Midnight Crest and Arkhady Wynter.

Grigor grunted his thanks, tossed a heavy sack of coin on the bar, and retreated to a table near the dark corner of the room.

The resident drunkards looked up from their empty mugs, watching Grigor with empty stares.

Leave it, Tyr thought, even as he moved across the tavern floor. Grigor didn't look up when he approached, so Tyr cleared his throat. "The coin. You overpaid."

"Nien."

"No, you did. It's far too much. Can I get you some stew?" He scolded himself as soon as he said it. There was no stew in the service pause.

"Nien."

"Then I must insist—"

"I paid for silence." Grigor seemed to shift his entire body to look up. He tapped his temple. "To think."

Tyr shook his head in confusion, but the steely look in the man's eyes was enough to crush any further attempts. He nodded, bowed, and retreated behind the bar just as the double doors swung open. Adeline emerged from the back.

Her smile died when she saw Grigor in the corner. She quickly signed, *Did he just arrive?*

Tyr nodded. He pinched his mouth to the side, nibbling the inside of his mouth and willing himself not to stare at the man who had paid their entire day's profits for two ales and some quality thinking time.

Something doesn't feel right, she responded.

He could've lied, but Addy reminded him so much of himself when he had been younger. Adults coating tough truths with soft lies had only made him bitter. *No. Nor to me.*

Is it Ana?

Tyr's heart sank. He'd never intended for Addy and Ana to get to know one another at all—anticipating the end of his and Ana's relationship before it had even really begun—but it had happened anyway. Ana had even learned to sign so they could communicate better.

Where is she, Tyr?

She won't be coming back, Addy.

Adeline's expression crumpled in sadness. *Please make it right with her. She belongs here with us.*

It's too late, he signed with a sinking feeling in his chest.

But you love her.

I don't—

Adeline thumped her chest with an urgent look. *You do love her. I know you do. And she loves you. If you won't make it right, I'll go to Fanghelm myself.*

Tyr balked so hard at Addy, it sent her skittering back a step. *Do not ever go up there. Ever. You understand?*

Addy just shook her head.

Tyr's attention traveled back to Grigor. The man was staring forward like he'd gone elsewhere in his mind. All evening Tyr had been thinking about the letters, about returning to his translations, and the service pause was supposed to be his time to dive back in, having finished most of his preparations while they had still been open. But there was no way he could focus the way he needed to with Ana's uncle acting strangely in the corner.

You should go home.

Addy scoffed. *I go when you go.*

You're too young for these hours.

Thanks, Father.

Tyr laughed without humor. *Then stay here while I run to the cabin to get work.*

Translations?

He nodded.

I'll help.

He almost said no, but he didn't, for the same reason he didn't shield her from the truth. *He's a good man. He won't trouble you. But you run to me if you're worried.*

I'll be fine. But something really isn't right, Tyreste.

Tyr nodded slowly, his eyes on Grigor's corner. He'd been starving an hour ago, but his belly had soured. *I know.*

Use your illusions.

It became a chant. A mantra. She sang it in her head on the flight back to Fanghelm—and as she stoked the fire, thawing her cold room. As she changed into her sleeping gown and as she drifted off to sleep.

Use your illusions.

She'd first learned illusory magic to alter her appearance when she had been five. It had been an accidental discovery, one that had confounded her mother so much, she'd nearly had a breakdown. Back then, it happened accidentally, when her emotions were at a peak... when she felt cornered or scared. Only as she aged did she learn to harness it and use it with intention.

But she couldn't simply snap her fingers and become someone else. Unlike shifting, which was second nature, illusions required continuous focus, a constant awareness of who she was and who she wanted to be, so she could hold on to one and dismiss the other.

Sometimes, when she wanted to go into town without feeling everyone's eyes follow her, she'd illusion herself into the same dark-haired, blue-eyed young woman she'd become earlier that night. She'd even created a new identity for this persona.

Nessa Arsenyev, long-lost daughter of the great Grigor.

Could it be coincidence it was Grigor himself who had given her the idea?

Maybe it wasn't what he'd meant. But still...

Keep your distance, he'd said, but also, *use your illusions*.

Anastazja Wynter couldn't be seen anywhere near Tyreste or the tavern, or everything she'd done to keep him safe would have been for nothing.

But Nessa Arsenyev?

Sweet, guileless, innocent Nessa, who was everything Anastazja wasn't? Everything Tyreste seemingly wished she'd been all along?

Ah. Well, *she* could do whatever she wanted.

Ana didn't sleep a wink that night.

SIX

NESSA

Dawn broke, signaling the end of Tyr's shift. He blinked his
bleary eyes, determined to fight the strong call for sleep. He
was behind on his translations, and Grigor showing up and acting
strange had only put him further in the hole. The stack of letters
behind the bar taunted him, waiting for him to snap out of the
trance he'd been in ever since the pause in service.

Grigor had departed a while ago. Adeline was asleep in the
back, curled up on the overnight cot. She'd refused to go home
until he did, and he hadn't had the heart to argue.

Rikard and Agnes arrived to relieve him. Agnes had one hand
over her eyes, a wide yawn spreading her mouth as she shuffled
behind the bar. Rikard slapped the double doors with a feral howl
and clapped Tyreste on the back on his way to the storeroom.

"Another hour. That's all I wanted," Agnes murmured with
another yawn. "I miss beginning my days at noontide."

Tyr chuckled politely, but his eyes were on the letters. Agnes
hadn't seen them yet, and as soon as he went for them, she'd be

nosy about it. "Ah! You know what... I forgot a stack of washed mugs in the back. Would you mind..."

Agnes narrowed her tired eyes and burst past him with a moody glare.

He snatched the letters up and tucked them into his vest, but with a glance outside the window at the snow and ice, he decided to wait for the sun to rise.

Tyr poured an ale and went to the same table Grigor had haunted for hours. Agnes shouted from the back, asking where the imaginary mugs were, but he'd already started to doze. His head fell back. The last thing he heard before he drifted off was Agnes telling Rikard someone should carry him home.

The bell above the door rang, startling him alert. He was still orienting himself when he noticed a girl with dark, buoyant waves, wrapped in a deep-blue cloak stitched with gold. She turned toward him, her sparkling blue eyes matching her smile, which seemed to be just for his benefit. Her fingers played with her necklace, a dazzling red that had the likeness of an apple.

Tyr bucked alert, spilling his ale in his sleep-addled daze. He saved the letters just in time but had nothing to mop his mess up with. Something smacked into the side of his head, and he looked down and saw a rag on the table.

Agnes rolled her eyes from behind the bar and returned to her work.

He was making awkward swirls of the fallen ale when a slight shadow forewarned him someone was approaching. The young woman appeared beside him, peering over his shoulder with an odd expression.

Tyr was both wholly positive he'd never seen her before and struck with the impossible sense he'd known her forever.

"*Dearest Par,*" the girl said, reading. "*I regret to inform you matters have become exceedingly worse.*"

Sputtering something nonsensical, Tyr pulled the letters back to his chest. "Hello, uh... If you're looking for a drink, uh..."

"Can I sit here?" Her glittering eyes were as wide as saucers. She didn't wait for his confirmation, brushing the back of her skirt with her delicate hands before sitting. "What are you doing with a Vjestik letter?"

"It's..." Tyr eyed his empty mug with a mournful gaze. His throat was a desert. "Do I know you?"

Her soft red lips curved into a delectable smile as she fingered a lock of hair. "No, I don't think so."

"But you must be native to the Cross. You know Vjestikaan."

"*You're* not a native," she said pleasantly. "And you have a letter written in that very language in your possession."

"Fair enough." He swallowed down a dry thatch. *Not just one.* "I can't..." He grimaced. "Can't read it. I translate documents for my business partners in the Easterlands." *Stop talking.* "Some of the letters are in... in a language I *can* read, and some... like Vjestikaan... well."

"The Easterlands!" She clasped both of her hands to her chest, looking oddly impressed. "That's where you're from?"

He nodded. "Well, Parth is technically in the *Westerlands*, but Riverchapel is just across the border, in the Easterlands."

"Never been there myself. Either place," she said with a slow nod. "I've heard it's beautiful."

"It's... nice. Yes." Tyr swept his eyes over her. She was breath-taking, like Ana but so different. That he was even comparing her to Ana was maddening. There were hundreds of thousands of women in the kingdom, and only one he never wanted to see again. "Where are you from?"

"Here and there," she said with a short wave.

"How do you know Vjestikaan?"

"I don't really know it so well. A handful of words is all."

"Yes, but how?"

"My father is Grigor Arsenyev. But I live with my mother's people... elsewhere."

Tyr practically choked. "You're a Wynter."

"*No,*" she stated. The word came out with surprising force. "I'm an Arsenyev. The Wynters are no friends of mine."

Tyr bowed his head with a laugh. "Nor mine."

"My name is Natasya, but you may call me Nessa."

"Tyreste, but you may call me Tyr."

"Tyr. You're not fond of the Wynters then."

He shook his head instead of answering.

Nessa tilted her head. "It's all right. You're in fair company on that matter."

"It's too..." He winced. "Can I pour you an ale?"

She tapped her painted nails on the table, contemplating. "I could help you with your translations, you know. That is, some of them. Perhaps. A little."

Tyr slipped them inside his vest. "Thank you, but I'm not authorized to show them to you." It wasn't *entirely* true. Asterin had said he could bring in help, but only if it was someone he trusted.

Nessa's pouty mouth parted with delighted mischief. "Now I *really* want to see them!"

"They're not that exciting, I assure you. Just confidential." He hated the way her face fell. It reminded him so much of the tender disappointment Ana always tried so hard to hide when she was upset. "Are you sure we've never met?"

"Quite," she said swiftly.

"Ahh. Well, about that ale..."

"How about a walk instead?" she asked, brightening again. She giggled. "For all the times I've been here, I still know the village so little. And with all this fresh snow, it all looks the same to me. I'm afraid I'd get quite lost on my own." Her smile eased. "Unless you're busy, of course."

"No," he said quickly. Too quickly. *What are you doing? Haven't you learned your lesson about spoiled, beautiful women, you fool?* "Not... not busy."

The beaming smile she gave him dissolved every opposition. She stood and held out her arm, waiting for him to offer his.

He was so spellbound by the woman on his arm, he left his questions about how and why she'd come into the tavern unaddressed.

Tyreste led Nessa Arsenyev out of the tavern and into the icy morning with a grin so broad, it made his face ache and his worries evaporate.

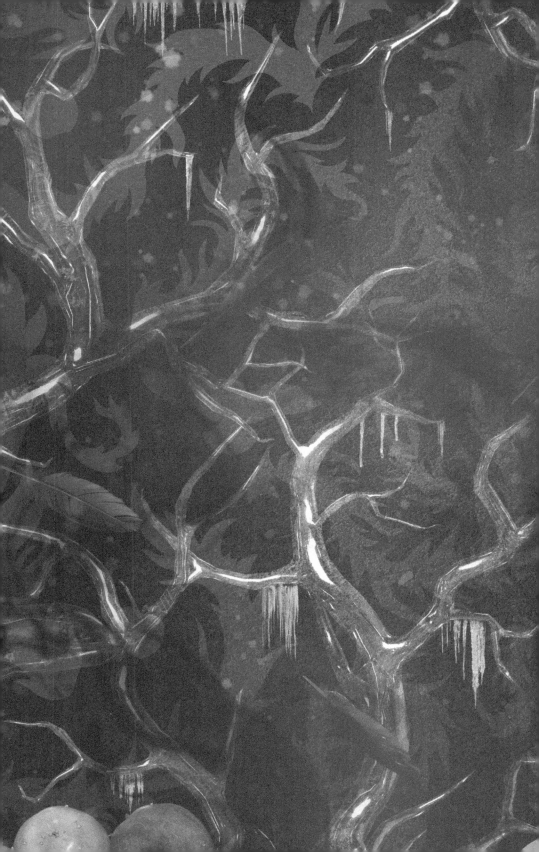

THE STRENGTH
OF HER ANCESTORS

SEVEN
THE MATTER
OF THE MYSTERIOUS TRANSLATION

Tyr stared at the two pages of vellum lying side by side on the small table. On the left was the original letter from Zofia Wynter—the one in Vjestikaan—and on the right was a translated version of the same.

Translated.

Not by him.

He'd risen and found both papers neatly arranged on his breakfast table, a tidy gift. But not only had the original *not* been sitting out when he'd gone to bed the night before, but Olov, Asterin, and Sesto were the only other people who even knew he was working on the letters. Addy knew he was working on something, but she didn't know how to read or speak Vjestikaan any better than he did. Ana might have known about the project, had she not rushed out of his life hours before his friends showed up unexpectedly, but even if she had known, she hadn't been able to expel him from her life fast enough. Even the idea of her sneaking into his cabin to help him was too absurd to entertain.

So he was back to where he'd started—exactly *nowhere*.

Nessa knew. She'd even read a piece of one of the letters, though she wasn't fluent. But he'd only just met her. She'd never been to his cabin. It wasn't a place anyone would stumble upon by accident either, as it was situated at the northern edge of his family's private property, near the forest line.

Thinking about her put an unexpected smile on his face. The expression barely fit, awkward and poorly placed upon his sour countenance, but it felt... good. Their carefree walk a couple of weeks ago, arm in arm under a fresh, soft blanket of snow, had offered a glimmer of the happiness he'd felt with Ana, before she'd sabotaged everything.

Tyr glanced around, half expecting to find some shadowy figure watching him. But of course, he was alone.

He pulled both hands down his face, groaned, and slipped into the chair. The heady aroma of yesterday's cider still brewing in the hearth wafted over, tempting him, but he was too consumed by the mystery of the translated document to rise and pour a mug.

Once more, he checked to ensure he was alone—he felt mad doing it, but not any madder than someone sneaking in during the night to translate a letter—and smoothed his hands along the edges of the vellum. He didn't recognize the handwriting, which was almost comically jagged, like the writer had gone out of their way to obscure their identity.

"Dearest Par," Tyr read aloud. He cleared the thickness from his throat and continued. "I, too, am alarmed. My father and grandmother are alarmed as well. They have not shared their concerns with me, but the high priestess of Midnight Crest has been to visit twice in the past month, both times arriving in the middle of the night. Before that, I'd only met her once."

Tyr sat back in his chair with a sharp inhale. It could be coincidence, the part about the high priestess visiting in the middle of the night. The alliance between the Wynters and Ravenwoods went back centuries. But Ana had told him their agreement was a "hands off" kind, where they respected each other's territories but didn't encroach upon them. *I've met her, once or twice, when my mother was still alive*, she'd said, about the high priestess. *But I would certainly not say I know her.*

He glanced toward the window. Dusk was shifting to darkness. He'd be expected at the tavern soon, and it wasn't a good idea to keep bringing the letters with him. *Someone* knew he was translating, and that same someone had taken it upon themselves to help. Kindness was the last motivation he'd expect, so why had he or she done it, whoever it was?

An image of Ana's flushed face watching him from on a pillow hit him so sudden and so hard, he had to close his eyes to re-center himself. Passing her in the village still felt like a violent ambush. The awkward aversion of glances... his fluttering heart betraying the cool pain he tried to hide. It had been weeks since she'd walked out of his life, but he couldn't shed her as easily as she'd shed him.

And he'd desperately tried.

Tyr waited for his heart to slow, for the heat to drain from his cheeks, before returning his focus to the mysterious translation.

I have never seen my grandmother so alarmed. Sometimes I'll catch Grandfather holding her, in complete and utter silence, and it terrifies me. The matter of the missing Ravenwoods is awful enough, but it's her reaction that tells me we have a much bigger problem on our hands than I can wrap my mind around.

What can it mean? I know not. Yet I have heard her whisper a name you'll recognize.

Mortain.

But that cannot be, can it? For the Mortain you speak of is from the time of our fathers, but Grandmother speaks of him as though he is quite a bit older than she. Are there more than one? Is her Mortain different than ours? He must be, unless the rumors about the Meduwyn are true, but though my mind is open to all possibilities, immortal sorcerers are far-fetched, even for me.

One thing I know for certain: Grandmother is terrified of him. Of what he might do. Of what he may have already done.

How are these matters connected? I don't know, but I intend to find out. But please, do not go snooping around Duncarrow, Par. Whoever—whatever—Mortain is, he's powerful enough to make the strongest woman I know quake with fear.

Please, please convince your grandfather to visit! I would love to see Onkel Octavyen, but mostly, I am dying to see you again. There are some things I cannot say in writing, even in code.

With love, Zo

Rikard leaped onto the table with a pebbly grunt. His tail twitched as he circled the letters in ruffled suspicion.

"You must have seen who it was, eh, boy?" Tyr gave him a loving stroke.

The mouser lifted his chin for more.

"It's too bad you can't speak."

Rikard rumbled a dark meow.

"Or maybe I'd rather not know what you're thinking."

This little one carries the world in his heart, Ana had said once. *Don't you, Riki?*

Ana was the only one who had ever spoken to Rikard like he was on her level. There were times Tyr suspected the mouser might follow her home one night and leave him for good. But it was Ana who had left.

She's in deep trouble. The thought swept through him like a gale.

"Yeah, well, I came to the Cross to get away from trouble, didn't I, Rik? And you can't help someone who doesn't want it. Someone who doesn't want *me.*"

Tyr carefully rolled the letters and tucked them away in what he'd *thought* was a pretty savvy hiding spot. There wasn't a better option in his modest cabin, unless he built yet another cubby. But he didn't have time to solve the problem.

Rikard meowed from the door.

"All right, all right, I'm coming."

Ana handed Varradyn the warm mug. He accepted it with a pitiful smile and sipped with his eyes closed. She leaned in, turning her head to the side, for a careful re-fastening of his cloak, the only thing covering his nudity below the waist. Until Magda removed the shackles around his feet, it was the best Ana could do for him.

Varradyn held the mug aloft in reluctant thanks. His dark eyes glazed over, aimed toward some distant spot beyond where Ana was crouched before him.

Two weeks Ana had been visiting him, and he'd said next to nothing. She came when she knew Magda was sleeping—or pretending to sleep, as she didn't believe for a moment the koldyna had the same needs as men and women—to ensure he had food and drink. She feared Magda was slowly starving the raven to death, a concern Varradyn himself had expressed on an earlier visit. He didn't know why he was still there at all, he'd said, perhaps not realizing the odds of him ever flying away from the observatory were grim.

Magda must still have had some use for him. Whatever it was, the koldyna hadn't shared it—or anything—with Ana. There'd been no further talk of Ana bedding the raven, nor requests for her to "endeavor" back to the Rookery for another raven.

She should feel relieved, but she feared Magda's silence more.

Ana rose to her feet. She crossed her arms and stared at the tea kettle, still hanging in the hearth. Tyreste would be awake by then and had likely come across the translated letter, puzzling over its existence. Did he suspect his new friend, "Nessa"? Next time she slipped in to help him, would he be awake, waiting to catch her in the act?

Now that she'd read Zofia Wynter's desperate appeal to her cousin, her heart pounding so hard she'd thought for sure it would have roused Tyreste, there was nothing in the world that could keep her away from reading the rest.

How had Tyreste even come across such a hoard? And what had it to do with the horrors Magda was inflicting upon the Ravenwoods?

Ana's one regret—and it was a big one—was translating the letter accurately and leaving the truth for him to puzzle over and, far worse, get involved in. In trying to help Tyreste, she'd instead thrust him into serious danger, the very thing she'd been trying to avoid in cutting ties with him.

"Ana." Varradyn's voice, low and scratchy, cut through her malaise. "It's past dusk."

Ana lifted her head and looked through the glass dome and into the night, where the auroras painted the sky with purple and the deepest turquoise. "So it is."

"I need to... ask you something."

She nodded, averting her eyes toward the fire. Anywhere but at him.

"Your mother—"

"That witch is *not* my mother," Ana stated through clenched teeth. "She swindled my father into wedding her, and she has done nothing but take from us."

Varradyn was silent for a moment. The logs in the hearth crackled and popped, adding an unsteady chorus to the standoff. "She's going to kill me... isn't she?"

Ana spun around and leaned against the stone. "What has she said to you?"

"She doesn't speak when she comes here. She pokes and prods my limbs like a physician, adds logs to the fire, and leaves." He glanced down at himself. "She must know someone is feeding and watering me, or I'd be dead already, wouldn't I?"

Magda couldn't be ignorant of Ana's visits to the observatory, but until that moment, Ana hadn't considered that perhaps she was being tested. Did Magda *want* her to feed and water the raven? To bond with him? If so, why?

"I don't know what she wants with you," she said after a pause.

The raven laughed. He slid his empty mug across the stones, toward the hearth. It tipped over on its side and rolled to a stop. "You're the one who brought me here."

"Usually she has me lure..." Ana shoved her tongue to the roof of her mouth. She wanted Varradyn to fly free when the ordeal was over. If she told him Magda had been behind the other Ravenwood disappearances, he would carry that knowledge home, and it would put her entire family at risk. "I don't know what she does when I'm not around. I really *don't* know what she wants with you. Or why she... why she chose the magic she did that day."

Varradyn wrapped his cloak tighter with a dark look. "If you hadn't stopped me—"

"It wasn't your fault," Ana said, eager for a subject change. "When she comes here, it's best if you say nothing you don't have to. She'll use every word she can against you." Ana again checked the darkening sky. She was as impatient to be away from the observatory when Magda arrived as she was to be *at* the tavern when Tyreste was working. He brightened every time Nessa walked in. Rikard the Mouser always pranced straight to the door to greet her, as he always had, as though he saw right through her ruse. She was more than a little grateful he couldn't talk. "You done with your bowl?"

Varradyn shoveled the remnants of the stew into his mouth with desperate grunts and then sent the bowl sliding toward the mug. His dark eyes glittered with competing emotions as he trained them on her.

Ana tapped the corner of her mouth to show him he needed to wipe his. He grinned sheepishly and buried his face inside the cloak with a hard rub, watching her as she gathered the dishes in her own cloak and wrapped them tight so the magic would hold them when she shifted.

"I'll be back again tomorrow," she said, already running by the time he wished her good night. She was aloft before she reached the door, then she soared down the mountain, toward the village.

And Tyreste.

The evening rush hadn't materialized. Tyr's father claimed it was the turn in the weather, marking the arrival of springtide, though their bloom season would be short and snow would still fall, just less of it. The Cross was accustomed to doing outside work year-round, but in the brief pockets of spring, villagers were outside *all* the time.

The Cider Festival was less than a week away, set at what was expected to be the warmest stretch of the season. Everyone prayed for a brief thaw that meant they could leave the layers at home and enjoy themselves.

For Tyr, it meant the revival of memories that hadn't always been so painful.

"I'm ducking out for a bit," his brother Rikard said, one eye squinted at the scruffy cat named for him. "Need to check on Faustina."

"Your shift isn't over," Tyr said. He eyed Adeline behind the bar, translating the assignment he'd given her. She looked up to watch their exchange.

Rikard gestured around. "Really need me, do you?"

Tyr shrugged and twerked the valve on the ale keg tighter, to no joy. The damned thing was warped, but Olov insisted it was still serviceable. Evert was the engineer of the family, but his shift wasn't until later. Tyr couldn't get even a drop of ale out of the cursed contraption. "Just be back before close. I did everything last night."

"Yeah, yeah." Rikard palmed the double doors open and disappeared into the back.

Adeline looked up from where she was sitting on the floor. *Faustina is pregnant. Be nice.*

Tyr rolled his eyes but smiled. *You're right. Sorry.*
We don't need him anyway. It's slow.
Did Mother and Father leave?

Adeline nodded. *Hours ago. While you were staring at the wall, brooding.*

Tyr snorted. *I don't brood.*

King of the Brooders. Adeline laughed with a distant look at the door. *I miss her too. Maybe she'll come back, and it will be like this never happened.*

She's not coming back, Addy. Tyr turned back toward the keg with a hard frown. He tried once more to tighten the spout, and it broke off in his hand, provoking a stunned giggle from Adeline. He shot her a look. "Fuck," he whispered. To Addy he signed, *Going to get the backup keg. Be right back.*

The backup keg is broken.

I thought Evert fixed it.

She laughed again.

Tyr groaned. *What about the spares?*

Father took them to the storage shed.

You mean the one with the old well?

Adeline nodded.

Tyr scanned the thin crowd before looking back at his sister with a reluctant groan. *I'll go grab a couple. Scream if you need me.*

I'm not an infant. She glowered. *Go, or I will.*

Ana shifted several yards from the tavern, landing beside a tucked-away shed that had fallen into disuse. It had once been the home of the town well, but the pulley system had been dismantled when toxic minerals had started coming up with the water. Villagers occasionally used the old structure as unofficial overflow storage for their businesses, but mostly it was a forgotten relic, making it one of the few places in town where she could take a moment to gather herself and find the concentration needed to hold her illusion.

The front side had a large doorless entrance, exposing the interior to the elements. The remaining three walls listed, rotting, one bad storm from total collapse. The top of the well had been sealed years ago, but time and decay had pushed the warped wooden disk halfway off the stone cylinder, and there it hung, matted in cobwebs, dust, and the neglect of several generations. *It was going poor in my time*, her grandmother had once said. *Should just tear the whole thing down and start anew.*

Ana stepped inside and bent down over her knees, catching her breath.

Her eyes closed as she let the force of the stone well support her. She breathed in fresh strength and exhaled unwelcome weakness. Again. Every day she was stronger. Every day she was weaker. Every day she learned another method to cope, to prevent her fragile world from toppling. Every day she teetered further and further over the edge of the threatening abyss.

"I am a warrior," she whispered, channeling Grigor, but the sound of the words, trite and meaningless, made her laugh bitterly. She was no warrior. Speaking the wish aloud didn't make it any more real than her fanciful dreams.

Boots crunching in snow preceded a furious "you have *got* to be kidding me."

Ana arrested mid-breath. Tyreste. He'd already spotted her, so there wasn't time for illusion. Fighting a cringe, she glanced up and saw his hair mussed, cheeks glowing from the cold—and maybe anger. It was certainly in his eyes, wild with accusation.

"What are you doing here, Anastazja?"

Ana fiddled with her cloak clasp at her neck. She drew in a rough breath, directing her gaze slightly past him. "Nothing. I'll go." She averted her stare and pitched forward, attempting to pass, but he thrust an arm out, blocking her way. The force of her sudden stop caused her eyes to lift.

"What are you *doing* here?" he asked again. His contempt landed like a boulder.

She was close enough for his scent to transport her to happier times. Of fires and ale and a trace of something softer, entirely him. She'd inhaled it enough lying against his chest and tracing the words on his flesh that she could never say aloud, and never in a language he understood. *Volemthe. Volemthe. Volemthe.* "I was up the mountain, and I landed here to catch my breath." It wasn't a lie, and for that she felt a small stab of pride.

"Why here?" He sucked in a hissing breath that took hers. Every bone in her body ached to be near him. To peel his arm from the doorless frame and wrap it around her, disappearing into the only safe place she'd ever known.

"It's just... It's where I landed," she said weakly. "I didn't know you'd be here. I didn't expect to see anyone at all."

Tyreste's arm tightened on the frame as he laughed, his muscles flexing under the thick fabric. "Why don't I believe you?"

"You don't have to believe me." Ana braced and tried to duck under his arm, but he corralled her farther in and backed her against the well. She bent backward with a light gasp, which made him retreat a step.

The concern in his expression was short-lived. He reached forward and cupped her chin between his thumb and forefinger, then turned her face in silent inspection. Whatever he saw caused him to release her. "What didn't you tell me that night?"

"Tyr—"

"Ana, *talk* to me." His smooth, controlled anger melted away, and all she heard and felt in its place was sadness. "I *know* something is wrong. I *know* you're in trouble. And, Guardians help me, I should just walk away and forget you, but I've tried, and I can't. I should take you at your word, but I *can't*. I know you. I know you better than you wanted me to, in spite of all your efforts to hide your world and all your troubles." He slapped a palm against his chest. His voice broke. "If anyone knows how to disappear, it's me. If anyone knows the temptation of closing out the world, it's me. But..." His hand fell away and he hung his head, the resulting silence heavy. His mouth parted in anguished surrender.

It was foolish, and she knew it even as she reached for him, but the moment she kissed him, none of it mattered. Nothing mattered more than his warmth, so intoxicating and perfect that no fire could replicate it.

Tyreste moaned in frustration, fighting it only briefly before he had her in his arms, lifting her up onto the broken disk.

Ana unhooked her cloak and let it tumble down around her. Together they scratched at the thick layers of her gown, clawing it upward in a bunch at her waist. She couldn't free him from his trousers fast enough, panting, kissing, and licking his face with every frantic tug.

Tyreste's cry was loud when he entered her. He cradled her face in one hand, restoring the broken kiss, and braced against the stone supports on the well for purchase as he moved in sharp, hungered plunges, stretching her to fit him. Ana threw her head back as a voice inside of her screamed to stop, to run away before she was so weakened by love and yearning that all the hurt and the pain would be for nothing, and she'd lose him in a way not even magic could reverse.

With his forehead anchored to hers, Tyreste locked her gaze. His mouth hung with breathless huffs, and she matched his choice of language as his generous thrusts woke her up, ounce by ounce, inch by inch, the entire surface of her flesh humming with rebellion.

"Ana." He whispered her name through a fissured grunt, which became an extended moan as he tightened and then shuddered against her, filling her and making her whole once more.

Still trembling, Tyreste ran his hands down her face in fraught passes, as though piecing together a memory. Her heart broke with every swipe of his palms... every recovered breath promising reality. He was laughing and crying, his expression shifting second to second, and she'd never seen a more accurate depiction of how she felt inside, all the time.

Ana had never asked the world to be fair, but she could not fathom how deeply *unfair* it had been to her.

Bloated tears pooled in her eyes and spilled before she could angle her face away.

He made a choking sound and followed her face with his. "There's nothing I wouldn't do for you, Anastazja. No trouble I'd stand down from. No evil I wouldn't face head-on."

She kissed both sides of his mouth and leaped off the well, tugging her dress down in a clumsy dance as she staggered away. "And that's the problem, Tyreste. I can't let you do that. Not ever."

In her misery, Ana did something she'd never done before.

She shifted right in front of him and flew away.

Long after she'd gone, Tyr saw Ana morph into a majestic orange-and-yellow bird and fly away. *Shift* into a *bird* and *fly away*.

It wasn't that he didn't know she could, but she'd always kept that part of herself shadowed from him. *I like to have some mystery between us,* she'd said, and anytime their conversations had veered too close to what her life was like beyond his walls, she'd diverted him with giggles, kisses, and poorly disguised angst.

He stumbled back toward the tavern in a daze. He made it halfway before he realized he'd forgotten the kegs and had to turn around.

When he finally returned, he found Adeline flitting about the tavern floor, clearing tables and signing to the handful of patrons. They smiled and signed the few things they'd learned over the years—thank you, please, and very good.

Enjoying yourself? He shook his head.

Addy grinned and skipped behind the bar to hoist the broken keg off the shelf. He started lugging the two he'd retrieved into the back, but she shook her head hard enough to pull his attention again, then flicked a nod toward the corner.

Nessa was sitting alone, her face splotched with pink and hands tapping the table in nervous beats. He looked back at his sister, who shrugged and set the keg down long enough to sign, *I can fill the kegs. Go talk to her.*

Do you know how heavy they are when they're full?

Was I not born in a tavern?

He locked her gaze with a playful glare that she matched with narrowed eyes. With a laugh, she grabbed the two kegs from him and disappeared into the back.

Tyr had been so caught in the exchange with his sister, his shock over the encounter with Ana had momentarily subsided. His groin ached from the unexpected interlude he couldn't forget if he tried. The perfume of her permeated his flesh, delivering painful reminders with every breath in.

He turned his effort toward boxing those emotions on his way to the corner table. Among them was guilt, for it seemed Nessa had taken a fancy to him. He liked her, more than made sense coming off of a broken heart, but offering her anything more ardent felt beyond his present capabilities. It wasn't her fault she didn't stir the fire in him that Ana did. He had a history of desiring the very things determined to destroy him.

Walking too close to the flames had almost been the death of him once. If he refused the lessons offered, he deserved to burn.

Nessa was...

Well, she was the opposite of her cousin Ana, wasn't she?

Demure. Sweet. Uncomplicated.

Tyr slipped into the seat across from her. The frazzled look she'd worn earlier was gone, and she was smiling. Smiling at *him*.

"I meant to come sooner," she said sweetly. One of her hands played mindlessly with her soft, dark curls. They were almost preternatural, shiny and luscious and perfect.

"I didn't know you were coming at all," Tyr said. When her face fell, he quickly added, "but I'm glad you're here."

Nessa's gentle smile returned. She focused her eyes on the table, on her folded hands, wrung tight enough to turn her knuckles white. She pulled her dark-blue sleeves down over the top of them. She seemed nervous, out of sorts. "The weather appears to be turning, at least for a spell."

"Everything all right?"

"Oh, yes, of course!" Her shrill giggle was laced with a nervous edge. She darted her gaze around the room. "Not very busy tonight, huh?"

Tyr frowned, watching her closely. "No, not really. When the weather turns, the place thins out for a week or so. Then they come back in droves, like they've just seen snow for the first time."

"Are you going to the Cider Festival?"

"Definitely not," he blurted. The started look she wore had him scrambling for a respectable answer. "I've been before, and it's not for me."

"Ahh." Nessa tilted her head in a slow nod, watching him closely. "And—"

The double doors squeaked, followed by grunts. Before Adeline had both kegs out, Nessa was out of her seat, gathering one in her arms. Adeline flashed a quick smile, and together they placed the kegs on the back shelf of the bar. When Adeline signed, *Thank you*, Nessa signed, *I'm happy to help you*, without missing a beat. Adeline hugged her, and Nessa hugged her back.

Tyr observed the exchange in bewilderment.

He made his way to the bar and sat on one of the stools, watching Adeline show Nessa how to attach the spouts and prime the kegs. Nessa got hers right on the first try, earning her a nod of respect from an impressed Adeline. When they were done, Adeline ducked into the back to finish cleaning the mugs.

Nessa smiled after her and turned toward Tyr. Something in his face made hers grow serious. "Something wrong?"

"No, it's just..." He shook his head, reframing the words so they didn't sound quite so much like an accusation. "Where did you learn to sign?"

Nessa blanched. "I don't... I don't know much. I've learned a few things over the years, here and there."

"You know more than patrons who have been drinking here for years."

Nessa glanced toward the doors to the backroom. She stammered before saying, "There was this girl. I cared for her very much. I learned what I could, but then I had to leave her behind."

"Why?"

101

She blinked hard and forced a smile. "Doesn't matter. I know you're not very busy tonight, but I'd love for you to put me to work, if there're things to be done."

Tyr nearly laughed. "You're serious?"

Nessa nodded earnestly.

"You want to... work?"

"I'm not allergic to it, if that's what you think. I suppose some highborns are."

"No, I—" But he had thought it. He'd thought it for years, ever since he had been a boy serving the rich as they passed through Parth on their way to do whatever it was they did. All highborns had been the same. Spoiled. Entitled. Demanding what wasn't theirs. Rhiain and Ana had both been surprises, but they were exceptions, and in the end, they'd still taken a part of him with them. "If you want to help Addy dry and carry the mugs out..."

Nessa brightened. She clapped her hands on Tyr's shoulders in excitement, then seemed to remember herself and eased off. "I'd love to help. Really."

It was only after he watched her disappear into the back that he remembered he still hadn't solved the matter of the mysterious translation.

EIGHT
A MUCH DARKER MOTIVE

Tyr's mother and sister, Agnes, ventured out twice a week to barter for meats, tubers, and the rare green vegetable for the tavern stew in the village shops. The weather had caused them to miss some trips, which had put them behind schedule, but the Cider Festival in a few days meant they couldn't put off a visit any longer.

Though he was exhausted, Tyr offered to come along and pull the wagon while they stocked up.

Fransiska shifted her basket high on her arm as they passed other shoppers on the road. She nodded to all, greeting many by name. She used the Vjestikaan greetings—hej for hello, or dobryzen for good morning, even a few kahk si's to ask after their health—which made her popular among villagers. Olov was the same way, memorizing the little details patrons shared about their lives.

Tyr followed, wondering how he'd inherited none of their charm. Rikard meowed urgently from inside the cart as if to say, *Faster!*

"We really might be in luck this season," Agnes remarked, cradling her very pregnant belly. Where the Penhallows had come from in the Westerlands, being unmarried in her condition would have made her a pariah; there'd have been whispers about her betrothed, Stojan, being trapped into wedding her to avoid scandal. But the Vjestik didn't subscribe to such archaic notions. Agnes loved Stojan, and Stojan loved Agnes, and that was all that mattered to Tyr, his family, and the village. "I can *almost* make out a hint of sun through the clouds."

Fransiska laughed. "We'd need more than a hint to melt all this ice." Her face curved into a scowl. She shook her head at a boarded-up butcher's stall as they passed. "Another poor season, thanks to the Hunt. It isn't my place to question their traditions, but another year of the import tax on meat is going to put us all out of business."

"Maybe we should raise prices to cover the taxes," Tyr said from behind them. His breath formed a white cloud as he shivered. *Hint of sun, my ass.* "The Vjestik lose the Hunt far more than they prevail."

"The people suffer as much as the businesses," Fransiska said. "If we raise prices, they'll be forced to choose between patronizing our tavern and putting food on their own tables. That helps no one. With luck, the next Vjestik son will triumph, and we'll have a solid hunting season ahead."

"Didn't your girlfriend lose her brother to the Hunt, Tyr?" Agnes asked.

"She's not my girlfriend," Tyr retorted, beginning to regret coming along. Agnes never missed an opportunity to goad him about something. "Stepan Wynter died in the Hunt several years ago, yes."

"Terrible," Fransiska muttered, clucking her tongue as she perused the stalls. "But what do they expect, sending their sons into the wilderness every year without even a bow?"

"They get daggers," Tyr said, unsure why he was defending a tradition he thought was arcane and ridiculous. "And for some, that's enough. Every few years, one of them comes home from the Vuk od Varem with the wulf's heart."

"Most do not, and we beseech the Guardians for their lost souls," Fransiska said.

"What would happen if men hunted the forests anyway?" Agnes slowed to examine a vegetable stand, but the pickings were sparse.

"I don't really know, darling," Fransiska said. She nodded at a group of women passing by. "There are more wulves in those forests than men in this village though. Their arrangement has worked for hundreds of years, so who are we to question it?"

"You're questioning it right now." Tyr's shoulders were already screaming, so he released the cart handles and took a rest.

"You don't *really* believe the Vjestik can speak to wulves, do you, Mother?" Agnes asked with a laugh.

"Not *all* of them." Fransiska clucked her tongue again and changed topics. "What shall we make for the party?"

Tyr perked up. "What party?"

"Is he serious?" Agnes asked with an eyeroll back at him. "Pern and Ev?"

"What?"

Agnes held her hands out with a slow shake of her head. "Mother, he's hopeless."

"Tyr, love," Fransiska said, sighing. "Their sendoff? It's springtide. Evert's apprenticeship starts in a few weeks, and Pern and Drago can't afford to put off leaving any longer, unless they want to be stuck in the Cross for another long winter. They're leaving in two days." She inhaled an excited breath. "Oh, Agnes, look! They have rhubarb again. Let's grab several bushels, and we can make apple rhubarb tarts for the festival. If you're feeling up to it, you could make some of your compote we all love so much."

"So soon?" Tyr asked, stepping forward. "Before the Cider Festival?"

"We've been talking about both departures for a year, Tyreste. I'm sure neither your brother nor sister will be terribly sad about missing another season of naked, drunken men crushing apples with their feet and 'lively' carols that sound more like dirges."

Fransiska looped her arm through Agnes's and enthusiastically ushered her to the crates of rhubarb.

Tyr moved the cart off of the road and leaned against the creaky stall wall, taking a moment for himself. He wasn't unaware springtide had arrived, of course, but how had he missed Pernilla and Evert were leaving so soon? He hardly saw them as it was, with both working opposite shifts as him, and it might be years before he saw them again. If ever.

From several feet away, he heard his mother and sister running down all the sweets they could make with their precious rhubarb as he fought the doze threatening to do him in.

He started to rest his eyes when he saw something unexpected.

Ana, in a dark-red hooded cloak, was purchasing a bowl of broth and an ale from a merchant three stalls down. She was facing away, but he'd know the shape of her anywhere... her slim waist flaring into hips he'd held a hundred different ways. The way she shrugged with just one shoulder and fiddled with her hair—the tips of her golden waves peeking out from the sides of her crimson robe—while waiting for the merchant to bundle her meal into a tight satchel.

She paid and lowered her head, shuffling quickly away. Tyr ground his jaw, predicting the path his next thoughts would take. *No. You will not follow her. She is not your business. She is not—*

MEOWWWWWWWW.

Tyr looked down at his little sidekick with a deep frown. "No." Rikard hissed.

"I said *no*. Shall I say it in Vjestikaan too? Old Ilynglass?"

"Brother, are you talking to your cat again?" Agnes asked from the other side of the wall.

"Nien! I mean... er... Ag, I'll be right back. The cart is right here."

"Whatever," she said dismissively and returned to discussing the virtues of rhubarb.

106

"Stay," Tyr ordered, and Rikard responded by lengthening his lean body into a comfortable, satisfied stretch.

Tyr darted off, sliding through the growing crowd of shoppers. He caught flashes of Ana's red cloak, dancing in and out of the pockets of villagers, evading him. He pushed on, nearly knocking an old woman sideways, and when he stopped to apologize and make sure she was all right, he spotted Ana again, ducking down a row of cider tents being erected.

He finally caught up to her, but before he could think of what to say, she spun around, her eyes flashing with rage... and something else. Fear. Of him?

"Why are you following me?" she demanded. Her jaw ground back and forth. "No need to think of a lie, Tyreste. I know what you're doing. Why?"

All he could think to do was nod at the wrapped soup in her hands. "Why are you eating in town?"

Ana tucked her chin downward in offense. "Why wouldn't I eat the food from the village?"

"It's not like you, is all."

She disappeared the bag under her heavy cloak and stared boldly ahead. "Why are you following me?"

"I *wasn't*. I'm here with Mother and Agnes—"

"Last night..." Ana sighed and glanced at her feet. "It shouldn't have happened. It was my fault for giving you the impression it was what I wanted."

Tyr took a step back. "I would *never* have forced—"

"I know," she said quickly, shaking her head at the ground. Her brows furrowed. "I *know*. That's why I said it was my fault. I'll take all the blame and leave none for you to carry. But please don't follow me. You said... You said if I walked out that door..."

"That I never wanted to see you again?" Tyr bit back a bitter laugh. He wished she'd look up, but meeting her eyes terrified him as much as the labyrinthine emotions holding his heart hostage. "How I wish I'd meant it, Ana. I would do anything to mean it."

"Then tell me why you're following me!"

Several villagers stopped to watch them. Tyr smiled, waved, and stepped closer, lowering his voice to a whisper. "I have never seen you so afraid, Ana."

Ana scoffed and cast her glance sideways. "Then maybe you should respect my wishes and leave me alone."

Something in the way she said it, *alone,* hit him like a sack of rocks. She *was* alone. For all her wealth and privilege, she'd been alone for years. He'd only seen glimpses of the pain she'd tried so hard to hide, even from him. "I don't..." He swallowed hard. "I don't need you to love me. And I won't try to win you back or convince you what we had was..." He breathed in. "But you are *not* alone. Do you hear me? I will always be here if you need me. I will always help you."

Ana's shoulders started to shake. He reached forward to hold them, and when she looked up, tears were streaming down her face.

"Ana," he whispered.

When her lower lip quaked, something broke inside of him. But then something worse took hold of her. Her eyes widened to saucers, terror slipping into every inch of her expression.

"Anastazja! *There* you are."

Tyr had only met Magda Wynter a handful of times, and they'd never had a conversation beyond dry pleasantries. Ana never wanted to talk about her stepmother.

He'd never told anyone how the woman gave him the dark chills.

"Sorry, Magda. I..." Ana's voice turned shrill and anxious as she divided her focus between Tyr and her stepmother. Her face had lost all color.

"And who's this?" Magda asked. Her plump mouth spread into a broad grin. It unsettled him so much, he had to remind himself that the urge to run from a harmless woman was silly.

"Tyreste Penhallow, ma'am," he said, his eyes flicking toward Ana as he extended a hand that the woman looked at but didn't take. "We've, ah, met before."

"Penhallow." Magda's nose curled upward in disgust. "Taverners. What would your father think, Anastazja?"

"My father loves all our people equally," Ana muttered with a defiant scowl. She winced seconds later though, and Magda noted it with a slow smile, crushing Ana's mischief in an instant. Tyr's confusion grew. "Anyway, we hardly know one another. He was just—"

"I wanted to know if the broth was any good," Tyr stated, cutting in quickly. "I've never had it before."

"Nor has she, I should think," Magda said, the corner of her lip tugging upward. "But go on, Ana, tell us about the broth."

Sheer, untampered panic spread across Ana's features, tightening around her eyes and mouth, and Tyr knew, finally, the source of her fear. The *why* was a mystery too big for a crowded market and a fraught exchange.

"Another time," he said with what he hoped was a polite smile and not a reflection of his own unease. "I have to get back to my mother and sister before they purchase all the rhubarb in the Cross."

Magda smiled thinly and wrapped her arm around Ana's waist, waiting for him to leave.

He caught Ana's eyes as he turned, and what he saw behind her gaze filled him with equal parts hope and despair.

She wasn't afraid for herself.

She was terrified. For *him.*

The last thing he heard was Magda hissing, "Is it him? Is he the one who's turned you into an insolent brat?"

Tyr forced himself to keep walking, cursing his cowardice at every step.

"Well?" Magda's soft facade cracked, revealing the koldyna's true form. Ana's heart lit up in hope that *someone* might notice, but the veil of deception returned. "Is he the one?"

Ana's mouth flapped in a useless attempt at rebuttal. Her eyes followed Tyreste, a foolish misstep that had Magda *ahh*ing. "I hardly know him."

"I have seen through every lie you have told me. What makes you think I cannot see through this one?" Magda seemed taller, wider. Her presence was like standing under shade when all Ana wanted was the sun.

Ana shook her head as she flailed for something close enough to the truth to appease her stepmother but far enough away to protect Tyreste. "The truth is..." She rolled her eyes in mock disgust, ridding her thoughts of Tyreste's soft dark hair, his mahogany eyes that made her knees weak when he trained them on her. "He's sweet on me, and I made the mistake of giving in to his affection a couple of times. Now he's acting like we're betrothed."

Magda cackled and licked her lips. Villagers milled around in the background, going about their morning business, oblivious to the horror transpiring in the middle of the market. "I can solve that trouble for you, girl. All you need to do is ask."

"It's not necessary," Ana said. "I think he understands now." She breathed out slowly. "I was just returning home."

"Another lie!" Magda's mouth hung wide through a protracted head shake. She ripped open Ana's cloak and gave the bag of broth a shake. "You don't think I know where you're taking this?"

"I—"

"Well, get on with it then!" Magda released the bag and stepped back. She flexed her bony fingers and tucked her hands inside her own cloak. "Wouldn't want him to starve."

Ana was dumbstruck. She'd assumed Magda knew she'd been taking Varradyn food and drink, but her encouragement was unexpected. "You *want* me to feed him?"

"Of course I do." Magda snorted. "Won't do at all for him to perish before he's served his purpose."

Ana's heart choked in her throat, but a bold stroke of courage forced her words forth. "What purpose is that, Magda?"

"There is no equity in our relationship, Anastazja. No balance, no tipping point where I determine you a worthy equal. Our arrangement is quite simple, isn't it? You help me, and your father and brother live."

Ana couldn't believe the koldyna was speaking so openly in public. But no heads turned toward the sound of her threats. No concerned villagers stopped to help. "You need Niko."

"I need either Niko *or* your father. I don't need both, do I? When you die, the designation of heir will pass to your brother. But if *he* dies... Well, I'm not heirless, am I? Really, if you were thinking about this objectively, you'd realize I don't need *either* of them because there will always be other Wynters."

"If something happens to Niko and me, my father will see you for what you are."

"Will he?" Magda's shoulders lifted in a chuckle. "You'll never know the answer yourself." She reached forward and wrapped one of her talon-like hands around Ana's cloaked arm. "You've done so well lately, Ana. It would be a shame to upset me just as I'm beginning to tolerate you."

Magda stepped backward. Darkness pooled in her dead irises. "Keep the raven's energy up. He'll need it for what's coming." She laughed. "And if you're lying to me about that tavern boy, you'll find I will deliver quite swiftly on my promise to serve you his heart for supper."

"I'm... I'm not," Ana stammered. She loathed herself more in that moment than ever before. Some warrior she was, unable to even form an unfettered sentence around the biggest threat her family had ever faced.

"Oh, and, Ana, you'll find I've implemented some changes at Fanghelm when you return tonight."

All the warmth in Ana plummeted straight into the cold ground. "What changes?"

Magda grinned. "The raven's broth grows cold."

Nessa didn't come to the tavern that night. Tyr watched for her until dawn, working his shift in silent reflection.

But though he'd hoped to see his new friend, it was Ana taking up the bulk of his thoughts all night. He couldn't unsee the fear in her eyes. The quake in her hands. The pure dread that had taken hold of her when her stepmother had found them talking.

And then the lie. *We hardly know one another.* He'd bristled at how easily the denial fell from her lips, but then he'd seen a glimmer of the truth behind it. The realization it wasn't shame he was seeing in her but fright.

As Tyr served ales and cleaned mugs, he tried to piece together what little he knew of Ana's family. Most of it was village fishwife gossip. Arkhady was a kind, doddering widower who had lost his eldest son to the Hunt and, in his apparent fear of losing his twins as well, had married a woman of unknown background who had come to Fanghelm looking for work. Many things were whispered about Magda, but little was actually known, and whenever Tyr had tried to ask Ana, she'd closed up and changed topics as quickly as wind whipping through an alleyway. She often spoke of her father and brother, but never Magda.

Tyr had always assumed her reluctance came from a place of grief. Losing her mother so suddenly had wounded Ana deeply. Another woman coming into her life, taking her mother's place, had to sting.

But there was nothing about Ana and Magda's interaction that seemed so easily explainable.

I'm going to bed, Addy signed from the other side of the bar. *Rik and Pern are here. You should leave too.*

I will. Tyr sighed and looked around. There was nothing left to do but go home. It was clear Nessa wasn't coming. *Be careful walking back. I heard whispers of an ice storm tonight.*

Some springtide this is shaping up to be, she signed with a theatrical eyeroll and flounced away.

Rikard burst through from the back room. "Do you hate sleep, Tyr? Because it feels like you're always here."

"Yeah. Yeah, I'm leaving," Tyr said distantly, his thoughts pulled in so many directions, there'd be no sleep awaiting him at the cabin.

Tyr took the longer route across his family's land. The direct path was a five-minute walk, but if he looped around the field and through the edge of the forest, it offered almost twenty minutes of head-clearing distraction.

The old Tyr had learned to compartmentalize when he was overwhelmed. With only a touch of guilt, he called upon that buried part of himself. He memorized the soft blankety scent of snow yet to fall, the earthy pine wafting across the field on the back of a fierce wind, and the satisfying crunch of ice breaking under his stride.

When at last he reached the cabin, the tension had lifted from his limbs, and he was calmer than he'd felt in days.

He was going into the kitchen to pour himself a cider when he noticed two letters lying side by side on the table. They hadn't been there when he'd left for work yesterday evening, which meant someone had left them during the night while he had been at the tavern. Even if he'd been keeping a lookout, the cabin wasn't visible from the tavern.

Cider forgotten, Tyr went to check on the stash of letters. All were there, he noted with heavy relief, then grabbed the next two letters written by Paeris.

He tentatively took a seat and reviewed both the Vjestikaan translations and the two he'd retrieved written in Old Ilynglass. He slid them back into proper order and read all four before sitting back in his chair with a heavy exhale. Then he read them again and again, but they made no more sense the second or third time.

Tyr couldn't reconcile the dark tone in Paeris's words compared to the light, upbeat nature of Zofia's responses.

Snippets of Paeris's dire proclamations promised terrible danger. *Mortain is up to something. I saw him speaking to someone, through a mirror, Zo. A mirror! My mother is scared, and my grandfather told me to be careful what I put in letters. Neither will explain themselves. I have the most peculiar, terrible feeling I'm being watched, and followed. You're the only one I can tell about any of this. I was only worried about the poor Ravenwoods before, but now I fear for everyone I love. Please tell me there's a way to stop this. But whatever you do, be careful, Zo. I'm so scared for all of us.*

The contrast in Zofia's responses was jarring. *We're having the most delectable springtide! Oh, how I wish you could see the blooms. Mother is making her famous tarts, and Father will not stop talking about them. I was just thinking you should come for a visit. The markets are full of all the best items right now, and it's a treat every time I go into the village. Have you collected any new books lately?*

He flopped back in his chair, rattling the uneven legs on the floor. Rikard leaped straight into the air.

Tyr jumped up to go back to the stash and rifled until he found the letters that had been translated. He brought them back to the kitchen and slapped them onto the table next to the translated versions. He might not be able to *read* Vjestikaan, but he knew the letters, the patterns.

There was no way to tell what all the differences were, but he was absolutely certain about one thing: they were not the same letters. The translated ones were shorter, in snappier cadence than Zo's usual flowery style. Even the voice was off.

They weren't the same letters.

Tyr dragged his hands through his hair and then down his face. His secret benefactor had duped him. Perhaps the first translation had been wrong as well, but that made less sense than the cover-up done on the two new ones. What seemed more likely was that whoever had translated the letters had seen something they didn't want *him* to see. But what?

He had no local friends, only acquaintances. Nessa was the exception, but she'd said the night he'd met her that she'd never learned much Vjestikaan either. But if it wasn't someone close to him, it could only mean that whoever had been sneaking in and translating had a much darker motive than helpfulness.

But how did they know he had the letters?

And why didn't they want him to know what they said?

"Fuck. *Fuck*."

Tyr shoved back from the table and screamed into the crook of his elbow.

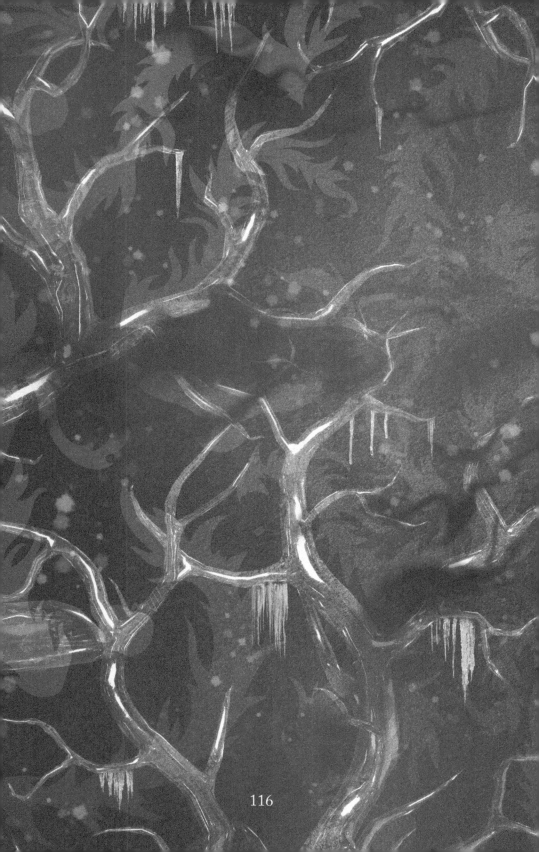

NINE
SEEING THE THREADS

"Nien." Ana stormed to the other end of the long table toward her father. "Nien! Ota, where? Where is he? Where did you send him?"

"Calm yourself before I do it for you," Magda said, carving delicate slices of boar's meat.

"It's not forever," Arkhady said with the same blank expression as always, staring at the roaring hearth. "But Niko must learn to be a man before he can take a wife."

"We don't send our men away to learn to be men, Father," Ana stated. She dropped to her knees before him, turning her back on Magda. "We've never sent our men away. This is *her* doing! She wants to separate us, to separate all of us!"

"Arkhady, control your daughter."

Arkhady sighed and closed his eyes. His head fell to the side. "Ana. Please don't disrespect your stepmother. She's done nothing but try to help this family."

"Tell me where my brother is!"

"He will not," Magda said firmly. She shoved her plate forward with a loud screech. "And now my appetite is spoiled."

"Do you even require food like the rest of us, *koldyna*?"

"Ana!" Arkhady exclaimed with more fire than Ana had seen in him in years. "You bring shame to this family with such vile words. Apologize."

Ana jumped to her feet. Her cheeks blazed with fiery anger and a boldness she knew she would regret later yet didn't care. "I will never, *ever* apologize to her, Ota. She hasn't helped this family; she's divided it. She's taken you from me." Her voice choked. "When I needed you most." She wiped her eyes and blinked hard to expel the tears. "But you know, my appetite seems to be spoiled as well, so I'll excuse myself, before I bring further shame to our family. Dobranok."

Ana raced away from the dining hall, darting down the long hall toward the stairs at a pace she hadn't commanded since she had been a girl. She didn't stop when she reached the stairs and kept pushing until she made it to her room, then bolted the door behind her with a victorious pant.

"You've had a difficult day."

Ana sounded a shrill scream. "Ludya! You nearly scared me half to death. And why is it I cannot even come to my room anymore without someone waiting to ambush me?"

"When have I ever ambushed you?" Ludya glided into the light. She wasn't smiling, but Ana liked that about her vedhma. While others employed kindness for deceptions, benign and not, Ludya spared hers only for truly joyous moments. Reading her was as simple as paying close attention to her choice of words and gestures. "I heard about Niko. I'm truly bereft for you. His place is here."

"It's *her*." Ana ground the words through a clench so hard, her teeth scraped.

"Tak. Of course it is. I told you the day she arrived she would cause great division in this household." Ludya held out a steaming mug. Her dark hair was plaited with ribbons of gold, which glowed in the warm light of the candelabras, giving her an otherworldly air. Ana had never been certain of Ludya's age, but she could have been fourteen or forty, and either would have made sense. "But you haven't made it easier on yourself, Pjika. You feed her with your anger. Your fear. Starving her would be far more effective."

Ana managed a grateful smile and took the mug to her favorite chair. She unlaced her boots and kicked them across the room, then pulled her achy legs up under her. "And how does one starve a creature that requires no sustenance?"

"None? You certain?" Ludya sat in the chair across from her. "Your anger blocks your cleverness. It represses you."

Ana squeezed the tears from her eyes before drawing a deep sip of tea. It had an immediate calming effect, which of course had been Ludya's intent. She always knew what Ana needed. "I've never been especially clever, Ludya, but I appreciate your confidence in me, however misplaced." Her foolishness with the letters came rushing back, affirming her words.

Ludya observed her in silence. "You forget how I can see the threads."

"I haven't forgotten," Ana said. "But seeing 'threads' isn't the same as divining the future. Don't look at me like that. You've said so yourself, many times."

Ludya folded her hands atop her lap. "I would argue it's more useful than divining the future, for what good is seeing something you cannot change, as a diviner does?"

Ana was too exhausted for one of Ludya's famous mazy lectures. "I would be forever grateful if you could just tell me and spare me the puzzles tonight."

"You already know the answer, but I'll indulge you, for I can see you truly are *not* in your best form," Ludya said. "Drink up. It will ease you into a restful night."

Ana sighed before taking another sip. "I'll need some grimizhna tea as well, when you can."

"I thought you ended your affair with the publican?"

Ana never had to tell Ludya her darkest secrets. The vedhma had her own ways of knowing, and it seemed wasteful, and a touch insulting, for Ana to act surprised. "I did, but..."

"Ahh." Ludya flashed a brief smile, a knowing one. "I'll have some sent up in the morning with your breakfast."

Ana lowered her face toward the mug and nodded her thanks. "So. Threads?"

"Threads," Ludya said. "As you know, threads are not the present or the future, but possibilities. Possibilities have not yet been woven and thus can be cut, frayed, woven, or destroyed altogether. I have seen many, many threads dangling along the tapestry of your life, Anastazja, and they are all so different. So confusing. Some leave my heart in tatters. Others fill me with such swelling hope, it brings tears to my eyes." She made a soft, clicking sound. "You already know I cannot guide you down the right path—the right thread to cultivate or cull. But it is imperative you know that there *is* hope. You can still weave a future that brings you and others joy. There are so many possible outcomes, I can hardly wrap my mind around them."

Hot tears stung Ana's eyes and poured over. "How? How can I do that when the creature has no weakness? No heart? Nothing to take or defeat?"

"You said she requires no sustenance. But even great evil needs air to breathe. Space to expand. What is Magda's air? Her space?"

Ana could only shake her head. The day lay so heavy on her heart, it choked the breath from her lungs. From the emotional confrontation with Tyr and Magda in the market to the morose visit with Varradyn, the loss of Niko, and her father's chilly reception, she had nothing left to offer anyone.

"*Your* fear, Ana. *Your* anger. Resentment. All these things, she devours like a ghoul, and you give them so freely."

"I cannot pretend to be what I am not!"

"Am I speaking to Ana or Nessa right now?"

Ana quieted and sat back in the chair. She laughed to herself with a roll of her eyes. "Ancestors keep us. Of *course* you'd know about Nessa too."

"But do you know who does not? Magda."

"*Yet.*"

"Tell me, when you are Nessa, do you feel fear? Anger? Resentment?"

Ana scoffed, but the question gave her pause. "I suppose I feel peace. Relief. Like I can be whoever I want."

"Now imagine if you were like that around Magda."

Ana burst into laughter. "I could never be that free around Magda. I realize you are all-seeing, but you really don't know the half of what she's capable of."

"You mean the Ravenwoods."

Ana tossed her head and nearly spilled the tea. "What do you know?" She leaned forward. "*Pros*, Ludya. Tell me. Tell me what she does with them when my part has ended."

"I don't know what she does with them, Ana, and that is the truth. What I do know for certain is not one has ever made it back to Midnight Crest. Have you ever been down in the cellar of the observatory?"

Ana frowned. "It has a cellar?"

"A deep one. Detached from the dome. Cellar may be the wrong word. Cavern perhaps? Magda spends a fair amount of time there, from what I know. I've seen..." Ludya's brows furrowed. "I've seen threads that take you down there. What I cannot see is whether any discovery you make there helps you or hurts you."

"A cellar," Ana mused aloud. "And you say she spends time down there?"

"Doing what, I cannot say."

She set the mug on the nearby table and cocked her head. "What has this to do with my fear of her?"

"Are you more scared of what you know she's capable of, or what you do not?"

Ana didn't bother answering.

"The mystery of her terrifies you. The *potential*. But if you discover what she's truly about, then there will be no mystery. And when you learn to control your fear, she can no longer feast

121

upon it." Ludya rose from the chair. "Never forget, Nessa *is* you. You created her for a reason, but you do not need her to become who you were meant to be. And when Magda has nothing left to take, then you will know what true power is."

Ludya went to the door and nodded but didn't bow. Ana had never liked deference from the staff, and Ludya was one of the few who respected her wish to be treated as an equal. "Sleep, Anastazja. Whisper to the Ancestors your need for clarity. And tomorrow, you will have more than you left the day with."

Tyr couldn't hear himself think over the rabble of conversation filling the tavern, which was stuffed shoulder to shoulder for the sendoff. Pernilla and her husband Drago held court near the bar, each carrying one of their children. Evert was surrounded by a large huddle of mates, all of them doubled over in laughter, probably about something inappropriate.

Tyr nursed his ale, swaying mindlessly to the music. His mother had hired a Vjestik ensemble for the evening, and the group was alternating between lively choral arrangements and cheerless dirges.

Adeline's waving drew his attention. A smile formed at the corner of his mouth as he made his way toward her.

Is this music as loud as it seems? she signed.

Tyr blew out a breath with an exaggerated nod, making her giggle. *Can't understand a word of it. They're singing in Vjestikaan.*

What if they're singing about wulf orgies or something? Would we ever know?

Tyr laughed and took another swig from his mug. *I might enjoy that.*

Plenty of Vjestik here tonight. Watch their expressions.

But there was nothing but the flush of ale and rousing conversation when he looked out into the swarm of people who had come to say good-bye to Pernilla, Drago, and Evert. At first he'd thought they'd come just for Drago, but Pernilla and Evert had just as many hugs and well-wishes.

We've become a part of this village, for better or worse, his father said from time to time, and Tyr at last understood the meaning. *Home is where we make it. Family is who we choose.*

Seeing so many gathered was what finally made Tyr realize he was losing a big part of his family, when he'd only just gotten them back. Five years with them didn't make up for the three that had been stolen.

"Your new girlfriend is here," Rikard said on his way to Evert's group of mates. He turned back toward Tyr and nodded at the door before moving on with a rousing *whoop!*

She's not your girlfriend. You know that, right? Adeline said with a pointed glance.

Tyr shrugged, sighed, and moved toward the door. He didn't see her at first, but then he clocked her standing alone near a window ledge with a faraway look. Her dark hair was pulled forward over one shoulder, both of her hands combing through it in almost tugging passes.

"Nessa." Tyr squeezed through the crowd and stepped in beside her. "You came."

Her expression changed so fast, he didn't know what to make of it. She rolled her bottom lip in and out of her mouth and lit up with a bright smile. "Of course I came."

He tried to respond, but for the briefest, strangest moment, he could have sworn he was looking at Ana.

Your mind is playing tricks. They're cousins. Of course there are similarities.

"Something wrong?" she asked.

"No," he said quickly. "Not at all. I'm glad you're here."

She gestured around with an appraising nod. "This is quite the turnout. Your family has truly won over the Cross. They don't always take so kindly to stranjak."

Tyr whistled. "I've watched them run more than one family of outsiders out of this village."

"The Penhallows must give more than they take," she said and went silent, her attention returning to the crowd instead. She seemed almost like she was looking for someone. "Your brother brings honor to your entire family. What did you say his apprenticeship was for again?"

"Evert? He's going to study with the Woodworkers Guild in Whitechurch. He's always been clever with his hands, as long as I can remember. I can't even list all the things he's done for the tavern. He built our first childhood fort and was the one who designed my cabin." Tyr chuckled, remembering. "I always tell people I built my own house, and I *officially* did, but the truth is I would have been lost without him directing every board and nail placement."

"Whitechurch," Nessa mused aloud. "What a tremendous accomplishment for a young man of the Cross."

"He's incorrigibly excited," Tyr said. "My mother, on the other hand..." His gaze followed his words and landed on Fransiska. She stood next to her husband as they chatted with a local miller, smiling through the bittersweet gleam in her eyes. "Would you like to meet her?"

Nessa looked surprised. "You want me to meet your mother?"

Her hesitation created his own. He rarely "introduced" his parents to anyone. All his friends back in the Westerlands had always just been there. Rikard described meeting Faustina's family like it had been the official demarcation between a casual dalliance and a serious commitment.

And what was Nessa to him? A friend? An acquaintance? He hardly knew her. He didn't even know why she'd been coming around or why she was still in town. Nor, as he thought about it further, did he know where she'd be going when she left.

"Why not?" If nothing else, his parents would have heard about Nessa from Rikard and Agnes, because neither were capable of keeping their mouths closed. Better to get ahead of it than wait for the whispers and questions.

Fransiska dabbed at her eyes when Tyr approached with Nessa. She smiled, but part of it faded to confusion and then wonder as she took in his guest.

"Mother, this is Nessa. She's Grigor Arsenyev's daughter, visiting from..." He used the opportunity to see if she'd share.

"The Westerlands," Nessa said pleasantly and bowed her head in a respectful nod. "It's very nice to meet you, Madam Penhallow."

"Madam!" Fransiska's face erupted in stunned delight. "You hear that, love? I'm a proper madam now."

Olov chuckled and returned to his conversation.

But Tyr was still stuck on Nessa's answer. The Westerlands. Hadn't she said before that she'd never been there? Had he misheard?

"I didn't realize Grigor had a daughter," Fransiska said. "How do you know my son?"

"She came in one evening," Tyr answered slowly. He couldn't say why Nessa answering made him nervous, only that he needed the explanation to come from himself. "We got to talking, and we've struck up a friendship."

"A friend. How lovely." Fransiska sized Nessa up with a long, sweeping gaze. "Are you hungry, dear? We have plenty of food, and more ale than we need."

"Thank you, Mad—"

"Fransiska will do."

"Fransiska." Nessa glanced at Tyr briefly. "Thank you. This is a lovely celebration, and I appreciate the invite."

Fransiska furrowed her brows at Tyr. "Well... of course. The fete is open to all, invite or no." She wrapped her hand around Tyr's arm with a quick squeeze. "If you'll excuse me, love."

"She's beautiful, your mother," Nessa said when they'd moved away. She looked behind her. "But did she know I was coming?"

Tyr was still mulling his mother's perfunctory reception. He had nothing to compare it to, but it seemed—

He suddenly realized he'd been wrong. He *had* introduced someone to his parents, and not so long ago.

Ana.

His mother and father had both swallowed her in near-inappropriate hugs, leaving him mortified by their gushing. Later, they'd expressed concerns about her being highborn and out of his reach. But what he hadn't felt, ever, was disinterest.

"Tyr?"

"Sorry," he said. "Can hardly hear myself think over all the noise. There's a table in the corner, if you want..." He trailed off in shock when his father climbed up onto the bar.

"Guardians, Olov, you'll break your neck! You're not a young man anymore," Fransiska declared to a roar of laughter. The small, clustered groups broke up and shuffled in closer as their attentions turned to the proprietor of the Tavern at the Top of the World attempting a wobbly scale of the bar.

"What is he *doing*?" Tyr muttered, waiting, along with everyone else, to find out.

Olov stretched to his feet, his balance wavering before he straightened with a triumphant smile. The tavern went silent. "My wife and I would like to thank all of you for coming to help us send two of our beloved children out into the world." He pressed his lips tight and inhaled deeply. "Evert has been recognized for his tremendous skill with building and design, and Whitechurch's gain will most certainly be our loss. Just be sure to remember us wee folk when you become a city man."

He paused and everyone applauded, shouting well-wishes to a beaming Evert. His mates nudged him from all sides. "And Pernilla... our sweet Pern. Our eldest. The light of our days and the joy of our nights. When she met Drago, we thought..." He laughed ahead of his joke. "Poor, poor man."

Tyr laughed along with everyone else. Nessa joined in, clapping.

Drago winked at Pernilla, who scrunched her nose, trying not to laugh.

"But at last our Pern had found a man who could hold his own with her. They've built a family, expanding both of ours. And now that love of family takes them on a pilgrimage to the once-homeland of the Vjestik, and Drago's people. They join several dozen other Vjestik in their quest to rebuild their old community and create another haven for their descendants. We wish them nothing but success, love, and joy in their endeavors."

The trouble began as a discordant flutter in Tyr's chest but then spread into his shoulders and down his arms. He stretched and twisted, but it didn't go away.

When the applause and shouting died down, Pernilla quipped, "Not going to ask *us* to remember you 'wee folk,' Father?"

Tyr's neck was on fire. He adjusted his collar and shifted, abruptly uncomfortable in his clothing.

"Oops. Caught me." Olov shrugged to more laughter.

Tyr rushed to the bar and poured an ale, then downed it in one sip. He tried to catch his breath.

Nessa was at his side seconds later. "What's wrong?"

The fire had spread down into his torso, and his breaths came shorter now. He was ravenous for air. He clawed at his neck, praying no one else had seen the panic stealing over him.

Nessa straightened. She looked around and looped an arm around his shoulder. "Come on."

Tyr tried to ask *where* or *what*, but she was already ushering him through the back. She didn't stop until they stumbled out into the cool evening.

He fell to his knees, gasping in a hungry lungful of air. His raspy, strained breathing didn't slow to an even pace until Nessa dropped down behind him and encircled him from behind, whispering, in a painfully familiar, soft voice, "I have you, Tyreste. Just breathe."

Ana ushered Tyreste up the small hill behind the tavern, to the edge of the forest line. She remembered the Penhallows had built a table underneath some massive firs sheltering a small open area that had been cleared. They hosted public events in the tavern, but private family time was held in the forest, when the weather allowed.

She ushered him up onto the table and then wandered the area, searching for kindling and logs that weren't too wet. She found neither, and the fire pit was a mess of blackened logs and ash, but beside it was an old stack of twigs. It might burn, but not for long.

I can't stay anyway, or Magda will get suspicious.

She'd already eased his suffering with her hands in the tavern, then some more on the short walk, but he didn't need to know that. As far as Tyreste was concerned, Nessa was the opposite of Ana. No magic. No fire. No troubles.

Tyreste shivered, hunched over his knees with a gentle rocking motion. She hadn't thought to grab his cloak on the way out, but she was still wearing hers—having planned a swift and uneventful exit from the party—and she draped it over the back of him, ignoring his mumbled objections about her freezing to death.

"I'm not that delicate. Vjestik carry the blood of the wulf," she said and hoisted herself beside him. She drew her knees up.

"How did you know about this place?" His teeth clacked between words.

Shit. "I didn't... I just started walking and it was here."

Tyreste's eyes narrowed in soft confusion.

"What happened back there?" she asked, diverting him.

Tyreste shook his head over the tops of his knees without looking up.

"We don't have to speak," Ana said and turned her face upward. Boughs of fir bent over the top of them, revealing flashes of the night sky. She'd been to the spot with Tyreste before, but only on walks. She'd never been invited to any of his family affairs.

Ana hadn't been invited. It brought her no joy to discover he'd been perfectly happy for "Nessa" to bond with his family.

Tyreste sniffed and pitched backward. He breathed out slowly, then in for a long inhale, and repeated this several times before turning his head to the side to smile weakly at her. "You really helped me. Thank you."

"I didn't do anything," Ana said with a demure smile.

"Can I ask you, Nessa... Why are you here?"

"You invited me."

"No," Tyreste said. "I mean here, in the Cross. And why spend so much of your time with someone you just met? You hardly know me."

"Well," she said slowly, forming a careful response to the question she'd been anticipating for weeks. "My father brought me to visit my family, and I'm not especially... especially close with any of them."

"Why?"

"It's hard to explain." Tears sprang into her eyes as truth and lie blended. As she thought of Niko, who had been sent away before she could even tell him good-bye, and was out there, somewhere, alone and perhaps suffering. "But when I met you, I knew I'd rather spend my time here, with you, than there, with them."

Tyreste rolled a hand atop her forearm. "Hey. Nessa, I'm sorry. I didn't mean to upset you."

Ana flashed him a quick smile. "You didn't. Promise."

He slowly withdrew his hand, watching her. "It's the strangest thing, but I feel like I've known you for years."

Her heart beat wildly out of order. She shouldn't be there, digging herself deeper into her deception, but she couldn't seem to stop herself. "I feel the same."

"There was..." Tyreste turned his gaze forward. "Someone. I loved her, though I shouldn't have. You remind me of her, but that feels strange to say because you're nothing like her at all. And yet I feel like I could tell you anything. Does that sound mad?"

Ana's eyes burned. Relief. Joy. Disappointment. She hadn't prepared herself for how she'd feel when Tyreste loved the illusion more than the woman. "No, it doesn't sound mad at all."

"Do you have siblings, Nessa?"

She *almost* nodded but caught herself. "No."

Tyreste nodded toward the tavern. It was too dark to make out the shape of the building, but the torches and candles burned bright. "I have five. I used to wish I had none." He laughed and swiped his face with the back of his hand. "But then I lost all of them. And it took years for me to get them back."

Ana stilled. She knew the story, but Nessa did not. "You lost them?"

His shoulders lifted in a hard inhale. "Yes," he said, breathing out. "Before I came to the Cross, I was from a small, forgotten post in the Westerlands. Have you ever heard of Parth?"

"Tavern at the Middle of the World," Ana said, feigning the same slow realization she'd come to when she'd heard the story the first time. "Well, now *this* tavern's name makes a little more sense."

"Suppose we'll have to move to the Southerlands next. They're probably feeling left out down there at the bottom of the world."

Ana laughed at the joke for the second time. "Might be right."

"I was born in Parth," he said. "And I died there too."

Ana turned toward him. "Died? How do you mean?"

Tyreste shook his head at his hands, laced around his knees. "You don't really want to hear this story."

"I would listen to any story you told me," Ana said softly. "But only if you wish to tell it."

Tyreste said nothing for a long time. "I had this friend, Rhiainach, and I just... just adored her. Loved her, maybe, but what did I really know of love? She was highborn, and I was only... the son of a taverner. But the thing about Rhiain was she never saw me as such. We were childhood mates, close as two people can be. One day, she came to me and said her father was marrying her off. She was miserable about it and wanted to run away together, and maybe I should have said yes, but I knew... I *knew* we'd be running the rest of our lives. Her father was a madman who had kept her purposely in the dark about parts of her life. Important parts. He'd never have let her leave without a fight."

"And did she? Run away?"

"She never got the chance. That same night, both our lives changed forever. Rumor spread about the few moments we'd been alone together in my room, and word got back to her father. Nothing inappropriate had happened, but the damage was done. He sent men to burn down the tavern and take me prisoner. The men who kidnapped me told me my family had died in the fire and that Mathias, Rhiain's father, had spared me because he had use for me. He sent me to the Reliquary as his spy, and as long as I reported back on the doings of certain men, he would spare my life." He twitched his brows. "For several years, Rhiain thought I was dead. My family thought I was dead. And in many ways, I was. I wanted to be."

Hearing the story a second time was just as powerful. Painful. She wanted to scoop him into her arms and kiss the hurt away, to give him the safe space he'd craved and she'd denied.

"Three years." His voice cracked. He cleared his throat. "Three years I spent in the Reliquary dungeon. And then fate brought Rhiain there. It wasn't her fault, what her father had done to my family, but I blamed her just the same. I wanted her to suffer as much as I had. But then I realized she was a victim too. Years of her life, of her memories, had been erased by her father in order to control her. But Mathias's plans fell apart when Rhiain fell in love with the same man I was sent to spy on, Asterin Edevane, and their love brought years and years of secrets and lies crashing down around both of us. Mathias eventually confessed to everything he'd done, but among his terrible revelations was an unbelievable one: my family was alive and had been sent to the Northerlands by Mathias to start a new life, without me. He'd told them I was dead and given them money and references to start anew." Tyreste bowed his head. He ran his tongue along his bottom lip. "Mathias threatened to have my family killed if she didn't marry the monster he'd arranged for her. She was going to do it too. For me." He squinted and tears spilled. "But I couldn't let it happen. Asterin and I were determined to save her from that fate." He chuckled under his breath. "Not that she needed us. She found her own way to hold Mathias and the other men who had hurt her to account. And when it was done, I went back for my cat, Rikard, put the Westerlands in my past, and traveled north to surprise my family. I left all the rest behind. My friends. My love of drawing. I used to draw day and night, draw everything... It doesn't matter. I could never do it again without thinking of those endless nights in the dungeon." He shook his head, sighing. "I've been here five years, but that part of my life feels like it happened yesterday."

It was no easier hearing the story for a second time. The way he spoke of those days was similar to how Vjestik spoke of the horrors of Nok Mora. "Tyreste. That's... a lot for one man to carry."

He shrugged, but she didn't miss the tight press of his mouth, the active effort to suppress the worst of his pain. "I suppose it is. But I was fine until Asterin showed up a few weeks back, to visit."

Ana stiffened. She wasn't aware his old friend Asterin had visited, which meant it had happened after she'd ended things. But the letters suddenly made sense. Asterin had to have delivered them. Even he must have seen how dangerous they were—too dangerous to trust them to a courier like the other translations.

"And now... Now I feel like I'm losing my family all over again. It's not the same, and I know that. But it feels..." He breathed out in a shaky exhale.

Ana slid a hand across the table and rested it against his outer thigh. The urge to hold him was so powerful, she had to close her eyes to restrain herself. "Of course it feels like you're losing them again. You've been through so much. But you deserve to be happy, Tyreste. Allow yourself to be sad, but allow yourself to see the joy as well."

"I *was* happy. For a while."

"Rhiain was—" Her pulse swirled rapidly skyward. *The one you loved,* she almost said, but she'd already tortured herself enough.

"No," he said distantly. "No, that was someone else." He looked down at her hand, and she almost removed it, but then he linked it in his with a brief smile. "I can't believe I just told you all of that. Only one other person in the Cross knows the full story, and I can't talk to her about anything anymore. I haven't even told my family most of it, honestly. It's not an easy thing to talk about."

"You can tell me anything, Tyreste. I want you to know that." Ana held her breath. It was what Ana would have said, not Nessa.

But he didn't seem to notice. "I believe you when you say it. I don't understand it, but I believe it." He laughed. "And you haven't run away screaming yet, so I suppose there's that."

"The night is still young," Ana teased, nudging him with her shoulder. She'd never felt so happy and yet so lost. To feel close to him once more was a gift she'd thought she'd surrendered forever, but it was Nessa he wanted, not Ana. Not *her*. And no matter how hard she worked to keep her secret, Nessa couldn't last forever, because Ana couldn't.

"You can—" Tyreste stopped and started again. "Tell me anything as well, Nessa. I don't expect you to, and I don't know why you chose *me* for friendship, but I'm grateful for it. More than I know how to say. You... Well, you came into my life when I needed a friend most, as though you knew."

Ana wanted nothing more than to stay all night with Tyreste under the trees and stars, but her illusion only worked if Magda didn't come looking for her. "I should go."

"And I should get back, before Evert and Pern take it personal." He snorted. "Though I kind of hope Evert does, the wiseass."

"This was nice," Ana said. Her flesh tingled with anticipation of the unknown future. *Kiss him*, something inside her whispered, but the objections were louder. Nessa was there to look out for him, not fall in love with him.

"It was." Tyreste jumped off the table and helped her down. He held her gaze, and for a moment, it seemed he would hold her as well. Then he whipped her cloak off and draped it back around her. His hands lingered at her neck as he clasped the fastener. "Thank you again, Ana."

Ana stopped breathing.

Tyreste winced and backed away. He looked down with a groaning exhale. "Fuck. I'm sorry, Nessa. I'm so sorry. Forgive me, it's—"

"It's *fine*," she said to assure him, her heart and head a mess and her illusion flickering so hard, she *knew* he could see it if he looked up. *Come on, focus!* "I left someone special behind too, and I... I understand."

He peered up with one eye squinted at the corner. "I messed up, didn't I?"

"No." Ana flexed her hands into fists under her cloak. *Breathe. Focus. And then leave.* "No, I promise you didn't. I'll see you tomorrow." She darted forward and pecked a kiss at his temple before racing away.

When she'd cleared the small hill, she flipped her hood up and released the illusion with a giddy, dizzying sigh.

TEN
YET

Ana couldn't stop thinking about the letters. The *real* letters, not the ones she'd invented in her head and made reality for Tyreste.

In her desire to throw him off the scent—to *protect* him—she'd gone too far, creating modifications too jarring to be plausible.

She shifted sideways, riding the wind's force down the side of the mountain. No, she'd really messed up. When he realized they were falsified, he'd find someone to validate them, and all would be lost. It was too late to change her translations, which meant she had to find another way to remedy the situation.

I have to get my hands on the originals.

Was she really going to *steal* the letters? And then what? His suspicions would *really* be ignited and then his stubbornness would kick in, and he'd be a dog with a meaty bone, hungry for the truth that would lead him right back to her. Or Nessa. If that happened, it would draw him closer to danger, when the whole point had been to remove him from it.

Ana weighed which was worse: Tyreste finding someone else to translate and learning what she had, or removing the letters altogether and spinning him up into a frenzy of suspicion and blame. One kept him safe. The other kept her in his life.

All that mattered was for Tyreste not to get wrapped up in something that would get him killed.

Ana surveyed the area around the observatory before landing. She'd already missed supper, but she'd not intended to join, not after the terrible revelation about Niko. Magda would be looking for her soon, but better she find her helping the raven than lurking around the tavern.

There was no one outside, and no sign of Magda inside either. Swooping once more over the glass dome, Ana could only see Varradyn lying on his side, staring into a dying fire.

Ana landed, shifted, and stepped through the doors. Varradyn looked up with a half smile and propped himself onto an elbow.

"You're late tonight," he said, scooting into a seated position as she approached with bread, cheese, and ale. He loved the cheeses she'd brought in the past, so she tried to find something new for him to sample every time she visited. On one of her prior visits, he'd told her the only cheese they ever ate at the Rookery came from the midnight goats, served only on rare occasion, for the animals were sacred and had to give full consent to be milked.

"I had something else I needed to do first," Ana said and lowered herself onto the fur beside him. He accepted his food and drink with a bitter but grateful grin. "I'll tend the fire before I leave." It was then she noticed the raw, angry flesh around his ankles. "Varradyn! What have you done to yourself?"

"It's nothing," Varradyn muttered. He tore a hunk off the loaf with his teeth, chewing with his mouth open. "Except more failure."

Ana knelt near the pile of chains. Her hands fluttered above his mangled skin. "Why haven't you healed yourself?"

Varradyn tilted his head toward the chains. "She's bound my magic. Remember?"

The chains. "I'll fix it."

"To what point?" He shoved more bread in his mouth. "Not getting out of here anyway, am I?"

"You don't know that," Ana said quietly. Healing was the simplest of her magic, the first of her gifts she'd manifested as a girl, but it required as much focus, or more, as an illusion. "Be still. Please."

Varradyn shook his head but complied. Ana closed her eyes and imagined his ankle whole. The soft, untouched flesh farther up his leg... spreading down and closing over the raw, exposed meat that would be infected soon if she didn't—

"Focus," she whispered.

"Don't fuss yourself, Ana."

His flesh was moving again, inching slowly closer to the wounds. Just as she'd imagined it, the fresh skin folded over the wound and closed it for a smooth finish. No evidence, nor scarring. No one would ever know he'd nearly torn the flesh from his feet altogether.

But he'd do it again. And again. Until he either succeeded or killed himself in the doing.

Time was not on their side, but only Magda understood how fast or slow the hourglass emptied.

"*She* hasn't been by today." Varradyn's lower lip jutted in impressed appraisal of her work. "Or yesterday."

Ana sat back to catch her breath. "What has she said to you lately? When she does come?"

"I told you before. She never says a damn thing to me." Varradyn tilted his head back and washed the dry bread down with some ale. His cheeks puffed with a sour look. "This is disgusting."

"I'll go back to bringing wine next time." Ana folded her hands and stared at the fur. She didn't know how to ask the question, and she was even less sure he would answer truthfully. "Varradyn, I—"

"Do *you* drink it?" he asked, forcing down another sip. He winced.

"Sometimes," she said, eager to get back to her question. "But I was raised on it. I don't know any different."

"Disgusting," he said again but drank more. "We make our own wine in the mountains. You'd probably find it off-putting, bitter, but we all like it."

"Look, I need to ask you something."

Varradyn's eyes rolled in bliss as he rolled a bite of cheese around in his mouth. His robe slipped off one shoulder. "I've already told you everything. When the witch bothers to show up at all, she just burns me with those dead eyes of hers."

Magda revealing her true form to Varradyn was the most certain indication of his fate Ana could imagine. "That's not what I want to ask you." Ana threaded her hands together. "You're not the first Ravenwood to disappear."

Varradyn chewed with his mouth open. "That's not a question."

Ana nodded. "But I wondered what your people think of it."

He snorted. "You want to know what we 'think' about our people disappearing and never returning home?"

"I want to know what the Ravenwoods believe is happening to them when they go missing."

"Shouldn't you know?" He shook his head.

Ana sighed. "It may not seem like it, but I'm trying to help you. We share a common enemy, which might not make us friends, exactly, but we're not on opposite sides either. I can't... I can't overpower her. She has far more magic than I do. She's been holding back, if anything. But maybe if I understood more about what happens when I'm not here, I can learn something that will help us both. Do your people have *any* idea why they're going missing? Why she's targeted them specifically?"

Varradyn pulled the brick of cheese away from his mouth. "Of course we know. We've upheld our end of the alliance all this time, but men are... Men are *greedy* and cannot help but take what isn't theirs to take." He fluttered his fingers with a dark, sarcastic scowl. "Our magic is so *unique*, you know."

"It isn't the Wynters doing this, Varradyn. I promise you—"

"Is your stepmother not a Wynter, Anastazja?"

"She's not one of us!"

"Was your father forced at knifepoint to wed her?"

Her face burned with shame. "She's taken *everything* from us, and she's not remotely done, is she? She'll keep taking and taking because there's no satisfying that witch."

Varradyn tilted his head back in annoyance and laughed. "You're still walking—*flying*—free, and you have the audacity to compare our situations as though they are even a little similar? The Wynters brought the old hag into their world and have done nothing to stop her from infiltrating ours. Forgive me if I have no pity for the one who sits before me untethered while I languish in *chains*."

Ana breathed out and nodded. "I wasn't looking for your pity. I'm sorry. You're right."

Varradyn seemed ready to respond but returned to eating in silence. Ana turned her gaze outside, watching the snow fall. Minutes passed, the silence slowly releasing its tension.

"The elders, they..." Varradyn hung his head. "They only whisper about it. They seem to know more than they'll tell the rest of us. But whenever anyone raises a concern, they make us all feel like we've imagined our missing brethren. Like *I've* imagined... imagined... my own sister—" He snapped his mouth shut.

Ana's heart seized. "I'm so sorry about your sister. I truly am."

"Do you even remember her? Or do they all blur together in your mind?"

"I remember every single one, Varradyn." Ana swallowed. It was true that she remembered them all, but she'd never learned their names. Learned anything about them. That she'd led his sister to her death was a revelation too painful to address then and there. "But I don't quite understand... If you know this keeps happening, then why—" She clipped the question, unable to make it sound like anything but accusation.

"Why do we do nothing?" He laughed. "What could several hundred do against thousands? The Ravenwood-Wynter alliance has always been unbalanced. We offer magic in exchange for protection because we cannot protect ourselves if men ever find a way up the mountain, can we? If we go to battle with men, they will lose some in the doing, but we could lose *everything*. Our entire existence hinges upon our safety in the clouds, but our sanctuary isn't even safe anymore, is it? Not when a phoenix can come lure us away with forbidden magic. No... No, they gloss over the whole thing, act like it's the rest of us going mad when we bring it up."

"I didn't—" She almost said *know*. Her conscience skated upon never seeing the aftermath of her endeavoring, but it wasn't the same as not knowing what happened when she walked away. "I don't know what to do."

He leaned back and propped himself up onto his hands. His robe lay open, exposing everything she'd already seen but still felt uncomfortable witnessing. "Only now coming to this conclusion, are you?"

"How can you be so flippant about your own life?"

"How would you like me to be, Anastazja? Screaming in terror? Sobbing in fear?"

Ana buried her face in her hands and moaned. "I don't know! I don't know how you should be because I've spent so much of my life in fear, I can't even remember what safety felt like. I'm sorry for everything, but I'm not giving up." She looked up and into his eyes. "I'm not giving up on you and getting you safely home."

"How very sweet of you," he said, his tone acerbic, "but you've already said what I've known all along. You don't know how to stop her."

Ana pushed to her feet and wiped her eyes. She had to get to those letters before the party ended, before Tyreste caught her in his cabin. And then... then she would take one of Ludya's draughts, slip into dreamless sleep, and try not to think about Niko, about Tyreste, about Varradyn, about her father, about the letters, or about any of it until morning.

"Yet," she said. "I don't know how to stop her *yet*. But she's going to kill me either way, so I've got nothing to lose for trying."

I'm afraid I have little to report. I've had limited success in translating the delivery and am now behind on other translations. Please advise whether I should continue or return to other projects.

Tyr tied the vellum around the raven's talon in the way Olov had taught him. He'd never sent ravens himself back in Parth, so had never considered there might be a proper way to secure correspondence for long journeys. There was a balance between the right tie and not harming the raven. Even with the perfect knot, there was always a risk of letters coming undone in flight. Some ravens had been trained to retrieve lost messages and carry them the rest of the way in their beaks. But the ravens of the Cross were stubborn, much like the Vjestik, and returned to their posts at the slightest hint of danger.

"Go on with you," he said, and the raven flapped its wings and soared out through the wide window of the rookery. He turned toward the ravener, who was busy trimming the talons of one of his messengers. "Anything new for me?"

"Not a thing," the ravener said without looking up. A blunt clipping sound followed and then an indignant squawk. "For a fee, I can tie your messages myself."

"You say so every time," Tyr said, almost smiling. He might have, had his heart not felt so heavy. "I don't mind doing it myself. A good skill to have."

"A good skill when there's no competent ravener," the man muttered. He ran a calloused hand along the raven's head and down its feathers. The bird stretched its impressive wings with a happy flutter. "Right. Bugger off now."

Tyr thanked him and turned to leave when the man called out to him.

"Oy, Penhallow."

"Yes?"

"Mind yourself, aye? There're rumors swirling. 'Bout ravens going missing again. The ones in the mountains, I mean. Not mine. Mine are smarter than that, aren't you, lovies?"

Tyr's blood cooled. "What has that to do with me?"

"Don't know. Just had a feeling I should warn you." He tapped his head. "Trust your feelings, they say. They're the closest thing you got to wisdom."

"All right." Tyr nodded. "Thanks."

He skipped down the seemingly endless stairwell and ran the rest of the way to his cabin, taking the longer way to avoid the tavern. The party would be ending soon, and he'd fully intended to go back after Nessa had left, but instead he'd worked up the letter to Asterin. He hoped his family would assume he was off with Nessa and tease him about *that* instead of honing in on his grief and panic.

His mother's reaction to Nessa had been curious. Her strained smile might have fooled a stranger, but not a son. *How lovely* was Fransiska's signature polite dismissal. The response made no sense when Nessa was everything they'd wanted for him in a mate.

They had to get to know her better was all. Really, so did he. Weeks she'd been visiting, and he knew almost nothing about her.

His cabin door was unlocked. He couldn't remember locking it, but he always did, so he must have. The door swung open and he stepped in slowly, listening to be sure he was alone.

Satisfied no one was lurking in wait, he threw both the bolts and went into the kitchen to pour himself a cider. It was cold and viscous, the fire having died sometime in the evening, but he drank it anyway, downing it in one long swallow.

Tyr leaned against the wall beside the hearth, breathing deep for the first time in hours. He'd sent his concerns to Asterin, and Asterin would advise what to do next. With luck, he'd ask Tyr to stand down and return to his other work. He hadn't understood

Asterin's and Sesto's anxiousness until *someone* had gone to great trouble to make sure he only read what they wanted him to.

While he waited for a response, he needed to find a new hiding place. There wasn't time to build a new cubby, but he had a small chest he could empty. He could bury it outside until he had word back from Riverchapel.

It was too late in the evening to be digging holes in the ground—a ground only just beginning to thaw for the season—but doing it in the daytime would draw unwanted attention from his family and patrons.

No, I'll do it now, he decided and went to retrieve the letters.

But when Tyr opened the not-so-secret cubby, there was nothing there.

The letters, all of them, were gone.

Ana divided her focus between her speed and her illusion, running as fast as she could as Nessa. It might not be necessary, but if anyone caught her fleeing his cabin, there would almost certainly be questions, and it was better for them to think Nessa was up to something than Ana.

She'd only meant to steal the ones in Vjestikaan, but then she'd spotted Tyreste from the window, heading down the back path along the forest line. With no time to separate the letters, she'd shoved the entire stack inside of her cloak and fled.

In her haste, she'd forgotten to turn the knob lock on her way out.

Ana slowed when she neared the tavern. In a few more feet, she'd turn off, and in a hundred yards or so, she'd be back on the main village road, blending into the evening crowds. She was close to being able to duck behind a market stall and emerge as herself before making her way home.

But Ana screamed and leaped back several steps when something jumped in front of her.

It was only Adeline, though her relief was short-lived.

I know your truth. I know who you really are, she signed, and Ana was too caught off her guard to hide her reaction to words she, as Nessa, had no business understanding.

Adeline lit up with mischievous delight. *I knew it! I knew it was you!*

Ana looked behind herself and then ahead. All she could do was shake her head, back and forth in a fruitless attempt to look confused.

"Adeline, I..." She cut herself off and sighed.

Adeline crossed her arms over her chest, stared, and waited for an explanation.

It's not what you think, Ana at last signed, cringing with every turn of her fingers. How Adeline had figured it out, Ana had no idea, but if she'd done it, others would as well.

The younger girl laughed and clapped her hands. *I knew it! Show me.*

Ana shook her head. She tossed another glance behind her.

Tyreste? He won't be out again until he's slept.

You can't tell him.

Why?

You just can't. I'm sorry, Addy.

Adeline ran her tongue between the gap in her lips, studying Ana closely. *Then show me.*

No.

Show me and I'll keep your secret.

Ana checked her surroundings once more and then slowly, grudgingly, let the illusion fade.

Adeline's smile increased by the second. *Incredible. How do you do it?*

I don't know, Ana signed. *I've always been able to. But it isn't easy. And it only lasts as long as my focus holds.* She looked around in a panic. *If anyone sees me here, they'll want answers. And I have no reason for being here.*

Adeline beckoned her closer to the road, between two buildings. *Why? Why would you break his heart and then return to his life with a lie?*

Ana grimaced and raked her teeth along the bottom of her upper lip. *It's hard to explain.*

I'm in no hurry.

Shouldn't you be sleeping?

Tell me, Ana.

Ana inhaled sharply through her nose. She tapped her feet against the cold ground. If telling Tyreste was off the table, telling his little sister was even more impossible. But Adeline was clever. Ana had spent enough hours with her, learning her language and accepting her secrets, to know she'd never let it go. *I can't tell you, Addy. But your brother is in danger. He would be in even more danger if he knew the truth. I can protect him this way. Nessa can protect him. Ana cannot.*

Adeline's eyes narrowed. *Danger from what?*

Talking about the danger makes it more dangerous for him. Ana sighed. *And for you.*

Adeline squared up with an indignant scoff. *I'm not afraid.*

No, I know you're not. But you should be. And if you have ever trusted me, you will listen to me now when I tell you not a single soul—Ana tapped her chest hard to emphasize the word *single. Not a single soul can know, or something terrible will happen. Something I cannot stop on my own. And no, I am not telling you any more than that. I'm sorry.*

Adeline shifted her jaw from left to right in cool scrutiny. At last she rolled her eyes and nodded. *I'll keep your secret. For now.*

Ana practically sagged in relief. *Thank you, Addy.*

Aren't you going to ask me how long I've known?

Ana half-heartedly urged her to go on.

Since the first day I met Nessa, Adeline signed and shifted her cloak tighter with a glance toward the tavern. *And if Tyreste wasn't so mired in his heartbreak, he would have seen it as well. But he's hopeless, isn't he? The answers are there for him to grab. You knowing how to sign. Grigor showing up and stalking the tavern corners every night. Failing to keep track of the lies you tell him.*

Ana mentally kicked herself. *It was a terrible idea. I'll stay away.*

No! Adeline's face knit into a panic. Her fingers flew. *Don't you dare. I won't let him lose you twice.*

But I can't... I can't be Nessa forever.

Then be Nessa until you can be Ana again. Adeline thrust an arm in the direction of Tyreste's cabin. *Until you can make it right with him.*

But Ana would never get the chance.

Better to let Adeline linger in hope than to tell her Ana only had months left to the world. Less if she could help Magda finish her experiments.

Good night then, Addy.

Good night. Ana.

Adeline spun and marched back toward the tavern.

ELEVEN
THE BLOOD ON HER HANDS

Ludya was standing in the courtyard at Fanghelm when Ana swooped down. Her dread returned as swiftly as her vedhma's harried approach.

"What? What's happened?"

"It's your father." Ludya glanced to the sides before continuing. "He's taken ill."

Ana charged past, but Ludya caught her in a firm hold.

"Listen to me, and listen carefully," Ludya said evenly. Her arm was still pinning Ana back, but her hold softened. "You and I both know who is behind this foul happening. If you go running to your father, furious and sobbing, she wins."

Ana's mouth fell open in disbelief. Her gaze fluttered to the double doors. "How can I *not* go to my father, Ludya? How bad is it?"

"He could recover, if she allowed it. She created his illness. She can cure it just as easily." Ludya's muscles stiffened again when Ana tried to break free. "*Listen*, Anastazja. She is trying to incite you. She knows you're pulling away. Becoming defiant."

"But—"

"And she will keep digging the hole and burying your life, piece by piece, if you let her."

Ana staggered back, staring at the doors, at the empty courtyard, and at Ludya. The blood left her face, plummeting toward her feet. Magda had sent her brother away—incapacitated her father. Ana didn't even want to consider what might come next. "I've done... I've done everything she's asked me to do."

Ludya lowered her voice. "Then consider she's preparing you for what she hasn't yet asked because she knows it will be a much harder persuasion to make."

"How could it be *harder* than it's already been?" Ana's voice screeched as she tugged at her curls, fidgeting in place. "Unless she kills us all, but she needs at least one of us, doesn't she?"

"She's been threatening you, using your father and brother... leading your mind down a path of fear." Ludya pursed her mouth. "But what if those are merely diversions?"

"What?"

"Diversions, Anastazja. There's an old Vjestik saying. 'If they're looking at the blood on my face, they miss the blood on my hands.'"

Ana tilted her head upward with an exasperated exhale. "I'm so tired, Ludya. So cursed tired."

Ludya lowered her arm back to her side and moved closer. "She has you so worried about your father and brother, you haven't stopped to wonder what she wants with *you*."

Ana grunted. "I *know* what she wants with me."

"If you were truly the nuisance she has claimed you are, she'd have killed you already. She has two other heirs at her disposal. *Pliant* heirs. And when they're gone, there will be other Wynters. Why does she need you? And why has she not been successful at taking over your mind, as she has with them?"

Ana crossed her arms and looked away. She was far too distracted to grasp her vedhma's point. No matter what Ludya said, no matter how it played into Magda's plan, Ana had to see her father. If Magda murdered him, she would never forgive herself. "I don't claim to know what goes on in that monster's head."

"You should take the time to learn." Ludya turned toward the entrance. "Fight the instinct to visit Arkhady. You will only waste time when you have so little. In your mind, you've already surrendered. Offered her the victory she's already confident in achieving. But in your heart..." Ludya turned back. She pulled one of Ana's arms free and placed her hand over her heart. "You know there's a way. There's always a way."

"And if..." Ana forced the well of emotion back. There was an entire ocean of feelings waiting to be addressed, but the void inside her was more useful. She could shove the rest into it and come back for it all later. "If you're wrong?"

"Fortunately for you, I'm not wrong." Ludya almost smiled. "Unfortunately for you, I have seen many threads, and I can neither predict which one you will take nor advise you which one is right. I can only remind you that the future has not yet been decided. *You* have the power to decide, but you will almost certainly have to face this alone." She gestured toward the doors. "Perhaps a visit to the kyschun will give you needed perspective."

"The archivists?" Ana asked, falling into step beside her. "Why them?"

Ludya leaned closer and whispered, "They might possess the perspective you seek with those letters you stole."

It took four guards to open the doors, an arduous effort producing a deep, yawning groan. Ludya nodded for her to go ahead, observing the same deference they both ignored in private.

"What if they're under her spell too?" Ana asked before ascending the steps.

"Wouldn't you rather know for sure than wonder?"

Ana hesitated. "Ludya, do you truly not know where they sent Niko?"

"Nien, I do not," Ludya said. "But I feel him. Here." She folded both of her hands toward her heart. "Wherever he is, he is safe. For now. I do not have to tell you it will not always be so.

149

She *will* use him. Not as she uses you. She will turn him into a weapon, the *only* weapon effective on a heart as true as yours. But Nikolaj is not her prize. Arkhady is not her prize."

"It surely cannot be me," Ana said with an incredulous laugh.

"Go on," Ludya said when she noticed a guard watching them too closely. "I've left several of your favorite teas in your apartments, just the way you like them."

Tyr ransacked his cabin, turning over every piece of furniture and lifting every loose floorboard. He looked under rugs, shook out his blankets, and climbed a chair to check the rafters. The stove he saved for last, worrying the culprit had burned them. Most of the translations he worked on were copies, to account for mishaps, but that was not so with the letters. *I didn't dare create more,* Sesto had said, just before Tyr had watched them ride away.

Tyr found no evidence in the ashes of the hearth either, but he shuffled quickly from relief into a deeper fear than he'd felt in years. Not since the Westerlands.

He didn't *want* to share Asterin and Sesto's paranoia, but what else explained the false translations? The stolen letters? Hundreds of years they'd survived just fine, and as soon as they were brought to Witchwood Cross, home of the Vjestik, they disappeared?

Maybe I left them in the tavern, he rationalized, though he hadn't been taking them to work for weeks. But he wasn't ready to cry surrender or admit they were gone. He should have found a better hiding spot the moment the first false translation had shown up on his table.

Rikard the Mouser watched him with his narrow yellow eyes, for once silent.

"Please, please, please," he whispered as he stormed off in the direction of the tavern. The party would have ended, making it easier to search, but another terrible thought struck him. What if the culprit had been *at* the party? What if it was someone he knew, someone he trusted?

But the list of people who spoke Vjestikaan and who also knew he had the letters in his possession was nonexistent. The last translations might have been forgeries, but the first wasn't.

"Tyreste?" Fransiska looked up from stacking barrels behind the tavern. She dusted her apron off and frowned. "You left early tonight."

"I had something to do." He grimaced and reached for the door, but she put a hand over his and stopped him. A familiar look snared him from the side. "It was hard, is all. Saying good-bye."

Fransiska tilted her head sideways. "Of course. Oh, of course, Tyreste. I was so consumed with planning that I didn't stop to think..." She sighed and shook her shoulders. "Can I make you some tea? With a blot of honey, the way you like it?"

Nothing sounded better than his mother's perfectly made tea, but if he didn't find the letters, he would lose his mind. "Later, Mama." He smiled to show her he was fine. "You didn't happen... you or Father... to find some of my work lying around, did you?"

"Your translations?" Fransiska cast her eyes sideways in thought. "No, darling. You're usually quite fastidious about your little side business. I never see you leave any behind."

Your little side business was how his mother described anything that wasn't taverning. Agnes's knitwork, lucrative enough to help fund an entire renovation the year before, was *her little side business*. Evert's efforts redesigning local shops to withstand the winds of Icebolt, the work that had earned him his coveted apprenticeship, was *his little side business*.

Tyr nodded and smiled, waiting to see the distress leave his mother's face.

"Don't forget your cat!" she called—wholly unnecessary, for his mouser had already strolled past him, headed for the tavern proper.

Rikard and Agnes were hustling around the back room like angry bees.

"I hope you've come to help," Rikard barked, carrying a precarious stack of dishes to the basin. "Pern and Evert already left.

151

Father is I don't know where, and Addy disappeared about an hour ago."

Tyreste drew a deep breath and looked around. He never did translations in the back because of all the grease and heat, but he had to rule it out. "I'll help, but first I need to find something."

"Your new girlfriend? She's not here," Agnes called from the cold room. She peeked her head out. "*Is* she your girlfriend? She's rather boring, no? Pretty, but..."

"Boring," Rikard said in agreement as he dumped piles of bowls and mugs into the soapy water. "If I didn't know better, I'd say it's why you're suddenly into her." He grunted and wiped his face. "Nothing like the women you usually martyr yourself for."

"Rik," Faustina warned. Tyr hadn't seen her when he'd come in, but he clocked her in the corner washing linens in a basin someone had elevated for her. She could no longer bend as she could before, so full with child.

He braced through the annoyance building under the surface. "Have you seen any of my translations lying around?"

"Mother didn't take to her either," Agnes muttered. "You can always tell with Mother."

Tyr turned toward her, frowning. "What was that?"

Agnes shrugged. "She was perfectly polite, as she always is. That's how you know. If she's all pleasantries, no enthusiasm, she's putting on a front so as not to hurt someone's delicate feelings."

Tyr laughed so Agnes wouldn't see she'd struck a nerve. He wasn't the only one who had noticed their mother's cool reception then. "Well, she's not my girlfriend, so it's really nothing to me, is it?"

"Whatever happened with Ana?" Rikard asked. He'd propped himself against the wall for an ale break. "And is her ox of an uncle in our tavern these days related or coincidence?"

"*Rikard,*" Faustina practically hissed.

"Nothing happened," Tyr muttered. He didn't address the Grigor question because he didn't know either and was tired of

152

guessing. "Because it was nothing. Have you seen any of my work lying around or not?"

Agnes shrugged. Rikard returned to his dishes.

"Great. Thanks. So very helpful." Tyr rolled his eyes and exited into the tavern proper. It had already been cleaned, the chairs stacked on tables and the floor mopped. He stepped carefully through the maze of still-wet spots and ducked behind the bar to search.

He'd finished rifling through several shelves, to no avail, when a hard creaking sound drew his attention back to the tavern floor. He slowly stood, scanning the tables, and then he saw her.

Magda. Ana's stepmother. She'd chosen the same corner table Ana had been sitting at the night she'd captured his heart. But there was nothing welcoming about the way she hovered, like a gargoyle. No softness in her expression nor life in her unblinking eyes. When her mouth parted, he could have sworn there were fangs.

He'd noticed none of those things in the market, and he wondered if it was a trick of the light.

More than that, though, he wondered why she was there at all.

"We're closed," he tried to say, but the words emerged as a series of embarrassing squeaks.

Magda watched him in silence. She sat in such absolute stillness, he almost questioned whether she was there at all.

"Stewardess Wynter, I apologize, but we're closed for a private event." This time his voice was strong and true, and it emboldened him to step out from behind the bar. He glanced toward the back room doors, where his siblings were still engrossed in their cleanup efforts. "But I could... Ah, I could pour you an ale if you wish?"

Magda didn't respond. She finally blinked. Her head fell slightly to the side.

A shrieking sound echoed through the tavern as she pushed back from the table, still ramrod straight and staring right at him. With her face turned his way, she moved sideways toward the door until she was standing right in front of it. Her mouth opened and kept opening, until it was so wide, it seemed her jaw had come unhinged. Like that she stayed for several excruciating moments, wherein Tyr stopped breathing altogether.

Magda's mouth closed. She grinned and reached for the door behind her, then opened it without breaking his gaze. Her gait was sluggish, almost a shuffle, as she backed herself out of the tavern.

And then she was gone.

Tyr rushed forward and dropped the barricade over the door. He felt her, just on the other side, waiting. He couldn't say how he knew for certain, but he had no doubt she was still there, still watching him.

Tyr sagged, gasping for air in silent, greedy gulps he prayed she couldn't hear.

He waited there until he felt her slow retreat.

It was another hour before he'd calmed enough to continue his search for the letters.

Ana fought every instinct she had and walked past her father's apartments, continuing until she reached her own. Once she was certain Magda wasn't lurking in some corner, eager to frighten her, she bolted the outer door. She waited for her heart to slow and her mind to calm.

She withdrew the stack of letters from underneath her cloak, but it was Adeline she was thinking of. The young girl cornering her was another problem to add to the ever-mounting pile. A rather *large* problem, but she could only solve one at a time.

Addy had promised not to tell, but for how long? Secrets were delicious at fifteen, and as far as secrets went, Ana's was a particularly juicy one. Addy and Tyr were inseparable. He cherished her above his other siblings.

If Tyreste were to find out, Ana prayed it was after she was long gone from the world.

He'd never forgive her for loving him twice.

For leaving him twice.

Ana arranged the letters on her desk, putting them back in order. She wasn't supposed to know the other language, Old Ilynglass, but Imryll had secretly passed her knowledge down the line. By the time Ana's generation came around, much of it had been lost, but she still understood enough to piece together the general messages from Paeris's letters.

She traced her fingers along the most damning of the words from each writer.

From Zofia:

High Priestess Avalyna came to visit. She refused to meet with my mother or father and demanded an audience with my grandmother. They were alone in a room for over an hour, and when they emerged, my grandmother looked more terrified, more pale, than I'd ever seen her. I asked her what happened, and instead of responding, she locked herself away for days. Even Grandfather couldn't rouse her.

From Paeris:

I know you said to stay away from Mortain, but I cannot. Five Ravenwoods missing, and no one has tried to stop him. Perhaps I cannot. Perhaps I'm sending myself on a fool's errand, doomed to catastrophic failure. But you can do nothing from there, Zo, and I am uniquely positioned to be near the creature. So tonight, I will take my father's dagger, dip it in poison, and catch the sorcerer unawares. If fortune smiles upon me, Zo, my next letter will be announcing we are rid of this evil for once and all.

Ana's hands shook as she traced Zofia's next words.

Par, it's been a month. A month. You have never gone more than a fortnight between letters, and I fear the worst has happened. Please, even a raven telling me I'm overreacting would be preferable to silence. I just need to know you're all right.

The final letter from Duncarrow didn't come from Paeris but from a woman named Annelyse. The message was succinct, cold.

Zofia, please cease your correspondence with Duncarrow. You've done more harm than you can ever know. I cannot read the letters you wrote my son, but I know all blame for his death falls strictly upon you and your childish incitement. Please inform your grandmother that my father, her brother Octavyen, succumbed to a brief illness days after Paeris died. His final visit several years past will be considered the last time any Rhiagain or Noble House of Duncarrow visits Witchwood Cross. With his death, the House of Glaisgain falls to me. Henceforth, the name Wynter will be forbidden upon our isle.

If Zofia betrayed her aunt's wishes and sent a letter in response, it wasn't part of the collection.

Paeris of Glaisgain had been killed for trying to stop Mortain. His grandfather, Octavyen, had died soon after from shock or grief—or maybe even something more sinister. Imryll had been so disturbed by a visit from Midnight Crest, she'd locked herself away. Familial relationships ended when the letters did.

The letters marked an abrupt end to a piece of Ana's history she'd never heard anyone speak of in detail. That they had resurfaced when she was embroiled in her own terrorizing of the Ravenwoods, hundreds of years later, had to mean *something*.

But where did *Tyreste* fit into the whole bloody mess?

He'd been doing translation work for years, but when she'd heard him speak of it, he usually dealt with boring legal documents no one but archivists would ever take interest in.

"Archivists," Ana whispered. She took a step back from the table.

Perhaps a visit to the kyschun will give you needed perspective.

Tomorrow, after she saw to Varradyn and helped Tyreste and his family prepare for the Cider Festival, her last hurrah as Nessa Arsenyev, she'd send the kyschun a formal request for a meeting. They might refuse to see her. If they granted an audience, they might tell her nothing. They alone decided who was worthy of the past.

But if Ana couldn't wrap her mind around the past, there was no hope whatsoever for the future.

TWELVE
DIGGING HER GOLD SLIPPERS INTO THE PIGPEN

It will be *fine*. It always is," Tyr said, reassuring his mother.

Fransiska stood in the middle of the tavern floor, her hands looped over her head, looking so frazzled, she had him stressing too.

"No one expects perfection, Mother. Just ale that doesn't stop flowing."

Fransiska leveled an exasperated look his way. "Really? Is pleasing the apple-loving masses as simple as that, Tyreste? Unending ale?"

"Evert fixed the stills. We brought all the old kegs back from the well house." Remembering his tryst with Ana there tripped him up. "We have enough. Besides, there are two new taverns this year that weren't open during the last Cider Festival."

"And you think that's what I want? To send business elsewhere?"

There was nothing he could say to ease her. She was like this every year in the final hours before the Cider Festival kicked off, and she'd find something to stress over even if they had a hundred kegs at the wait.

"All I'm saying is—"

The warning in his mother's expression kept him from finishing.

"What can I do to help, Mama?"

Fransiska softened. "Nothing, dear. Nothing until this evening, when we start the prep. You're right, anyway. We've done more than enough. We will either thrive or fail tomorrow. It's up to the Guardians which side we fall on."

Tyr had little love for the Guardians, after the years he'd spent toiling in the dungeon of the Reliquary, the center of spirituality in the realm. Telling his mother that, though, was a surefire way to send her over the edge. "I'll see if Evert needs any help in the back."

"Oh!" Fransiska shook a hand at him. She had the other wrapped around her torso. "Did you ever find your papers, love?"

Tyr shook his head. He'd managed to go almost an hour without thinking of his failure.

"Have you asked Addy?"

"Addy?"

"I saw her this morning with a stack. When she saw me, she tucked them inside her dress, which was odd, but..." She exhaled with a short laugh. "We know our Addy, don't we? Could be anything."

He hadn't asked his little sister because he trusted her. She'd never take anything from him, especially not something so important. But shoving papers into her dress made little sense either, because everyone already knew she was learning to translate.

"Did you... Did you invite your little friend tomorrow?"

Tyr looked up. "Nessa? I invited her tonight, actually. To help with our prep."

"Hmm." Fransiska turned away with a distant look. "All right then. Lovely."

Tyr shook his head, laughing. "I know you, Mother. You clearly have thoughts you're not sharing."

"No, no." She blinked in unconvincing denial. "It's really none of my business, dear."

He crossed his arms over his chest. "You've never let that stop you before."

"I don't know, Tyreste," she said, sounding utterly exhausted. "I just don't see you brighten around her. She's perfectly nice, but I'm not sure she lights the spark you have inside of you."

"Lights the spark?" Tyr's brows shot upward in amusement. "Really?"

"Oh, bah." Fransiska swatted a hand at him and half turned, facing the front windows. "I know I was... *critical* of Anastazja... but she inspired something in you I hadn't seen since you were a boy."

"More than critical, Mother. You said she was, and I quote, *dipping her gold slippers into the pigpen* by spending time with me."

"Well, what of it? Was I wrong? She left you, in the end."

"Yes," Tyr stated firmly. Heat flooded his cheeks. "Yes, she did leave me. And yet *Nessa* is here. Other than being highborn, she's the opposite of Ana in almost every way, so that should make you happy."

"Doesn't matter if *I'm* happy, love." Fransiska smiled sadly. "If you are, that's all that matters."

"I am." He pinched his shoulders back as his defensiveness kicked in. "I've been with women who 'light my spark,' as you say, and every one of them has broken my heart. Maybe my spark belongs in a metal box, where it's safe and can't catch fire, burning me and everything else to the ground."

"As you say," Fransiska said, which was right on par with *that's lovely*.

"You think I'm wrong?"

"I think my eldest son has always been strong-willed. Always done as he wanted. I would not expect this to change now." Fransiska pulled a rag out of her apron. "Addy is in the back, if you wanted to ask her about the papers."

"Thanks," he muttered, still mulling her words as he stepped through the double doors.

Addy was sitting on a stool, slicing potatoes over a large vat. Her face was flushed from exertion, her tongue wedged between

161

her front teeth. She glanced up with a grin when he stepped closer.

How many potatoes is that now? he teased. *Three?*

The riotous look she gave him almost made him forget he'd come to ask her a serious question. She shifted the paring knife to the hand holding a potato and signed, *Try three hundred, brother.*

Three hundred potatoes. For a festival about apples.

Everyone else is serving apples. We're "special." She smirked and returned to peeling.

Tyr pursed his mouth and moved closer to catch her eyes again. She wouldn't lie and wouldn't steal, and he needed to approach the question with those facts in mind. *Have you seen my letters? The ones Asterin and Sesto brought.*

Addy's chin dimpled in a frown. She shook her head.

You certain?

She nodded. *Did you lose them?*

I don't think they're lost. I think someone took them.

Why would anyone do that?

Tyr hadn't told her about the false translations, and there was nothing in her face suggesting her question was for show. *That's what I'm trying to find out.*

Addy's mouth twisted in contemplation. *If I see them, I'll bring them to you.*

Tyr shifted in discomfort. He didn't want to press it, but their mother had seen Addy hiding *something*. There was only one way to clear it up. He breathed in and signed, *Mother said she saw you hiding some papers in your dress. She thought they might be the missing letters.*

Addy froze. Her eyes shifted to the side and then back at him. *She saw wrong.*

Tyr balked. She'd just lied to him. *Mother wouldn't have said it if she hadn't seen it.*

She saw wrong.

All you have to do is tell me. I won't be angry. I just need to find them.

She saw wrong, Tyreste.

Tyreste? Are we fighting?

You tell me. Her fingers flew with furious speed. The bloom in her cheeks reddened. *If I say I don't have your letters, then I don't.*

He'd come into the conversation fully expecting to rule his baby sister out, but she *was* hiding something. Not just from their mother but from him. *Addy. Please.*

Addy chucked a potato across the room. It slammed into one of the doors with a wet thud. *Either you trust me or you do not. But I don't have your silly letters!*

She leaped off the stool and shoved past him, knocking him sideways as she burst into the tavern proper.

Ana rushed through the village, head down. She knew everyone she passed but didn't greet a soul. Her illusion would require all of her focus soon, and her thoughts were so scattered, so utterly disarrayed, she'd considered canceling on Tyreste. If she hadn't felt so certain it was the last time she'd ever see him, she would have.

She'd ignored Magda's summons. *Meet me at the observatory at dusk,* the koldyna had commanded, though it wasn't boldness but cowardice at the source of Ana's disobedience. If Magda wanted her at the observatory, it had to mean her need of Varradyn was waning. Ana could neither save the raven nor participate in his demise.

She would pay later for her insubordination. Perhaps dearly.

As she brushed tears away from her face, she prayed her hood was enough to hide them.

"Hej! Ana!"

Ana kept walking, pushing her pace. She felt someone coming up fast behind her, and she quickened further, but then an arm landed on her shoulder.

It was Evert Penhallow.

She squinted away her tears and turned. "Evert. Hello."

He gave her a lopsided smile, his brows knit together. "I missed you last night. Did you get my invitation?"

"Sorry?"

He chuckled. "My party? My going away?"

"Oh." *I* was *there.* "Apologies."

"You were there when I got the letter about the apprenticeship. Remember?" He smiled at her from behind a mountain of furs. "You were the one who convinced me to try for it."

Ana recalled the two of them sitting by the hearth, writing and re-writing his entrance thesis until they were both speaking and thinking gibberish. She'd almost written to the guild as his sponsor, but after watching him work at his craft with such earnest passion, it would have been doing him a great disservice not to let his merits stand on their own. "I'm... I'm happy you took the advice. You have a rare talent, Evert. Whitechurch will gain much with your arrival." She half turned and gestured toward the path. "It was good to see you, but I really must be going. Take care of yourself."

"You broke his heart," Evert blurted. "You really hurt him."

Ana stiffened.

"And mine. And Addy's. We both believed you were the one—"

"Evert!" Ana barked in exasperation. "I *wasn't* the one. I wasn't... What does it matter now? I hear he's moved on. With my cousin."

Evert snorted. "With that boring little princess? There's a word for what he's feeling right now, broken as he is. But it isn't 'love.'"

"I can't talk about this with you. I'm sorry." She reached a hand out and squeezed his arm, too quickly for him to react. "Best of luck in Whitechurch, Ev, not that you'll need it. They'll quickly see what a rising talent they have in Evert Penhallow, and you'll be a guildmaster in no time."

Ana hurried off, and mercifully, he didn't follow. She held her swift pace until she was sure he wasn't watching anymore, and she ducked behind a clothier to transition into Nessa.

She watched her clothes transform, revert, and transform. The coloring of her hands shifted, flickering.

"Nien. Nien, pros, pros. Focus. Focus!" She slammed her fist against the building and tried again.

And again.

Ana groaned and leaned against the building. She closed her eyes and whispered a plea to the Ancestors.

The illusion held. But her concentration was already slipping. She could feel her hips threatening to widen, her breasts aching to fill out. It wouldn't be hours, but minutes. Despair stole over her as she realized she would need to leave Tyreste almost as soon as she arrived at the tavern.

She rushed the rest of the way without stopping. When she stepped inside the Tavern at the Top of the World, Tyreste was alone behind the bar. The rest of his family wasn't around, but the tavern was swiftly filling with patrons warming up for the festival the next day.

He set aside the stack of mugs he was holding and rushed to greet her. "I thought you'd changed your mind."

"No, but—" Ana shivered, despite the wave of warmth flowing over her from the sweltering tavern. "I can't stay long. I wish I could, but my father needs me."

"Oh!" Tyr smiled. "Well, he's here now." He turned and pointed toward the corner, where her uncle Grigor sat nursing a still-full ale. "Grigor! Your daughter's here!"

Her uncle stared directly their way.

Ana backed up a step. Grigor's eyes narrowed, locking onto hers. He sliced his jaw back and forth with a wrathful scowl that froze her insides. The illusion had been his idea, but the way he glared at her had her reassessing the advice.

Grigor made his way over, his long gait purposely slow. She reached for her hair and saw blonde creeping into the ends. The visual shape of her body began to shift, stretch.

"I have to go. I'm so sorry." Ana leaned in and pecked the corner of Tyreste's mouth. His hand moving to the spot and his eyes brimming in bewilderment were the last things she saw before she shoved past him and raced back out into the night. She heard Tyreste calling after her, but Grigor exited right behind her, grumbling something that stopped Tyreste from following.

"What is *wrong* with you, girl?" he hissed and took hold of her arm. He dragged her onto the road and kept going until they were several yards from the tavern. After a look both ways, he practically hurled her into an alleyway behind a row of leatherworking shops. "You've been a right fool, Anastazja." He snorted and ran his eyes over her. "Are you always so careless?"

Ana followed his gaze to confirm she'd fully transitioned back to herself. Back to the weak, helpless debutante who had failed at everything that had ever mattered. "It was... It was *your* idea, Grigor! You said to me *use your illusions.*"

Grigor grunted. The sound started low and hollow and escalated to a near yell before he clipped it off. "I should not have had to remind you to also use your intelligence."

"What does *that* mean?" she demanded.

"He suspects something." Grigor ground his teeth and paced in the melting snow. "You'll get him killed."

"Nien, Grigor. He suspects nothing," Ana replied. "He's hurt and confused, but he's far too rational to ever think Nessa is me."

"Did you know *she's* been to see him?"

Ana felt herself paling. She backed into the cold wooden siding and pressed her hands to the cracks. "She doesn't know."

"Ack, girl. She knows everything. If he's still alive, it's because she has use for him still." Grigor blew out a rough breath and shook his head at the sky. He paced, gripping his neck. "I should have come home sooner."

Ana tossed her head and laughed. "Why? To do what? You did nothing when she took hold of my father... my brother. You did nothing when she spread her evil over the staff. Come to think of it, Onkel, you did nothing when she destroyed my mother—"

Grigor grabbed her by the shoulders and shook her against the building. "Do not speak of my sister around me. Ever."

Ana shrugged him off and stepped sideways. "Why? Does it call to your guilt? Or your apathy?"

He turned away and spat on the ground.

"Apathy then." She sniffled and rolled her eyes.

Grigor spun back around. His eyes glowed with intensity. "I couldn't save Ksana. But I *swore* to her I would save her daughter."

Ana's flesh turned to fire. "What do you mean... swore to her?"

"She knew." Grigor palmed his face and shook it in his hand. "She knew what that koldyna was the day she showed up. I didn't believe her. I told her she was being absurd. Histrionic. But when I watched her burn upon the funeral pyre, I promised her spirit I'd not make that fatal mistake a second time."

"It wasn't your fault." Ana exhaled, digging her boot toes into the muddy snow. "We are all powerless against her. You couldn't have saved my mother even if you'd believed her. Just like I couldn't save my father and Niko. Like I'll never save all the ravens she takes. I know that now."

"You're still here. Still breathing. Still thinking your own thoughts, making your own choices," he said.

"So?" Fat tears spilled from her eyes and ran down her frozen cheeks. "All that means is I've had a clear mind to watch her destroy everyone I love."

Grigor returned to looking at the sky. He fell into a heavy, breathless silence.

Ana sucked in a gulp of cool air and decided to tell him about the letters. "Onkel, I've come across something terrible."

He turned just his eyes her way.

"There are these... these letters." Ana pushed off the wall and paced away from him, trying to decide how best to approach her secret. "They're old. Hundreds of years. But they speak of Ravenwoods disappearing, even back then. Of a sorcerer from Duncarrow, Mortain—"

167

Grigor charged toward her and clapped a thick hand over her mouth. He shook his head wildly. "Say not another word."

Ana wrapped both her hands around his to peel it away from her. "You *knew*."

"This is bigger than you, Anastazja. Bigger than all of us." He broke away and pulled a hard breath through his nose. "You think you're fighting a war now? You've never seen war. You start this one, you'll find you lack the power to end it."

Ana's heart raced and raced, alongside her thoughts. Grigor knew. Why had he done *nothing*? "If you know—"

"All battles are wageable but not all are winnable." Grigor returned to her side. He towered over her, casting a shadow wide enough to block the last of the day's sun. "The only one that matters to me now is keeping my promise to Ksana."

Ana shuddered a laugh. "So that's it? We just... let her win? Let them both win?"

Silence stood as his answer.

"Ludya said I should ask the archivists."

His eyes flared. "Nien, Ana. *Nien*. Do not engage them. They are not on your side."

"The kyschun work for us!"

"Nien," he said with a short, acerbic laugh. "They work for no one. They work for themselves."

"What does that mean? Work for themselves?"

"Their sole remit is to protect history and keep the future intact. Your vedhma has been feeding you lies. There is no *changing* anything."

"Then why protect me at all? If my fate is already decided?"

Grigor didn't answer. She hadn't expected him to. His devotion to her and his promise to his sister—these were the product of fear and emotion. He couldn't save Ana any more than she could save herself.

She wiped her tears with her knuckles. "Right. Well, it's as I've known all along. I'm on my own. I'll handle this on my own, as I *always* have."

Ana backed away, skipping into an ungainly jog, and once she'd put enough distance between herself and Grigor, she shifted and flew away.

Ana flew straight to the ravener at Fanghelm, where she sent a formal request for an audience with the kyschun.

Watching the bird fly away with her message, she made a decision.

It was the worst one yet, but what did it matter?

She was doomed either way.

If she was going to die at the hands of a monster, she'd rather go out knowing precisely who had decided her fate.

Ana took flight once more, this time headed for the observatory.

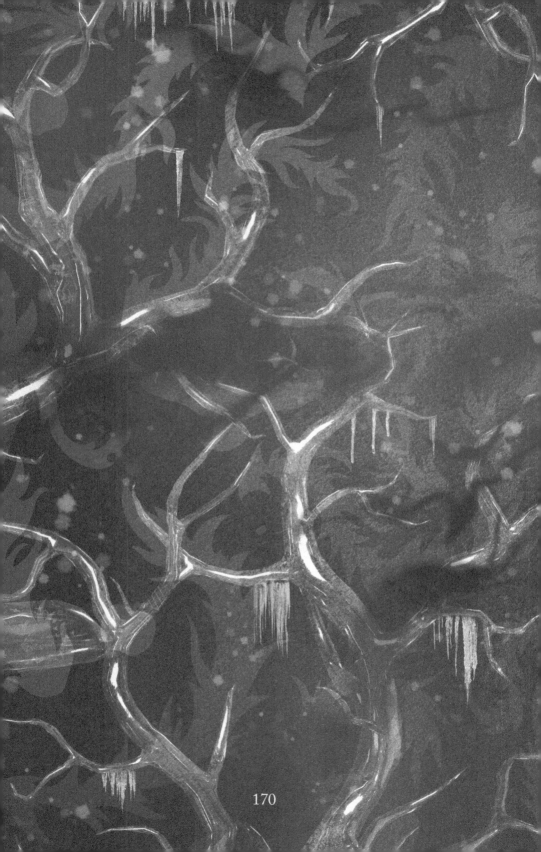

THIRTEEN
FIFTEEN HEARTS

Ana landed outside the observatory and staggered through the doors, catching herself on the handle before she went sprawling. Varradyn looked up from the fur where he'd been sleeping, but she shook her head at him and marched back out into the cold.

Wind whipped her sideways as she stormed alongside the massive glass dome. She stayed close to the structure to minimize the gusts, but she was knocked to the side more than once on her way to the small, disused courtyard.

Ana whipped her head around for what she knew was there, but not *where*.

Have you ever been down in the cellar of the observatory?

It has a cellar?

A deep one. Detached from the building proper. Magda spends a fair amount of time there, from what I know. I've seen... I've seen threads that take you down there. What I cannot see is whether your discovery there helps you or hurts you.

A cellar. And you say she spends time down there?

Doing what, I cannot say.

"Doing what, I do not ever wish to know," Ana whispered to the sky and stars, even as she looked for signs of the very thing that would rip off her blindfold and expose the rest of the horrible truths she'd been so afraid of.

She turned back toward the dome and saw Varradyn staring at her from inside, chains running from both of his legs. The raw panic on his face was discernible even from outside.

"You don't even know what I'm doing, but you know it's a bad idea, don't you?" she said, wind and glass and time separating her words from his ears. He didn't look away, but as she started to, she caught him raising an arm. Pointing.

Ana followed and saw it immediately: a protrusion of wood peeking up from the snow, between two trees at the back of the courtyard.

She turned back toward him. He shook his head again, with less enthusiasm. He seemed to know she'd already made up her mind.

"I won't promise I can save you. Or even myself," she said, breaking his gaze and starting toward the cellar doors. "But I won't live in ignorance a moment longer."

Ana bent low to examine the doors. The wood was rotted. The metal bars where the bolt went were so rusted, one was crumbling away at the edges. But the rust had been disturbed; the wood was damp but not sodden.

She slid the wooden bolt back and tossed it into the snow.

After she verified Magda wasn't lurking over her shoulder, ready to pounce, she tugged on the handles. A low, burping groan emerged from the musty darkness. She regretted not bringing a lantern, but it was too late now.

Ana angled her body to lower it onto the first step when she backed up and decided to bury the bolt in the snow, out of sight. The last thing she needed was for Magda to see the open doors and lock her in.

She stepped slowly, blindly, down what seemed to be the longest staircase in the world. But it wasn't a cellar so much as a cave, she noted, at last reaching ground and a corridor that could have ended in several feet or several thousand. Her vision reached mere inches.

Lair was the word that jumped into her head. But the area was old, judging from the condition of the door and hinges, so it wasn't Magda's creation. Whoever had built the lair, they'd had more than storage in mind.

With one hand on the dirt-caked wall, Ana moved tentatively down the dark path. Something large and fur covered skittered over her hand, and she screamed, slamming against the wall on the other side. It had to have been a spider, those mythical arachnids the vodzhae, their spiritual leaders, preached about. It was ever too cold in the Cross for any but the most hearty creatures, but under the ground, in caves, and in the mountains, lurked all kinds of horrors.

"What horrors will I find at the end of *this* row, Magda?" The sound of Ana's voice steadied her, grounding her. It helped her dust herself off and keep moving forward, despite doubts of different shapes and sizes nagging at her to go, to turn back... to run and keep running until she was back to safety.

But safety was an illusion. It had been since the day Magda of No Family Name had arrived at Fanghelm and claimed it as her own.

On Ana pushed. One foot. The next. She counted each step to give her anxiety something to chew on, but it was also the right thing—the practical thing—to memorize details she'd need on the return trip. *Audacious of you to assume there'll be a return trip.*

The air grew colder the deeper she traveled, the wall harder. Running water trickled ahead but seemed so far away, but soon she was passing her hands over a tiny system of waterfalls pouring down the walls, turning them to mud.

Ana left the peace of the waterfalls behind her. The soothing rush faded into the distance, as though she'd stepped from one world to the next. The air thinned, leaving the sound of her harried, raspy breaths her only companion. She turned her flimsy courage into a chant, to battle the urge to race back to the entrance.

"I will not run. I will not close my eyes. I will call upon the strength of my ancestors, who are always with me. I will not turn. I will not blink."

Niko's sweet face filled her scattered mind. Her inhalations were strained, wheezing. "I will not run. I will not close my eyes."

Her father's bright laughter rang in her ears. She ran her sleeve across her eyes to clear the sweat. There were tears there too, but she could no longer discern the difference. "I will call..."

Ana paused to catch her breath. She felt Tyreste's hand cupping her face, the warmth of his breath as he whispered about a future she could never have. "Upon the strength of my ancestors, who are always with me." Varradyn's hopeless stare seized her. She bowed over, gasping and steadying herself to continue. Straightening, she slapped the wall and took another step. "And face whatever waits for me. I will not turn." Another step. "I will not *blink*."

The passage narrowed. Ana slowed her pace to anticipate the rest of her course. She couldn't know if she was halfway there... almost there. The mountain range was the deepest and tallest in the kingdom. It could be miles before she found anything, if she was even on the right path, which she couldn't be certain of because she hadn't checked to see if there were others before marching bravely down this one.

Two thousand and twenty. Two thousand and twenty-one. "I will not run." Ana coughed through fatigue. She spat the bile rising into her throat. It disappeared into the darkness. "I will not close my eyes, not even for a fucking second, you wretched, cursed hag."

Ana lost her count somewhere around three thousand and thirty. She stopped thinking of Niko or Father or Tyreste or even the raven up on the surface, who was probably wondering if she was ever coming back. She murmured her chant in a daze,

174

shuffling forward by sheer will alone. Her hands fell away from the walls, and she swayed with each step, no longer bothering to clear the sweat or tears or dirt. The creatures crawling over her feet became an afterthought, a surreal nightmare she didn't have the strength to address.

Ana screeched when the floor dropped out, and she went sputtering forward. She looked up and found herself in a small room. The ceiling was covered in crystal protrusions, glittering off the light.

Light. Ana straightened and looked around. Seven torch baskets hung around the perimeter of the space, half of them lit. Her eyes squinted to adjust as she stepped farther in. There wasn't much else in the passage. Just the torches, a chair, and—

Ana narrowed her eyes and approached the far wall. What *was...* She recoiled, taking a backward step. Was that a series of drawers—a chest—built *into* the cavern wall?

She folded her arms over her chest with a hard shiver. She was both cold and scalding hot somehow, sweat and chills fighting for dominance.

Torches didn't light themselves.

Magda had been there recently.

She might still be there, lurking in corners and shadows only she understood well enough to command.

"I will not run," Ana said, rallying her courage as she inched toward the rows of drawers. "I will not close my eyes. I will call..." She stretched a shaking hand and snapped it back. With a grimace, she tried again. "Upon the strength of the Ancestors, who are always with me." A sharp, inward gasp rang across the cave as she wrapped her hand around the metal handle of the left uppermost drawer. "Imryll, hold me close," she whispered, and pulled it open.

Ana's hands flew to her mouth to stifle a scream. She had never wanted—*needed*—to look away more, but she'd promised herself not to close her eyes, not to run. She lifted onto the toes of her boots and widened her eyes to keep them from shutting involuntarily. Then she made herself look closer.

The organ was old and shriveled, no longer fleshy but gray and crumbling. Ana had helped her father dress enough deer and swine to know a heart when she saw one. The one in the drawer was neither deer nor swine though.

She licked her cracked lips, opened a second drawer, and found another shriveled heart. The next revealed the same, and she flung them all open one by one, each slightly less decomposed than the one before, turning the wall into a macabre tableau of time and horror.

Fifteen drawers she'd opened before she found an empty one. *Fifteen* hearts.

"The most useless organ of all." Magda's garbled voice came from behind her.

Ana tensed but didn't turn. She'd brought no weapon, not that it would have mattered. Not even her magic was a threat to the crone.

"The others, my predecessors..." She laughed to herself. "I'd never collected hearts, but when I found them like this, I couldn't abandon the tradition. Preserving the font of life from the very much dead. What do you think, Anastazja? Be honest with me. You already know I won't kill you *yet*, and I much prefer your candor to your caution."

"Predecessors," Ana whispered, her voice hitching and her breath lodging in her throat. Whether or not she'd meant to, Magda had confirmed she'd not been the first to pursue and murder the Ravenwoods.

"What's that? You're mumbling again, girl. It's so unbecoming."

"You didn't start this madness at all, did you?" Ana spun around. Heat flooded her face and throbbed in her clammy hands. "You weren't the first. You aren't even the one in charge, are you? You're just *following orders*."

Magda's cruel smile froze on her face. "There is no one in charge in this world, girl. There are only orders and those who

176

follow them. Like you, for example. Luring all these beautiful subjects to me. You never wanted to know how it ended for any of them. Now that you do, will you defy me? Feign indignance over what I've asked you to do, whilst pretending you never, deep down, knew their fates ended at my hands?"

"*Your hands* maybe. But the command didn't come from you." *Say it. Say it. Say his name.* But she couldn't. There was no way to know, until the words were unleashed, whether calling upon the name of Mortain would surprise or enrage the koldyna, and there was nowhere to hide.

"You split hairs when others see potential." Magda moved closer. She was in her deceptive form, all beauty and light and lies. "But I do not care what inspires you. What compels you. You have but one use, and when you're gone, there will be others. There are always others. The gift doesn't die with anyone, does it? You, your brother, your father. His sister and on and on and on. Once you're all gone, there will be more still. Once I am gone, there will be more like me. There is no end until we prevail, and I have no qualms using and discarding a hundred Wynters if that's the cost. It has always been in your best interest to keep me satiated." She flicked a nod upward. "His time is coming. But it will not be Magda carving his still-beating heart from his chest."

"*Nien*." Anastazja added force to the word. "I have done everything you have asked, but I will *not* take a life. Not ever."

"They who wield the knife are not the sole claimants of death, are they? You have already taken many lives, girl."

"You gave me no choice!"

"Oh, there are always choices." Magda grinned. She tapped her fingers along the outsides of her arms. "But you valued your own life... the lives of your family, more than *their* lives." She aimed her gaze at the wall. "You can cry your excuses, but *that* is the sum of the matter. You were always able to say no, Anastazja. You *chose* to help me, and this is the price."

Ana was frozen in place. She could no longer feel the icy cavern air whispering across her flesh nor hear the irregular beat of her heart throbbing behind her ears. She had no answer for the koldyna's charge. No defense against what felt like a damning judgment belonging to someone else.

But Magda was right. She had chosen. She'd chosen her father, Niko, Tyreste... even herself, if she was being honest, and it seemed sheer, brutal honesty was the only path available to her now.

You chose to help me. This is the price.

Niko was gone. Her father was no longer a man she knew. Tyreste might still be safe as long as she never returned to the tavern—as herself *or* Nessa.

As for Varradyn... She was powerless on her own. But an anonymous call to aid could send a hundred villagers up the mountain to secure the observatory and free him.

"There is no danger to you greater than the one you offer yourself," Magda said. "Do not test me, girl. You only think you've seen the worst of me."

"You..." Ana unclenched her jaw and stepped forward. "You no longer hold any sway over me, koldyna. You played *your* hand too early, and now you can't hurt me." Ana threw her head back and laughed. "Even killing me would be a mercy, Magda. It truly would. But know this. I am no longer afraid of you. Do whatever you want. But your hold over me has ended."

Feeling returned to her hands, a great, buzzing tingle that empowered her to move closer, to meet the dead eyes of the crone as she stood before her in bold defiance and then brushed past.

"You only think you understand regret, Anastazja." Magda's gravelly voice, her *true* sound, echoed as it followed her.

Ana ran the entire way to the stairs, shedding her hesitation to make room for the hubris coursing alongside the blood in her veins.

She was a reckless fool for provoking Magda like that, and she would pay for it. But if she made it back to Fanghelm first and could convince her father to leave with her, it wouldn't matter. Away from the koldyna's influence, he'd return to himself and tell her where Niko was, and they would all travel to the Sepulchre, the governing body of magic for the realm. The magi would know what to do about the koldyna and her wickedness. They would send help to Witchwood Cross and fix the terrible wrongs done there.

Ana had no doubt she'd make it back first. Magda could do many improbable things, but flying wasn't one of them. If it was, she'd never have needed the Wynters at all.

The challenge would be breaking through the powerful spell that had taken root in Arkhady.

Ana burst through the open cellar doors and gulped in a ravenous swallow of air. She fell to her knees in the wet snow, panting so hard that spots throbbed behind her eyes. She forced herself to her unsteady feet and had launched into the sprint that would ensure a smooth shift when motion caught her eye.

Varradyn was working his arms up and down to get her attention. When he had it, he thrust one entire arm out to the side in a wild gesticulating motion.

Ana shook her head in confusion, but he only pumped his arm harder. Still bewildered, she was trying to follow his frantic gesturing when she saw it.

The wooden bolt.

He jumped up and down in excitement, nodding furiously.

Ana glanced back at the doors. She'd not considered, until that moment, how she might solve the greatest trouble of her life with something as simple as a locked door.

She shuffled to the buried plank and lifted it from the snow-bank, but she didn't move back to the cellar doors right away. Her hesitation was a mystery even to her. Was she really going to murder the woman? It was exactly what Magda deserved, but could she, Anastazja, be the one responsible?

She could feel and hear Varradyn's panic behind the domed glass.

"You have a choice," she said to herself, to her conscience, and yet to no one. "You always have a choice. It's the price you have to live with."

Ana settled the bolt onto the doors and locked it into place, choosing peace for her family and the Ravenwoods in exchange for what remained of her conscience.

Ana flew faster than she'd ever flown in her life. She landed just outside the doors of Fanghelm in a dead sprint, sending guards and courtiers scattering in the wake of her urgency.

Hope sent her bursting into the Great Hall, but her father wasn't there enjoying a meal. The room was cleaned and cleared. On her way back out, she ran into Ludya.

"What's happened to you?" Ludya demanded, pacing her on her way to the central stairs. "I can see it in your eyes, Anastazja."

"The witch is dead. Or will be," Ana said and raced up the stairs so fast, she stumbled and landed on the heels of her hands. She groaned and pushed on. "Please tell me my father is in his room."

"As far as I know. But Ana—"

"What?" Ana asked without stopping. She charged down the hall toward her father's apartments. "But what?"

"He doesn't want to see you." Ludya stopped in the middle of the hall.

"*Her* doing. But she won't be a problem anymore." Ana rapped on the door.

Her father's footservant answered. She didn't wait to be invited in, brushing past him to Arkhady's bedside.

Her father lay under the covers, gaunt and blank-faced. He stared up and into nothing, his eyes pools of hollow despair. She hardly recognized the man in the bed at all.

"Ota." Ana lowered into a crouch and reached for one of his hands. She folded it into her own and brought it to her mouth with tearful kisses. "Ota, we're leaving. Tonight. Right now."

Arkhady cleared his throat with a rattling sound. His dry, cracked lips parted. "You are..."

"It's me, Ota. It's your Anastazja. Your Pjika. Your little bird." She kissed his hands again, sobbing against his bony flesh. He'd deteriorated so fast, he couldn't last much longer.

"Who?" He puffed the word on the end of a ragged breath.

"Your daughter. Anastazja."

"I..." His jaw flapped. "Have no daughter."

Ana whipped her head at the servant, but he had disappeared. To inform the koldyna, probably, like they all had been doing for years, but he'd be on a fool's errand. Ana's evil stepmother would never emerge from the cave of horrors, and it was a fitting place for her to meet her end, surrounded by the hearts she'd stolen.

"We can discuss this later." She jumped to her feet. "On the road. We'll... It doesn't matter. It doesn't matter. But we have to go now, before—" *Before they figure out what I've done.* "Come. Forget your trunks. We'll send for whatever you need, or buy it when we get where we're—"

Ana stumbled back into the wall, her hands clapped over her ears. The wail emerging from her father was preternatural, deep and morbid, like death itself had clawed its way up from his chest to announce itself. She watched in creeping dread as he rose from the bed, compelled by an unseen force.

He stayed like that, his arms out and his mouth crooked and hung unnaturally wide, howling for so long Ana, started to scream with him.

Then he stopped. His head—only his head, the rest of him remained disturbingly still—slowly turned her way. His mouth gaped even wider, flesh splitting at the corners. Blood ran down his face, dropping onto his nightgown and blanket in fat, grisly blobs.

His bloody lips stretched into a grin so wide, it transformed his entire face. He was no longer the great Arkhady Wynter but a ghoul, a vessel for the damned.

"All you had to do was aid me." The words came from his throat, but his mouth didn't move at all. But they were not his words, nor his voice. "You have no idea what you've done."

They were *hers*.

"Everyone you have ever loved is marked for death. I will become you, and through you, I will do *everything* he has ever asked of me."

Ana sobbed against her hands, digging her back into the wall.

"You have no *idea what you've done*," the koldyna rasped, then the decrepit man who had once been her father crumbled and collapsed onto his bed like a sack of flour.

Ana tried to return to his side, but Ludya had her in a firm hold from behind. "Come. Now!"

"I won't leave him, Ludya!" Ana wrestled against Ludya's grasp, but she was too weak to overpower her.

"We'll return for him when we can. But *you* must go. *Now.* Now!"

Ana screamed for her father as Ludya dragged her from the room and toward the servant staircase at the opposite end of the hall.

"Where are you taking me?" Ana rasped as she half stumbled down the steps.

"Somewhere safe," Ludya said, shifting her hold to steady Ana. "Safe for now, anyway. Tomorrow... nien, nien. For now, we will not think of tomorrow. There is only tonight." Ludya sniffled and pushed a faster pace. "Just tonight."

FOURTEEN
THE CIDER FESTIVAL

Despite the rain threatening the horizon—at least it wasn't *snow*, the villagers said—everyone in Witchwood Cross was down in the market. Even the stalwart hermits had emerged for the treasured annual tradition, a celebration as odd as it was cherished.

Apples only grew in one orchard in the Cross, the one behind Fanghelm. The rest were brought up from Wulfsgate in an endless stream of overflowing wagons, which were still pouring in from the North Compass Road. Tyreste stood in the doorway of the Tavern at the Top of the World and marveled at the Vjestik's ardor for a simple fruit.

Men and women alike salivated as the wagons passed on their way to the market center. Merchants and traders had been preparing their booths for weeks, and now they waited, breaths swirling in anticipation.

"People used to come from all over the Northerlands for this." Agnes appeared at his side. She propped her hand on the doorframe with a washrag as they watched the wagons roll in. "Or so Stojan says, but the man has an imagination on him like you wouldn't believe."

"I don't understand it," Tyreste said, shaking his head. "But I understand the coin it brings into the tavern. So, two cheers for apples." He unenthusiastically pumped a hand into the air.

Agnes chuckled. The mirthful sound died into a soft sigh. "I didn't think I'd miss Pern and Evert so soon. Evert especially used to love the Cider Festival. Or maybe he just enjoyed the lawful opportunity to smash applesauce in the faces of his elders. We may never know the truth." She nudged a hip against him. "Where were you when they left? Headache, my eye."

Tyreste kept his gaze on the road. He watched some children, their little animated arms shaking their entire bodies, wave at the waggoneers as they passed. He hadn't joined the family at dawn to see his siblings leave, begging off with a headache that wasn't *all* lie. His head did hurt, as well as his heart, his mind... his everything. He carried so much grief on his back, he didn't know where to set it down.

But even more than Pern and Evert, he missed Ana. Time had softened the things about her he'd found maddening. He woke in pain; he fell asleep in pain. Only in his dreams was he whole again, lost to the shape of her.

She was alone and afraid, and in an effort to respect her wish to be left alone, he'd left her even more alone and even more afraid. After his encounter with Magda in the tavern, the one he still couldn't quite believe had been real, he'd doubled down on convincing himself staying away was the right choice, the only choice.

There was a word for that.

Fucking coward.

Two words.

"I couldn't do it." Emotion clogged his throat. "Saying good-bye is different for me than it is for all of you."

Agnes had seemed ready to level him with another good ribbing, but she sighed softly and ran a hand between his shoulders instead. "I know, brother. I think they know it too." She tilted her head back and inhaled the cool air. "Something happened between you and Addy, didn't it?"

Tyr flicked his eyes toward the side in a warning.

"Make it right," Agnes said. She stepped back and swatted him with the rag. "For the same reason you couldn't say good-bye to Pern and Ev. Yeah?"

Tyr nodded without looking at her. He waited for her to leave before checking the sky. Close to noontide. Nessa should have been there already.

Why her absence bothered him, he couldn't say. She was an enigma, a passel of half-truths he didn't know how to address, if he even should. From the signing, to the weirdness about the Westerlands, and really *all* their interactions, if he was being honest, he couldn't shake the sense something was off. Even the way she called him Tyreste. Yet there was something about her that stirred the same passion Ana had ignited. It came and went, like the tides of the Howling Sea, often so fast, he wasn't sure he'd felt anything at all. And while he *should* feel something for the beautiful, kindhearted girl who had taken a fancy to him, of all people, everything he felt was what he'd convinced himself to feel.

Maybe it wasn't the worst thing that she'd stood him up again.

He closed the door and returned to the tavern to finish last-minute preparations for the night ahead.

"Are you sure you're willing to take such a risk?" Ludya chided Ana as they dressed her in so many layers of dilapidated, frayed fur, it would have been a miracle if her own family recognized her.

Ana stared straight ahead into the dying hearth and the empty kettle hanging from the center hook. She was starving, but even the thought of food turned her stomach. They'd slept in an inn right in the center of the village. Hiding, Ludya had said, wasn't about pockets and corners but stealth. No one would expect the steward's little bird to be holed up in a cheap room, so they'd see what their mind expected them to see.

"I *could* read your thoughts," Ludya said pleasantly, tugging at the hooded layers to stack them around Ana's face. "But I do not deal in violations. Thus, I would appreciate your openness."

"She's *dead,* Ludya. Or will be." Ana swished her jaw back and forth. It was painfully stiff, like the rest of her. She'd insisted on sleeping in the chair with one broken leg, and Ludya hadn't argued. "I fear only her influence on the people of the Cross until that time. When she's gone, I'll tend to the mess she left us at the keep. But it could take days before she's gone. Maybe longer. What if she has a stash of food and drink down there? And why am I... How can I speak so casually of her starving to death? Of *me* starving her to death? If I'm not there to wield the dagger, it *is* still murder, right? Oh, Ancestors, it's not too late to go back up there, to just quietly slide the bolt and pray she won't murder the entire village to spite me."

"You're rambling."

"I'm..." Ana had only just risen and already she was exhausted again. "No, I made a choice. She knows I made a choice. If I let her go, she'll... She'll follow through on every terrible threat she's ever made. I have to wait... is all. Stay the course I've chosen."

"Can you not wait until *then* to see your beau?"

"He's not my—" She refused to finish. "I promised him I would spend the evening with him at the festival."

"A promise that hardly seems prudent to keep, given the turn of events. Does it truly matter now?"

Ana turned her head upward, to look at Ludya. "When I have failed to keep all others, keeping this one feels like the *only* thing that matters." She straightened with a shiver, rolling her head. "And unless Magda has taken over the entire village with her witchery, I'm still safe walking our roads and shopping our markets, aren't I?"

Ludya backed up and sat in a nearby chair. "She's not that powerful. Not even her master is, or he'd be here doing his own bidding. But to assume she's gotten to *none* of them is an ignorance beneath you, Anastazja. If she can speak through your father—"

"Maybe I imagined it," Ana retorted.

"Maybe you did," Ludya said evenly. "But I did not. I saw and heard every painful moment. You must assume she can do the same with anyone she's taken hold of."

Ana snorted and tucked her long braid into her furs. "As though she has an entire network of spies. Sounds even more foolish when *I* say it."

Ludya went silent.

Ana spun on the stool. "You don't really believe that, do you?"

Ludya rose and returned to her side. She placed a soft hand on the side of Ana's face. "I believe you are only pretending to be impenetrable right now. You're in shock. I feel your unspoken fear, and something even worse."

Ana tensed in annoyance. "What?"

"Guilt." Ludya lowered into a crouch. "The fear you carry for your soul, after locking the koldyna away."

Ana started to rebut but turned her mouth into a tight, tense line instead, knowing anything she said would just be torn apart by Ludya.

"You know the world will be safer without her, but you toil. Your soul toils. You suffer for what you've done but also for her crimes, a burden too heavy for even the strongest to carry."

"If I could have, I'd have stopped her *years* ago," Ana hissed through her teeth.

"And that's where you and I differ even more," Ludya said calmly. She stood and moved to the door. "For you always had the power to stop her."

Enraged, Ana leaped from the stool. "You say such things to me, after all that's happened! Do you not think I'd have done *anything* to keep her hands off my family? Off the Ravenwoods? I accepted the fate she set for me, *my own death*, and *still* pulled myself out of bed every day, doing whatever she asked to keep as many people safe as I could. How dare you accuse me of being idle while the monster stormed the village!"

Ludya shook her head, unruffled. She wore a sad, placid look, angering Ana more. "You haven't been idle. But you *have* been negligent. Blind. You call upon the Ancestors like you're entitled to their wisdom, but like any 'gods,' they expect you to come to some conclusions on your own."

"What does *that* mean?"

"Have you been to see the kyschun?"

"I sent them a raven. You know that."

"In your entire life, Ana? Have you *ever* been to them, to ask about yourself? Your people? Have you ever bothered to learn anything beyond what the scholars teach in the village about the Vjestik?"

"Why..." Ana scrunched her face, which was burning hotter by the second. "Why would I when I already know our history?"

"Why do we have archivists if you can learn everything you need to know from scholars?"

"I—"

"Why have you never asked your father? Your grandparents?"

"Asked them *what*?"

"*Who you are!*" Ludya's voice thundered loud enough to send Ana scrambling back a few steps.

Ana's nose flared, her eyes dilating in a defense that didn't quite make it to her lips. Her heart vibrated in her chest like an explosive ready to detonate. And she thought it might, if she didn't leave the tiny, oppressive room, which smelled like mildew and felt like a prison.

She blinked hard, swallowed, and stepped forward. "I will be back by midnight. I don't expect you to stay with me. You've done enough, and this mess—this problem—is mine to solve. It's always been mine to solve." She moved beside Ludya and rested her face against hers. "Volemthe, Ludya, but I release you of this burden."

Ana ripped the door open and ran before Ludya could see her crying.

Tyreste wandered down to the festival just before midnight. Nessa hadn't shown up, and between the bittersweet memories attached to the Cider Festival, his fallout with Addy, the stolen letters, Pern and Evert leaving, and the strange matter of Magda, none of it felt right. Even Rikard the Mouser had stayed in the cabin.

But a part of Tyr *did* want to see the men stomping apples in a vat with perverse delight. To smell and taste the creative ways bakers turned the fruit into sweet and savory dishes. The poetry contest, the games, and the mummer's show. It was all so bizarre and yet curiously appealing.

As he meandered the rows of tents, assaulted by scent and sound, his heart relaxed.

Tyr dropped coin to a merchant selling apples dipped in honey. It was mounted on a stick, but the viscous, sweet trail ran down over his hands, and soon he was licking his fingers like a savage. He remembered Ana licking honey off of another appendage of his, and the memory sent him stumbling into a nearby tent pole, dizzy with grief.

He dropped the apple on the ground, and a couple of rats rushed to devour the remnants.

Tyr closed his eyes, ignoring the whispers from passersby. He didn't care what they thought. He was finding it hard to care about *anything* anymore.

Shrieks of indignation and laughter filled the air as the sudden storm hammered the fairway. Celebrants exchanged befuddled looks, frozen in indecision, but it wasn't long before everyone was back to their activities, the rain a mild nuisance to the guilty pleasures they'd been waiting seasons for.

Tyr started to duck back into the main row of tents, but something looped around his waist from the sides, startling him into a yelp.

He turned and saw Nessa, her dark hair soaked and falling in waves around her smiling, flushed face.

"Hi," he said weakly, as she pulled him into a narrow alleyway between the tents.

"I'm so sorry I wasn't able to come help. There was nothing I could do." Her words came out in such a rush, he had to replay them in his mind to understand them. "I swear to you, I wanted to be there. I really did, Tyreste."

"It's all right," he said, thinking again of the way she called him Tyreste, but his words trailed when the air around Nessa changed, *shimmered*. She became Ana. His heart stuttered. "Ana?"

Her face seized in alarm, but then she was Nessa again. The change was jarring, his eyes struggling to adapt to what no longer felt like his imagination at all. But how could that be? She wasn't Ana. She was her cousin, sharing enough blood to trick his mind and heart into believing what he wanted. It wasn't the first time he'd made the mistake.

"What... did you call me?" Nessa asked.

"Forgive me, I—"Tyr buried his face in his hands. He clenched to keep the sadness down. "It's been a long day, Nessa. Not my best one."

Soft fingers plied his away from his face, one by one. He saw her through a haze of tears, and she was again Ana, because that's what his heart most desired. Who his soul needed, to be whole again.

So when Nessa kissed him, planting her pliant, gentle lips against his, he decided to let it happen, to allow the rest of the world to fall away—all his troubles, his pain—and embrace the joy that had been his, if only for such a short, tortured time.

"Ana." He moaned, wrapping her wet hair in his hands to pull her closer. This time, Nessa didn't correct him. She pressed her body as close to his as she could, held apart by their layers of furs that he needed *off* before he exploded. "I've missed you so cursed much."

"I can be her, if it helps," Nessa said between breathless kisses. "Tell me what you loved about her, and I can be all those things.

Tell me what you hated about her, and I'll never be any of those things. I can be everything you wished she could have been. I can be so much more."

Her words put a sudden halt to his escape. He closed his lips against hers, taking a half step back.

"What? What did I say?"

Tyr breathed in a pained whimper. He reached for her face again, but this time pressed his forehead to hers, repressing the well of anger and sadness that seemed without end. "Forgive me, Nessa. I like you. And if anyone could... should... stand a chance of breaking through this wall around my heart, it's you. But the truth is—" He winced. "I'm in love with someone else. And though she may not feel the same, it doesn't mean my heart doesn't belong to her." He turned his head to the side and exhaled through a gap in his lips. "It wouldn't be fair to you to pretend."

Nessa slowly backed away. Through his tears, he saw her once more change, flickering between Ana and Nessa, Ana and Nessa. It was Magda all over again. He was seeing things that simply weren't possible. Of all the trauma he'd endured over the years, none had left him hallucinating; he'd never questioned his own sanity.

"Tyreste," she said, measuring her words. "What if I were to tell you—"

She was cut off when screams rang out from their left. They both turned toward the sound but then more came from their right.

"Someone *help us!*" a voice called from several tents over. A chorus of desperate shouts followed, and the market swiftly dissolved into chaos.

Tyr and Nessa exchanged stunned looks. Nessa shook her head. She took off running.

When Ana returned to the main fairway of the market, it felt like she'd stepped into another reality. Men and women were screaming for help, howling for physicians, and leaning over a haphazard line of convulsing bodies. Some were covered in blood. Others had gone dangerously pale.

Some of the tents had already collapsed, and the rest were being pulled down to place under the dying and dead. *Dead*. Yes, she realized some had already succumbed to the unknown horror ripping through the market. She searched for signs of anything that might explain what was happening, but there was nothing.

Ana regarded them all in utter helplessness. Her legs tried to go one way, her head another.

"It's the apples!" someone cried. The person ran through the crowd, her hands waving above her head. "Don't eat the apples!"

Shrill, sharp pounding pulsed in Ana's ears. The screams and cries turned into an ambient hum, like she'd been pulled away from the scene and was viewing it through the lens of a distant memory.

Several feet away, a little boy tore out of his parents' arms and retched a spray of blood. It coated his father, who tilted his head back to the sky and begged for mercy.

A cart thundered down the road, knocking Ana into a tent. The cacophony of dread and despair climbed to a crescendo once more, and she started screaming herself, to drown out the terror that yet had no name.

But of course it had a name.

You only think you know regret.

Ana started moving through the crowd. She crouched near the boy, asking his parents for any information they had about what had happened, but the mother was incapacitated with sobs. She pulled her boy—her already-gone boy—to her chest and rocked him in the rawest grief Ana had ever witnessed.

If she'd only moved faster, she might have—

"It was the apple," the father said, swaying on his knees with a soulless look in his eyes. Beside him she saw a honey-covered apple—or what had been one before the child had eaten it. Only the stick remained, coated in remnants of honey and dirt clumped around the discarded instrument of death. "It was the fucking apple!"

"We need physicians!" Tyreste cried, his voice rising momentarily over the din of terror. Ana couldn't see him; her senses were too overloaded to place where he was. "Where are the physicians? The healers?"

Ana stumbled to her feet. She blinked the sweat and tears away and scanned the crowd. Magda's words bored holes through her. How had she done it? Had she taken hold of a villager and turned them into a murderer?

She found Tyreste standing over another situation too far gone, his hands laced over his head. The helpless look on his face broke her.

"You're a healer," she whispered, low enough just for the two of them. "We can help people."

"I tried... I..." He turned back toward her, wan-faced, and lowered his shaking hands so she could see them. "How do you know I can heal?"

"Does it matter?" Ana was too agitated to be concerned about the slipup. "We need to act fast, faster than whatever is killing our people."

"I can't. Nothing... I can't. I don't know what's wrong with me."

"Does your family have other healers?" Ana knew the answer, but Nessa didn't. She'd already given away too much.

"My father used to, but he stopped when the arthritis set into his hands, said it was that or the bookkeeping and only one fed his family, and now..." Tyreste's shoulders shuddered as they lifted. "It's just me."

"We can—" Ana looked around. Things had only gotten worse. There was more blood. More agony. More bedlam. "All right. Here's what we'll do. Let's recruit some help in taking as many of the sick or injured back to the tavern as we can. Maybe you'll do better somewhere safe, and there's plenty of room to get everyone laid out safely. While you do that, I'll go find the physicians."

"Right." Tyreste nodded furiously. He met her eyes in relief. "Let's do that."

"Guardians, there you fucking are!" Rikard cried out and rushed over. "Tyr, we need you *now*."

"What?" Tyreste asked. "What is it?"

Rikard's throat jumped. "Addy."

"No." Tyreste shoved his brother. "No, don't lie to me. Don't you dare lie to me—"

"She's *alive*, but she needs you *now*."

"Go!" Ana screamed. "I'll find the physicians, *go!*"

She watched Rikard and Tyreste sprint away and turned back toward the scene in the market. Where *were* the physicians? All she could see was blood and terror blending into a single stream of reality.

"Where are the physicians?" she cried out, running down the fairway. "Someone tell me where the physicians are!"

"One is dead. The other two are over there," a man said hurriedly as he passed. He jutted a thumb behind him and rushed on.

Ana followed where he'd pointed. They'd cleared out a section near the field, and atop a sea of canvas, pulled from tents, were dozens of dead and sick. The two physicians tending them both looked as though they'd been run over by a cart. One vomited off to the side, narrowly missing a young woman.

She was astounded at how fast everyone had come together in a crisis, but she knew better than to be relieved. Magda would take as much as Magda wanted. Not a drop less.

"There's no help coming," she muttered to herself. There wasn't time to wait for more to arrive. Nor was there time to help everyone. She had to choose, and there was only one choice she could make. It would expose "Nessa," who had said she had no magic in her, for a liar, but did she care anymore what anyone thought of Nessa? Or her, for that matter?

Addy.

Ana gathered her skirts, turned, and ran straight into—

Magda.

She tried to gasp, but it emerged as a pitiful squeak.

"You thought a bolt could stop me," Magda said with a slow smile. She turned her eyes toward the side in appreciation of her work. Her shoulders lifted with a little shudder of pride. "How did you suppose you were ever going to best a warlock when you're still thinking like a child?"

Ana shook her head, wide-eyed and unable to speak.

"I told you what would happen." Magda stepped forward, and Ana retreated. They kept up the dance, moving backward down the fairway. "If you crossed me."

"These people are innocent!" Ana cried. "They had nothing to do with us!"

"You made the choice for them to suffer. You had all the power here."

Ana laughed through her sobs. "What power? What power have I, koldyna, against you? Why would you feel the need to show me what I have already seen and know I cannot beat?"

"*I* alone know where Niko is." Magda pushed her pace, causing Ana to stumble. "*I* alone can release your father from his pain. *I* alone decide what happens to the pitiful tavern boy you'll run to seconds from now." Magda stretched her hand out and hooked a nail under Ana's trembling chin. "So go to him. *Save* his baby sister. And then come back to me, girl, for we both know there's only one way this ends."

Ana turned toward the direction of the tavern, and when she turned back around, Magda was gone.

Shivers seized her from head to toe. She stumbled sideways and gripped a bare tent pole, fighting for calm.

But there was no time for *calm.*

Ana dropped her hood, lifted her skirts, and raced for the tavern.

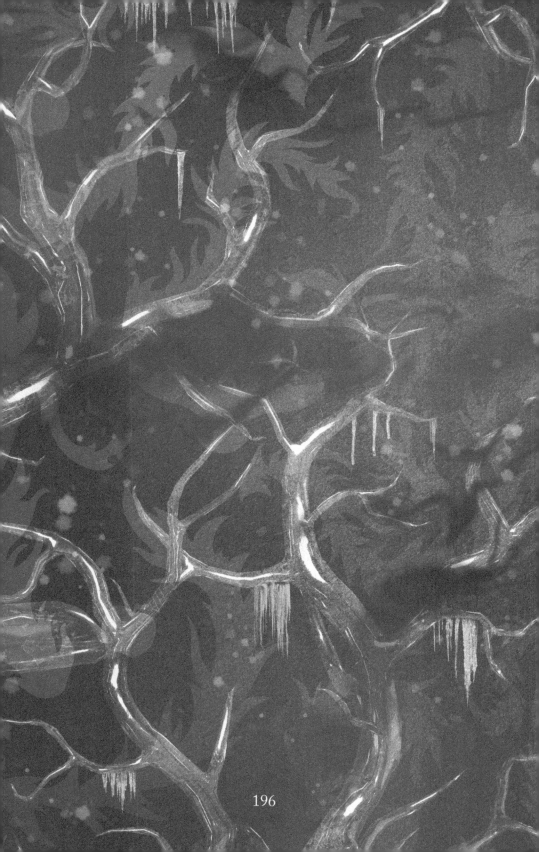

196

FIFTEEN
I WOULD SWIM THE HOWLING SEA

Tyr would never forget the sound of his mother screeching as Addy convulsed atop a table in the center of the tavern. Nor his father's soundless, desperate pacing, set to creaks in the floorboards that would never again feel anything but sinister. Rikard and Agnes rushing to the back in shifts to get more useless rags and waterskins, which would do nothing for their dying sister, only magnified the horror.

He hovered over the chair he'd pulled to her side, both of her hands clasped in his as he pleaded with the part of himself that had muted his magic. His tears ran onto his sister's face, joining with hers. She'd stopped seizing, but she'd gone so utterly still, he had to muster his courage long enough to check for a pulse.

The patrons had left to help in the market. A few had lingered in loyalty, but Olov had sent them away to check on their own families. There was nothing they could do anyway. Nothing anyone could do.

Rikard the Mouser leaped onto the table and rubbed his purring head along Addy's outer thigh. It was the most affection Tyr had seen the tomcat offer anyone.

Was that what finally broke him?

"I'm so sorry, Addy. For everything I said to you. Forgive my hotheaded foolishness. I didn't mean any of it. I know you didn't take the letters. I know you weren't lying. Just please... *please* come back. Please don't leave me."

Agnes slammed a bowl of water onto the table she'd pulled close. "Look at her face, Tyreste! We need to keep cooling her down. She's hot. She's flushed. We just need... need to cool her down."

Tyr looked up into his sister's eyes, reading the haunted despair they all felt.

The tavern doors flung open.

Anastazja marched through. She bolted the door behind her.

Rikard squinted at Tyr in confusion, but he didn't understand what was going on either.

"I couldn't find—" She closed her eyes and sucked in a short, hard breath before trying again. "I couldn't find any physicians. I tried, but they were..." She reached a hand out and steadied herself on the wall. Her gaze traveled to the table. "Addy."

Tyr choked the words out. "Did you run into N—"

"I lied to you about magic. I do have it. I just didn't want anyone to know." Ana rushed over, grabbing a chair on her way. She dropped it on the other side of the table and started running her hands along Addy's motionless face.

"I *know* you have magic," Tyr replied. "*What* is going on?"

"Thank the Guardians," Fransiska said, breathless. "*You're* here. Please, we'll give you *anything*..."

"All I want is to see her smiling face again," Ana said distantly. Her hands traveled Addy's face in slow, circular paths. Her eyes fluttered, then closed. Her mouth moved in muted whispers, following the same cadence as her palms.

Fransiska sobbed and covered her face in her hands. The sharp sound stirred Olov from his stupor, and he reached for her, then pulled her into his arms without a word. Rikard stood frozen in the center of the floor, Agnes several feet away holding dirty rags in one hand, clean ones in the other.

They all watched Ana.

No one made a sound.

Time passed too slowly. Ana looked up. Her eyes rolled back, and she started to topple backward. Rikard reached her before she fell altogether and caught her in his arms. He lifted her up off the chair and helped her stand, but she was out again before she found her footing. Agnes dropped the rags and joined him, and together they dragged her to another chair.

All Tyr could do was stare, stunned.

A guttural gasp ripped through the quiet tavern. Addy's chest rose so high, she nearly bucked off the table. She rolled to her side, sputtering pink foam everywhere.

"Adeline!" Fransiska cried and tore away from her husband. She shoved Tyr and curled her daughter into her arms, lifting and carrying her away from the bloody table. Olov hurried to her side, and they rushed her to the bar, where Fransiska mopped Adeline's face and fed her gentle sips of wine.

With one hand on her belly and the other behind her neck, Agnes waddled toward Tyr. "I'm gonna assume Addy will be all right now?"

Tyr nodded, staring blankly.

"Ana's all right, but she might lose consciousness again, so you should... I don't know, check on her. Rik and I are going to go help in the market."

Tyr nodded, still caught in the iron grip of his daze. He watched as Agnes and then Rikard went to the door, leaving Ana alone in a chair, huddled over her knees.

He needed to go to her. To say *something*. She'd arrived at just the right time to save the most important person in his life. Another few minutes...

Rikard the Mouser jumped off the table and padded toward Ana. She didn't look up, but one hand stretched down to give him a loving pat, same as she always had. Same as Nessa had, now that he thought about it. Rikard had only ever *liked* Ana, Addy, and Tyr. He tolerated everyone else.

But he'd taken to Nessa right away.

Tyr forced himself to stand. He moved slowly to where Ana sat, vaguely aware of his parents sobbing over Addy's miracle recovery at the bar. Each step readied him to confront truths his mind hadn't wanted him to see, and his heart still didn't understand.

He lowered his hands to the table beside her and leaned close. "Ana?"

She didn't react, so he said her name again. Before she looked up, he caught the flare in her eyes, the panic settling around her jaw.

Ana locked his gaze, unblinking. Her hands turned to soft fists, her lower lip moving in strange twitches.

Tyr looked back at the bar for only a moment, but it was long enough for Ana to bolt. She was halfway across the tavern floor, her dark-blue dress flapping like a sheet behind her, before he was even on his feet. He raced after her, watching her unlatch the door and rush out into the night.

He caught up to her as she turned the corner, slowing her by grabbing her arm. She tried to shake him off, but he held tight and guided her into the alley behind the tavern.

When he released her, she paced away but didn't run. She traced her hands down her arms, her head shaking through some unseen battle she was waging with herself.

"Talk to me," Tyr pleaded. "You just—" Grief clogged his throat. "Saved my sister. You appeared, out of the blue, as though you knew. You *knew* she was dying, and you came, at just the right time... You *had* to know, but *how*, Ana?"

Ana ran to a nearby tree, grasped the bark, and retched into the dirt. Nothing emerged except the most devastating cries.

Tyr came up behind her and smoothed his hands along her back, pulling her hair out of the way in case she vomited. Her harried breaths began to normalize. Her head came up and she stared, glossy eyed, into the forest.

When he tugged her back to her feet, she didn't stop him. There was no resistance left in her as he gathered her in his arms and pressed her to his chest, one hand behind her head, the other nestled against the small of her back.

The silence lasted so long, Tyr began to feel the entire night had been a dream.

"I'm in desperate trouble, Tyreste." Her voice was no longer bold and strong, but small and scared. "I'm drowning in a sea I cannot swim through."

Tyr tightened his hold on her and brushed his lips across her matted hair. "Please talk to me, Anastazja. Tell me what's done this to you."

"Do you not understand? Do you not know?" Ana tilted her head back to look at him. Her beautiful eyes sparkled with tears he had to stop himself from kissing away. She swayed in his grasp, so he tightened his arm around her back. "I have done—" She sucked her lower lip in. "I had to keep you safe."

Tyr pressed his chin to the top of her head, hugging her close to him. "Do you not think I can protect myself?" He pulled back and met her eyes with a sad smile. "I would walk through fire... swim the Howling Sea... for *you*."

Ana rolled her lips in and nodded. Tears rolled down her pink cheeks. "I know you would. But I can't..." Her eyes squeezed shut as her face crumpled into sobs. "Lose you."

"I don't understand, Ana. *Please* help me understand."

Ana withdrew one of her hands from her cloak and slid it along the side of his face. He closed his eyes, surrendering to a return of warmth, familiarity. "Love isn't just knowing when to say good-bye. It's finding the strength to do it when everything inside of you would do anything to just be weak, for once."

Tyr mouthed the word *love*, but she had started to pull away. He felt her slipping further from him, not just physically, and he reached for her face, desperate to stop it from happening.

He cradled her soft flesh in his hands, letting her see him, his tears and his truth. "We can be strong *together*. We *are* stronger together. Don't you see?"

Ana's eyes closed. Her face went limp in his palm. "You only think you know evil, Tyreste. But you have no idea."

"Magda." He snarled the name. "It's her, isn't it?"

Ana's eyes flashed open. "Why do you say that?"

"I saw her with you in the market. I've seen her since. She came into the tav—"

"WHEN?" Ana seized his face and shook it. "*When?*"

"I don't... not that long ago. She didn't buy an ale or come to meet someone."

Ana ripped away and staggered back to the tree. She seemed distressed but not surprised. "Grigor was right. She came for you."

"Why?" It hadn't occurred to him that Ana might know about the strange visit, or her stepmother's intentions.

"Why? Because she's on a mission to take everyone from me. Everyone I have ever loved. And I tried to keep you out of her sights—"

"I'm not afraid of her!" Tyreste yelled. "I'm not afraid of anything in this world except *losing you*."

Ana held her silence. With one of her hands on the tree, her shoulders lifted with her labored breaths. "There's evil... and then there's Magda. You want to know why Addy almost died tonight, Tyreste?" She turned to regard him over her shoulder. Her eyes glistened in the moonlight. "The koldyna poisoned an entire village to teach *me* a lesson."

Tyr could only shake his head. "But—"

"People *died* tonight because I refused to do her bidding any longer. More people will die." She turned all the way around and wrapped herself in her arms—a sad, fractured hug. "*You* will die, if I can't let you go."

He ran a hand down his throat and turned his head toward the night sky. "I know death. I've dined with it... danced with it. But I have never known what it is to give my heart away so willingly, knowing that to do so means I am entirely at the mercy of the one I gave it to. Knowing that even if she gives it back to me, I wouldn't even recognize it, for it's no longer mine at all. So I don't fear death, Ana. I'm already dead."

Ana threw herself into his arms. It happened so fast, he couldn't decide what to do with his hands, but it didn't matter—nothing did—because she was kissing him the way she used to, spreading his lips with hers. Her legs climbed his sides until he leaned down to lift her. The rest of the world fell away, and there was only the slide of her tongue lapping his and the warmth of moans he'd feared he would never hear again beyond his dreams. The clench of her fist in his hair... the squeeze of her thighs locking around his hips. The tiny, fraught scream she sounded before climbing higher, until she was no longer kissing him but looking down on him through tearful eyes.

She slid slowly back down until her feet touched the ground. "If you love me, Tyreste..." She pursed her mouth and cast her eyes toward the side before looking back. "If you truly love me, you'll pretend you don't. You'll do as you threatened months ago and ignore me when we pass on the road. You'll act as though I'm the last person in all the world you'd want to see again. And you'll do it so convincingly that Magda's eyes will pass over you."

"How?" His voice croaked. "How?"

Ana shrugged with a sorrowful smile. "If you figure it out, let me know, will you?"

"And Nessa..." The truth felt within his grasp, but he needed to hear her say it.

"I have to go." She swallowed. "I'm going to try to save as many as I can. If you can find your... your magic, you should do the same."

Tyr nodded. "And then what?"

Ana huffed a short, bitter laugh. "I can't run anymore. And it's probably futile to keep fighting when there's no way for me to win." She nodded to herself. "But that's what I'm going to do. It may be the last thing I ever do—"

203

"*Ana.*"

"But this has been going on for centuries, and no one has done anything to stop it. Someone has to try. *I* have to try."

"What do you mean centuries..." Tyr's mouth fell open.

The letters.

It had been Ana all along. The false translations. The theft. She was the only one who knew every inch of his cabin. His hiding spot.

The answer was so obvious. He'd been such a fool.

"If I survive this... if I *can* even defeat her..." Ana's cheeks puffed out with a held breath. She released it and smiled tightly. "I'll find you again."

"No, Ana, wait. *Wait.* I'm coming with—"

"Don't you dare," she warned, moving sideways, toward the alley and escape. "Don't you *fucking* dare, Tyreste Penhallow."

Ana's eyes locked onto his and then she broke away and fled into the night.

Tyreste's objections never made it past his clogged throat, but they were still more than alive in his heart, beating so hard, it was the only sound left.

He would respect her need to fight her own battles.

But he was fucking done with not fighting for *her*.

I Would Swim the Howling Sea

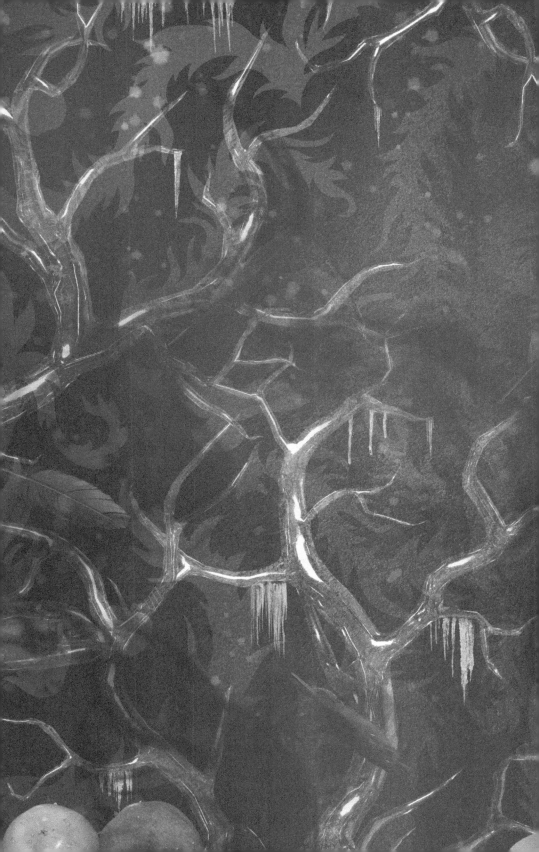

SISTER OF ASH,
BLOOD OF THE WULF

SIXTEEN
DEATH NO LONGER SCARES ME

Anastazja wasn't afraid of dying. She'd claimed it as her truth for years, never understanding that sometimes words were just words. They had to *mean* something. It wasn't until the message streamed across her mind in a swift, bold stroke—*death no longer scares me*—when she understood the monumental shift that had occurred within her after the horrors at the festival.

Her once-fear of death wasn't without value. It had kept her alive. It had pushed her blood through her veins, filling her heart, beating as swiftly and strongly as it ever had. But fear came with dread, and dread had stayed her hand many times over. Had eclipsed her creativity, demolishing any confidence she'd had in her own abilities.

Magda had to be stopped, and if Ana died trying, was there a better cause to surrender her life to?

Words were just words, until they weren't.

For the bitter truth was, she thought as she flew to Fanghelm, building her offense with every wing stroke, she was never going to save Niko, her father, or Tyreste unless she was no longer

209

around for them to be dangled as motivation for her compliance. Magda would use Niko next and then her father, but accepting those were already foregone conclusions was freeing, in a way. It freed her to storm into Magda's room without a plan and go wherever her instincts guided her.

But Ludya flagging her down on the road, just before the Fanghelm gates, made the fear return.

"Anastazja!" The vedhma wrapped her robe tight and raced down the road to where Ana had landed. "You're safe." She sagged, sighing. "Glory to the Ancestors."

"I am," Ana said, her fire returning and eyes on the keep, "but many others are not. She *poisoned*—"

"I know." Ludya's hand clamped over Ana's arm. "The word is all over the village now. We've sent the other vedhmas and veduhn down to the market to help save as many as we can. The situation is stable, as much as it can be."

"How many?"

Ludya looked at her.

"*Dead*. How many did the koldyna murder?" Ana seethed the words through clenched teeth.

"Fifteen," Ludya said. Her eyes fluttered closed in a brief moment of reverence for the dead. "The rest will recover, we believe, but only time will reveal their fates."

"Fifteen Vjestik dead." Ana's mouth fell wide, her head shaking as she pieced things together. "Fifteen hearts in the cellar."

Ludya didn't seem impressed by the connection. She squeezed Ana's arm impatiently. "The kyschun have answered your request, Anastazja. They want to see you."

"So why do you look as though someone shat in your porridge?"

"*Now*," Ludya said with a nervous look. "They've summoned you to come now."

"Summoned me?" Ana balked. "I don't answer to them."

"You do if you want an audience. They meet on their own terms or not at all."

Ana crossed her arms and angled away. The keep was half-hidden by the descending fog. Magda was no doubt inside, relishing in her destruction. Ana's blood ran hot. She was *ready* for a showdown.

But she needed the archivists. Why or how much, she couldn't know until she'd spoken to them.

And what if I can stop Magda with whatever they tell me? What if it doesn't have to end with me dying at all?

Even the idea was dangerous. She was either resolved to die or she wasn't. Hope was the last thing she needed.

"All right," she said. She squinted against the hard wind. "Where are they?"

"Somewhere you cannot fly." Ludya turned her and then released her arm. "You've been to the Shrine of the Ancestors before."

"Enough times I know I can *fly* there," Ana replied.

"That is not where we are going." Ludya pointed toward the mountain path she used to climb on foot as a girl, before Stepan had died and she'd inherited his wings. It was a long trek, one she didn't miss. She wasn't even sure she *could* walk it, in her present state of exhaustion. "I can feel your angst. We are not going up. We're going *down*."

Ana turned toward her. "What?"

"The kyschun are underground. Far, far beneath the shrine."

"How have I never known this?"

"Even if you had known," Ludya said with an apprehensive glance toward the path before starting down it, "it would not have made a difference. You wouldn't make it a single step inside their antechamber without an invitation. Besides, you've never *cared* until now, have you?"

Ana skipped steps to keep pace. "That feels an awful lot like condemnation, Ludya."

"Truth simply *is*. If truth feels like condemnation to you, then by all means, accept it as such."

Ana scoffed and jogged faster. "We were never raised to—"

211

"Arkhady has visited the kyschun many times," Ludya said, cutting in. She slowed as the path climbed, a short hill that would then drop them into a small valley.

"If that were so, then why has he been so blind to the koldyna?"

"He was not asking the right questions. What your father most wanted was a cure for his unending grief, a way to bring Ksana back. But there wasn't one. And the archivists do not share what is not asked. They often do not even share what *is* asked." Ludya paused at the peak of the hill. She pointed down into the valley, but at what, Ana couldn't tell.

"What am I looking at?"

"Do you see the place where the trees part?"

Ana looked again. The forest was a solid line at the base of the foothills, except in one spot where the patch of trees thinned. She nodded.

"The entrance is there."

"Where?"

"You'll see it when you're close."

Ana spun toward her. "You're not coming with me?"

"I was not invited," Ludya said. "But I will wait for you here."

"You can't come in with me? Even if *I* invite you?"

"I could," Ludya said, "but they may or may not reveal what you want to know in front of someone else. And you are not at liberty to take such risks right now, are you?"

Ana sighed and turned her eyes back toward the quiet, foggy valley. "What if—"

"No matter how you choose to end your question, Anastazja, I have no answer for you. But *they* might. Go, now, before others discover where you are. I'll be here when you're done."

Tyreste made it all the way to the gates of Fanghelm before he spotted Ana. She was walking away from the keep, but she wasn't alone anymore. He recognized the woman with her, though they'd never been formally introduced: Ludya. Her beloved vedhma.

He followed from a distance and hung back when they reached the short hill. He waited for what seemed like more than enough time and slipped behind a tree to spot where they'd gone.

But Ana was on her own now, marching through the valley floor. Where she was going wasn't clear, but she was headed toward the foothills. Her vedhma sat on a fallen log at the top of the hill with her eyes closed, her face flushed with something resembling grief as she comforted herself with words he couldn't hear—and wasn't sure he wanted to.

Whatever was going on, wherever Ana was going, Ludya had left her to go on alone—which seemed highly unlikely unless necessary. If so, avoiding Ludya's notice was crucial if he wanted to make it wherever Ana was headed.

There was no way he was letting her walk into a dangerous situation alone again. Isolating in her darkest hour was her way of punishing herself—for what, he intended to find out.

Tyr slipped into the forest from the north side, keeping close enough to the path to follow Ana's progress. He checked on Ludya every few paces, but she continued her strange meditations, unaware.

He fell behind, slowed by the patchy layers of ice and snow, so he slipped into a sprint that had his side aching in seconds. Each land of his boots came with a new discovery. Something hard. Something sharp. Something slippery. Something soft. Something *moving*. He kept losing sight of her, so he veered closer to the path, knowing the risks yet too excited to care.

Tyr inched out onto the path in time to see Ana disappear between two trees and go...

Down.

Into the foothills.

If he hadn't actually seen her do it, he wouldn't have believed there was anything there.

He couldn't waste a breath. With one final, hopeful glance back at the hill, comfortable that Ludya was still occupied, he launched onto the road and ran so fast, his feet barely touched the ground between strides.

Tyr slowed as the earth descended into a muddy embankment, at the bottom of which was a small arch. Angling sideways, he allowed himself to slide, arms out for balance, and came to a tumbling halt at the bottom. His hands landed on either side of the narrow arch: an entrance. He could make out nothing beyond the darkness.

The only thing to do was step inside, so he did.

Tyr moved slowly down a slim stretch of earth. The path was barely wide enough for his feet, an abyss—how deep, he couldn't see, nor was he interested in finding out—calling on either side. The cave walls glittered with crystals, catching light from an unseen source farther in. There were also drawings. Words. In Vjestikaan. The depictions, of men and wulves, seemed to tell the story of Vuk od Varem, but the glittering reflections and carvings, faded with time, rendered the tale incomplete.

The cave stories guided him deeper into the cavern. Further back in time they seemed to go, from before the Vjestik came to Witchwood Cross as refugees. He'd never heard those stories before. He wondered who had made the drawings, and why. Though paper was valuable, it still seemed an easier method of preserving histories.

Then again, he thought, who even knew the place existed?

Another few steps and he heard low, sonorous voices. It sounded like singing but was mournful and searching, a call to some deeper place existing within everyone. He felt suddenly, overwhelmingly sad, and the impulse to cry was so powerful, his eyes sprung with tears.

He came to a damn near devastating halt when one of the voices boomed, shaking the cave. Crystals shimmered and twinkled, creating a symphony that started and ended everywhere. *"ANASTAZJA WYNTER, HEIR OF OUR KIND, SISTER OF ASH, BLOOD OF THE WULF, BELLE OF HER FATHER,*

PRIDE OF THE ANCESTORS. STEP. FORWARD. TWICE. STOP."

Tyr held his arms out, wobbling for balance. He crouched to fend off vertigo before he stood again.

"YOU REQUESTED A COUNSEL WITH THE KYSCHUN, AND WE HAVE GRANTED IT."

"Hvala! Hvala, hvala, hvala! I am weighted with a great burden, and I believe you are the only ones who can help me," Ana cried out. Tyr recognized the word *hvala*, as a form of gratitude. She sounded so small and insignificant amid whatever colossal creatures had announced her. Her voice trembled, a shrill edge peaking certain words. "I am utterly at your mercy, and pray the Ancestors show you my heart is true in intention."

Fear pushed Tyr back to his feet, and he inched closer to the sounds, moving far faster than felt safe. Kyschun, kyschun. He didn't know that word. He needed to know *that* word. What they were. Why Ana had thrown herself at their mercy, and why, despite knowing having none of those answers, he was petrified.

"YOUR INTENTION IS NOT OURS TO FACILITATE OR COMMAND."

Tyr wobbled as dirt sifted down from the cave walls, set to a fresh song from the crystal chorus. His eyes stung but he pushed on, slower until he found surer footing.

"WE ARE NEITHER JUDGE NOR JURY. WE ARE KEEPERS. WE ALONE CHOOSE WHO MAY SHARE IN OUR TRUTHS. WHICH IS WHY WE WILL TELL YOU NOTHING TODAY, ANASTAZJA WYNTER."

"I... I don't understand!" Ana yelled. Tyr could barely hear her over the cave melee. "You invited me here!"

"YOU. WE INVITED YOU." The voice didn't speak again until the cave settled once more. *"BUT YOU DID NOT COME ALONE."*

Tyr went shockingly still. He even held his breath.

"I did! I did come alone! My vedhma stayed outside. It's only me here."

215

"YOU WILL LEAVE US NOW."

"No! Pros, I beg of you, there is *no one* with me. I desperately need your help!"

"YOU WILL LEAVE ON YOUR OWN, OR YOU WILL BE REMOVED."

"You don't under—"

The cave shook harder than ever before. Ana screamed. Tyr clung to the edge of the walkway to avoid being thrown into the nether, but he had to get to her. He pulled himself along with one hand, then the other.

Tiny but forceful steps pounded, growing closer, and he looked up just in time to stop her from tripping over him and flying into the darkness.

"Tyreste?" Ana huffed his name. "What in the Ancestors are you doing here? How did you—" She whipped her head around. "*You.* They meant *you!*"

"Come on, Ana, we have to go. Now."

"No, *you* have to go! I need them to talk to me! I need—" The cave shook so hard, she slipped and started to go over. Tyr yanked her arm and pulled her against him.

"Be angry with me later." He panted and nudged her in front of him. "We have to get out of here *now.*"

Ana shrugged his hand away when he tried to guide her. He stayed close, reaching for her every time the crystals sang, but she didn't want his help. She pushed on until she disappeared back into the dusky night.

By the time he made it to the arch, she was out of sight. He scrambled up the muddy embankment and found her waiting at the top, staring away from him, into the valley.

He swallowed hard and asked, "Nessa?"

Ana whipped around, her eyes as wide as saucers. She patted her dress... her breasts.

Tyr lost his footing. He stumbled sideways in the tall grass and raked his hands through his hair, trying to find another rationalization for what he'd seen.

"I... can explain," she said weakly. Her voice trailed.

He had every reason to be angry. Every right to feel deceived and wronged and lied to. But he clung to the silly thread of hope that she'd become someone else because she couldn't bear to really leave him.

His head split down the middle, sadness battling frustration and bewilderment swathing both. There was no battle to be won though, only a heart to be lost, and so he went to her, gathered her in his arms, and whispered, "I'm here now, Ana. Everything is going to be all right."

"You're well within your right to hate me." She sobbed. "I would hate me."

"Oh, Ana." He sighed, laughing softly. "I've already tried hating you, and it's not for me. Nothing you've done these past weeks erases the mark you've left on my life."

The sky opened for the rain, which came on with sudden swiftness. It swept sideways on the wind whipping through the valley, roaring off the foothills. He could still hear the sound of the crystals, of the cave turning on them. But all he could *feel* was the collapse of the wall she'd built to keep him out, crumbling brick by brick.

Her eyes were spidered with red when she leaned up to look at him. "I don't really have a cousin, Tyreste."

His solemn facade cracked, and laughter took hold of him. He shook his head and pressed her tighter. "And Grigor?"

"The man has never been with the same woman twice. I'd be stunned if he didn't have lads and lassies running all about the kingdom, but if so, he's unaware of it."

"I'm sorry for messing things up with... whatever that was." Tyreste nodded behind them. "I was afraid for you. I *am* afraid for you. What... *are* they?"

"The kyschun and kyschuna." Ludya appeared at the top of the embankment with a stern frown. "The archivists of our histories. And you, publican, just turned their anger Anastazja's way, a problem that will not be easily remedied."

"I didn't mean—"

Ana turned away to look at her vedhma. "It's not his fault, Ludya. He did what I would have done, had I watched him leave, distressed, headed for Ancestors-know-where." She glanced back at the cave, still rumbling from the aftershocks. "What I *have* done, in the creation of Nessa."

"You do not owe this boy explanations," Ludya stated. She slid partway down the hill. "Anastazja, it is already quite late. If you're not back soon..." She leveled a cool glare on Tyr that made him slide back a step.

Ana's mouth parted with an incredulous gape. "What, you don't want me to anger the koldyna? After everything she's done?"

Koldyna, Tyr mouthed, trying to recall the meaning. He'd heard the word before, from Ana, but his thoughts were too scattered from everything happening. The exceptionally weird trip into the foothills. Ludya's hostility. Whatever the fuck *Nessa* had been.

Ludya's eyes widened in warning. "What I want is to continue this conversation in private." She flicked another glare at Tyr. "Consider your words and who you are speaking them in front of."

"Tell me... how you did it," he said, finding his voice. "Ana. I want to know who—*what*— Nessa was."

"*Anastazja,*" Ludya practically hissed.

"An illusion," Ana said, her eyes cast away from them both, her voice quiet and distant. "I've been doing it since I was a girl, but it's not easy for me. I... have to focus to hold the illusion or it breaks. Flickers. Sometimes disappears entirely."

Ludya moaned. "Ancestors keep us."

"He's always known I had magic, Ludya," Ana said with a halfhearted eyeroll. "This isn't exactly a radical revelation."

"So that's why..." The past weeks caught up to Tyr in a series of bizarre revelations. "Sometimes I looked at her and saw you."

Ana nodded.

"And I thought I was losing my mind, but it *was* you."

Ana nodded at the muddy ground. "I'm sorry."

"Sorry? But..." He didn't know how to finish. *But* she was doing it because she loved him? *But* she was doing the right thing? *But* she was telling him the truth now?

"We must *go*," Ludya barked and gathered Ana from the side. But Ana didn't move. "You'll get him killed if you continue telling him things he has no reason to know!"

"I've almost gotten him killed anyway, haven't I? And Addy..." Ana's chin quivered and she spun away from them both, pressing her hands to the cluster of stone rocks. "Magda is a dangerous, dangerous creature, Tyreste. Even if I told you everything—"

"Do not dare say another word!"

"Ludya..." Ana's sigh was laden with exhaustion. "It wouldn't matter if I did tell you, Tyr, because there's nothing to be done. I thought, perhaps, the archivists... but they won't see me now. Their counsel is no longer an option."

"I really fucked up. I'm sorry."

She shook her head at the rockface. Her wet hair hung around her face, clinging to her jaw. "This is what happens when we hold our secrets too close. You care about me, and you did as I would have done. I should have seen it. Perhaps... perhaps Nessa was the true miscalculation, but I was greedy. I was *weak*. I couldn't say good-bye, even though I knew there was no other way. And now, I've kept you from moving on and put you in even more danger."

A single stitch closed on the wound rent through Tyr's heart. "I wish you had known you could tell me anything."

"It wasn't that." Ana half turned with a sorrowful smile. "She would have come for you. She *will* come for you. And now I have no fathomable idea how to protect you."

Ludya groaned through her nose and stepped between them. "Grigor and I will ward the tavern."

Tyr and Ana both looked at her. "*Ward* the tavern?" Ana asked. "This is something you can do? And what has Grigor to do with it?"

"Grigor has Vjestik magic, like many of us. Like you."

219

Ana flung her arms out. "Why did we not do this sooner, then?"

"Warding is not without limitation, Anastazja," Ludya said through strained patience. She squinted through the rain. "It thins with distance. When I am at Fanghelm, it will be far less potent than if I was nearby. When Grigor leaves the Cross, it may fade altogether."

"No," Ana said slowly, eyes darting right and left in thought. "Magda is stronger than our weakest magic. She'd sniff it out and know we're protecting something very, very dear to me. She already has her eyes on Tyreste."

Tyr desperately wanted to ask more questions, but Ana's unhindered speech revealed more than she ever had in all their private moments put together.

"Then there is only one way," Ludya said gently. "But you already know that."

Tyreste watched them both, his blood racing with fear he couldn't ascribe to anything specific.

"Go home," Ludya said, when Ana just stared into the distance. "Show your defeat. Let her see it, so she thinks she has won. Grovel if you can bear it, but you *must* disarm her, and your only weapon now is to play the part she's written for you."

Tyr had to turn his hands into fists to keep from roaring. "No. No, like fucking *hell* is Ana going back and offering herself to someone you both are so clearly terrified of. What if the... koldyna *hurts* her? She's already scared her half to death. No, I'm sorry, but it's not happening. We're not leaving her. There's no fucking way."

Ana looked up at him, her eyes sparkling above the flushing high apples of her cheeks. She seemed on the verge of laughing, but tears came instead, blending with the raindrops streaming down her cheeks. She tucked her lower lip inside her mouth and turned her head downward, but he caught her in his arms before she could shut down completely.

"You are not alone. You are *not* alone, ever." He tilted her chin up and kissed her. "*Ever.*"

"I don't care what she does to me," Ana answered. She let him kiss her again and then squeezed her eyes shut, expelling more tears. "But I am utterly *terrified* of what she will do to you if I don't obey her."

"I'm not afraid of her either, Ana." A lie, but how he wished it were the truth.

"You should be. She poisoned this village to hurt *me*."

Tyr's arms slackened.

"Yes. I'll say it again, so it really sinks in with you, so you *really* understand. Magda *poisoned the apples,* and now fifteen lives are lost, and more are forever changed. *Addy* almost died tonight. Because I could not—" Ana's voice choked. "Because I could not bear to lose those dearest to me, she sent a message that others will lose dearly instead."

"All right," Ludya said, in the placating tone of a long-suffering mother. "Tyreste, Anastazja has shared with you things she should never, ever have shared. But the price is your trust in her. Trust she knows what must be done, for you do not."

"But—"

"You will go home. If you want to protect your family, you'll stay in your cabin. Take a leave from work, and keep away from them."

Tyr shook his head sideways. "Ana, I don't like this plan. I don't like it *at all.*"

"She's right." Ana wiped her face and peered up at him. "I do have to go back. The only way to slow her destruction is to offer myself in her service once more."

"Her *service?* Ana, what the *fuck* does that mean?" Tyr's head shook wildly.

"Not tonight." She stretched up to kiss him, and for one fleeting moment in time, everything was all right. "If I can, I'll come to the cabin tomorrow. As Nessa."

"Teach me your illusions, and I'll come with you tonight!"

Ana tried to smile, but her mouth sagged. "Do you trust me?"

"Trust you?" He repeated the question because he wasn't confident in his answer. *Did* he trust her? Should he?

"*Can* you trust me is what I should have asked. You have no reason to, and I have no right to expect you to. So what I'm asking you for is faith... faith that I haven't earned. Not yet."

Yes, he decided. He might come to regret the choice, but it was the right one in the moment. "I can. And I do."

Ana kissed him again, suffocating the balance of his protestations. He could live in her kisses and require nothing else. No water. No food. No shelter. Just the promise of a moment entirely theirs.

"Then do not come for me until I come for you."

Tyr swallowed, glancing slightly away. "And you will? You're not saying this to get rid of me?"

Ana's head shook. "No, love. I think we're..." She sighed and glanced at Ludya, who nodded. "We're beyond that now."

Love. It wasn't quite the admission he'd hoped for, but it was enough. Enough to trust her and to do as she was asking him, despite everything within him aching to throw her over his shoulder and run as far as his legs could take them.

"Tomorrow, if I can. But I *will* come. I promise." Ana gathered his cold hands in hers and brought them to her mouth. "I wish I'd never gotten you into this mess."

"And I'm so grateful you did." He kissed their joined hands and reluctantly released her.

He waited for Ana's little wave as she and Ludya climbed back into the valley. Even expecting their departure, his heart wasn't ready, and the resultant fluttering forced more tears into his eyes.

She would come for him. He believed her. He had to believe her.

But when she arrived, he had no intention of being empty-handed.

SEVENTEEN

THE BLOOD WE ARE BORN WITH

Ana sat on her bed, hands folded and head bowed, flinching with every fifth or sixth condemnation Magda flung at her. She prayed all Magda saw was a contrite, broken girl who knew she had lost, ready to accept whatever mercy the koldyna chose to reap upon her.

Magda stormed from one end of the room to the next, no longer speaking. It seemed she was trying to outpace herself, to lift her speed with each pass.

She screeched to a sudden halt, planting her true form, broad and gnarled, in front of the blazing hearth. Serrated shadows cut across the room, in malignant lashes. Ana started to fight the resulting shiver down her spine, but Magda would love seeing her so unsettled, so she let it happen.

"I will be away for a couple of days," Magda said. She used her disarmingly melodic voice, the one that had charmed so many.

"Away?" Ana couldn't stop herself. "You've never left the Cross before."

223

"Need I remind you where questions fit into our arrangement?" Magda's upper lip twitched. "Nonetheless, I *will* be away. I tell you this because you will ascertain as much yourself soon enough, and I need to remind you that your behavior while I am gone will very much decide how much you suffer upon my return. Do you understand?"

Ana bit her lip and nodded, making up for her bold question. Magda's slow grin confirmed it was convincing enough.

Ana held the pitiful look, but there were fresh ideas buzzing around her head. Magda leaving the Cross might be a temporary relief, but it was wiser to assume her departure was so unavoidable, she had no choice but to leave Ana, the hearts, the hostage raven, and her work behind for something that was, somehow, even more dire.

Still. Two days without Magda.

"While you may choose to see these two days as a respite, when I return, you will either be ready for what comes next, or I will begin collecting the hearts most dearest to you. Have I been clear enough? Do you believe me now?"

What comes next? Ana fused her mouth shut from sheer will alone and forced her head to nod in the blind obeisance Magda expected.

But it wasn't pure acting anymore. Magda gone for two days, no matter the reason, meant two days when Ana could *breathe*. Could *think*.

Two days when she could see Tyreste without the fear her presence would condemn him.

Magda stepped away from the hearth, and the sinister edge to the room faded. "Plans have changed. If you do as I command when I return, your life will be yours to live a while longer. How long, I cannot say. But your purpose is greater now. Much greater."

"My..." Ana bit down the question, but Magda didn't punish her for asking, for once.

"Yes, girl. Your purpose. It seems your usefulness may have years left before expiry. If you obey me without more of your untenable defiance, I may even consider returning to you that which I have taken."

"Niko?" The word was out before she could swallow it.

"Niko," Magda stated. "And I may heal your father and soften his heart toward you, so you may bask in his adoration once again. Would you like that?"

Ana's nod was sincere. She knew better than to trust anything the koldyna dangled before her, but the witch was the only one with the power to return her father and brother to her.

For the first time in a long time, Ana had hope.

If she could summon the fortitude to do whatever Magda had in mind for her—whatever this new "purpose" was that she'd failed to define—Ana could have her life back. Not forever. Magda would find new demands, and she would take far more than she ever returned. But it could be long enough to buy time.

Magda *must* be defeated. The war would never end until she was.

But Ana could only handle one battle at a time.

"Stay out of trouble these next two days, do as I ask when I return, and you may find your joy returned to you." Magda stormed toward the door. "You have already witnessed what I will do when tested. Try to imagine what I might do next."

Ana slid from the bed to the floor when the door slammed closed. She fell to her side, clutching her knees to her chest and shaking in a fit of complicated laughter and horrified sobs.

Tyr worked his final shift in silence. He left the tavern floor to Agnes and Rikard and took up the labor of closing and prep in the back room. As soon as his mother or father showed up in the morning, he would tell them his intention to take a leave. It wasn't the best timing, with Evert, Pern, and Drago having just left. Even so, he didn't think they'd be upset about it, but they would be curious. Worried. He had only until then to find the right words to allay both.

But it was sweet Addy he struggled the most to find words for.

She'd stubbornly insisted on working, so Agnes had assigned her to peeling potatoes. But instead of sitting on her stool in the kitchen, she'd dragged it and the vat of tubers into the curing room and shut the door on everyone.

Tyr pushed open the back door, wiping his forehead sweat on his arm, and watched the sun rise beyond the trees. His parents would arrive soon. When they did, he'd be sent home for rest, and so would Addy and the others.

He returned to the kitchen, the door swinging hard behind him, and marched into the curing room. Addy didn't look up. Her violent peeling, set to anxious grunts, continued. Thousands of discarded skins painted the floors and walls, and as he watched her take the knife to the poor tuber in her hands, he saw how the gory scene had come to life.

Tyr took another step in. The candles flickered, and she finally glanced up. She swiftly ripped her attention back to peeling, chewing on her lower lip.

Addy, he signed, ducking low so she couldn't ignore him. *Can we talk? Please?*

She shifted the potato to one hand and signed with the other. Her fingers snapped in and out of place with furious twitches. *Nothing to talk about.*

There is. I need to apologize to you.

Don't want it.

Addy. Please. I fucked up. He carefully reached for the potato and knife and held them for a moment, waiting to see if she'd stab him, before he set them aside on a nearby table. The glare in her glistening eyes was more devastating than any wound she could inflict. *I was scared. I thought someone was stalking me, and it was easier to believe you had stolen the letters. It was safer if you had. I wanted it to be you, even though I didn't believe you would ever do it.*

Addy slammed the signed words against her chest, tears running down her cheeks. *I told you it wasn't me and you refused to believe me.*

I know. And I know now who it was.

Addy snorted and blinked hard. *Ana, right?*

Tyr sat back on his heels. *How did you guess that?*

Addy's eyes rolled hard. *Because she loves you, you fool. She wanted to help you. Did she tell you her big secret?*

You mean... Nessa?

Addy blinked. *I knew she was Nessa the day I met her.*

What? How?

When you choose to be blind to the truth, you are.

Tyr grunted. *How did you know?*

I saw what you refused to. And then I asked her. She didn't deny it.

Tyr didn't know what to make of that. *You talked to her about it?*

Addy nodded. *Can I have my potato back? And my knife?*

He could berate himself later. It didn't matter who had known what or when. He was beginning to realize how little most things mattered. *I love you, Adeline. I have never been more sorry, or more wrong, in my life. Seeing you so sick...* Tyr's words caught. *I owe Ana a debt I can never repay.*

Adeline watched him without signing back, but her eyes softened.

Tyr gathered her hands in his and brought them to his cheek. He inhaled the scent of her, his baby sister, the one who had saved his life so many times when his heart had been heavy. Why had he never told her so?

He kissed her hands and released them so he could sign again. *You are the sunshine on my darkest day. My best friend. I need you, Addy. I suppose I need you more than you've ever needed me—*

Adeline leaped off the stool and threw herself into his arms, knocking them both back. He held her, laughing, until she pushed back onto her knees and signed, *Do you want to know what I was hiding from you?*

Tyr did, but he shook his head. *No, it's not important.*

But it is, you dumb man. It is to me. Addy scampered to her feet and left the curing room. He followed her into the kitchen and found her climbing a shelf, her tongue wedged between her teeth as she slapped her hands around.

Need help? he signed.

The offended look she flashed him had him lifting his hands in surrender.

Her eyes brightened finally, and she jumped down. She held the papers in her hand, shaking them to get him to take them.

Tyr sifted through the stack and looked up.

I learned more Old Ilynglass, and I wanted to show you I was getting better.

Tyr tucked the papers under his arm and signed, *How?*

I re-read your old translations. Then I made a cipher, like the ones you make for yourself.

You made a cipher? His eyes filled with fresh tears. *All by yourself?*

Addy nodded. *I wasn't ready to show you. I wanted it to be perfect first.*

Addy. Tyr's cheeks puffed. He blew out a breath. *This is incredible.*

I know.

He laughed. *I really am proud of you. You're a far faster learner than I ever was. Father used to throw up his hands at me almost every day in exasperation.*

He still does.

The back door opened, and their mother stepped through. Fransiska made a beeline for Addy and yanked her in for one of her famous hugs that made Tyr nostalgic in a way he wasn't prepared for. It reminded him of how she'd held him to her bosom with enough force to choke him the day he'd returned to his family from the "dead."

You snuck out while I was sleeping, Fransiska signed furiously, though the accusation in her eyes was pointed at Tyreste. "She should not be working, Tyreste."

This wasn't my doing. You know how she is, he signed in defense, and Addy laughed.

Waited for me to fall asleep. Little demon, you are. She pulled Addy in for another hug and mussed her hair. *Go on home,* she signed when she pulled away. *That's an order.*

Addy rolled her eyes but nodded and pranced away. She turned back at the door and made a heart with her hands, looking straight at Tyreste. She nodded.

Emotional, he nodded back.

"I'm glad to see the two of you have mended things. All I want to do is hold her against me for the rest of her life, but she's almost a woman now, and she needs herself more than she needs her mother," Fransiska said. She swept her scrutinizing gaze over him, but exhaustion seemed to dull her usually acute observation skills. She breathed in through her nose and looked past him. "We almost lost her, Tyr. It was so close. Minutes maybe."

For the rest of his life, he'd see Addy convulsing on the table, bloody foam crusting around her mouth. "It was close."

"I don't know how Anastazja knew to come when she did, but..." Fransiska shuddered through a breath. Her mouth trembled closed. "Fifteen dead, Tyreste. Fifteen poor souls. Some are already calling it the next Nok Mora."

"Because it is a nightmare," he said. "I can't think of a better word for it."

"Nor can I. So many Vjestik are still wounded from what happened back then, and now they've been dealt another terrible blow. Perhaps it's true, and they really are cursed."

They're cursed all right, but only a few know the name of it.

"Anyway." She tried to smile. "I never should have said what I did about Ana before. It was terrible and untrue and, more than that, unfair. We don't choose the blood we are born with, do we?"

"I appreciate that, but Ana loves Addy too," Tyr said, switching topics before his mother's kindness had him crying again. "Look, Mama, I want to take a leave from the tavern for a while. Not forever, just for a little while. I just have so many translations, and—"

229

Fransiska tugged him close with one arm and kissed the side of his head. He was far too tall now for her to kiss the top, as she had when he'd been a boy. "I don't need an explanation, son. None of you are indebted to us. Take whatever time you need."

"Really?"

"Really." Fransiska kissed him again and let him go. "But I *would* like to ask something of you. I've been mulling it all night, and I know why you may have good reason to refuse, but I believe you have more reason to grant it."

Tyr waited anxiously for her to tell him.

"The weather has broken, though probably not for long, and that means we are long overdue for a family campfire."

He laughed. "Obviously I'll be there. It's a family campfire, Mama."

"Not you." Fransiska shook her head. "Well, of *course* you. But I would like you to invite Anastazja."

Tyr's expression froze. "Ana?"

"Will you do that for me?"

"But..." There had never been an invite extended to anyone outside the family. They'd only started inviting Stojan after Agnes had made it clear she intended to marry him when she "looked fetching in her gowns again."

"I don't know what happened between the two of you." Fransiska frowned and held a hand up. "And I do not wish to know, for you're a man, and your business is your own. How *I* feel about it has no bearing on your life, and I know that. I know it."

"Mama—"

"But when she saved our Addy, she became a part of us in a way no law nor blood could ever displace. And it would be my *honor* to include her in the last truly sacred thing we have as a family." Fransiska met his eyes. "So will you do this for me? Will you ask her?"

His eyes stung as he nodded. He cleared his throat. "Of course. I don't know if she'll come, but I'll ask."

"She'll come." Fransiska smiled and wiped the exhaustion from her eyes. She reached for her apron, hanging from a series of hooks on the wall. "Don't worry about your shifts, Tyreste. Stojan has already offered to come in more, and once Faustina delivers and is healed, she's eager to return as well. We will never need more than we already have. The Guardians have always provided, and after watching another child of mine return to life, I know now they'll never forsake us."

232

EIGHTEEN
THE FUTURE BELONGS TO NO ONE

Ana had been expecting Tyreste or Addy. Tyreste's raven had said only, *If you can, come to the tavern at dusk for a surprise. It would mean a lot to my mother. And me.*

But Olov was the one waiting when she knocked on the locked tavern doors.

"You closed Top again?" she asked, before realizing who had answered. "Oh. Mr. Penhallow. Hello."

"About twice a year, we shut it down for a special occasion, but I believe this is a first, in the history of our business, to have done it twice in the same week," Olov answered and stepped aside so she could enter. He threw the door bolt and secured it with a lock. "I'm glad you came. Everyone else will be too."

Ana looked around the empty tavern. "Tyreste said Mrs. Penhallow wanted me here?"

"We all do," Olov said and swallowed her in a hug. His eyes gleamed when he let her go. "There is no gratitude in this world adequate for what you did for us, madam."

"Oh..." Ana didn't know how to respond. "There's none necessary, Mr.—"

"Olov," he said with a fast, gentle grin. "And my wife is Fransiska. There is no need for formalities with us, especially not now. If there's one thing a taverner understands, it's that family is a choice."

"Then please call me Ana." She hesitated before saying her next words. "It's what my friends and family call me. Even my mother was not madam to those who knew her best."

Olov nodded. "And that is why we asked you here tonight, Ana. We would like for you to know us better... and if it pleases you, we'd love to know you better as well."

Ana tingled with the potential of such a gift. She fixed her stare on the same bar where she'd first spotted the man who had stolen her heart with a crooked smile. To know him better, his people better, though... how utterly terrifying. A glimpse into a life that could never be hers.

She nodded anyway.

"Come then." Olov held out an arm and ushered her into the back room. She moved ahead, knowing her way through the kitchen. She turned when she reached the back door, and he gestured for her to exit.

Once outside, he carefully stepped around her and led the way. At first she thought he would take her to the spot she'd been with Tyreste before, the one she wasn't supposed to know about, but they went right past the campsite and moved deeper into the forest.

"Watch your step for this next part. The logs are covered with slick moss," Olov called from ahead—a timely warning, for Ana nearly upended herself when her boots failed to grip. She righted herself, dodging ludicrously oversized toadstools and rough thatches of brambles, eventually catching up.

Farther on, there were two logs stacked, and she had started to search for a way to go around when Olov doubled back and lifted her over the obstruction like she was nothing more than a doll. "As a tall man, sometimes I forget not everyone has my long legs," he said sheepishly, and instead of going on ahead, he hung back and walked by her side.

The canopy of bowing pine branches thickened the deeper they went, and before long, darkness had obscured the path entirely. She moved slower, guided only by the sensations greeting her boots, but Olov gently looped his arm through hers and helped her through the absence of light.

Laughter cut through the solitude of the forest. A dance of light flickered through the occasional gap in the trees. "Almost there," Olov said, smiling from the side. "Are you hungry? Thirsty?"

"A little of both," she said. Her appetite had been nearly non-existent for weeks, but her stomach suddenly rumbled, and her tongue longed for something to wet it.

"Agnes made a rhubarb stew, and Tyreste, well, I'm sure you're familiar with his cider."

"Very." Ana smiled and quickened her pace to catch the light revealing the path.

Olov shuffled down a short, slippery hill and turned to help her navigate it. When she reached the bottom, they were in a clearing, centered by a roaring bonfire contained by boulders. All the Penhallows were there, save the ones who had left. Fransiska. Adeline. Agnes and her betrothed, Stojan, someone Ana and Niko had played with when they were children, before Magda had stolen their innocence. Rikard and his wife, Faustina, another person Ana had known her whole life. Faustina and Agnes were both full with child, and Ana's heart swelled to see Vjestik and stranjak so united. The Penhallows had integrated into their society so smoothly, it was hard to remember they weren't Vjestik at all.

Tyreste had spotted her first and was looking her way, his eyes lidded. He moved sideways on the log to make room for her.

Ana removed her cloak and draped it over the log before sitting. She glanced around, expecting some of them to be laughing at her for wanting to keep her gown tidy, but no one was. They only waited for her to get settled.

Tyreste kissed her temple and handed her a cider. "I wasn't sure you'd come, but I'm so glad you're here."

Ana's face flooded with heat. She brought the cider to her mouth. Suddenly bashful, she pulled it away. "Me too."

One by one, the others came over to thank her. They embraced her, kissed her, and whispered their gratitude. Fransiska was last, sobbing through her words and holding so tight to Ana, it seemed she'd never let go. But Ana didn't want her to. The sobs hit her next, remembering how wonderful and pure it was to be held by a mother figure, as she mourned her own mother again.

"You will never know anything but love from a Penhallow. You are one of us," Fransiska said as she pulled away and kissed her on both sides of Ana's mouth, like her mother used to do. "And I mean that, Anastazja." She was still sniffling as she returned to her own log.

Addy smiled at Ana from across the fire. She signed, *We love you. You belong here.*

Ana bowed over her knees to hide her embarrassing weeping.

"Hey," Tyreste whispered. "You belong here. And you're safe. Tonight is for joy."

Ana pulled herself up, blinking away the sting from her eyes. She passed a smile around the circle. "Thank you for inviting me. I know you feel I've done something exceptional, but I love... I love Adeline." She signed the words to Addy. "And I..." She glanced at Tyr, her chest full of fear and the other emotion, the one not safe to feel.

"It's all right. You can say it. None of us can stand Tyr and his whinging either," Rikard quipped.

Everyone laughed, including Ana. Tyreste rolled his eyes and nudged her in mock offense.

The other Rikard, her favorite mouser, ripped a shrill howl from somewhere in the woods. Ana stretched her hand out and was rewarded with a soft headbutt moments later.

"That's bloody shite," Rikard said. "Named a cat after his favorite brother, and the cursed thing won't come anywhere near me."

"Favorite brother?" Tyreste asked. "You think *that's* why I named him Rikard? Couldn't be because I loved screaming 'get your shit together, Rik' so much?"

Rikard the Mouser hissed, and everyone was laughing again.

"The little bugger is a fabulous judge of character. Aren't you, Riki?" Agnes said.

"Cats are a good omen in Vjestik lore," Faustina said. "Unless, of course, you're my husband."

Rikard squinted at her from the side. She laced their hands tight and brought them to her mouth with a laugh.

"It's been a long time, Ana," Stojan said from across the fire. "Kahk si?"

"How am I... Where would I even start?" she said lightly, her eyes flaring. "I'd be lying if I said things had been good since Oma died, Stoj."

"Ksana was such a bright light," Faustina said wistfully.

"That she was," Stojan agreed. "May the Ancestors forevermore preserve Ksana. And Stepan, a good man taken young, to help keep our people fed. We remember them as the ones who came before so others could come after." He raised his mug, and everyone else followed. "By the wings of this life or the bones of the next."

Ana and Faustina repeated the old Vjestik refrain. Tyreste clinked his mug to Ana's, his eyes still fixed on her as he took a swallow.

"Thank you." Ana wiped her mouth. A soft calm stole over her, one she hadn't felt in a long time. She was safe with the Penhallows, in a way she hadn't been since her mother had been taken. "For all of this. For inviting me."

"You might be singing another tune when Agnes's stew gives you the—" Rikard was cut off when something sailed from the other side of the fire and hit him in the shoulder. "That fucking hurt, Ag!"

"There's a word for that. What is it, darling..." Agnes fingered her chin. "Ah, yes. Justice."

Faustina passed Ana a bowl. "Don't listen to Rik. It's really quite good."

Ana nodded her thanks. "I'm sure it is."

"Ana, love, we haven't seen Steward Wynter in the village in some time. How is your father these days?" Fransiska asked. She knelt to add more logs to the fire.

"I'm afraid he's been unwell," Ana said cautiously. Tyreste's hand slid to the outside of her thigh. His fingers tapped along the edge of her dress, a reminder he was there.

"I'm so sorry to hear that. We'll beseech the Guardians for his swift return to good health," Olov said. "And your stepmother?"

"Ana's stepmother is not worth wasting our breath on, and we won't speak of her tonight," Tyreste said. He brushed his thumb along her thigh. "We've known our share of those people, haven't we?"

Everyone nodded, muttering agreement. Agnes translated the message with her hands for Adeline, as she had been the whole time.

Ana smiled at Tyreste from the side, nearly losing herself in the dreamy look he had trained on her.

She loved him so much.

She had always loved him.

Fear had taken so much from her.

Let's play a game, Addy signed. She practically bounced on her log.

"Let me guess, Addy, you already have one in mind," Rikard said, signing the words as he shook his head.

Ana looked at Tyreste for an explanation, but he was laughing, signing, and speaking at the same time. "Finish the Story, right?"

Addy nodded exuberantly.

Rikard grumbled.

"Finish the Story?" Ana asked.

"Just watch." Tyreste stood. "I'll start. There was this cat, and he was *very* charming." He winked at Ana as the others laughed and groaned. "He was named after a boy no one much liked but tolerated, for he occasionally did good work in between his favorite pastime, which was complaining about everything."

Ana laughed into her mug as Rikard jumped to his feet. "You failed to mention how *handsome* the boy was, and charming to boot. The cat, however, was a proper asshole, and one day, when it was busy shaking its ugly tail for no apparent reason, the handsome lad scooped it into a bag—"

"Nope, my turn!" Agnes cried. "No bag could hold the champion mouser, and so it fled, taking a flap of cheek from the not-quite-handsome boy. He devoured it, thinking, if only I had more, it would make a right good stew."

"Ass stew," Stojan muttered, shaking his head at the dirt.

Rikard's chest puffed. He turned his head right and left. "You b—"

"Not your turn anymore, darling," Faustina said. She pecked him on the cheek and stood. "The cat was known for far more than its mousing. When no one was looking, it snuck up onto the shelves in the kitchens and learned to read from Tyreste's stacks and stacks of translations. And not just *any* language, but all of them. He didn't even require a cipher! For mousers are particularly smart kitties. Smarter than handsome boys even, if you can believe it."

"Lies," Rikard groused.

Addy waved her hand, indicating she wanted to go next. *But the cat, most of all, was loyal. He loved those who loved him. Particularly the one who had saved him, Tyreste, but there was another he loved even more.* She smiled directly at Ana. *For he saw through her hard outer shell, straight to the woman's heart, and he knew there was so much goodness there.*

Ana's throat dried up. She reached for her mug, and Tyreste scooted it her way. But instead of taking a sip, she surprised herself by standing. "I'll go, if that's all right."

"Your turn," Olov said, grinning.

"The woman, she..." Ana looked down at Tyreste and immediately she wished she hadn't. His gentle, patient expression ripped her heart out. "Well, she knew a proper mouser when she saw one. Just as she knew a proper man when she saw one. Like herself, he was tortured by a past that had wounded him beyond belief. But through him she saw there could be... could be another way. Far from the pain. The fear." Ana ran her thumbs under her eyes. "But it *really* cannot be overstated how smart this mouser is, and so the woman ran away with the cat and left the world behind."

"What an ending!" Olov exclaimed. He clapped his hands. "Another round?"

"Yes!" Agnes and Faustina cried, at the same time Rikard pursed his mouth with a disgusted frown.

Ana set her mug aside and drew her knees up. Her eyes fluttered as she enjoyed the cross talk and banter, and when Tyreste looped his arm around her and pulled her close, she let it happen. When he kissed her head, pausing to trade barbs with his brother, and then gave her a gentle squeeze, instinctual and warm and perfect, she realized there could be nothing better in all the world than these moments she wished would last forever.

The games turned to conversation. Her inhibitions fell away, and she joined in as easily as if she'd been a part of their circle forever. They teased her like she was one of them. She moved to the cauldron and refilled their mugs, bouncing between logs as the night wore on. She laughed so hard with Agnes, her face ached. She cried with Fransiska, conversed with Olov, and sparred with Rikard. Reminisced with Stojan and Faustina, and swapped secrets with Addy.

But the best part of the night was how natural it felt to be a part of Tyreste's life—to fall into his arms without looking over her shoulder.

"You're fading," he said, brushing her hair away from her eyes and kissing the spot where it had lain. "Shall I walk you home?"

Ana remembered the first time Tyreste had walked her home, after they'd shared a magical night under the stars. She hadn't stopped buzzing until morning. There'd even been a moment when she'd thought perhaps happiness *wasn't* out of her reach.

But tonight she didn't want to go home.

"No," she whispered, her voice husky with drink and brashness. "Take me home with you."

The veins in his jaw flexed. "Is that really what you want?"

Ana nodded.

He pulled her to her feet amid whistles and *oohs*. Rikard made a snide comment about Tyreste going to bed alone. Noting the flush of embarrassment in his cheeks, she brazenly gathered her hands behind his head and kissed him deeply enough to warrant an apology to his parents later.

"Oy, there are children out here!" Rikard cried.

Agnes and Faustina whistled.

Ana laced her hand in Tyreste's and looked around at the gathering of people she wished, desperately, could be her own. "Thank you for a night I'll not soon forget."

"You won't have to," Fransiska said softly. Her warm, knowing smile passed over them both. "For we expect to see you at the next one as well."

"I would love that," Ana said, her voice breaking, and let Tyreste lead her away.

Tyr added logs to the fire to bring it back to life. He had one eye on Ana, who was perusing his sparse cabin with her arms crossed over her torso in a protective hold.

She's nervous, he realized. He was nervous too. Though he'd dreamed of bringing her back to the place they'd made so much magic before, with each passing day it had felt more and more like fantasy.

But Anastazja was very much *not* a fantasy. Her blonde curls were a tangled mess from the wind, quite the opposite of his imagination, where she always appeared without a hair out of place. He'd seen her as thus in his dreams because that was what she'd always been to him: a dream.

Seeing her dress wrinkled, her boots coated in mud, and her hair affright... Ahh, he loved *this* Ana because she was real. She wasn't a dream or beyond his reach at all. She was there because she wanted to be, and though he didn't know how to help untangle her from the bonds of her evil stepmother, that seemed a problem for another day.

"Ack," he muttered as his boots veered too close to the fire, in his daze.

"Everything all right over there?"

"Fantastic. Almost lost a foot. And you? Anything new on the empty wall that wasn't there before?"

Her laugh had a smoky edge. "Just eyeing this crack here in the board, trying to decide if it was a few inches longer than before."

Something else is a few inches longer at the moment, he thought and then cursed himself for assuming she'd come for that. "I think they're all spreading, truth be told. Gonna send a nasty letter to the architects when I get around to it."

"I thought Evert designed the cabin?"

"*Designed.* I built it and, ah, didn't really follow *all* of his advice. Hence..." He gestured around, and her giggle in return made him weak. He didn't know how he was going to last a night without pulling her on top of him.

"Say no more." Ana clicked her tongue. "Did I ever tell you Niko and I built a fort in the forest behind the keep?"

Tyr turned and leaned against the bricked hearth, crossing his arms. "All by yourselves?"

"Well, mostly. Grigor was in town, and he stopped by every few hours to grunt at us about something we'd done wrong."

Tyr chuckled. "Sounds like your onkel."

"Onkel?" Ana arched a brow. "Your Vjestikaan is improving."

"I know a few words, like all stranjak." He shrugged. "Wasn't good enough to translate the letters."

Ana's soft smile froze, then faded. "It was safer for you not to know."

Tyr pushed off of the hearth. "The first one..." He had to tread carefully. The last thing he wanted was to scare her away. "Was translated correctly though, wasn't it?"

Ana cast a thoughtful look toward the side and nodded. "It was foolish to leave it like that, but I wanted to... to do something for you. To help you. Only after did I realize how dangerous the letters were, and I regretted... I should have changed the message the first time, but by then, it was too late. And I knew as soon as I'd placed the fake ones on your table that you'd know that's what they were."

"Then why did you?"

"I don't know, Tyreste." She tilted her head upward and pressed her mouth tight. Her irises sparkled with fresh tears. "I don't know anything anymore."

Though what he most wanted to do was pull her into his arms and love her, he peeled her cloak away instead. "Go on, have a seat by the fire. I can heat up more cider and then... then I'll take the cot Addy sometimes sleeps on, and you can have my bed."

Ana turned partway and craned a hand up. She cupped one side of his face and slowly breathed out, drinking him in. Her mouth formed a small, desperate O. "Or you could take me to bed, and we could pretend, for one night, that this is how it was always meant to be."

Her invitation shattered his resistance. He leaned down and kissed the inside of her palm, breathing her in before scooping an arm underneath her and lifted her. Her light whimper made his cock so hard, he almost speared her through his pants.

His room was a mess because he hadn't made time to tidy after tearing it apart, looking for the letters she'd stolen. The letters she'd snuck in to translate because she couldn't bear to be away from him, no matter what she'd said the last time she'd come there with him. The letters she'd forged to keep him safe.

All this time he'd wasted.

He laid her gently on the bed. Even the way she wriggled to get comfortable stirred something both protective and primal within him.

But that wasn't what she wanted, he realized, as he watched her head loll sideways on the pillow, her glazed eyes following his every move. Nor was it what he wanted.

He climbed in beside her and brushed his lips along the hollow of her throat, enjoying the rumble underneath her flesh. He groped for the stays on the front of her dress, trying to become the calm gentleman the moment demanded. Her hands moved faster than his though, and he let her take over, the lump in his throat growing thicker as more of her soft, pale flesh was exposed.

Ana had hardly reached the last lace before he tugged the heavy, untenable fabric down, shimmying it over the flare of her hips, and down, where it caught on her feet. She kicked several times and sent it fluttering off the bed in a heap.

She went for his tunic next, yanking it up and over his head. He rolled sideways to free himself of his pants and was barely out of them before she had his face in her hands, demanding another kiss.

She moaned softly as her tongue slid from his mouth. "You're going to get yourself killed."

"And what life is worth living if you have to give up what you love most?" Tyr dragged the inside of his bottom lip along her jaw, stopping at her ear. "You may as well kill me yourself. It would be quicker than the slow death I've been dying since you walked away. The thousand tiny little deaths I've died every day since."

"Tyreste." She moaned. The name trilled on her tongue, and no one had ever said it in such a way that left him so bare and exposed and needing. "We're doomed, the two of us. But I do love you, Tyreste Penhallow. I was afraid to say it, and I am still, because such a thing can never be unsaid, can it?"

She licked her lips and sucked them in, but he pushed against her mouth with his thumb and released them, kissing away a small piece of her fear. He was still reeling from her confession, still plumbing the depths of the past months for a proper response. She'd said it at last, not in an indirect, searching way but leaving no room for guessing or interpretation. *I do love you, Tyreste Penhallow.* "Tomorrow we might—"

"There's only tonight, Ana." He rumbled the words along her lips, parted to receive more of his words, his kisses. "The future belongs to no one."

Tyr no more believed the words than any other lie he'd told, but to waste a single precious moment dwelling on Magda or whatever else Ana wasn't telling him was to rob themselves of what they both needed so much. What they'd both earned, in their suffering.

"Volemthe," she said. "You know the word?"

Tyr nodded. "It means... I love you, right?"

"It means so much more in Vjestikaan. The word is never wasted. Never frivolous. And I could say it to you, over and over—volemthe, volemthe, volemthe—and it would still never come close to how I feel." She closed her eyes and exhaled. "Are we fools, Tyreste?"

"Anastazja," he said between kisses. He arched his back and lifted to meet her eyes. "I won't ever pretend again I don't love you. To those who wish to do us harm, fine, but to you? Never again. If this is all we get..." He bowed his head, and it was her turn to break *his* reticence, sliding her finger under his chin to lock their gazes again. "Then you'll know it was real. That I loved you in a way I never imagined I could love anyone. The last thing I'll ever know, before the Guardians declare my promise spent, is my love for you, and if they so allow it, volemthe from beyond and forever."

Ana lunged upward and wrapped her arms around his neck, burying her face against his pulse. "It's always been so... hungered with us." She articulated her words slowly, putting voice to what they'd both already decided. "But that's not how I want it tonight."

"Nor I." He swept the words through her mussed hair. "Do you trust me?"

She nodded against his neck. Her short, quick breaths were evidence of her vulnerability, and he would give her no reason to regret it.

"Open your eyes, my love." He gently laid her back onto the pillow and gazed at her. "Look at me."

Her soft, wide-eyed blinks pushed his heart into his throat.

"Don't let them close, not even for a second," he whispered and reached down, circling his cock to guide himself. He pushed against her core, his eyes fluttering back when he felt how ready she already was to receive him.

Her throat jumped when she nodded. A throaty gasp rippled off her tongue when he entered her, her hips lifting in encouragement.

Tyr planted his elbows on the pillow and rested his forehead against hers as he moved in her, measuring each plunge to draw it out and quieting his urge to go faster, to consume her. Her eyes stayed fixed toward his, just like he'd asked, but they rolled back every time he filled her full, and it made him want to do it over and over and over again, until there was nothing left to do but lose himself in her dreamy gaze. "Like that?" he asked.

Ana moaned, raking her teeth along her bottom lip. "Like that."

Tyr slowed his pace more, enjoying every soft and pliant and soaking inch of her as he dragged his cock in... out. With each stroke, he gave her what she needed, sinking as deep as he could and then pausing for the reward of her delicious response. Her hips trembled and bucked for more, but he didn't move until she clenched so hard, he nearly exploded.

"You're not playing fair," he teased, sliding all the way out. He slammed back in, jolting a gasp from her.

"Just following your lead," she said and hooked both legs around his back. She inched her heels higher and higher, until they were near his biceps. "Seems like you wanted to go deeper."

"Never deep enough." Tyr grunted and draped her legs over his shoulders, pounding and thrusting. His mouth watered with longing, and he flexed his hands on her calves to keep from losing control and injuring her.

Ana exhaled in disappointment when he pulled out, but her eyes widened again in delight when he gripped his cock and ran the head along her clit in teasing circles.

Her eyes threatened to close, but she braced, gripping the sheets tight enough to rip them from the corners of his bed.

"You deserve to feel pleasure. You deserve everything. Look at me, Anastazja."

Her breaths were labored, as stilted as the rest of her. But she set her eyes on his with a look so vulnerable, it was time to reward her for it.

Tyr crawled on his hands and knees, relishing the heave of her breasts as she panted through her confusion. With his eyes still fixed toward hers, he licked his lips and glided his tongue from ass to clit in long, deliberate passes. Once. Twice. Three times. He felt every muscle in her legs tighten and watched her belly go concave from tightening. When he was satisfied she'd been patient long enough, he breathed deep and sucked her swollen bud through his teeth, the way she'd always loved.

Ana's scream rocked the cabin. She thrashed into her release but he held tight, his arms hooked around her thighs as she came undone. He didn't relent when her orgasm faded to spasms, and it was a short climb before she was moaning and crying his name, coming again and again.

Tyr sat back on his heels and ran his tongue along his lips to taste her again. He climbed over her, but she peeled up off the bed with a feral squint and shoved him backward. Before he could topple off the end, she lunged for him and dragged him back, shoved his cock to the back of her throat, and slurped and whimpered as her fingers dug against his ass to drive him even deeper. Stars exploded behind his eyes, every inch of him roaring to life in the most intense stab of pleasure he'd ever known. He feared choking her, but she dug her fingers deeper, like it wasn't

247

enough for her, and as she peered up, her pupils blown, he spilled his release along her tongue and down her throat.

Somehow, spent as he was, he still found himself back on his hands and knees, backing her up until she was again lying down, pliant, her legs spread in anticipation. He settled between them again, nestling inside her.

"You deserve pleasure as well." Ana's words were cropped, incomplete from the force of his lovemaking. "You deserve everything."

Tyr slowed his pace and spread his palms down her face, planting them on either side of her head on the pillow. "I *have* everything. I have you."

Sadness crept into her eyes. Her lips moved without speaking. He didn't need her to say anything, because everything she was thinking lived in her tortured expression.

"I love you, Ana. And I believe, with my whole soul, that there is nothing in this world more powerful than a heart that beats for another."

Ana brought her hands around his and peeled them away from the pillow. She turned to the side with a pained sob. "Will you hold me, Tyreste?"

"Will I hold you?" He drew a shaky breath. "Of course. Of course I'll hold you." He slid out, but she shook her head.

"Stay inside. All night if you can," she said. "Until morning."

Tyr blinked his own fresh tears away and nodded. "I can do that."

He carefully moved in behind her and tugged his quilt over the both of them. Her smooth, warm flesh fit so perfectly against his, he wondered how they'd never held each other like that before—how they'd wasted so much fucking time protecting their wounded hearts from clinging to something real.

When he found the perfect spot, he entered her and secured himself in place. He tangled one leg through hers to keep them joined and nuzzled his face between her shoulders. "Like this?"

Ana murmured something in a sleepy, distant voice. She trailed a hand along her outer thigh, offering it to him, and he laced his fingers with hers. "I want to feel... your seed inside of me. I want to wake up with it inside of me."

Tyr swallowed back a furious wave of desire. That wasn't what she'd asked for. But even the slightest movement from her had him baring down, fighting another swift finish. Each moment was exquisite torture, every slide against her tight, warm pussy a gift and a curse.

"Don't hold back," Ana said, reading him as well as he'd been reading her all night. "Give it to me."

He rocked into her with a climax even more powerful than the last, giving her everything he had left. When the release subsided, he snuggled her, creating a tight seal between their bodies he hoped would hold all night. The sound she made when they locked into perfect place, a contented sigh, made all the rest seem so inconsequential.

She was his, and he was hers, and no matter what he'd said, he would never be satisfied with just tonight.

Tyr was prepared to die if it was what the Guardians demanded, but he was never, ever again turning his back on the keeper of his heart.

Never.

Ever.

Again.

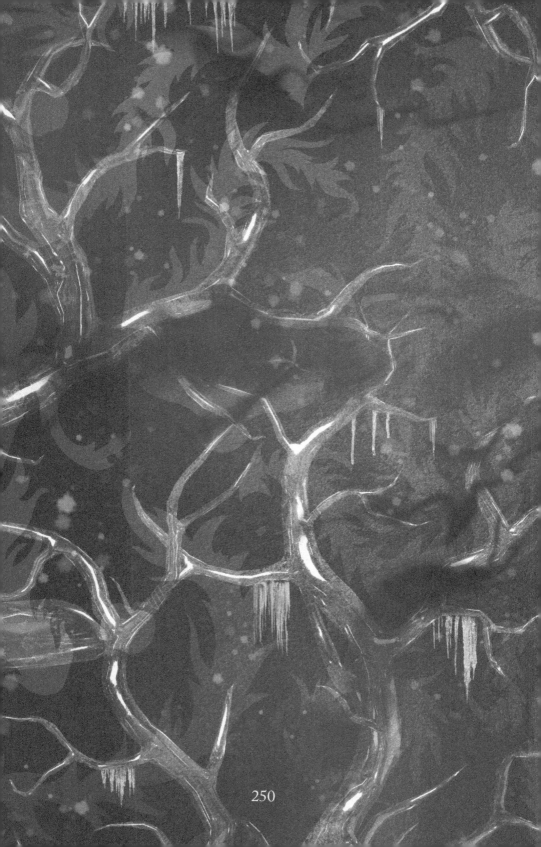

NINETEEN
KISSED BY HAPPINESS

The delicious aroma of pan-fried bread and Tyreste's famous hot cider stirred Ana from the best sleep she'd had in years. She rolled forward in the bed, a touch sore, the throb between her legs reminding her how she'd spent her slumber hours.

She felt a flush meet the ends of her smile. The entire night had been amazing, better than her most indulgent fantasy. The warmth of a family who only needed each other. A lover's safe and gentle caress, and a much-needed restoration after.

Ana reluctantly peeled herself away from the bed. She was still nude, but her gown, crumpled on the floor at the foot of the bed, was a muddy disaster. The idea of anything so foul touching her skin after she'd been kissed by happiness seemed an affront to the gift the Ancestors had given her last night.

She pulled the quilt from the bed instead, wrapped it around her shoulders, and padded into the kitchen.

Tyreste was at the small stove, flipping bread in an old iron pan. But that wasn't what caught her eye, nor what stirred her desire. He hadn't bothered putting on a shirt and wore only trousers, that, without his buckles, sagged around the edge of his hips. His muscled back rippled as he tossed the bread in the air and deftly caught it, chuckling to himself in approval.

Ana, smiling, tiptoed across the usually creaky boards, avoiding detection until she craned up to kiss the back of his neck.

Tyr leaped, pan swinging, and nearly clocked her with it. "Woman!"

She covered her mouth with laughter at his narrowing eyes. He set the pan on the stove and charged forward, scooped her up, and tossed her over his shoulder, growling playfully through her squeals.

"All right, I'm sorry!" Ana protested, swatting his ass as he spun her. "But that smells *so* lovely."

Tyreste sat her down, offering another squint of warning before he returned to the stove. "Damn right it does. When do you ever get to eat fry bread at Fanghelm?"

"I don't eat breakfast, so I wouldn't know what they serve," Ana replied. "At least, not anymore."

"Don't care for it?" Tyreste asked over his shoulder.

"It's more the company than the food," she muttered.

He nodded to himself and didn't probe further.

"If my father ever tasted your cider, he'd pay you a fortune for the recipe."

"No recipe," Tyreste said. He dumped the last piece of bread from the pan onto the others stacked on a plate and pushed the pan off the flame. "It's just... the way I made it when I was at the Reliquary."

Locked away in their dungeon was what he meant, but if he'd wanted to talk about it, he would have elaborated more. "Well, I love it. It's a comfort to me. It feels..." She trailed off, feeling silly.

He turned and leaned against the hearth. "Feels what, Ana?"

"It's nothing." She lowered her eyes.

"We're past that, right?"

"What?"

"Holding back. Keeping our truths from each other."

She nodded and shrugged. "It feels... safe, I was going to say. Like home should feel."

Tyreste's mouth stretched into a grin. He tapped his hands on the stone behind him and pushed off. "Have a seat. Go on. I'll bring everything over."

Ana breathed deep and sat in the chair she'd always chosen. He'd often fed her before their acrobatic sessions, but in the years she'd been coming to his cabin for sex, they'd never just shared a meal because they wanted to.

Everything was different now, and she wasn't sure what it meant.

Tyreste hummed to himself as he flitted about the kitchen, gathering the plate of bread, the mugs, and linens for them both. He set it all on the table and snatched a thin jacket from a nearby rack, then shrugged it on, to her dismay.

"Eat up," he demanded, nodding at the plate and then her. He swallowed a mouthful of cider and dug in without waiting.

Ana just watched him, her heart swollen with confusion.

"What?" he asked, his mouth full of bread. "Not hungry?"

"Famished," she said softly and pulled a piece of bread from the plate. She picked at the corners and pushed a delicious bite into her mouth, forcing herself to chew. She *was* famished, but her mind was heavy, and she had things she needed to say to him before she lost her courage.

"You're being polite," he said without looking up.

"No, it's very, very good," she said truthfully. Her eyes stung, a sure sign tears were on the way, but if she let them fall, he'd want to comfort her. "But there are some things I need to tell you."

Tyreste wiped his mouth on his shirt and nodded with a frenzied look. "If this is anything like what you had to tell me the last time you were in my cabin—"

"No," she said in a rush. Her hand traveled across the table and clamped atop his. He looked down at it with a blank stare. "I'm sorry for what I said that day. Not a word of it was true, Tyreste. I was just so afraid she would hurt you, and after years and years

253

of her taking and taking and taking, I'd given up trying to beat her and just tried to... to mollify her. Before you scold me again for not telling you, understand that I *would* have, had I thought you had any more power to defeat her than I did."

Tyreste swallowed. His gaze hadn't left her hand.

"Look at me."

He groaned. "Ana—"

"Tyreste, *look* at me."

He set his jaw and looked up.

"Volemthe." She let the word settle.

The veins near his temple throbbed. His eyes twitched in a hard blink.

"That's what I *should* have said that day, but I was weak, a coward who hadn't earned her courage. I was alone, and afraid—"

"Stop." His voice croaked. He took a sip of cider, held it in his mouth, and washed it down. "Stop. I am just as much a coward as you. I could have come for you. I thought about it, many times. But my pride was wounded. My heart was... broken. And I convinced myself you meant what you said, because it was easier to feel slighted and wronged than to step up and be there for you when you needed me most."

Ana squeezed his hand. She bowed her head for the next part, for though she was brave enough to make the confession, she wasn't nearly brave enough to look into his eyes when she said the words. "Magda is not just anyone. She's not... Well, we've both known awful people, haven't we? You certainly have, before you came here. Evil people, even. But they are not what she is. *She* is something else, something I lack definition for and, frankly, I don't *want* to define."

"I believe you. I saw a glimpse of it myself, but I'd believe you even if I hadn't," he said. He brought his other hand atop their joined ones and shifted her hand between his two. "Go on."

Ana nodded swiftly. She had to do it. She had to. "The letters... the missing Ravenwoods..." She paused to catch her breath.

"It's all right, Ana. I'm listening."

"When I said I didn't know *what* Magda is, I don't. I don't believe she's like the others, the sorcerers. Meduwyn. Mortain and the like. But she answers to them." She forced herself to look up. "What happened back then, what Zo and Par talked about in the letters, is happening again."

Tyreste pursed his mouth. "Was it Magda back then too?"

She shook her head. "Magda is just a tool for terrible creatures. Before her, there were other Magdas. From the letters, I now understand the reason it's Magda here, doing the sorcerer's bidding, instead of the sorcerer himself. Zofia and her grandmother, Imryll, found a way to push Mortain from Witchwood Cross forever."

Tyreste watched her, expressionless. "How?"

Ana's shoulders lifted in a hard exhale. "I don't know. It wasn't in the letters. I had hoped... the kyschun..."

"Fuck. I am *so* sorry—"

"No, it's not your fault. And it's not what I wanted to tell you." Ana withdrew her hand and plucked off more of the bread, then shoved it into her mouth. "Sorry, I really am hungry."

Tyreste's grin returned. "Nah, go on. Eat up."

Ana covered her chewing mouth and shook her head. "No," she said and swallowed. "I have to tell you now or I may never." She moved her hands to her lap, which Tyreste noted with a slight frown. But if his touch faltered for even a second when she spilled her darkest secret, she would lose her nerve. "Magda is the one murdering the Ravenwoods. Of this, there is no doubt. I'm confident everything she does is on the command of Mortain, but *why*... I don't know why. The answer wasn't in the letters. I really don't know what he wants with them."

"I wish I could say I was surprised."

Tears abruptly spilled over her lids and dropped onto the table. Tyreste's face lit up with concern, but she shook her head and pointed it at her hands, laced so tightly in her lap, they were bone white. "The reason Magda chose the Wynters to infiltrate..." Her voice quaked. "Is because she cannot fly herself. And so... and

255

so... and so... She cannot lure the Ravenwoods down from their Rookery."

"Well, then maybe she waits for them to land down here. Or shoots them out of the sky. Or—"

Anastazja silenced him with a look he read—she could see it so clearly in his eyes—before she ever said a word. "She has her own slave with wings to do it for her." Ana ground her knuckles against her legs. "No, *no*, I will not understate my own culpability in this madness. I could have chosen death, but instead I choose to live, knowing those poor Ravenwoods were never going to be released. And I did it because I, selfishly, couldn't bear to be without my father and brother, and no matter the lies I tell myself, I know the truth is I valued *their* lives, and yours, well above the others, and I deserve no forgiveness for this choice, nor will I accept any. And before I completely lose my voice, Tyreste, I want to take you up the mountain and show you what my explanation never could. I want you to see that it was more than fear of your safety that drove me away from you, but rather a fear... a fear you would see me as I am. As I really am. But it's enough for me to say it. You won't believe me until you see... until you see Magda is not the only monster in Witchwood Cross."

He studied her in the space between the seconds, ticking slower with each passing moment. She searched his face for what she *knew* had to be there, disgust, hatred, revulsion, pity...

"My love," he said finally. He nodded to himself, casting his gaze to the side before continuing. "You can show me whatever you want. But let's just agree that when we're done, we're just going to kill the fucking bitch and end this."

Ana trudged several paces ahead of him. Her gown, still filthy from the evening in the forest with his family, was bunched in her fists, hiked high as she huffed and panted up a path so steep, he wondered how she visited so often.

Then it dawned on him. *She usually flies. She has to walk because of me.* A strange thought, no matter how he attacked it.

But Magda climbed the hard way every time, which must have required a level of determination powered by a prize so great, there was nothing that could keep her away.

Ana hadn't said what they were going to see. He hadn't asked. She was so visibly rattled, he feared questions would unhinge her further. He wanted to assure her nothing she'd said and nothing she could show him would change his commitment to her, but even that seemed unsafe in her state of disarray.

She'd given him an illusion for the trek. He'd never had any desire to look like Ludya, but there he was, trekking up a mountain in the guise of a wise vedhma. Every time he looked down at his thin-toed boots and flowing skirt—which he could very much *see* but still felt like trousers and thicker shoes—he was wracked with a powerful dissonance.

Despite wolfing down three thick slices of fry bread, he was ravenous. He thought about the food Ana had wrapped in her cloak for the trip, and his mouth watered.

"Almost there," she called back after they'd been walking for nearly an hour.

Tyr squinted through the fog, searching the mountainside for signs of anything resembling a place they might end up. All he could see was a white haze and the hint of fresh snow, the last thing anyone wanted to see in the brief season of springtide. But the Cider Festival had been canceled after the horror in the market. He'd heard whispers it might never come back.

The path veered into a wicked switchback that had him gripping low shrubs to keep from losing his footing. Ana marched on with astonishing determination, not slowing at all.

There were two more turns just like it, then they seemed to be heading *into* the mountain. The ground evened out until they were standing at the edge of a small enclave, in the center of which sat an obscenely large glass dome, dusted with the fresh snow, the view above only sky.

"The observatory," he muttered. "I've never seen it before. Not even from the ground."

"You wouldn't have," Ana replied, dropping her dress. She tilted her head back and breathed in. "It's meant for the sky, not the earth."

"What's it—" *No, not that question. Not yet.* "Why was it built? Did it have a purpose beyond the view?"

"My ancestress Imryll," Ana said. She rubbed her arms under her cloak. "You recall it was she who founded Books of All Things, the coterie of scholars and students in the village? Where Addy takes her instruction?"

Tyr nodded. He glanced around to guess what she'd brought him there to see.

"She had a partner in the endeavor. A man from Duncarrow, who had been her teacher there. His name was Rahn Tindahl, but most called him Duke Rahn. He had a particular fascination with the stars and, unlike most of the realm, didn't grow up believing in the Guardians. He had other hypotheses about all this light in our sky, and he and his disciple, Aesylt Wynter, built this place so they could explore those ideas. The observatory was used for generations, but interest eventually dwindled, as those things go. I don't think they ever found satisfying answers." She turned toward him. "But... They shared all their findings with the Reliquary, which was still being built back then. The Reliquary then stole their work and claimed it as their own. Or so the tale goes. But one thing is absolutely certain, which is that Imryll opened Books of All Things in the Cross two full years before the Reliquary named their realm compendium *The Book of All Things*."

"Can't say I'm very surprised," Tyr said. "I spent my entire tenure there translating documents that had either been purchased or stolen from their rightful owners. I have read *The Book of All Things* front to back."

Ana arched her brows, impressed. "All tomes and volumes and chapters? That must have taken you months."

"At least once, maybe twice. It's all I had in the Reliquary dungeon, time. I can assure you no one ever gave your ancestress credit. She was given reverence as a matriarch of Witchwood Cross, but I don't remember anything about her contributions to science or discovery. Or Duke Rahn."

"Of course not." She turned back toward the dome with a hard shiver. "Let's go."

Tyr had avoided dread the entire exhausting climb, but as they neared the unusual structure, the sense they'd approached the point of no return pulsed in his temples.

Movement inside the dome stayed him a second time. He saw it again, noting the flickering light, reminiscent of candelabra or a hearth fire, catching and reflecting off the glass.

"Ana. Ana, wait. There's someone inside!" he whisper-screamed.

"I know. It's why we're here." She turned just outside the arched doorway and swept her gaze over him with a curt nod. His illusion faded away. "I didn't want anyone to see Tyreste Penhallow following me up the mountain. But it's Tyreste who should enter the observatory and meet the person inside."

"Who... Who's inside, Ana?"

"Not her, if that's what you're worried about." She held out her hand to him, then seemed to think better of it and tucked it inside her cloak. "Come on. He can't hurt you. You'll see why soon enough."

"He?"

Ana dipped under the arch and disappeared inside the dome. Tyr warily followed her in.

"There you are," a man—a *naked* man, barely covered by a cloak half draped over him—said in exasperation. "Gods, I'm starving."

Tyr could only gape at the dark-haired man, who was around Ana's age, if not a little younger. He was definitely naked under the cloak, but Tyr had already moved on from that because he was fixed on the thick chains wrapped around the man's raw, red ankles.

Questions formed and were swiftly answered. The man was a Ravenwood. He was a prisoner of Magda.

"I'm so sorry, Var, I thought the last loaf of bread would hold you longer. I should have come last night," Ana said as she went to him. She lowered into a crouch and held out a pouch that contained the remaining fry bread—Tyr understanding why she'd eaten so little herself—and a small cask of cider.

The raven tore into the cold, soggy bread, rolling his eyes with pleasure. "This is far better than the other bread you've been bringing." He moaned, his mouth stuffed full.

"Uh... thank you," Tyreste muttered in a daze.

The raven frowned at Ana. "Who's this? He doesn't... He's not..."

"No, Varradyn," Ana said to assure him. "He's with me. This is..." She glanced back with a hard smile, but she wasn't looking at Tyr at all. He sensed her nerves, her fear, rising with the next revelation in their crusade for shared truth. "This is the man I love, and I brought him here to meet you. And to show him I am not innocent in what Magda has done to your people. He and I promised no more secrets, and so here I am, revealing my darkest one."

"Varradyn." Tyr turned the naked man from fantasy to reality with one word. He *was* real. He was a captive in the strange glass dome, and Ana had played a part in getting him there, however involuntarily. And now she was... what, feeding him? Looking in on him? "Why is he still here, Ana? Why have you not let him go?"

Ana pushed to her feet and aimed a curt nod at the chains. "Go on. Give it a try."

"Just watch the ankles, will you? I know she can heal them, but it still bloody hurts every time," Varradyn said.

"I don't have the tools for it," Tyr said but moved closer, circling the fur the raven sat upon. "We should have brought a mallet and a chisel."

"You want a mallet and a chisel?" Ana jogged to a basket positioned under a large table. She lifted it. "You'll find several sizes in here. I've tried them all."

"So have I. It's rather pointless," Varradyn said. The frivolity in his voice was jarring. He might have been talking about what to wear to supper. "The crone's magic is the only thing that will spring these locks unless I want to saw my feet off, which *has* occurred to me, more often than I wish to admit. Ana, do you think you could regrow feet?"

Tyr shook his head to dislodge the competing questions. "I don't even know where to start."

Varradyn raised a hand. "Well, it's simple, you just point the chisel at the lock, and once you have solid purchase—"

"I know how to break a chain!" Tyr cried. His skin tingled, both icy cold and furiously hot, alternating between the two sensations. He marched away toward the window, his thoughts racing wildly out of control.

"Not going to try?" Ana asked, still holding the basket. The misery in her voice was a jolt of reality.

"If you say it doesn't work, it doesn't work." He crossed his arms and bowed his head. There was nothing he desired more than turning around to find the raven had been in his imagination, and Ana had been toying with more illusions. But her distress was real. The raven was real. Magda's genocidal quest was real, one that had started many years earlier, long before the crone had even been born. Maybe even before the Nok Mora itself.

And if he didn't quickly assure Ana she had done the right thing, letting him in on her secret, he would lose her.

"Put the basket down," he said gently. He stared out the thick panes of glass, into the snowy crags. "And come here."

It was a moment before he heard the slow creak of reeds as she returned the basket to its place under the table. Longer still before her boots clicked on the stone. The only other sound was the animated chewing of the raven, too occupied with his meal to care about the exchange.

Tyr held out his arms, and Ana walked into them. He wrapped her tight, planting kisses in her hair. "You did what you had to do, and now we have to set matters to rights. But we're going to do it together." He pulled her back to look at her. "*Together*. You've lived in fear too long, Anastazja. I've known fear and even preferred it, because it meant I was powerless, and to be powerless absolved me of the need for action. But neither one of us is powerless. It's time we start believing it. You understand?"

Ana nodded and tipped her face back against his chest.

"At least she's not coming back today," Varradyn said from the rug. He slurped a deep sip of cider and belched. "The crone, I mean."

Ana stiffened in Tyr's arms and turned. "How do you know that?"

"Well, she was here this morning, and she only comes once a day, so you missed her."

Ana's face paled, panic spreading through her expression. "You're sure she was here *this* morning? You're not confusing time?"

"She was here long enough to add logs to the fire and glare at me," Varradyn said with a shrug. He frowned at the empty bag. "You don't have any more?"

"I'll bring you more later," Ana said distantly. She peeled away from Tyr. "We have to go. Now. She was supposed to be out of town, but if she's not... This could be another one of her traps. Tyr, we have to go *now*."

Tyr pointed an arm at the raven. "We can't leave him here."

"We can't take him unless she releases her magic," Ana replied. The pace of her words grew desperate. "I've been searching for ways to free him for *weeks*. I don't even know why he's still alive, Tyr, because the others are all dust now, their hearts locked in boxes in her underground lair, like prizes to be kept."

"Her underground..." He shook his head. "Where is it?"

"I'm not taking you there," Ana said. She turned back toward the raven. "Var, did she say *anything* to you this time?"

"Never does."

"Didn't mention where she'd been?"

"The day she actually says a word to me, Ana, you'll be the first to know." He cackled, a sound tinged with madness. "The *only* to know, because who else ever visits me? Unless you intend to bring your boyfriend every time? Did you tell him how I tried to take you right here by the fire?"

Tyr's face rushed with heat. "He *what?*"

"It wasn't his fault." Ana swatted the air with a dazed look. "The magic she chose for him, it was different than the other times. *Everything* about Varradyn's capture has been different, and if I could just discover *why*, we might find a means to end this and save him."

"Oh, I'm dying here, no doubt about it," Varradyn quipped, followed by another grating laugh. "This cider is good. Better than the wine and ale you've been bringing."

"Thanks," Tyr muttered. He reached for Ana, but she angled away. He couldn't get the image of the raven trying to mount his love out of his head, nor the anger that came with it. "Ana."

"We have to go," she said again. She jogged toward Varradyn and knelt.

Tyr flexed his fists, restraining a foolish wave of rage at the sight of them so close, despite the chains marking the raven a prisoner, a victim.

"See if you can get her talking when she returns."

"You've lost your mind if you think I'm saying one word to her." Varradyn snorted. Then his eyes clouded. "Ah, wait. She did speak. I just forgot."

"What did she say?" Ana planted her hands on his shoulders.

"Not to me. She was talking to herself, something about the cellar. And then off she went, down, down, down."

"She went *into* the cellar?" Ana probed. "When?"

"Right before you two arrived."

Ana stumbled back into a stand. "And she went *into* the cellar? You're certain?"

Varradyn nodded. "Hasn't come back up. I would know. Nothing else to do but watch the birds shit in the snow and the crone travel to her lair."

"Is there a lock on the outside of the cellar by chance?" Tyr asked.

"Tried that already." Ana screwed her mouth to one side. "She must have another way out."

"No," Varradyn said. "No, she always comes out this way. The day you locked her in, I watched the bolt slide on its own. She emerged looking no worse for it."

Ana gathered the bag and the cask and shoved them under her cloak. "I have another idea."

"Don't keep it to yourself," Tyr said.

"You won't like it," she warned. "You're going to return to your cabin. And I... I'm going to search her room, while she's occupied."

Tyr's mouth dropped open with a hard laugh. "You're damn right I don't like it, and you're not doing it. Not by yourself."

"I wasn't asking your permission." Ana went to him and looked up. "I'm doing my best to let you in, but there are some things I must do for myself. If she catches me, she'll berate me and that will be it. She still needs me, for a while longer anyway—for some foul purpose she hasn't bothered to explain. If she catches *you*, you'll be dead. And I will *not* lose you again, Tyreste."

"Ana, no, this is foolish and reckless, and—"

She craned up to kiss him. "You asked me last night if I trusted you. Do you still trust me?"

"That's beside the point, and you know it."

"It's the entire point. Do you *trust* me, Tyreste?"

Tyr squeezed his hands into fists at his side. "Yes. You know I do."

Ana swept her eyes over him. The air shimmered, and he saw the feminine boots again appear where his had been, under the hem of an ungainly gown. "I can only hold this from afar for so long, and perhaps not at all once you're out of range. Descend as fast as you can, go straight to your cabin, and I'll meet you there."

"When?"

"As soon as I can—"

"*When*, Ana? Give me a time, or I'm not going anywhere."

"Tonight. I'll be back tonight, after she's retired for the evening. I don't think the koldyna sleeps, but she does lock herself away until morning."

"If you aren't there by midnight, I'm coming to Fanghelm," he stated. "I *mean* it."

"Midnight it is," she agreed and backed away. "Please go. If she sees you, and the illusion doesn't hold..."

"I'll be right behind you," he said. He tapped his chest, where a hard lump of fear had reformed.

Ana nodded before turning to face the door. She straightened, breathing deep, and launched into a sprint. As she passed under the arch, she came up off the ground, shifting into a brilliant orange phoenix, and disappeared into the dawn sky.

It wasn't the first time he'd seen her shift, but it felt like it as he stared after her in stunned silence.

"She's going to get herself killed," Varradyn muttered and curled up on the rug. "But so are you if you don't listen to her. If the witch sees you here, won't just be Ravenwood hearts in her collection anymore."

TWENTY

A PERFECTLY ORDINARY MIRROR

Fanghelm was unexpectedly quiet. The usual bustle of staff was missing, and the smell of breakfast, which should have been permeating the air at that hour, was absent as well. No one greeted Ana when she entered except the guards, who nodded in acknowledgment but otherwise paid her little mind.

She passed Lenik, her father's vodzhae, but the spiritualist was whispering to himself in a language she didn't recognize.

"Lenik?"

He paused his walk but not his murmuring. His dark eyes pierced her with half his attention.

"Has something happened here?"

Lenik's eyes turned upward, he muttered something, and with an affronted air, he finally addressed her with a direct look. "Nien, Miss Wynter. Nothing has happened that was not wholly expected to happen."

"I don't understand what you mean," she blurted in impatience. The vodzhae were even worse about riddles than the vedhma, claiming the spirit realm could not be understood in plain language. "Why are the halls so quiet?"

"There is more simplicity to this answer than your question seems to require."

Ana waited for a clearer explanation.

"Your father has requested rest and gave the staff the day off."

"Has he left his room at all?"

"You'll have to be more specific with the time frame in which your question references."

"Lenik." She sniffed a hard inhale through her nose. "Since... Since the stewardess has been gone, has he left his apartments? At all?"

"Ah, well then, no. He has not."

Ana's spirits plummeted deeper. She hadn't taken a normal breath since leaving Tyreste on the mountainside. "Is he... worse?"

"Well, that all depends—"

"Pros, Lenik!"

Lenik straightened. His nose crinkled. "He is neither worse nor better than he was when he took abed."

Ana wilted in relief. It wasn't good news, but it wasn't the news she'd feared either. What she needed most was for every other terrible thing happening around her to just *slow down* so she could focus on the one thing that might fix it all. "I'll go see him then, a little later."

"Unless you intend to visit him within the span of one of your rare visions, Miss Wynter, or he wakes and offers a reversal of wishes he made quite clear, that will not be happening."

"Pardon?"

"Your father has forbade any visitors until further notice."

Ana scoffed, narrowing her eyes. "My father made this wish? Or *she* did?"

"Your father, after she left."

"Right." She scrutinized Lenik, trying to read his allegiances through his stoic expression. But it was impossible to know if the eccentric spiritual adviser was under the koldyna's sway or simply being his usual maddening self. "Surely he'll make an exception for his daughter."

"And I wish you all the luck of the Ancestors convincing the twelve guards standing watch outside his door that Steward Wynter did not mean you when he said, 'I do not wish to be disturbed, not even by my own blood.'"

"Of course she would," Ana muttered as she brushed past Lenik and turned down the hall housing the family apartments. Just as Lenik had said, an entire division of guards were huddled around her father's door. *He's safe. Let it go for now. You can't solve that problem without solving another first.*

The guards all paused to show respect, some tensing in anticipation of what she might do, but she smiled, as warmly as she could manage, and moved on toward the end of the hall.

She lingered, waiting for them to return to their conversation. When they were occupied again, she reached inside her cloak for the key that unlocked every door in the keep. She hadn't used it on anything but her own apartments since she was a little girl full of curiosity, and it was unlikely Magda even knew she had it. She half expected the door to be enchanted, impervious to any key, but to her happy surprise, the lock clicked and the door creaked open.

Ana checked the hall one last time.

She'd never been inside Magda's apartments. Ksana and Arkhady had always shared their living quarters, but Magda had demanded her own and never invited others in.

Ana half expected to be walking into an elaborate torture chamber, but the place looked like every other guest apartment in the keep. There was a sitting area and, on the other end, a bedroom nook. Two doors, one on each side, would lead to a privy and a closet. The furnishings matched the decor of the rest of the keep. Her eyes skimmed the desk and tables, searching for anything incriminating, but they were accoutred with only the usual items, like hairpins and potted ink.

She looked closer anyway. Opened every page of what appeared to be a journal but was merely a ledger of accounting for Magda's needs, detailing the cost of her gowns, slippers, bedding, and more. Each useless item Ana examined wound her nerves tighter, and with a sinking feeling in her chest, she began to accept the apartments were *not* where Magda kept her secrets.

"If I were dark magic, where would I hide?" Ana said, scanning the same items, the same furniture. There was nothing out of order. Her bed was perfectly normal, her bureau like any other. The desk, the tables, the mirror—

The mirror.

Her blood turned to ice. Paeris's words returned to her. *Mortain is up to something. I saw him speaking to someone, through a mirror, Zo. A mirror!*

But surely it couldn't be *that* mirror. Paeris had witnessed Mortain's strange conversation all the way in Duncarrow. There was no evidence in any of the letters that the person on the other end of his shadowy conversation was in Witchwood Cross.

You're being a dramatic fool, she scolded herself, her eyes sweeping the absolutely ordinary mirror as she passed it. But she couldn't pass without trying. No matter how silly she felt, there was no one around to see her act so ridiculously and, therefore, no harm in saying, "Hello, you perfectly ordinary mirror, you. What secrets will you reveal today?"

Ana laughed to cover her discomfort and made her way to the privy. She was still scolding herself as she searched around the toilet and under the vanity. Of *course* nothing had happened. Of *course* no one had responded because—

"Well, well, well. Hello to *you* as well, Miss Wynter. Do you prefer Anastazja? Would Ana be too casual for such a relationship as ours, which is only just in its inception?"

Ana was frozen solid. *I've imagined it. I'm exhausted.*

"Why not step into the light, where I can better see you? I would so like to know if you match the whims of my imaginings or if I've been so far off the mark as to be laughed at."

No. No, it was *definitely* a real voice. A man's voice. And it was there, in the apartment, despite the austere, faint intonation that sounded more like words traveling across a great distance.

"Have I scared you? I would be most aggrieved if you are avoiding me because I've given you an unintended fright."

"No, not at all," Ana cried out. She squeezed her mouth and eyes closed. *Idiot.*

"Ahh, and I thought I might *never* hear your lovely voice again. Please. Or shall I say pros? You have nothing to fear from a mere mirror. And you have expressed a desire to learn its secrets, but how will you do so when you cower in a privy, afraid of that which you do not now, and never did, understand?"

Everything the voice said was a lie. Ana *knew* this, in her soul, but still she put one foot in front of the other and forced herself to return to the sitting room.

"Closer," the preternatural voice beckoned. "So I can see you."

Ana crept slowly across the stones until she was again standing before the mirror.

The face staring back at her sent her hands to her mouth in alarm.

Dark hair... wan, pale flesh that was nearly translucent. Those were enough for her to think, *Not a man,* but it was his *eyes.* Oh, Ancestors, his *eyes* were pools without end, a place where a person could disappear and never again be found.

"Mortain." She hadn't meant to say the name aloud, and the way his entire sculpted face came to life made her instantly regret it.

"How delightful. We may forgo all necessary pleasantries and proceed as though we know one another. For I certainly know you, Miss Wynter, and how curious to find that *you* know *me.*"

"I don't... know you." Her trembling voice was horrifying. Why had she said anything at all? Why hadn't she ignored the voice calling to her in the privy and pretended none of it had ever happened?

Why, why, why?

"No," he agreed pleasantly. "I should say not, for anything you believe you do know was compiled from the unreliable recollections of others. To truly know someone, you must go to the source. No?"

"I suppose so. Yes." She was desperate for something to clear the dry thatch spreading down her throat.

"You look so much like her. It's all in the eyes. It's almost startling." He shook his head with a wistful sigh.

"Who?"

"My daughter. Imryll."

Ana breathed deep. "She was your daughter."

"Mm." Mortain's face wavered, as though speaking through water. "Imryll was precocious. Intelligent. Insightful. Were I a man, I would have fostered these traits in myself. Though she did not much approve of me, she did everything I ever asked of her. She married the wulf and founded a dynasty. *My* dynasty."

He's lying. This time, the words were not her own, but she heard them as clear as if they were. *There is truth in his words, but only some.*

"What..." Ana cleared her throat. "What is Magda to you? Another part of your 'dynasty'?"

"You must already know she's nothing to me, or she would be standing where you are and not clawing her way to a more promising future. In fact, as we stand here, enjoying the company of one another, she has gone deep into the mountain in search of answers to old Vjestik riddles, hoping to learn the means by which to subdue you as she has so easily subdued the others. You are a most vexing puppet, it seems." Mortain's thin smile was chilling. "Yet now that I have your *rapt attention*, I cannot see a need for her at all."

Do not trust the excited race of your heart. He knows what you most desire. He will offer you anything you want but will fail to tell you the price until you have no choice but to pay it.

The voice was certainly not her own, but it was distinctly female. She'd heard it before, at various points in her life, never often enough to strike more than a passing wonder. But as she reflected upon those times, Ana realized this voice had come to her in her hours of need—not every one, but enough to believe it wanted her to succeed.

"I could... dispose of my need of Magda. If I had known I had such a curious Wynter right there in the keep, I might have never summoned her at all."

You are a warrior, she heard, though that voice was no mystery. Grigor had never dealt compliments frivolously, and while she didn't understand, his belief in her gave her enough confidence to speak clearly and confidently to the only creature with the power to end the terror. "You're right, sorcerer. You don't need Magda. It is I who has done all the luring. It is I who keeps them alive while she toils in a cellar, collecting hearts for her own wicked indulgence. Tell me what it is you want with the Ravenwoods." Her voice faltered ever briefly, but she recovered quickly and prayed he couldn't see it. "Tell me and I shall see it done."

Mortain disappeared from the mirror. All that remained was her own reflection and the blooming horror that she'd not just scared him away but assured her family's destruction. But then he was back, flashing a placid smile that did the opposite of putting her at ease. "You must forgive the disturbance. It is ordinarily *I* who does the summoning." He offered no further explanation. "I could rid you of the foul witch. What is the word you use again?"

"Koldyna."

"Koldyna." His tongue lashed across both of his lips like how she imagined a snake might do. "What a colorful language is Vjestikaan. Would you like to be rid of your koldyna, Anastazja? To live beyond the cruel end she has chosen for you?"

Her heart did somersaults in her chest. "Very much so, Mortain."

"Very well." He tilted his head. "I will not ask you to lie for me. You would lie, if I posed this question directly, and that would not do at all for our new relationship, would it? So instead of asking you whether your heart is *truly* invested in my vision, when I already know your answer, I will instead ask you this: If you could end the murder of the Ravenwoods and the persecution of your loved ones by doing one simple thing for me, would you do it?"

You must know the price.

"In exchange for... for what?"

"Answer the question, Anastazja."

You must know the price!

"But the question is impossible to answer without knowing what must be given in return," she stated. She linked her sweaty palms behind her back. One hand wouldn't stop shaking. "My father would say no good deal was ever struck without first understanding the weight of the bargain."

"Has your father done much bargaining with a Meduwyn?"

Ana could only shake her head.

"No, for if he had, he might not be caught in the sway of a creature hardly worthy to eat at his table. So I will ask you once more and *only* once more. Your answer will be final and will determine whether we speak again or whether I trust in your koldyna to deliver what I require instead." Mortain's chin lifted. Something traveled the length of his throat, moving in anticipation of his next words, and she realized he *wanted* her to see it. "Will you do this one thing for me, and in return, be rid of Magda forever? You would get your father back. Your brother. The tavern boy not fit to lick your boots but whom I will not begrudge your love for. They can all be yours again. What say you?"

You must refuse! It only seems like a gift because he knows to name the terms would repel you. There is no bargain to be made—with a demon—that comes with a price any less than the ownership of your entire soul. If there is anyone who would know, Ana, it is me. His daughter.

Imryll.

Had Ana dared hope that was who had visited her across time, imparting wisdom? Could she trust it was even Imryll at all and not a fulfillment of her desperation?

"Anastazja? Your answer?"

I'm sorry, Imryll. Ancestors. Magda dangled all three of my beloveds as threats, but Mortain offers them as a promise. There is no cost, not even my own life, that would not be worth paying.

Forgive me.

Ana pinched her shoulders back and boldly met the sorcerer's icy gaze. "I accept your offer."

Her breath suddenly caught in her throat. She swatted at it in futile slaps, choking and gasping. Mortain watched her suffering with the same lineless expression he'd worn all along.

Ana lowered to her knees and pitched forward, still clutching her neck. The room darkened, and she felt her life slip away, inch by inch.

Then, abruptly, it stopped. She wheezed in, swallowing enough air to render her dizzy.

"*That* was not the price," he said with a lighthearted chuckle. "That was merely a demonstration of my authority over you now. I will not exercise it unless you give me cause to, but you now understand how simple it is for me to reach across time and space and take anything I want."

"Then... what..." Ana couldn't speak.

"What must you do in exchange for my gift?" Mortain asked. "Magda's efforts, as with the efforts of all who came before her, have failed, over and over and over again. They have failed because the Ravenwood blood that was once so vital to the Wynter legacy has dimmed over the years. We must replenish it. *You* must replenish it."

What? Her throat was too swollen to speak, so she mouthed the word. *Your purpose has shifted,* she heard Magda say.

"The raven you feed and keep will become your mate. With him, you will bring me heir upon heir upon heir, until I am satisfied your body is too spent to bring another life into the world. And on *that* day, Anastazja, I'll release you from your fruitful obligation, and you may enjoy whatever is left of your life in whatever way you see fit." Mortain stretched closer to the mirror. He seemed like he would climb out of it altogether, but she was too paralyzed to move aside. "If you decide reneging on your word is more to your benefit, then you will find your hands about the necks of those you love dearest. Your cruelty will be the last thing they see as you choke the life from their miserable existences. And then I will possess you utterly, and you will become the vessel you promised to be, at *my* command."

Mortain bowed his head. "You will soon see I am a creature of my word. Magda will not trouble you a moment longer. Until we speak again."

The sorcerer disappeared.

Ana passed out.

Grigor hesitated before entering the Tavern at the Top of the World. He'd never enjoyed ale. Crowds. People. He could turn on the charm when conditions demanded it, but avoiding such conditions was its own form of magic, one he'd perfected.

He'd left the Cross after Ksana died. Thrown himself into helping Arkhady establish more and better trade lines in the other Reaches. *I want to be useful,* he'd said. Guilt, though, had been the real catalyst.

Guilt had brought him back to the Cross when Ana had started to go downhill, and it compelled him to enter the tavern, again and again and again, to keep watch over the Penhallows.

Olov Penhallow tossed a friendly nod at him from behind the bar, where he was drying mugs. Grigor nodded back, though he did not share the man's enthusiasm. For anything, really.

His boots echoed with every clomping step he made toward the bar, rising even above the din of the crowd. Some paused conversations to follow the sound and the shadow, two things he'd not found a way to hide.

"Light or dark?" Olov asked, aiming his thumbs over his shoulder toward the two kegs.

"Neither," Grigor said. "I'm looking for your son."

Olov set the mug aside and picked up another. "Which one?"

Is there more than one fucking my niece? almost escaped his mouth. "Tyreste."

"Ahh." Olov gave a slow nod. "He's taken a leave from the tavern. He'll be at his cabin, most likely. I can have Addy show you the way."

"I know it," Grigor muttered. He rapped his knuckles on the bar and grunted. *Say it.* "Much obliged."

"All right then," Olov replied with a suspicious look, likely wondering how Grigor knew his way around their private property. Then again, Olov had daughters. He'd understand a man keeping an eye on the closest thing he'd ever come to having one. "You can cut through the back. It's faster."

"Aye." Grigor nodded once more and left before someone tried to engage him in needless chatter.

A few minutes later, he was knocking on the cabin. Tyreste answered fast enough to make Grigor wonder if he'd been standing on the other side, waiting.

"That was *much* faster than I thought, but thank—" Tyreste's mouth dropped open. He craned his neck upward to sweep Grigor's height, then locked eyes with him. "Grigor. I wasn't... Is everything... Is it Ana?"

"Yes," Grigor said curtly and shoved past him. He grabbed a chair from the table, tapped it to indicate Tyreste should sit, and took the one on the other side for himself. He felt like an ogre in the tiny, rickety chair, but if he was used to anything, it was the unsurprising discovery that almost any chair, save a throne, was too small for him.

Tyreste approached the table but gripped the back of the chair instead of sitting. "Please just tell me. I need to know."

"Sit."

"*Tell* me."

Grigor bolted up in an unspoken threat, and Tyreste quickly slid into his chair.

"I found her on the floor in the stewardess's apartments. Unconscious."

"Unconscious... *Why?* What happened to her? What did Magda—" Tyreste's eyes were a bit too wild for Grigor's liking. He sensed he'd have to subdue the lad before they were done with the conversation.

"You can ask Ana when she wakes," Grigor explained. Others touted patience as a virtue, but for him, it was a weapon. There were times for the fist, and there were times for the siege. He'd been in a decade-long siege with the koldyna destroying his family. Patience had kept her eye from settling upon him.

"Where is she?"

"In my wagon."

"In your *what?*" Tyreste tried to leap out of his chair, but Grigor was faster. He clamped a thick hand atop his arm. Tyreste regarded the restraint with a blend of horror and disgust, but he settled back down. "What do you mean, in your wagon?"

"I'll bring her in here when I've said what I need to say." Grigor withdrew his hand. "My niece has been reckless. Courting danger. The stewardess has returned. By now she'll be aware of Ana's sojourn into her room."

Tyreste stared blankly at the table. His cheeks blazed. "Then it's not safe for her there."

"It never was." Grigor sighed. He was familiar with Tyreste's history. He understood the boy craved stability. But he had to try. "I came to you today, Tyreste Penhallow, to appeal to your love for Ana. She needs to leave the Cross immediately. I would take her myself, but I already know she would not leave without you."

Tyreste held out his hands. "When do we leave?"

Grigor had been expecting a fight. "You're willing to do this? Leave your family?"

Tyreste sat back in his chair. He crossed his arms and looked away. "Would she be safe anywhere?"

"That, I cannot say." Grigor pushed back from the table before the negotiation became a conversation. "But the time for defeating the koldyna has passed."

"What about her father? Niko? She'd never leave without them."

"I will find Niko and send him wherever you end up." Grigor couldn't meet the man's eyes for the next part. "Arkhady is already too far gone. He would not want Ana to stay on his account. She will heal if she has you and her brother."

"And this is the only way?"

Grigor nodded.

Tyreste whipped his cloak from the rack. "Take me to her."

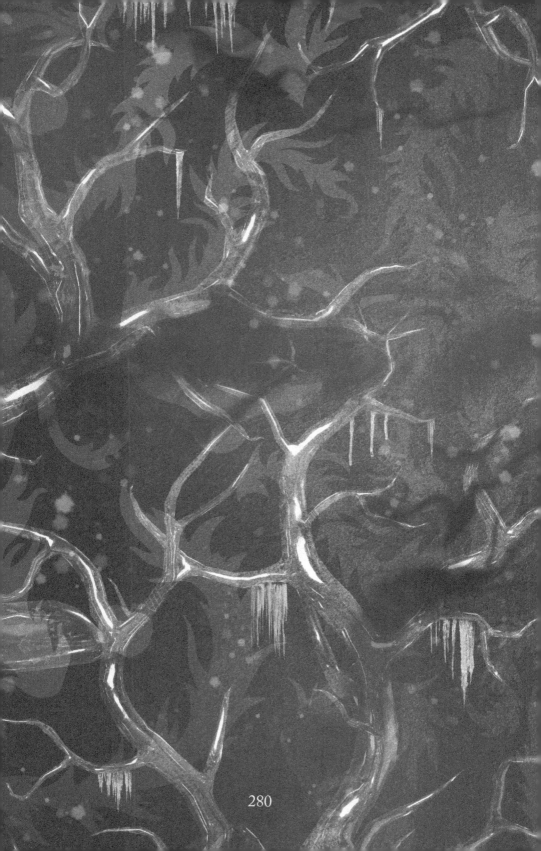

TWENTY-ONE
FIRE WATER

Grigor left as soon as they'd had Ana settled in the cabin, but Tyreste wished he hadn't. Ana had been shivering from the moment they pulled her out from under the tarp in the wagon, and the convulsions had only grown more violent. He'd triple bundled her in furs, placed her in front of the fire, and put a mug of hot cider in her hands, but nothing seemed to offer relief.

"Talk to me, love," he coaxed, crouched on his knees beside her. "What's wrong? What happened that made you like this?"

"I... cold..." Ana's jaw clacked so hard, he shook his head to stay the rest of her words, fearing she'd chip or break her teeth.

Tyr surveyed the room helplessly. The cabin had always been drafty, and there wasn't a warmer spot than where he'd parked her. But she was deteriorating right in front of his eyes.

There *was* a place he could take her, but to get there, she'd need to get colder first.

He stood and enveloped her from behind, holding her tight to battle her tremors. "I can ease this, Ana, but we'll have to go outside to do it."

281

Ana's eyes were wild with panic.

"Do you trust that I wouldn't tell you there's relief unless it were true?"

Her jaw smashed in response. She buried her face in the sea of furs and nodded.

He thought about leaving a note for Grigor, who would be returning with gold and a small trunk of Ana's things for the long journey ahead, but another look at Ana's intense shaking was all it took to discard the idea.

Tyr gave her his own cloak. It did nothing for her shivers, but it was a ten-or-so-minute walk to the hidden spot at the forest's edge, and he wasn't even sure she had that long.

But he'd lose his composure if he acknowledged the fear he was watching her die, so he redirected his focus to getting her there. He'd never taken her before, though he'd thought about it plenty. He'd held onto the idea of surprising her with a romantic picnic in the most magical place he'd ever seen. Carrying her against his chest through a dead sprint, tears stinging the backs of his eyes, was not the vision he'd had in mind.

The forest sloped downward near the base of the foothills, revealing a hidden enclave he'd discovered purely by accident. Bowing pines stretched their long, sweeping branches low enough to cover the entrance. It had been the steam rising from the pool, from the waterfall itself, that had drawn his notice the first time, but he'd had to touch the scalding water to believe what his eyes had seen.

Magic was the only explanation he could conjure for why there was scorching, flowing water in the foothills of the coldest place in the kingdom.

Magic had harmed his love, so it stood to reason it could fix her too.

Ana clung to him, whimpering and clacking, as he reluctantly peeled away her layers of furs. She mumbled her objections against the side of his neck, her head whipping as he draped her clothes and furs over a low branch.

When she was nude, he quickly lifted her and stepped into the water that was warmer than most baths. It was risky to shift her temperature so fast, so he guided her feet in first, counting to ten before sinking her deeper. Her chokehold eased, and slowly, so did the tremors, until her shivers normalized and eventually eased off altogether.

She gripped the rocks on the other side of the small pool. Her eyes were closed, her breathing fitful. He wanted to go to her and wrap her tight, but she seemed to crave distance.

The waterfall splashed steam and warm sprays onto his face. He closed his eyes and let it wash over him, cleansing him of all he'd done and would do to save her.

The roar of the falls dulled the world beyond, heightening the sense they'd stepped out of their realm and into another.

"Ana," he said, softly but loud enough to be heard over the crash of water. "Tell me what you need. Tell me how I can help."

Her hair was plastered to her face, covering one eye, but she didn't seem to care. The muscles in her arms strained through the hold she had on the rocks. "What I need..." She wiped her face on her arm and looked his way. "Is to forget what I need and just be free."

Tyr swam toward her and scooped her face in his. He brushed the hair from her eyes with his thumbs and kissed the places where it had lain. Every moment they lingered in Witchwood Cross was a dangerous one, but they couldn't run until she was ready. "I've never felt more free than I do when I'm with you."

Ana leaned her forehead against his. The backs of her fingers swept down his torso, moving slowly through the water's resistance. He spasmed when she trailed the length of his cock and again when she slid through the water, fastening her legs around his back. "I have swam in fire water since I was a little girl."

"Fire water?" Tyr caressed the underside of her thighs. "That's what this is?"

"Ahen vodah." Her mouth parted with a moan as she angled herself into place. "The scholars say it's a rare but natural occurrence in the Northern Range. I don't know what it is or why it happens, and even if I did, I wouldn't tell you because all I can think about is you fucking me until I forget my own name."

Tyr's cock jumped to life, hard in an instant. They'd never had sex in water. He didn't even know if it was possible, but the yearning clouding her lidded eyes made him willing to drown to find out.

Ana circled his cock in her fist and guided the tip inside her. He gently peeled her hand away to slide the rest of the way, until he was seated as far as he could go, flexing until her eyes fluttered back in surrender. Her tiny feet curled against his back. Not even the ahen vodah could wash away how wet she was.

Tyr gripped her face and dragged his cock slowly out. He nested it against her core, savoring the raw wanting in her eyes, the demand she was preparing to voice. She had asked for escape, to be brought to the brink of pleasure so she could safely crash over the edge, and he would deliver precisely that.

"Please," she whimpered. She dug her heels into his ass to spur him on, but he was immovable.

He crushed his mouth to hers in a fiery kiss and then ducked beneath the water. The last thing he heard was Ana's delectable gasp.

Tyr spread her legs wide and fixed his mouth on her clit, creating a suction to avoid inadvertently drowning himself. Breath held against her core, he dragged her through his teeth. She bucked and thrashed, knotting her hands in his hair, riding his face. He felt her lift into her release and tighten, and then she was crashing, her nails digging to his scalp and her feet carving down his back in desperate kicks.

He emerged from the water, gasping for breath. She swam forward and slid her tongue into his mouth, brushing it against his. Tyr pulled her onto his cock, tracing a thumb along her still-swollen clit to make her come again, desperate to feel her desire choke the life from his cock.

Ana threw her head back and screamed as she writhed, twisting and contorting, and came hard enough to bring him over the edge in a sudden, violent explosion. He poured his seed into her womb with a stilted cry, but she squeezed his ass to keep him inside, waiting for more with her eyes locked to his.

It happened so fast, he didn't have time to recover. The sight of her nodding and biting her lip, urging him on, was enough to make him come again.

Tyr breathed deep to gather himself. He watched her lift herself from the water, his eyes drawn to the way her pussy dripped with water and pearls of his spend. She beckoned him to follow, and he hoisted himself up, barely out before she'd rolled him onto his back and was climbing over him. He was inside her before he even had time to think, looking up in dazed awe at her perfect stride, the sway of her milky breasts, and her hand slipping between her legs.

She lifted to slide him all the way in, then all the way out with every thrust. He bore down on her hips and slammed upward, her mouth open wide in a never-ending cry of pleasure.

Ana's thighs clamped against his as she came. He pinned her onto him, starved for every tremor, every clench. As it came to an end, she lowered her hands onto his chest to catch her breath, and the sensation of her nipples brushing his flesh sent him spiraling into another forceful release. She arched her back, pushing down on his cock to receive everything he had to offer.

Tyr rolled onto the damp stones, panting. He didn't see Ana climb onto her knees and lower her mouth over him. For the fourth time that day, his cock roared to life, hardening with every flick of her tongue tracing the underside of his sore crown... each drag of her warm lips. He tugged on her legs, his mouth watering for more of her, indicating he wanted her to climb over him so he could enjoy her as she was enjoying him.

When she was in place, he ran his tongue down the length of her and spread her wide with his thumbs. Guardians, he had never wanted anyone more. Body, mind, heart, and soul. He wanted

285

all of her. Every inch. Every breath, every moan, every tear, and every smile.

He devoured her cunt as she worked his cock in her mouth, bringing him all the way to the back of her throat. He lapped at her, starving for more and tasting himself as well, something he'd never done before. The realization drove him wild enough to do something else he'd never done, flitting his tongue across her ass. Her whole body responded to the fresh assault, more than enough encouragement for him to spread her even wider and bury his tongue inside of her ass until he couldn't push it any deeper.

Ana was the first to give into the pleasure, arching as the release flowed through her. Tyr was right behind, erupting into her mouth with a thrust upward.

They lay that way—her on top, resting against his inner thigh, him below, caressing her ass—until their breathing slowed.

She climbed off and sat back on her bare heels. "I need to tell you what happened in that room today," she said, low and heavy, "but unfortunately for you, I still know my name, Tyreste, so we have some work to do."

Something primal stirred within Tyr, and he was on his knees, crawling toward her like an apex predator starved for fresh meat. "Nothing unfortunate about it, love." He licked his lips, tasting all her different flavors in one pass. "And if you think it will be me crying for mercy, you've underestimated the situation and me." Tyr climbed over her, and she clambered onto her back. He brushed his cock along her core. "I'm afraid I'll be carrying you out of here when I'm done with you."

They'd found a pleasant spot behind the waterfall, a small cavern warmed by the water. Tyr laid out the furs, and there was just enough room for them both.

He wanted to know what had happened, but the problem was Ana didn't *know* what had caused the attack on her body. The last thing she remembered was losing consciousness after

Mortain's terrible demand, then she was waking in the back of a wagon rumbling through town, shivering harder than she ever had in her life.

"We can talk on the road if you prefer," Tyreste said. His hands moved in slow circles around her belly. She could be vulnerable with him. She wanted to be vulnerable with him. But how could she ever tell him he would have to wait for her to bear child after child for Mortain, until she was bent and broken and lost, before she was free to love him?

"On the road?" she asked, only half-present.

"We can't stay here," he said. "Grigor said—"

"Grigor knows nothing," she said. Mortain's preternatural face haunted her thoughts, his terrifyingly calm delivery of her sentence repeating in her head.

"Magda knows, Ana. She knows you were in her room. She'll come looking for you soon, if she isn't searching already. It won't be long before she stumbles upon my empty cabin and keeps going."

"Magda won't be a problem much longer." Ana nuzzled her cheek against his chest.

His hand stopped moving. "What? What do you mean, she won't be a problem much longer?"

"We aren't leaving, Tyreste." Ana propped herself up so she could look at him. "Magda is only a foot soldier for someone much more powerful."

"Mortain," he said. "We already know that."

Repressing was so natural to Ana, it took sincere effort for her to stay the course they'd set together when they'd promised full disclosure. "I talked to him, Tyreste."

Tyreste shot up in a flash. "*Talked* to him? He's *here*?"

Ana shook her head. She looked at her hands instead of him. "In Magda's mirror. It's how they communicate. He speaks to her from Duncarrow, through some foul magic. Paeris mentioned it in a letter to Zofia, and I'd thought he was imagining it. I felt silly compelling a mirror to answer me. But then it did."

"Fucking Guardians deliver us," Tyr said, breathless. "You're sure it was him?"

"Tyr."

"Okay. Okay but, Ana... This is madness. Whatever he said to you, you know you can't trust it, right? Even less than you trust Magda. His evil goes back hundreds, maybe thousands, of years. Even saying that is utterly insane! But you know he's a professional liar who has had lifetimes to perfect his trade."

"A trickster," Ana said slowly, "but that is not the same thing as a liar. He said he could rid me of Magda and return my father and Niko to me. Keep you safe. And all I had to do was say yes."

Tyr seemed to grow bigger, taller, his skin reddening as he blustered through failed attempts to speak. "You and I both know he wants more than a yes from you. Demons don't make deals that benefit anyone but themselves."

Ana's pulse slowed, spreading a fearful tingle through her limbs. "You're right." She continued nodding. "What he wants is worse than anything Magda ever asked of me."

"But you didn't agree," Tyreste said. "So it doesn't matter. Right?"

Ana bowed her head lower.

"Ana."

Her head shook. "The thing about demons... They may pose the deal as a choice, but there isn't one. There never is. You either accept or they take everything anyway."

"*Ana.*" Tyr's breathing quickened. He leaned in to catch her gaze. "*What* did you agree to do for the sorcerer?"

"I'll tell you," she said, "but then we have to get to the observatory and tell Varradyn as well. He should have a choice, as I did, even if it isn't really a choice at all."

"What does the raven have to do with this? What choice?"

She wasn't ready to answer.

"We *really* need to get the fuck out of town, Ana."

"I'm not asking for permission. I'm telling you what's going to happen. I need to see him, and I will go with or without you.

Without you is quicker, but... but I'd rather go with you by my side."

He pulled his hands down his face with a groan. "All right. Fuck. All right. But first you're going to tell me what the raven has to do with this."

"Everything," Ana said, then she told him.

TWENTY-TWO

UP THE MOUNTAIN

The trek up the mountain felt longer the second time. Every step was agony, a steadily accumulating weight Tyreste couldn't shed. Every breath filled his head with the image of Ana chained to a wall for the next ten years while the raven bred her until she was naught but a husk of the woman she'd been.

She'd been so forthright in describing her negotiation with Mortain that Tyr hadn't had the heart to push her when she'd failed to answer the biggest question of all.

You aren't seriously considering following through. We're going to fight, right?

Or maybe he hadn't asked, because he had nothing to offer except rage and heartache and a love bigger than all of it.

A chill carried down from the mountain. Springtide was an illusion, an unmet promise. Anything that had thawed was already re-freezing. In the dark sky, a tempest swirled ominously around the crags of Icebolt, waiting for the right moment to upend the entire village.

Tyr held tight to Ana's hand. Her pulse pounded through her flesh, magnifying the helpless dread clawing through his limbs.

Badly he wanted to throw her over his shoulder and run. She'd be furious, but she'd be alive, and they could figure things out once they were safe somewhere. But those were lies born of cowardice and the bone-shattering fear he was losing her, bit by bit, as they moved up the mountain path. There *was* nowhere safe, not from a sorcerer who seemingly had no spectral limitations.

Everyone has a weakness, he heard in Rhiain's voice. And though she'd been speaking of mortal men when she'd said the words, she'd gone up against those far more powerful than her, exploited their weakness, and bested them. Could Mortain have a weakness, powerful as he was? If so, was it possible to find it before Ana...

Tyr decided he'd risk her leaving him and loathing him forever to keep her from that fate.

Near the top of the path, Ana suddenly broke away and ran. It was another few paces before he saw what had startled her.

The scene blocking the path was both a relief and a portent of doom.

Magda lay on the ice, broken and contorted, her lifeless expression frozen in permanent horror. Her final moments had not been pleasant, that much was clear, but what she'd seen and felt as her life had been ripped away would forever remain a mystery.

Ana screamed. He looked down and saw why.

In Magda's hand was a freshly extracted heart. Blood pooled under where her hand had fallen and had frozen with the ground.

Ana's head shook as tears flooded her eyes. "We were too late," she croaked. Her chin trembled. "Tyreste. We were..." She clambered back and away from the corpse, her limbs and arms flailing for balance. She made it to her feet and ran off again.

"Ana, *wait*! We don't know anything yet. Let's get there and then we can decide—" He broke off when she burst into feathers.

"Dammit." He grunted and shoved himself into momentum, huffing to catch up.

By the time he reached the observatory, there was nothing he could do. Ana lay over Varradyn's corpse, prostrate, howling and rocking his limp body in her arms. The image of Varradyn's arms flopping against the rug would stay with Tyr forever.

He took his time approaching her. "Ana. Love," he said, his voice low and gentle. "He's gone."

"I did this. I did this. I *did this*!" she screamed. The sound left her in a passionate wave, bouncing off the glass. "Weeks. Weeks. Weeks. Weeks. He's been here weeks. Weeks. I did nothing. *Nothing*!"

"Anastazja," he said again, taking another cautious step. He purposely avoided looking at Varradyn because he couldn't afford to lose it, not when she was so close to the edge herself, dissolving piece by piece. "You didn't do this."

"Don't tell me what I didn't do! He's not dead because of you! I can't even... He can't even go home in one piece, to be mourned by his people. They'll never know how their son died, how *all* their sons and daughters died!"

"The magic holding him should be released now, with Magda gone. Let's..." Tyreste scrambled for the right words. "We'll take him down the mountain and then we can decide what to do. How to honor him."

Ana rolled back on her heels and sprung up. She paced away, coated in blood from chin to boots, her arms twitching at her sides, and her gown a tableau of remorse. But it was the dead calm in her eyes and the astonishingly abrupt shift from frenzied rambling to whatever was happening to her now that made his head spin with bewildered fear. "There is no honor for Varradyn Ravenwood. No justice. His murderer is dead, and there will be *no* retribution for him or his family. Not the one they deserve." She wiped the blood from her chin onto her sleeve and laughed. "But I will offer myself to the Ravenwoods just the same, and they can do with me as they will."

Tyr's jaw dropped. "Offer yourself... Ana, *no*. No. Whatever you're thinking, it's a terrible idea, and it will solve nothing. If you fly up there—"

"It was I who lured him," she said, stone cold, "and so it is only fair they decide what happens next."

"No," Tyr stated. He reared back and said it again, louder. "*No*, Ana. We're in this together. You're not going where I can't follow."

Her cheek twitched in the start of a grin. "You're the one who thought he could follow. I always knew that where I was going, there was no room for another." She swayed on her feet and he rushed forward, but she put both hands out. Her eyes rolled like she was being called to slumber.

"Ana?" He lunged forward as she teetered sideways, and he caught her before she hit the ground. She went limp in his arms. "Ana, wake up." He shook her against him, to no avail. "Ana!"

She bent upward and shot out of his arms with a deep, croaky breath, sending him back a step. Her head shook in wild, concentric jerks, her hands clenching and unclenching at her sides so rapidly, her fingers twitched out of pace. All he could do was stare in horror as she fixed her feral stare on him, clicked her jaw, and launched into a grueling sprint, her arms pumping and her feet climbing the air in anticipation of the next lift, the one that turned her into a phoenix and carried her into the darkening skies.

Tyr, thunderstruck, watched Anastazja fly off into the storm and disappear.

When Ana came to, she was flying. The experience had all the qualities of a dream. The sense of detachment, covered in the soft haze of surrealness... Even the air felt different, as though she were floating adrift rather than commanding the skies.

The cumulative sensations came to a crashing halt, ripping her off course and sending her spiraling downward through the cloud, hurtling toward the mountainside. She flapped her wings in furious demand, straining to rise above the clouds, but it took twice the effort to go half as far.

Only when she was safe did the questions form.

Ah, but I have answers, little phoenix. Or what does your father call you? Your word for it? Pjika?

The voice was Mortain's, but there were no reflections nearby. It must be a part of whatever daydreaming had sent her into the skies with no memory, her imagination gone sideways.

What she *needed* to do was find a safe place to land, recover, and figure out what had transpired between finding poor Varradyn and waking up in the sky. But when she flapped her wings and angled closer to the mountains, nothing happened. She could go neither forward, backward, or sideways.

Only up.

You know I am no mere figment of your imagination, Anastazja. I am here, with you. I was with you when you found the crone. I was with you when you came upon her handiwork. I was in you when you succumbed to your weakness, and it was I who stirred you to life and pointed you toward your purpose.

Her mother used to say it wasn't a problem to hear voices in your thoughts; it was responding to them that sealed your fate. But Ana was certain Mortain was the one controlling and impeding her flight, and she was already exhausted from aimless flapping. *Release me, sorcerer. Whatever you've done to me, undo it before you kill me.*

I have fulfilled my end of our bargain, have I not?

She murdered the same raven you commanded me to mate with!

Unfortunate, yes. You were on a mission in the observatory. Do you remember?

Let me land, and we'll speak about whatever you want. Please.

Then it would be prudent to remember.

I need to land—

You will land nowhere but Midnight Crest. Covertly, as you always have. To find a replacement for the one Magda inconveniently dispatched.

No... Ana strained against a barrage of hail. She remembered the storm they'd watched arrive from the mountain path, but that seemed hours ago. *No, that was not my mission.*

You were going to fly to Midnight Crest, find a suitable mate—

No! Ana was hit by a ball of ice large enough to knock her off course. She recovered, but Mortain's hold on her grew stronger with each passing moment. *I was... I was going to Midnight Crest, but not for that.*

If not that, then what? Certainly you were not going to do anything foolish that would ensure the deaths of everyone you love?

Of course not, she lied, feeling a bold stroke of mischief unexpectedly take hold of her. She couldn't say why, but she didn't think he could read her thoughts. He could be with her, watch from afar, and even control her, but her thoughts were her own. To be certain, there was only one way to test it. *You're right. Whatever you did to me turned my thoughts into a jumbled mess. I remember now.*

What do you remember, Anastazja?

Her avian body lifted, tugged upward by an unseen force. She stopped fighting. She had intended to fly to Midnight Crest, so did it matter whether she was in control of the flight when the destination was the same?

I remember... thinking you would be so mad at me when you saw Varradyn.

Oh, my darling girl. That was not your fault. I would have eliminated the witch for that alone. She lost sight of my vision and pursued her own interests. But she has done nothing that cannot be remedied. Now, go on.

Ana stopped flapping her wings, and as expected, they continued without her focused effort. She let it happen because she would need all the strength she could muster when she landed at the Rookery.

I was going to Midnight Crest to find a replacement. So I could deliver on my end of the bargain. It wouldn't be enough to repeat what he expected, to tell him what he wanted to hear. She needed more to sell her obedience. *I was thinking it may befit us to select more discriminately than Magda liked. She always forbade me from choosing from the direct line of the high priestess. But if you wish to strengthen our bloodlines, Mortain, it is my belief we should take the son of the high priestess. The one they say will be high priest when her daughter comes of age.*

She was well above the clouds, the dark spires of the Rookery looming in the distance, before he spoke again. But his voice was shaky, dissonant, as though whatever magic that had fixed him to her was fading. *You are truly of my blood. Bold. Brave.* The next words cut out entirely, until she heard, *Any mirror will do. I will wait to hear from you.*

Ana was shoved forward in the air. She detected quickly that she'd been released, so she flapped her wings and soared higher and faster, determined to say what she needed to say before Mortain returned and realized her deception.

As she neared the great stone palace in the mountains, something was different. The east ramparts were lined with what seemed to be guards, watching the skies with solemn stares and rigid stances. The south and west ramparts were the same.

She angled around to the north side, to where the Courtyard of the Regents was carved into the rocks. It was a sacred place, where only the high priestess and her heir were allowed to step. Landing there would place her in violation of the Ravenwoods' most treasured law, and who knew how they would choose to hold her to account, but the guards on the ramparts were for *her.* The Ravenwoods were at last shoring their defenses, and if they were so prepared on the outside, she'd be a fool not to expect a ready offense as well.

Ana swooped low, dodging the icy trees some said were thousands of years old. She spotted a silver-maned beast milling about at the edge of a garden. Her mother had told her tales of the mythical midnight goats, but she'd never believed they were real.

Her boots hit the icy floor and she stumbled forward, nearly crashing into a broad, intricately carved throne. She gripped the arm, her chest heaving with wheezing breaths and her mind a spinning mess of words and thoughts she hadn't had a chance to sort.

Heels clicking on ice drew her attention forward.

"How fitting you would see no problem violating consecrated land after all you have done to eviscerate our blood and ways." High Priestess Elyria wore her raven-colored hair in a series of braids coiled around her head. Her dark-leather gown clung to every inch of her. She flicked a hand, and the goat disappeared. "Stewardess Wynter."

"High Priestess." Ana lowered to her knees and prostrated herself, forehead kissing the ice. The same trembling that had taken over her in Magda's room returned. "I have come not for your forgiveness, which I do not deserve, but to offer answers for what you have lost and submit myself for whatever penance you see fit."

"Rise and face me, you coward."

Ana scrambled to her feet, clutching the throne for purchase. A bolt of lightning shot from Elyria's hands, and the sharpest pain Ana had ever felt sent her flying across the ice and into a tree.

"You will not defile our throne as well," Elyria said. Her heels created a dance of sharp sound as she approached Ana, still slumped against the base of the tree. The high priestess towered, high and foreboding, as beautiful as she was dangerous. "The last time I saw you, you were a girl, and your brother was the one with wings. Had I known then you would bring such pain and death to my people, I'd have snuffed the life from you and left you for your pitiful father to find."

"My father... Please don't place the blame with him. It was all me."

"But that's not entirely true. Is it?"

Ana braced her hands in the dirt. The force of her ragged breaths coiled her forward. "It was all me, High Priestess. I have done terrible, unforgivable things—"

"For someone else," Elyria stated. "We know all about the witch who enchanted your father and claimed the village as her own. I wonder if *you* know how she poisoned your mother? How she stalked your elder brother in the Hunt and, right as he prepared to claim his victory and return to your people a hero, cut his throat and watched as the wulf devoured him."

Ana's heart skipped. "Stepan too?"

The priestess shrugged with a brief laugh. "I would imagine reflecting upon all the terrible things that have befallen your family would reveal the presence of her evil hand. But *she* is not the one huddling like a cornered animal in my courtyard, is she?"

"No, High Priestess. For she is dead, and now *I* will answer for the totality of her crimes. I do so willingly, if not fearfully." Ana wiped her eyes and looked up. The bewildering combination of vengeance and compassion in Elyria's searing gaze was blinding. "I have never in my life been more afraid of anything, but I am..." Ana's jaw clenched to keep her tears at bay, for she deserved no sympathy from the woman she'd taken everything from. "I am here because you should not have to live in fear. But you must know the threat to the Ravenwoods did not end with Magda's doom or with the punishment I'm prepared to accept from you. There is a sorcerer—"

"Mortain. Yes." Elyria glared downward. "He has been an unrelenting adversary, and long before we ever came to the White Kingdom."

"Ilynglass?" Ana was stunned.

"That's what *they* called it. We had another name, from the days when there were no Meduwyn haunting our lives. When they arrived, they decided what was ours was theirs. We fled here, to your land, to be rid of them, but Mortain gathered his highborns and followed us. Made those weak men kings, all in the guise of finding *us*."

Ana realized Elyria was only telling her so much because she planned to kill her when the conversation was over. Though she'd come prepared for that outcome, sensing the end was soon coming was sobering. "Why... What does he want with you, that he would go to so much effort?"

"His grandmother was a Ravenwood." Elyria's brows shot up as she swept her gaze to the side. "Thousands and thousands of years ago, Mortain was an abomination. He was unlike the other Meduwyn, who came into their power at birth and never had to work for it. Weaker, you might say, for though our magic is strong, it is nothing compared to theirs. His phoenix form, the very one you inherited, resulted from this atrocity. Among other things."

"*Mortain* is why..." Ana fell back against the tree. "We were told it was a gift given to the Wynters, by the Vjestik."

"Yes, well, men always believe they're more exceptional than they'll ever be," Elyria quipped, "as Mortain has always believed about himself. But for all his confidence and bluster, he fears the Ravenwood blood within him has held him back. That if he could only study us, he would uncover the 'spark' that makes us what we are, so he could excise it from himself. He compelled the weak king, Carrow, to march upon the Cross and burn it to the ground, to put into motion the series of choices and events that led his own daughter here, opening a fresh path to what he wanted. Us."

"Mortain was behind Nok Mora?" The revelation was as stunning as it was believable.

"But he could kill a thousand Ravenwoods, Stewardess Wynter, and he would never find what he was looking for. Can you guess why?"

Ana shook her head.

"Truly? Not even going to try?"

"In the moments I have been here with you, High Priestess, all I have learned is that I have known so little. I have understood so little. And I will die in ignorance, just as I have lived."

Elyria scoffed but didn't disagree. "There is no spark, girl. Our hearts and souls make us who we are. All of us. Ravenwood. Man. Yes, even Meduwyn. Mortain can no more change who he is than you or I could. But you're right about one thing. He won't stop. He will haunt our flight for the rest of his days." She lowered to a crouch and looked straight into Ana's eyes. "But we will not make it easier for him, will we?"

"No," Ana said. "But I beg of you, do not lash out at my father and brother. They had no part in this. They're innocent. And everything I have done... It was to keep them safe."

"I don't believe your heart is dark either, but it was corruptible. And I see in your eyes that they are even more susceptible to it than you were. I will not wage a war I cannot win, but nor will I hesitate to clip the wings of any phoenix who dares circle our skies, ever again."

"Then let me get word to them—"

"I have nothing more to say to you, Stewardess Wynter, except this: shift."

"What?"

"Shift into your phoenix form."

"Now?" Ana pushed up from the dirt, sliding her pained back up the tree. She hadn't known how broken she was from the impact until she tried to stand.

Elyria caught her before she could fall. "Now."

Ana sidestepped Elyria and stumbled out of the way. She didn't even know if she *could* shift, in as much pain as she was in, but the request sent fingers of dread spiraling through her. "Why?"

"Did you or did you not come to me intent on answering for your crimes?"

"Yes, but—"

"Shift, or die where you stand."

Ana wrapped her arms around herself. The shakes had escalated to the point her teeth clacked when she tried to speak, so she gave up trying. Did it matter why the high priestess wanted her to shift? Elyria was right. Ana had come to answer for what she'd done, and it was not up to her how the Ravenwoods exacted their justice.

She shook her arms out at her sides and rolled her face upward. The convulsions might follow her when she shifted, but they would not plague her for long. Nothing would.

Tyreste, volemthe. Forgive me.

Ota. Niko. Grigor. Addy. Ludya. I will see you again by the wings of this life or the bones of the next.

Ana's mouth became a beak, her arms stretching and shaping into majestic, fiery wings that she'd been proud of until Elyria had told her where they'd come from. Her phoenix form was not simply something she could call upon but an intrinsic part of herself, as much as her lungs, her heart, and her mind, so how could she ever separate herself from Mortain's foul magic? She *was* his magic. Perhaps it was fitting to die in the shape he'd given her.

Elyria's mouth twisted in scorn. Her nose twitched with every sprouted feather and elongated or coiled limb, as though witnessing the birth of evil.

As she marched toward Ana, one hand came out, and something cold and firm clamped around Ana's neck. She flinched from instinct, but her neck was frozen in place, and she could not move the rest of herself either, only hover above the ground.

The high priestess lifted her dress and removed a dagger from her thigh strap without slowing. She paused long enough to look at Ana and say, "No bird can land without their claws. My council knows this. My people know this." Elyria grasped both of Ana's talons in her fist and severed first one, then the other. The pain blinded Ana until it was all she knew, the high priestess's pronouncement relegated to another part of her mind. "And I will show them I have clipped the power from the evil haunting our halls. Fly now, bird, until your wings give out and you fall from the sky to the death of your own choosing."

Elyria held the severed talons high for Ana to see. She slipped them into a pouch attached to her dress and gave them a loving pat. "There was a time when I called your father 'friend.' When he discovers his only daughter has been taken from him, I hope he understands our history is the only reason I am not now holding your heart in my hand. Your debt is paid, phoenix, and so long as he respects our skies, so is his." She released the magical chain from her neck. "Now go."

Ana commanded her wings to lift her higher, but she didn't budge. Pain eclipsed everything else. Blood flowed from the place where her limbs had been severed, painting the stones in further evidence Elyria had dealt indiscriminately with the Ravenwoods' enemy.

Elyria reared back, pursed her mouth, and blew. A fierce wind whipped around Ana, sending her spiraling up and into the air. Higher, higher she soared, caught in Elyria's gale, until she was released and sent hurtling through the hail and snow hammering from the dark sky. Soon she couldn't see the spires or the ramparts or anything at all. Her wings finally answered her commands, but without direction, she flapped in disoriented arhythmic jumps and falls, not knowing right from left or up from down.

I'm dying. It wasn't a revelation but a call to action. She couldn't die like *this*, lost in mountains her people couldn't reach. There was still time to make it to the village, and she only needed to reach as far as the paths went, and someone would find her body. She'd never again see her father or Niko or...

Tyreste. I love you. Forgive me. Forgive me.

Heartache fractured her focus, and she went hurtling downward. She called upon the last of her vigor to push her wings, strong and fierce even in their final throes, to find her way again, bracing through ice and snow and wind and leaving trails of blood in her wake. She opened her beak in what would have been a scream had she been Ana, but she would never again be her. The high priestess had heard her last words, and all that was left was to reach her people to offer closure.

I'm coming home.

For the last time, I'm coming home.

303

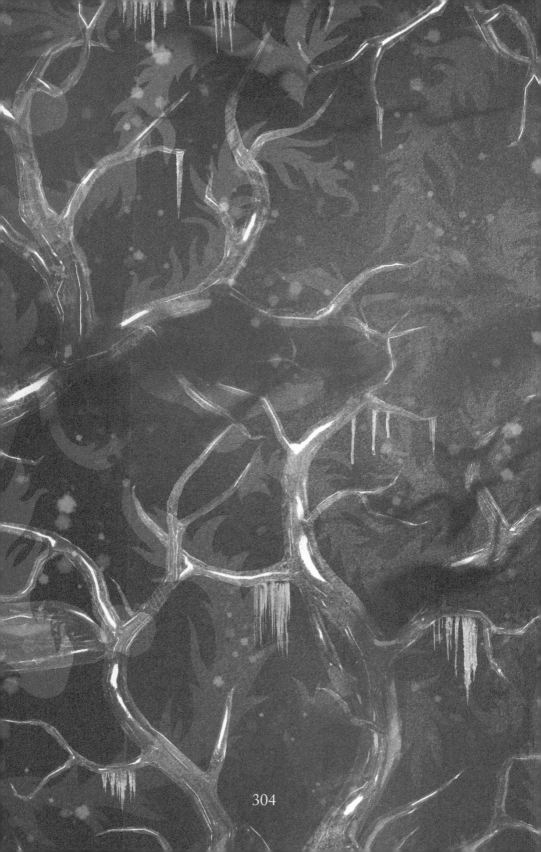

TWENTY-THREE
THERE WILL BE NO REST

Tyr shoved past Ludya, swiping the unlit candles, papers, and stack of mugs onto the floor with one pass of his arm, beckoning wildly to Grigor with the other. He rushed to the bed, tore the sheet from the thin mattress, and returned to spread it haphazardly atop the wooden tabletop just as Grigor and Ludya eased Ana's limp body onto the makeshift gurney.

There was so much blood, but it wasn't the time to dwell on it.

"The bed would be simpler," Grigor said, rifling through the bureau.

"She'll need it for rest, once we've saved her," Tyr answered as he joined in the search for anything useful. He chose to overlook the bigger man's skeptical frown, because *hope* was all they had left, and Tyreste would hope enough for all of them.

He didn't even know what he was looking for, but *anything* was better than realizing they'd taken her to the wrong place. Ludya had rented the room after they'd found Ana's broken body twitching at the base of the mountain path.

Tyr found a half-drunk bottle of spirits and froze. He looked around. "Where's Ludya?"

"Summoned."

"What? Where?" Tyr hadn't even seen her leave.

Grigor held up a poorly folded sheet, tearing it into rough strips. "She didn't say, and I didn't ask." He tossed a few of the scraps to Tyr, who caught them on the way back to the table.

Tyr dropped the fabric into piles and set the liquor near Ana's shoulder. He pulled the knife from his boot and cut jagged lines down the middle of her dress to remove it. "She better be back soon. We don't have time."

"Nien." Grigor pulled his own flask from his vest, took a nip, and sprinkled some onto Ana's mangled legs. There was far too much blood to make sense of her injuries, but without a healer, without *Ludya,* she would lose both legs to infection. "She won't be."

"How's that?" Tyr asked, panic settling in. He'd harnessed it through finding her, through watching her bounce, limp, on Grigor's shoulder covered in so much blood, but those had been constructive actions, needed to get her to safety so Ludya could fix what had been horribly broken.

"She said you would know what to do." Grigor tore another strip with his mouth and wrapped it around one of her bare thighs, pulled it taut, and moved on to another. He glanced up long enough to share his impatience. "So fucking do it already."

"But I—" Tyr mopped at Ana's wounds, but cruel memories of Adeline dying in front of his eyes eclipsed the hope he'd felt. His failure had nearly cost her—and their family—everything. If not for Ana, it would have. He hadn't healed in years, and in that time his talent had been squandered, forgotten. "Ludya... She was mistaken. I can't do anything more than you can."

Grigor blinked away sweat, his nose flaring. "If Ludya says you can, you can. But Ana will die on this table if you stand there overthinking it. If you love her, save her."

Grigor was wrong. Ludya was wrong. They were both horribly, terribly wrong, and their wrongness would be the end of Ana.

If Tyr was all Ana had, and his choice was to stand, immobile, in helpless defeat, she had no chance at all.

Another memory invaded. Rhiain, bringing Asterin to him after the man had been beaten near to death. The desperation in her eyes as she'd begged him to save the man she loved... and then he *had*, even as his own heart broke.

Tyr reached behind him and dragged a chair to the table. He dropped onto it and peeled Ana's bloodied hands away from her chest, gathering them into his. "Don't you dare die on me." He rubbed her hands in his, searching for the place in his mind he used to go to find the healing magic. "You... You are the breath in my tired lungs. The beats of my fractured heart. The peace in my tortured mind. And if the Guardians or the Ancestors asked me to be the breath in your lungs, the beats in your heart, the peace in your mind, for the rest of our days, just to keep you with me, there would be but one answer for me to give." He kissed her hands, enveloped by his trembling ones, tears running down his face and over blood both dried and fresh.

A full, stuffed feeling spread across his chest and down his arms, then into his hands. He caught Grigor observing him from the corner of his eye as the man tied tourniquets.

Tyr slowly climbed onto the table, careful not to brush the angry gashes slashed across her poor, battered body. He hovered over her on all fours, pulled in a deep, swollen breath, and pressed his mouth to hers, turning off any part of him not fully connected to her.

The room disappeared. Grigor. The acrid scent of cheap spirits. The cold from a room not yet warmed.

Only Ana remained.

Tyr's tongue parted her lips, allowing air to flow into her and through her lungs, and breathed for her while she could not, waiting to feel her giving as many breaths as she took.

Thrumming pulsed in his ears, swiftly increasing its pace, his heart beating where hers failed to, beating *through* her. He could spare no thrill in the victory, though, because there was so much left to do before her heart could again beat independently of his.

You still have everything to stay for. He'd sent the same words to Asterin, telepathically, as he'd pulled him back from the brink over five years ago—the same words he'd sent to everyone he'd ever helped. But his next words were solely for her. *You are brave, beautiful, and perfect. You are strong. You see the hurt you've caused but fail to see the joy. You saved me, not once but many times. You saved my sister. You have saved your father and your brother, every day of your life since the one she came into it. You are not the terrible thing you were forced to do. And if you leave us now, Anastazja, you'll never get the chance to prove it.*

He sent these thoughts from his mind to hers, waiting for her thoughts to become her own once more.

Guardians, hear my prayers. You have left every one I've ever sent unanswered, but you must hear me now. For if you brought me back from the edge of life only to wound me beyond measure, to watch me say good-bye to the love of my life, then you may as well take me too.

Ana's pulse jumped to life. He imagined his heart moving back into his own chest, to give hers space to beat on its own. She sputtered, gasping, so he tilted her head back to clear her airway. She huffed out one breath. Two. Another. Short, stilted, desperate... but each one more productive than the last.

Grigor rushed over, but Tyr shook his head, to wait.

Tyr hovered over her, frozen. The next part would be the hardest. It had nothing to do with magic.

Come back to me, love.

Nothing.

Grigor grunted and paced. He threw the remaining scraps at the wall.

Ana, come back to me. We'll find Niko. We'll help your father. We'll make everything right. You and me. Together.

He watched her eyes for signs of movement. She sent nothing back.

"Where the *fuck* is the vedhma," Grigor muttered, followed by a long grumble of agitation.

They'd switched places, Tyr realized. Grigor had lost his hope, and Tyr had never had more.

I know you're there. I know you're fighting my efforts. And I think I know why. Do you still trust me, Ana?

Seconds ticked. Grigor's pacing continued.

I do.

Tyr fell forward from the weight of his relief. He kissed the side of her mouth. *Open your eyes. Open them and come back to me, and I'll make it all right. I'll make everything right again.*

You can't, my love. You shouldn't have brought me back. The high priestess sentenced me to die, and I have earned this death.

Tyr sat up in shock. He glanced at Grigor to see if he'd picked up on the subtle shift in Ana, but the man had both hands pinned on either side of the window frame as he stared into the storm.

The high priestess did this to you?

I asked her to.

Ana, I don't...

I can't live with what I've done, Tyreste. Magda has been punished, and so must I be. You were only supposed to find my body, so you didn't spend your life searching for me. You weren't supposed to save me.

Find your body? Ana, I have already mourned you and decided it's not for me. I'm sorry, but you are not in the right mind to choose death. Your soul is wounded, and it can be mended, but a broken soul cannot make such a choice. And I won't accept it.

Tyreste, you don't—

Tell me this, Anastazja. If it were me on this table, begging to die, would you abide my wish? Would you stand back and watch me die?

No answer came.

It was the only answer he needed.

He kissed her and broke away, leaping off the table. Grigor left the window and stormed over.

"We need to clean her up," Tyr stated. His hands twitched, already imagining her flesh made whole. "Anywhere there's a wound must be free of blood and dirt before I can close it. You clean. I'll follow your path until we've taken care of all of it."

Grigor reached for another sheet and started tearing. "We'll start with her legs."

Ana listened to the voices for hours. She could've woken sooner, but she craved the solitude of private rest, loath to surrender it until she had to.

It was far too soon for any thinking on a deeper level. Tyreste had healed her, and she was so proud of him—would've been prouder if it were someone else he'd saved. But with some rest under her, she finally understood *why* she had been saved. Why the Ancestors had intervened and given him his magic back.

Dying was a coward's way out of a problem she'd been an integral part of perpetuating. Mortain would still be free to terrorize the Ravenwoods. And though she would act surprised when Ludya gave her the news, Ana had heard Ludya explaining to Grigor and Tyreste where she'd been and why. Both men had argued, and how she loved them for looking after her, for loving her so, but Ludya was right.

"She needs to rest!" Tyreste cried. "She almost *died.* I don't even know if I got everything, if there's still some internal bleeding, or... or..."

"Your remediation was sufficient," Ludya said, as placidly as ever. "I have confirmed this myself. A proper healer you are, Tyreste Penhallow. I hope I am forgiven for speaking coldly to you when we last met."

"I don't care how you speak to me! I care that you want to drag Ana away from here, into that cursed fucking cave, to the... the *beings* that almost killed her the last time!"

"The kyschun are not wicked, nor murderous. And they have at last decided to offer Ana the information she seeks."

"Then she can go *later*, when she's well enough."

"We are beholden to their time. They are not beholden to ours."

"No." Tyreste's heavy steps echoed through her rest like low, slow drums. "She needs to rest, Ludya! The kyschun can wait another day or two."

"There will be no rest for Ana," Ludya said. "Nor, if you love her, for you. Not until this madness has ended, one way or another."

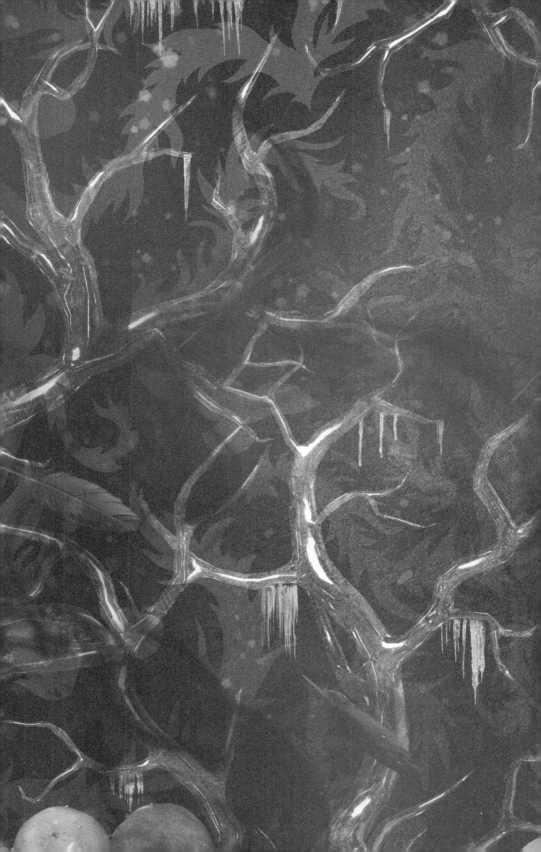

BY THE WINGS OF
THIS LIFE
OR THE BONES OF
THE NEXT

314

TWENTY-FOUR
THE HISTORY KEEPERS

The trek down the narrow walkway of the archivists' lair was less treacherous the second time. Ana had been too distracted to note the details on her first visit, but she remembered the bizarre sensation of blood running down the walls, filling the space on either side of the thin platform that divided life from death.

Though Tyreste had healed her well, phantom reminders of her pain lingered. Her flesh had memorized every gash and would feel the high priestess's blade severing her talons for the rest of her life. She hadn't tried to fly again, because she wasn't ready to discover not everything could be mended.

Tyreste, close behind her, was unusually silent. He'd been invited this time and hadn't hesitated to come, but he clearly didn't trust the motives of the kyschun. Ana didn't know them any better than he did, but she believed in her heart they were not evil. Nor were they good. Such designations had no place in the role of a history keeper.

The long cavern was almost tranquil. No tremors knocked them off course. Every few paces, Tyreste stretched a hand toward her back and offered a soft, comforting touch, to remind her he was close. She was glad he was there. She hoped she would still feel that way after the kyschun had imparted their knowledge.

The path flared into a broader platform. It was no less dangerous against carelessness, but there was room to spread out. Tyreste stepped beside her with a wary look from his peripheral. She felt the same but smiled for them both.

"Where are they?" he asked, looking around at the room barren of anything but stone. He hadn't gotten that far the first time, when the kyschun had tried to shake him from the mortal coil for venturing where he hadn't been invited.

"Look up," she said, pointing toward a series of six archways carved into the stone like little windows. Before she could explain the kyschun and kyschuna would appear there, they did, one by one. The glow surrounding them was dazzling as they each stepped into place, and as with the last time, she could make out nothing but outlines within the emanating light.

"Are they... like us?" Tyreste asked, leaning in to whisper.

"Yes. And no," Ana replied, watching in the same rapt awe as him while the archivists finished settling into place. Their glow died to an ambient radiance, but their features were no more discernible. "They were born like us but were chosen for a different life. It's often a designation carried through familial lines. The Petrovashes have long been among the kyschun, and there are three here now, as I understand it. Mishka and her daughter, Raisa, who I used to play with as a girl. Mishka's brother, Olek. I don't know who the others are." She sighed. "I probably should. My father would."

"Petrovash." Tyreste twisted his mouth in thought. "I know that name."

"I'm not surprised. They're a prominent Vjestik family in the Cross. Here, they serve their family and our people with honor."

"Are they going to say something?"

"Eventually." She tried to smile. "Don't be afraid. This time you're invited. They *want* you here."

Tyreste gaped at the glowing arches. His head slowly shook. "Hopefully not to correct their mistake of not killing me the first time."

"YOU HAVE RETURNED TO US WITHOUT DECEPTION. WE WILL HEAR YOUR PLEA."

The cavern rumbled. Tyreste reached for her hand and clasped it tight.

Ana swallowed and raised her chin high. "Hvala for hearing my plea, kyschun and kyschuna. I should have solicited your wisdom sooner, but my fear, and perhaps bravado, chose isolation instead. I stand in full admission of this failure and beseech you to hear me when I say I come to you not for the good of myself but for the good of my people. For the good of the Ravenwoods, who do not deserve the torture that Mortain and his sycophants had inflicted upon them."

"WE KNOW WHY YOU ARE HERE, ANASTAZJA OF THE WYNTERS. WE KNOW WHAT KNOWLEDGE YOU SEEK. WE HAVE CONFERRED AND DEEMED YOU WORTHY OF RECEIVING IT."

Ana opened her mouth to thank them, but another voice eclipsed hers, this one female. She recognized it. Raisa.

"TYRESTE OF THE PENHALLOWS, YOUR FIRST VISIT WAS NOT SANCTIONED, AND YOU ARE FORTUNATE WE ALLOWED YOU TO LEAVE HERE AT ALL."

Tyreste cleared his throat, nodding. "Yes, and I thank you for that mercy. I was only trying to help Ana, to keep her safe, but I didn't know the rules. I will do whatever you ask of me." His mouth twitched as he eyed Ana from the side. She nodded to confirm he was doing fine.

"YOU ARE HERE, TYRESTE OF HOUSE PENHALLOW, BECAUSE YOU WERE PUT IN ANASTAZJA'S PATH TO SHOW HER SHE WAS DESERVING OF LOVE. SO SHE WOULD EMPOWER HERSELF WITH THAT LOVE AND KNOW IT IS NOT ONLY HER LOVED ONES WHO ARE

WORTHY OF SAVING. BUT SHE MUST LEARN TO FIGHT **FOR** *HERSELF OR SHE WILL CONTINUE TO FAIL."*

Ana shook her head in confusion. "But it is selfish to love oneself more than one loves others. I would gladly lay down my life to protect Tyreste, my father, my brother. The Ravenwoods."

"AND THIS IS WHY YOU HAVE FAILED. YOU HAVE NOT PLACED APPROPRIATE VALUE ON YOUR LIFE. YOU DEFINE YOURSELF BY YOUR PAST, WITH NO EYE TO THE FUTURE YOU WILL CREATE. YOUR DEATH INVITES DESTRUCTION. THE WYNTERS END IF YOU END BEFORE YOU HAVE BROUGHT THE FUTURE TO LIFE. ARKHADY HAS PRODUCED THE LAST OF HIS BROOD. NIKOLAJ IS NOT BUILT AS YOU ARE. IF YOU DO NOT PREVAIL, ANASTAZJA, THEN NO ONE WILL."

Ana glanced at Tyreste, but he was staring at the arches. "What does that mean? I don't understand."

"WE WILL NOT WASTE PRECIOUS TIME EXPLAINING WHAT YOU CANNOT ACCEPT. YOU WANT TO KNOW ABOUT THE MEDUWYN BLOOD FLOWING IN YOUR VEINS. HOW THE CREATURE HAS USED HIS DESCENDANTS AS PAWNS IN A TERRIBLE BID FOR POWER. WE WILL TELL YOU WHAT WE KNOW."

"Please. Pros," Ana said, battling the urge to turn and bolt. "I will receive your knowledge with gratitude."

"IMRYLL OF GLAISGAIN BROUGHT THE MEDUWYN BLOOD TO YOUR LINE," said another voice, male. *"MORTAIN WAS HER FATHER. HE WAS THE ONE WHO WHISPERED THE NEWS OF SEDITION INTO THE KING'S SUSCEPTIBLE EAR THAT BADE HIM RAZE THIS VILLAGE, THE NOK MORA. TEN YEARS LATER, HE ORCHESTRATED IMRYLL'S MEETING WITH DRAZHAN WYNTER, IN A BID TO PLACE HIS BLOOD CLOSE TO THE RAVENWOODS, WITH WHOM HE SHARES A DEEP HISTORY. IMRYLL REFUSED HIS PLEAS. SHE TURNED HER BACK ON HIS EVIL. THROUGH THE POWER OF*

FEAR, SHE LEARNED TO WARD HERSELF AND HER CHILD, ALEKSY, FROM HIS SIGHT, BUT SHE DID NOT APPRECIATE THE DEPTH OF HIS PERSISTENCE. NOT UNTIL HER GRANDDAUGHTER, ZOFIA, WAS CAUGHT IN THE WAKE OF HIS EVIL."

"The letters," Tyreste whispered.

"YOU KNOW THIS STORY," boomed a kyschuna. *"YOU HAVE READ THE LETTERS BETWEEN THE ILL-FATED PAERIS AND HIS COUSIN. BUT THE LETTERS ARE NOT THE END. ZOFIA WENT TO HER GRANDMOTHER AND CONFESSED EVERYTHING. IMRYLL SHARED WITH HER GRANDDAUGHTER THE WHOLE SORDID HISTORY. TOGETHER, THEY CREATED A NEW WARD, ONE THAT PROTECTED ALL OF WITCHWOOD CROSS. AND SO MORTAIN WAS CLOSED OFF."*

"You're saying he cannot come here?" Ana asked. "And that is why he sent Magda?"

"FOR TWO HUNDRED YEARS, THERE WAS CALM. TO AN IMMORTAL CREATURE, TIME IS NOTHING. HE WAITED FOR THE LEGEND OF MORTAIN TO BECOME HISTORY, BELIEVING THE STORIES WOULD DIE OVER THE YEARS, LIKE HIS DESCENDANTS DID, ONE BY ONE, AS THEY AGED OUT OF THIS LIFE. MAGDA WAS CHOSEN FOR DEVILRY AS MUCH AS HER POWERFUL MAGIC—WAS SENT TO DO WHAT HE COULD NO LONGER DO HIMSELF."

"So he'll just send another Magda," Tyreste said bitterly. "And this will never, ever end."

Ana's mind was spinning too fast to speak. Both Elyria and the archivists had now confirmed Mortain was not just anyone, but her ancestor. Imryll's father. *Her* grandfather, however many generations apart.

"HE WILL NOT STOP UNTIL HE IS STOPPED. HISTORY SHOWS US THE PERSISTENCE OF THIS CREATURE CANNOT BE QUELLED. YOU MAY CHOOSE TO END

THE WYNTER LINE TO SUPPRESS HIS BID FOR POWER, BUT HE WILL ONLY CHOOSE ANOTHER FAMILY AND BEGIN ANEW. HE HAS AN INFINITE SUPPLY OF TIME, THE ONE THING YOU DO NOT POSSESS."

"Then how do we defeat him? What good is knowing any of this if he cannot be stopped?" Ana cried.

"DEFEAT IS NOT A STRAIGHT PATH. WE ARE KEEPERS OF THE PAST, NOT THE FUTURE. WE WATCH, WE RECORD, WE LISTEN, AND WE CONVEY. WE HAVE WATCHED YOU TRY AND FAIL TO STOP HIM. WE HAVE RECORDED YOUR FAILURES, AS WE HAVE RECORDED THE ONES OF THOSE WHO CAME BEFORE YOU. WE HAVE LISTENED TO YOUR QUESTIONS AND READ YOUR FEARS. AND WE HAVE CONVEYED WHAT WE KNOW. OUR POWER HAS NO REACH BEYOND THESE CAVERN WALLS. YOU ALONE, AS THE WYNTER HEIR, CAN DEFEAT HIM. WHETHER YOU WILL OR NOT IS A MATTER FOR TIME AND FATE."

Ana turned toward Tyreste, her head shaking. "I don't know what to make of this. All they've done is confirm that we're dealing with an overpowered creature who has all the time in the world. When I'm gone, he'll find another. You heard them. The ward wasn't enough."

"That's not all they've done," Tyreste said quietly. His brows furrowed in a deep frown. "I have an idea for when we leave here. It may lead us nowhere, but we have to try anything, don't we?"

"WE HAVE EXHAUSTED OUR KNOWLEDGE UPON YOU. YOU ARE DISMISSED."

"That's it?" Ana yelled. "There's truly nothing else you can tell us that will help?"

"WE ARE ARCHIVISTS, ANASTAZJA WYNTER. THE ANSWER TO YOUR QUESTION LIES BEYOND OUR WALLS. YOUR INVITE HAS BEEN RESCINDED."

"We used to be friends, Raisa," Ana muttered. Tyreste yanked on her hand and pulled her away from the platform. She stumbled into motion, looking back over her shoulder in desperation, but the glows of each arch receded one by one. There would be nothing more from the archivists.

He held fast to her as they rushed down the narrow passage. He didn't stop until they exited into the light of day, and before either of them spoke, he had her in a crushing hug.

"Ana, what do we know about your people? Beginning with Imryll?"

She shook her head against him. "I'm too tired for guessing."

"They were archivists themselves, weren't they? Imryll created Books of All Things. She and the duke, Rahn. They documented everything they could. Where do you think Zofia picked up her love of letter writing and ciphers? It *must* have been her grandmother."

Ana laughed and pulled back, looking up at him. "And?"

"And why would we ever think the letters are *all* that exist on the matter of Mor—"

Ana pressed a hand to his mouth. "Don't say his name. Not out here. I fear he can hear us when we do... like a summons."

Tyreste nodded. "There must be other documents. Imryll wouldn't have left it all to chance, not after everything she did to keep him away."

"If there are," Ana said, sighing, "I've never seen them."

"Well, you wouldn't have, would you? Not unless you knew where to look." Tyreste released her, running his hands down her arms. "Where would Imryll or Zofia have kept their secret writings?"

"I don't... I don't know, Tyreste..."

"Think!"

"The library at Fanghelm, perhaps. If there was anything at the observatory, I'd have found it years ago. Maybe in Books of All Things. But, Tyr—"

"Time is the one thing we don't have," he said quickly. "I'll go into the village, into Books, and see what I can find. I'll open every volume, shake out every page if I have to. You need to go home, to Fanghelm, and do the same. But Ana…" He reached for her face and cradled it in his hands. "I need to know you're protected. Ludya. Grigor. Whoever else you can trust. Enlist them to keep you safe, until we're together again. We meet back at my cabin at midnight, no matter *what* we have or have not found."

Ana tore away and turned her eyes on the ground. She pulled in a deep breath and released it, then again as a violent wave of nausea took hold. It had come on about a week ago and was worsening by the day. "Yes. All right. Midnight?"

"Midnight." He crushed his lips to hers. "Volemthe."

"Volemthe." She didn't tell him Mortain was there too, a whisper of death. He was always there—and always would be if she could not find a way to be rid of him.

And she must, for the kyschun and kyschuna had affirmed that the future of the Wynters was hers to sacrifice or save. The very thing she'd been fighting to protect all along hinged upon her own survival, changing everything.

"Midnight," he said once more when she broke off for Fanghelm. "There is an answer. I believe it in my bones. We just have to find it."

"Then we will," Ana said. "Oh, and Tyreste… You'll need a code if you want the scholar to grant you access." She gave it to him.

Tyreste nodded and headed down the road into town.

Her smile died the moment he turned toward the village.

Ana rushed to a patch of bushes and retched.

TWENTY-FIVE
LOOK TO THE SKIES AT DUSK

Tyr nudged his shoulder against the weighty entrance to Books of All Things. A series of bells went off in a shimmer of tinkles. Scholar Haldyr looked up from the tall, ominous counter—carved from a massive amount of ebony wood from the Great Darkwood—blinking dramatically as though the only light he'd seen in days was from the half-burnt candles huddled around the bulging tome he was reading. His spectacles slid to the tip of his nose as he cast a dark, suspicious eye on Tyr's arrival.

"Hej, Scholar Haldyr, kahk si?" Tyr asked, giving the desk a wider berth than felt reasonable. The man had to be nearing a hundred years old.

Haldyr's nose twitched at Tyr's atrocious pronunciations. "Do I know you?" The man didn't speak the words; he culled them, as though they'd been burned onto his tongue and needed excision.

"I'm here on behalf of Stewardess Anastazja Wynter," Tyr said, with a cough in the middle, in case the scholar didn't realize how unnerved he was. He glanced around at the endless rows of bookshelves with a pang of nostalgia for the days when he had so many works at his own disposal.

"Hmm." The scholar slid his spectacles to the bridge of his nose and narrowed his eyes. "You're no Wynter." He sniffed. "Nor Vjestik."

"You can *smell* that?" Tyr felt immediately foolish for asking. The man was clearly deriding him.

"What business have you undertaken for Miss Wynter?"

Tyr, not totally convinced Haldyr *hadn't* sniffed out his foreign-ness, decided a lie would get him thrown out. But so would the truth. "She has sent me to study any books or papers written by her ancestors. Or... ones her ancestors took a particular interest in."

Haldyr's expression thinned to a dry grin. "Well, that would be all of them, *stranjak*, wouldn't it?"

Tyr balked at stranjak, but at least he hadn't said uljez, the slur many Vjestik still used for outsiders. "Of course, but—"

"Unless you have a more specific request for me to entertain..." The scholar gestured his robed arms around. "You can see I am quite busy."

Tyr didn't need to turn around to recall the place was empty. "I won't require your aid beyond pointing me in the right direction. I can take it from there."

Haldyr folded his wrinkled hands atop the desk and waited. Tyr, flummoxed, was lost for words, until he remembered what Ana had told him just before she'd broken off for Fanghelm.

Sceptre of Ilynglass.

Tyr coughed. "I, uh... Yeah, uh, Sceptre of Ilynglass?"

The old scholar's brows shot up in a flash, widening his eyes to saucers. "Well then, stranjak. You must know a great many secrets you should not, but my charge does not involve the solving of such salacious conundrums. Follow me."

The scholar shuffled out from behind the tall counter, his head down and his hands straight at his sides, as he moved toward the back left corner of the rows of shelves. He stopped and ran a bony finger across a line of books, before tapping three times on one with a blue spine.

Tyr jumped when the entire shelf moved, bowing inward. The scholar stepped through the opening and disappeared.

Seeing no other choice, Tyr followed him into the secret passage.

For the first time in years, Ana did not step daintily through the halls of Fanghelm, hoping to remain unnoticed.

She stormed in like a soldier announcing a war.

The many eyes fixed on her belonged to people she'd known most or all of her life, staff she'd trusted for years before Magda had corrupted them. They gawped at her in a heady, dazed blend of confusion and sorrow, as though they'd awakened from a long nap and found their world much changed.

As they swarmed into the central hall, they each showered her with apologies, prostrate with horror at their inability to fight the thrall of the crone. They begged for Ana's forgiveness, something she didn't even know how to offer.

Ana didn't have time to relieve their anxiety, nor the heart. They had all, wittingly or not, played a significant role in subjugating and isolating her. The love she saw as she swept her attention across them, one by one, was not the consolation it might have been if she had still been the same subjugated, isolated girl who had nearly thrown her life away to find the light again.

She gripped a column when searing pain ripped across her mind. Mortain. He'd been trying to break in for hours, and her only reprieve had been the cave, a place he seemingly had no power. But relentless and determined, he'd come raging back, wearing her down, the moment she'd exited.

"Mistress?" asked Feyhan, Stepan's once-vodzhae. All Wynters were supposed to have one, but Magda had driven Ana's away years ago. Feyhan had stayed on, aiding Lenik in his work with Arkhady, but she knew his true intent in staying had been to eventually convince Ana he would be a suitable replacement for the one she'd lost. He might have made a persuasive argument had he not eventually, like the others, succumbed to Magda's sway. "This is everyone. As you asked."

Everyone was more than she had realized. Could there really be over a hundred staff in Fanghelm? Had she been so inured to the world around her that she'd forgotten so much?

Ludya pulled up beside her. "Breathe, Ana. You are stronger than your doubt would have you believe."

"Where's my father?"

"Lenik is with him. He's improving, but he's experienced some confusion." Ludya patted Ana's arm. "It may take time for him to return to the man you remember."

Ana nodded, drawing a shaky breath. "And Grigor?"

"Here." The man stepped in from the hall. "Discovered two trying to escape. Minions of the crone." His nose and mouth twitched. "They work for no one now."

Ana arched a brow at her uncle's casual delivery of confessing the murder of two people. But she would spare no tears for traitors. She turned back toward the gathered staff. "I'll keep this brief. Magda is dead. She can plague us no longer. I will not hold over your heads the terrible deeds you committed on her behalf. The pain you caused. For I, too, hurt others in her name. But Magda was not the source of the evil that haunted our halls. She answered to a being far more powerful, one whose name I will not speak. Whose name will *never* be spoken in our halls again. Never be written in our caves, our histories." Ana paused to gauge their reactions.

They were all listening, rapt.

"I intend to defeat him and end this. But I need to know my father is safe. That Fanghelm is safe." Ana gestured toward Ludya. "Ludya here, along with her fellow vedhma and veduhn, will guide you all in how to protect your minds from malicious infiltration. Until this is ended, Fanghelm will be a fortress—impenetrable, even from a monster such as the one who has chosen us for his diabolical deeds. I require verbal acknowledgment from all here that you understand what I am saying and asking."

Murmurs rippled through the staff. Some wore uncertainty in their eyes, others excitement. But she'd done her part and had to trust Ludya to do hers.

"One more thing, in the event this is not already clear to you now that your minds have been released. The Ravenwoods are our *allies*, not our enemies. Henceforth, anyone who harms them, unless acting in justifiable self-defense, will be held to the same laws that govern harm to our own people. Understood?"

More affirmations followed. Ana breathed deep and turned toward Grigor. "Follow me to the library?"

He nodded and fell in behind her.

When they were safely inside, Ana bolted the doors and faced her uncle. "Can I count on you to do something for me?"

Grigor leaned against the door with a stoic nod. "You know my answer."

"The observatory," she intoned. The idea felt extreme, even under the circumstances. Could a *place* be evil? Or was it evil that rendered a place unfit for use? Did it matter, when her heart told her this *must* be done? "There is a cellar in the courtyard behind it."

"I know it."

"You do?"

"It's no cellar."

Ana scoffed. "Nien. And you may wish to take reinforcements, for I cannot be certain there will not be other sycophants of the koldyna lying in wait to avenge her."

"Unnecessary. What is the ask?"

She told him.

"This is what you want?" he asked.

Ana nodded. "I would do it myself if there was time. But I have..." She staggered into a desk. Grigor rushed forward, but she stopped him with a head shake. "I have no time to waste, and I need to know what my ancestors knew. What they *did*. Because it worked. It wasn't perfect, but it worked, and there must be a way to do it better."

"Who will stay with you?" Grigor hovered over her.

"Well, I have all of Fanghelm, don't I?" She forced a smile, but he didn't appear fooled. His solemn stare was unwavering. "I'll be *fine*, Onkel. Ludya will join me once she's trained the staff. And I'll be meeting Tyreste after I finish here."

"I'll speak with her on my way out," Grigor muttered. He marched to the door and turned back. "Look to the skies at dusk."

Ana nodded until he left. When he was gone, she allowed a single, vexing wave of tears, wiped them away, and went to work.

Tyreste's nerves balanced on a razor-thin edge. He hadn't expected the Wynter's secret documents to be in a dungeon, down a long, winding stairway that was far too similar to the one leading down to the place he'd wasted years of his life.

You can leave anytime, he reminded himself, mopping sweat from his brows every few minutes. *You chose to come here. This is not that.*

The room was far smaller, more cramped than his Reliquary living space. It was practically a closet, the walls lined ceiling to floor with books, stacked in haphazard piles lacking any cohesive organization. Most clearly hadn't been touched in many years, and when he disturbed the stacks, dust plumed and swirled in the condensed space, sending his sinuses into a tailspin.

He didn't know what he was looking for. He couldn't even read half the works, many of which were written, unsurprisingly, in Vjestikaan. Looking back on his suggestion to split up, he realized the foolishness of it. If the answer was in the claustrophobic box he'd willingly locked himself in, he might never find it.

Tyr's thoughts turned to delirium right as he heard someone descending the staircase, into the vault.

He prepared to inform the scholar he needed more time, but when he turned around, the words died on his tongue.

328

It wasn't Haldyr at all, but Adeline.

"What..." He shook his head and signed, *What are you doing here?*

Addy thrust a note toward him.

He leaned in to read. *Your brother will need a Vjestik cipher. I found this one in our library. I only hope it is not too late. You will find him in the vault of Books of All Things, and to get to him, you will need the passcode, which I am writing here, in the language of Old Ilynglass, in case someone other than you reads this.*

Addy passed the cipher over. It was more of a journal, wrapped in old leather.

Tyr swallowed hard. *Thank you. This will be a great help to me.*

To us, Addy signed, tapping the words on her chest for emphasis. *I'm not leaving until you do.*

Tyr shook his head, but she plopped herself on the floor in between piles of books and grinned.

Perhaps you should tell me what we're looking for.

Tyr groaned, realizing they could argue the point for hours and he'd still lose. *All right, but afterward, you go straight home. Deal?*

Addy beamed with excitement. *Oh! I almost forgot. A letter came from the Eesterlands for you.*

And let me guess, you took it upon yourself to read it?

Of course I did. It was from Rhiain. Asterin and Sesto are still on the road, but she said she received your last message, and she understands.

Understands? Tyr signed back.

Adeline frowned and dug into her dress pocket. She withdrew a crinkled wad of vellum. *She understands...* Her eyes scanned the paper. *Here we are. I understand you've exhausted your efforts and appreciate them.*

Let me see that. Tyr took the paper and read it himself. Seeing Rhiain's lovely scrawl choked him up. "If Asterin were here, he would release you to return to your other projects, but since he is not, I will say it. One last thing..." Tyr wiped his eyes on his sleeve. "Be happy. With love."

He dropped the letter and breathed deep. If only she knew... If only they all knew everything that had happened since Asterin and Sesto had slid the stack of correspondence across his table.

But the letters had brought Ana back to him. If they'd never landed in his hands, she would still be fighting her war alone.

He smiled at Addy. *All right then. Let's get started.*

At dusk, Ana moved to the east window and turned her face toward the mountains.

She braced herself on the frame, too exhausted to stand without aid. Sweat rolled down her temples and disappeared into the bosom of her dress. Failure burned through her weary limbs from the hours and hours she'd spent searching books and scrolls and pamphlets, coming up with *nothing*.

Not a single thing.

She pressed her forehead to the cool pane, her breathing shallow, and watched the sky dance with flames of gold and red. They licked the stormy sky like wispy tendrils, becoming one with the turquoise-and-violet auroras.

Ana didn't hear the door open, nor the steps drawing nearer. She didn't notice Ludya at all until the vedhma wrapped a protective arm around her from the side and joined her in watching the observatory burn.

"It's almost beautiful, isn't it?" Ludya remarked. "Destruction often is."

"It solves nothing, but... I couldn't let it..." Fatigue took the rest of her words.

"I know." Ludya ran her hand along Ana's lower back. "I would have done the same, Anastazja." Her hand came to a stop. "You didn't find what you were looking for."

Ana bowed her head and shook it.

"Perhaps Tyreste will have met with better fortune." Ludya breathed deep. "But I did not come here to enjoy the final throes of the observatory with you."

330

Ana rolled her face along the glass until she was looking at Ludya.

"I fear you are not in the right mind for such a revelation, but there is no better timing than now, when you are battling yourself on the proper strategy... on the energy you're willing to give a fight you are afraid you cannot win."

Ana shrugged and closed her eyes. "I never know what you're trying to say."

"Then let me speak plainly," Ludya said. She leaned in and pressed her lips to Ana's ear. "I know what exhausts you, and it is far more than the wickedness of a rogue sorcerer."

Ana's eyes opened.

Ludya spoke plainly.

TWENTY-SIX
THE LIFE WE'RE FIGHTING FOR

Ana used the last of her vitality to become Nessa. She no longer had a koldyna to hide from, but she'd never in her life needed to disappear more. To be unseen by the world.

Villagers in the market turned their heads to look at the pretty girl, but they saw only what she wanted them to see, their minds sorting her with the other scenery. Some stalls were still decorated for the ill-fated Cider Festival, but most had been shuttered after the tragedy. Yet life went on for a village that was always one terrible storm—and one damaged storehouse—from starvation.

She couldn't fool Mortain though. He knew her from within, and boy, was he determined she know it. He rattled the bars of her mind like an insolent child trying to gain their mother's attention. On and on, pushing her queasiness to a peak. She stumbled into a boarded shop, retched, and pushed on.

Ludya had wanted to come. Grigor had wanted to come. She'd sworn to return soon, this time with Tyreste, a promise that barely sated either of them. It seemed that was what her life

333

had devolved to, a system of coming and going and promising to return.

What she had to say to Tyreste, she had to say to him alone.

She didn't bother knocking on the cabin door. He'd still be at Books, more than likely, and she looked forward to letting herself in, heating some cider, and closing her mind for a few precious moments of uninterrupted thought.

But Tyreste *was* home. And he wasn't alone.

Addy leaped from her chair and flew across the room, throwing herself into Ana's arms. Ana closed her eyes and held her. The warmth of the younger girl, the closest she'd ever come to having a sister, pushed Ana's tears forward.

Tyreste's chair screeched. Ana opened her eyes and shook her head.

Volemthe, she signed to Addy, because she'd not told the girl she loved her before. There wasn't time to address all of life's regrets, but she could remedy that one. *You are the sister I always wished I could have had.*

I am your sister, Ana. In all the ways that matter.

Ana crushed her into another hug, meeting Tyreste's eyes over the top of Addy's head.

She kissed Addy's forehead as she pulled back. *Can I speak to your brother alone?*

Addy's mouth pursed. Her eyes flicked to the side, narrowing. *I know why you've come, and I can help. I want to help.*

I really don't want to involve you in this. Neither does your brother. We couldn't bear pulling you into danger.

He said I could be here.

Ana looked at Tyreste for assistance.

"She helped me at Books," he explained, glancing away.

"The cipher." Ana sucked in through her teeth. What had she expected when she'd sent Addy to the shop? "Did you find anything?"

Tyreste nodded. "We did. Will you sit down, and we'll walk you through it?"

She realized that even when he'd been looking at her, he hadn't been looking *at* her. "You're both making me nervous."

Addy signed something behind her that she didn't see. Tyreste shook his head and signed back, *I should do this alone. We'll come get you after.*

Ana whipped around to read Addy's response when a violent bout of nausea sent her crashing into the table. She took a chair with her to the floor.

Tyreste was at her side in an instant. He shoved the chair to the wall and cradled Ana's head in his lap. "Talk to me, Ana."

"It's worse..." Ana panted. "When he's trying to get in. It's so much worse." She nestled her face against Tyreste's thigh and focused on breathing.

Tyreste's hands left her for a moment. She couldn't see the exchange between him and Addy, but she felt the air shift as their messages flew back and forth.

Boots thumped on the boards. A door opened and closed.

"I promised we'd come get her before we return to Fanghelm." Tyreste brushed her hair off her face in gentle strokes. "You said it's worse when he's trying to get in. You mean who I think you mean?"

Ana nodded against his trousers. She wasn't ready to open her eyes.

"But you also said 'trying.' You're fighting him off, aren't you? He can't get in if you don't let him."

"I think... yes. If I focus on keeping him out, I can." She rolled her head upward to look at him. "But I'm so tired. And... There's something else I have to tell you, but I don't know how to find the words."

The solemn, loving look Tyreste wore as he cupped her face, caressing her cheek with this thumb, brought fresh terror to the surface. She had lost him before and could lose him again. She might lose him in that very moment.

"Use whatever words feel right." He tried to smile. "Unless you're planning to rush headlong into death again."

"It's not that," she said quickly and sucked in a greedy breath. Mortain had gone silent, but she didn't trust for a moment that he wasn't waiting in the shadows of her mind, biding his return. "I swear to you, I thought I had done everything right, Tyr. I took all the right precautions, I never meant for this to happen, to do this to you, to saddle you with such a burden."

"Don't suffer by holding it in," Tyreste said gently. He leaned down and kissed the corner of her teary eye. "Whatever it is, we'll figure it out together."

"I tried to solve it before it even happened," Ana said. She squeezed her eyes closed and rolled her face downward. "It's why I was so vigilant with the grimizhna tea, drinking it almost every night."

Tyreste's hands stopped caressing her cheek. He stilled entirely, then started to withdraw.

Ana's heart skipped in dread, and she lifted off of him and tried to scoot away. "I'm sorry, Tyreste. I truly am."

His arm shot out to draw her in again. He pressed her to his chest. "Do *not* misread my shock as horror, Ana," he stated, giving her a soft but firm shake. "If you think I would ever *not* want to raise a family with you, if *I* have ever led you to believe that's not the life I'm fighting for... then shame on me. Shame on me."

Ana looked up right as he tilted her chin to kiss her.

"I would burn the world to make it safe for the three of us. But we might not have to," he whispered against her lips. He ran his mouth along hers. "When I tell you what I found, you'll know fate is smiling upon us. The Guardians smile upon us. Just as they smiled upon Imryll when she fled her father's evil hold."

Ana pushed up to sit beside him. "Tell me."

"Addy found a letter, written by Zofia," he said. "It was *meant* to be found, though by you, not us. It was stuck in the middle of a book titled *The Witchwood Observatory: A Spectacular History*. When she picked it up, I felt this tightness in my chest, and before I could take it from her, she'd found the letter wedged between the pages." He reached into his pocket and handed it to her. "Want me to read it to you?"

Ana nodded, grateful not to have to move her eyes too much. "Please?"

Tyreste cleared his throat. He flashed her a quick smile from the side before beginning. "If you are reading this, it is because you sought the knowledge I hope to impart, the knowledge required to save your people—and theirs. And if you are who I believe you to be, I do not need to define who 'they' are, do I?" He glanced over. "You're not going to believe what she says, Ana."

Ana's mouth lifted in a frown. She looked at Tyreste, but he was searching for his place.

"My grandmother Imryll is the daughter of..." Tyreste mouthed the word, and she loved him for remembering she couldn't bear to speak or hear it. "You by now may understand he is no mere man at all, but a powerful Meduwyn, those terrible sorcerers from Beyond, a place they called the Sceptre of Ilynglass. Imryll was born in the White Kingdom, but *her* parents were part of those who arrived on a fateful passage. It saw thousands of Rhiagain dead in the sea and just as many from the Noble Houses. If you do not know the term Noble Houses, it was the moniker ascribed to highborns in their land. Dukes, duchesses... titles we do not know or use here. The man believed to be Imryll's father was the Duke of Glaisgain, a vain, dangerous man who tried to sell Imryll to a king, but she instead fell for a knight. The rest of the tale is as shocking as it is sordid, and if you wish to learn more, there is a book in the vault called *The Claw and the Crowned* that tells the whole story. What you need to know is..." Tyreste again redacted the name. "*Wanted* his daughter and Drazhan together. He orchestrated a terrible genocide in the Cross, one that pushed the surviving heir, Drazhan, on the path that led him to Imryll. The sorcerer wanted Imryll to beget a dynasty in the Cross, so that through her and her descendants, he could control the Ravenwoods. But Imryll, terrified of being his pawn, came into her powers and discovered her gift of flight. She flew from

Duncarrow and holed herself away in a place she felt safe, for many months. No one found her, not even her father, for she had found the secret to keeping him out of her mind."

Ana's mouth had dried out. She tried to wet it, to swallow, or to do anything, but she needed to hear the rest. She nodded for Tyreste to go on.

"The sorcerer made the mistake of telling my grandfather Drazhan, who had been searching for Imryll for many months, that she did not want to be found, and so she would not be. Drazhan learned the sorcerer could hurt no one sharing his blood. He could get into their minds, attempt manipulative tactics... but even then, only if they allowed him. The shared blood acts as a shield for both sides. It is why he cannot be killed by his kin, but neither can he kill them. He will not want you to know this, and of course, this is precisely why I am telling you." Tyreste took a deep breath and switched to the next page. "But he can and will kill those you love. To hurt you. To control you. He took my dearest cousin, Paeris, from me, as he took my grandmother's oldest friend, King Torian, from her. But Imryll, in her desperation and helplessness, discovered it was this *very love* that gave her power against him. When she was hiding, in a small cabin in the Easterlands, her fear and love created a ward that kept her and her unborn child safe from detection. Drazhan only found her because he was keen enough to read through the monster's message, and he knew Imryll as well as he knew his own heart. He knew where she would go to keep herself and her child safe." Tyreste glanced over to check on Ana, but she nodded for him to finish. "When I came to my grandmother and confessed that Paeris had been murdered, and by whom, she folded me into her secrets. Together, we placed a new ward over Witchwood Cross, barring the monster from ever crossing our gates. It worked. If it ever fails to work, I will come back and leave another letter with this one. But while I do not expect it to fail, not in my lifetime, I know the creature is patient. He has what we do not have: endless

338

time. One day another ward will be needed, and so I leave you with the secret to creating one."

Tyreste wiped his eyes and kissed Ana's forehead. He folded the letter and put it back in his vest. "Do you want to know what the secret is?"

Ana looked up and nodded. "A spell? Magic we haven't seen yet?"

His eyes were ringed with red as he watched her. "No, Ana. It's love. The fear of losing what makes your heart beat. Imryll was so terrified for her unborn child, she turned her fear into protection. When Zofia went to her grandmother, pregnant from an affair with a boy she'd loved from childhood, Imryll bade her to channel her terror into power, and she did. Imryll used the monster's *own magic against him* to keep him away."

Ana bowed her head with a deflated scoff. "But I have been afraid every single day since Magda showed up in our lives. I have loved to the depths of my soul. If that were all it took, I would have driven the evil from this land a decade ago."

"Anastazja," Tyreste said slowly. "There is a different kind of love for those you hold as equals than there is for those whose entire existence depends on your ability to provide safety."

Ana brought a shaky hand to her belly. She was almost scared to touch it, to acknowledge the life growing within, the life she already knew she would die to keep safe. When Mortain discovered it, he would rage at the wrinkle in his plan. There was no telling what he would do to return her to the path he'd set her on.

"I do love them. I don't even know them, our baby, but I love them so much," Ana said. Her face crumpled in sadness, and Tyreste tugged her close. "I understand Imryll now. I only thought I understood fear before."

"I know," Tyreste agreed. He nestled his face in her hair. "I know what you mean."

"We don't have much time." Ana wiped her eyes and sat up. "I think my... my biggest failure of the past years has been believing

339

I could do any of this on my own. That I was ever going to solve this without letting others in."

"You're talking to the king of Never Admitting Weakness," Tyreste said in a hushed tone. "The past isn't our concern, Ana. No one has the power to change it, not even the monster deciding fates. There's a fallacy in thinking a trail of sadness behind us means we can only pave the road with more of the same. We know we need each other, and we know we need help. So let's embrace those things and finish this."

"Your family stays out of it," Ana said hotly. "And I mean it. I want them safe. If this doesn't have to be their battle, we don't make it their battle."

"Well," Tyr said, hands tented under his chin. "I won't argue that. But if we don't invite Addy in, she'll invite herself, and then we lose the power to protect her."

Ana sighed. "You're right. Okay. We need to return to Fanghelm, share Zofia's letter, and let those who would stand with us stand with us. Let them decide whether the risk is worth taking. Everyone gets a choice. No one is required to stay or to help."

Tyr stretched to his feet and reached a hand down. His mouth was drawn in a solemn line, but the warmth in his eyes betrayed the hope his findings had given them both. "Let's grab Addy and go."

TWENTY-SEVEN
BLOOD OF THE MEDUWYN

If someone had told Arkhady Wynter he'd been sleeping for years, he would have believed it. No command his mind gave had put his limbs into motion, even with hours and hours of Lenik coaching him through what the vodzhae persisted in calling, with careful hand pats every time he said it, "*your terrible ordeal.*"

Arkhady had asked after Stepan and had been given news so soul-crushing, he might have returned to wherever he'd been for the past while, if a sharp, dark memory hadn't reminded him he already knew his son, his baby, had perished in the Vuk od Varem. Five years it had been. Five years and Arkhady could still feel his son's presence like he'd only left yesterday.

The rest was a mess of twisted, rotted vines, flashes of thorns and honey, and so much bewilderment. He ordered Lenik to bring Niko and Ana to his chambers, but Niko had been "ordered away" by the stewardess, and Ana's whereabouts were unknown.

His entire family, gone.

And the stewardess...

In his nightmares, he remembered everything. The way she'd come to Fanghelm, when Ksana was still alive and floating through Arkhady's days like a dream he never wished to wake from. He couldn't recall which of them had made the case to bring Magda into their lives, but he alone shouldered the blame for wedding her. Grief was a powerful yoke. It would never be reason enough for the suffering his family and people had endured when he was too distraught to confront reality.

"The witch is dead," Lenik said, throwing wide the curtains with aplomb. He'd only said it a hundred times, each time casting a knowing glance Arkhady's way like it was the first time, like he wasn't quite certain the steward was done with his long sleep.

"I need my children, Lenik." Arkhady slapped the nightstand for a glass of water to wet his throat.

Lenik fluttered over and placed it in his hand.

"Someone must know where Niko is. And Ana..." The sound of her name in his mouth recalled a hundred heartbreaking moments. Ana pleading with him to see the truth... him ordering her to fall in line. If only he'd said the words he should have: *we must fight.* How much might have been different...

"Grigor knows where Niko is, and has sent men to retrieve him," Lenik explained. He crossed his arms and frowned at Arkhady, still in bed. "Ana will return. She said as much to the staff earlier when she gave her speech."

"Speech?" Arkhady's forehead knit tight. He willed his legs to move, but they may as well have been boulders. "What's she up to, Lenik?"

"I couldn't say, sir." Lenik cast an odd look toward the hearth. Arkhady never got the chance to push further because a knock sounded on the door, and Lenik flew into motion.

Arkhady swallowed more wine and tried to pick up the conversation between Lenik and whoever was on the other side of the crack in the door. All he heard was *uninvited.*

Lenik clicked the door closed and turned, his back pressed to it. "Steward Wynter, you will *never* believe who has arrived to Fanghelm Keep. I daresay if I gave you a dozen guesses you'd waste all of them."

Arkhady capped the wine with a groan. "If it isn't one of my children, then I don't care."

"Oh," the vodzhae said with a slow grin. "You will care about this one. Shall I fetch a wheeled chair, or do you suppose your legs may finally obey you?"

Arkhady closed his eyes. He could almost reach for the escape, the dangerous void where he'd lived, guileless and guiltless, for too long.

No, not guiltless.

The guilt was more powerful than any sway Magda had held over him.

"Help me to my feet," he said, deciding. "And we'll see if today is the day the Guardians deem me fit to fight."

Your father is in the dining hall was all Ana heard before she went flying down the corridor. Had she lingered a second longer, she might have saved herself from the shock that followed.

"Ota!" she cried, searching for Arkhady and finding, instead, a table full of beautiful men and women bedecked in black leather and feathers. She passed her eyes over every one, including the enigmatic High Priestess Elyria, deciding it was a trap until she finally spotted her father, thin and small, at the other end.

Ana staggered backward and into Ludya. She felt Tyreste's presence at her side, felt him make himself big.

Elyria rose, prompting a flutter of rustled feathers and squeaking leather as the rest joined her. Ana darted her gaze around in a dumbfounded bid to decide whether to fall at the raven's feet or turn and run.

Arkhady planted his palms on the table and tried to stand. He wobbled and returned to the chair. Lenik rushed to assist, but Arkhady swatted him away.

"My beloved Pjika." He sounded so small, so unlike the formidable man who had been both sword and shield of her young life. "You need not fear the Ravenwoods. Sit. Listen."

"With respect, Steward, I think we'll stand," Tyreste stated from beside Ana. He reached for her hand and clasped it tight in his.

"I understand our presence has alarmed you." Elyria gestured for the others to sit but remained standing herself. "I've thought a great deal about the troubled phoenix who approached her penance with bravery and resolve. When my scouts returned and confirmed what we'd heard about the stewardess, I came to offer my congratulations to your father and rekindle the alliance we enjoyed for so many years, before recent tragedies."

Addy yanked on Ana's other hand to get her attention. She signed, *I sense sadness but not anger.*

Ana nodded briskly to keep Addy from catching the ravens' attention, nudging the girl behind her. She swallowed the fear she couldn't afford anyone in the room seeing. "High Priestess..." Ana sucked in a breath.

Tyreste's hand twitched in hers, his eyes narrowing at the high priestess in warning.

"I was ready to die. I had accepted it. Others had not." She turned her gaze toward the ground. Her heart pounded in her ears. "But upon being saved, I learned something that compelled me instead to fight. I returned home to help you, to help us all. And while I will not hide from the penance I avoided, I would ask that you... you allow me first to safely deliver my child to my family, as the child is not responsible for the crimes of their mother. They are the future of the Wynters. You have no reason to care, but my descendants have not wronged you. I have. It is not our way or yours to punish those who have done nothing to deserve it."

"Ana." Arkhady wobbled to his feet. He swayed, but Lenik was there to steady him. "*Anastazja.*"

"No. Fuck that," Tyreste hissed and bolted forward, releasing Ana's hand. "High Priestess, you had your chance—"

Elyria held out a hand, and Tyreste stopped mid-lunge, frozen in place. He strained, gaping at himself in disbelief. She flicked her wrist and released him, but she cocked her head in warning. "I didn't come here to harm you, Anastazja. Your resilience has stayed with me, nagged at me. I haven't been able to stop thinking about you."

"Ota, I'm sorry you had to learn this way," Ana said gently, allowing a soft smile to linger on her aged father before moving on. He looked so old, sitting there, but he seemed to be improving right before her eyes.

Arkhady shook his head without looking at her.

As she swept her gaze back to Elyria, it was caught by a young woman with the most captivating eyes Ana had ever seen. She was younger than Addy but wore her regal pride in the lift of her chin and lengthening of her delicate neck. Elyria's daughter, Ana realized, the one who would soon take her place in the highest role. Ana had no doubt that the younger girl would not have shown her the same mercy as her mother had. "High Priestess—"

"Please. Sit. You have my word no one here will be harmed." Elyria gestured around. "You don't have to trust me. Trust the hundreds of guards who would have us all subdued before we could eliminate more than one or two of you."

"Comforting," Tyreste grumbled.

Ana nodded to tell him it was all right. She took the seat at the farthest end from her father, turned half to the side to show she wasn't planning to get comfortable. Tyreste reluctantly sat beside her, and Addy slid in opposite him.

"High Priestess, this is Tyreste Penhallow, my... my *love*, and this is his sister, Adeline. Should you prove yourself a deceiver and any harm comes to either of them or their family, you can be assured I will take to the skies and burn your Rookery to ash."

"Can you even fly anymore, sparrow?" quipped the violet-eyed heir. She rolled her eyes at another next to her, who laughed coldly. "My mother wisely stole your ability to land."

"Who says I need to land to destroy?" Ana asked.

345

"Enough," Elyria stated. "Raelyria."

"Mother." Raelyria's nostrils flared as she folded her hands on her lap and glowered forward.

"Pjika," Arkhady said from the other end. His thin voice was swallowed by the roaring hearth. She felt his vigor returning to him piece by piece, but only time would reveal how fully he'd recover. "High Priestess Elyria has told me everything. There will be other times to rehash it, to decide—" He coughed into his sleeve, and Lenik shoved a goblet of wine under his nose. Arkhady glared and the vodzhae recalled his arm. "To *discuss* the news you are unwed and with child."

Tyreste tensed.

"But today we find ourselves evaluating the past years with the dark lens of new information. Had I known Magda had been sent by a wretched creature, determined to use our people to harm our friends... Well, it does not matter what I would have done, for our foe is strong and wily. He is resourceful and does not suffer under the limitation of time. Perhaps if we had all been working together more cohesively... Well, there is no room for 'perhaps,' is there? We did not, and here we are—fractured and dispirited, but not vanquished. As long as I draw breath..." He lifted his eyes to meet Ana's. "I will use my strength toward whatever conclusion we require to excise this rot from our land."

Elyria pulled a hard breath through her nose with a sharp turn toward Adeline. She lifted her hands and signed, *Will you please show my daughter and the other Ravenwoods to the sitting room?*

Adeline's eyes widened in stunned surprise. She whipped her head toward Ana, but Ana was just as confused.

"One of your ancestors taught us the language of the deaf," Elyria said, signing the same words to Adeline. "Ravenwoods are not impervious to the troubles of man. I have just asked young Adeline to accompany the other Ravenwoods to the sitting room, or elsewhere, if you prefer it, Steward. But I would like for the three of us to discuss this next part privately."

"Four," Ana stated. She flicked her eyes at her restless lover.

Arkhady lifted his shoulders at Elyria, and she nodded.

Tyreste signed to Adeline that everything was fine, to do as the raven asked. He told her where the sitting room was, and that he'd come find her soon. She wasn't pleased, but she beckoned the others to follow.

The four watched the room empty in silence. Ana looked to the high priestess and waited for her to begin.

"I assume we are all now apprised and there's nothing new to share," Elyria said. "So let us discuss what we will do."

"High Priestess," Ana said, cutting in. She glanced at Tyreste, who still hadn't settled. "We do have something new to share."

Elyria swept her hands at Ana.

"We have been..." Ana tried not to look at her father. Every time she did, she faltered, whisked back to a time when he had been her hero. Before her was the husk of that man. The font of power in the room had shifted, to her, and she wondered if he could sense it as well. If Elyria could sense it. "Searching for answers in the old Wynter writings. As you know, my people were scholars and scribes, just as much as they were witches, and if there was going to be an answer anywhere, it would be within those writings."

"It's all mostly clinical though," Arkhady said. "Documentation of people, creatures, places, scientific phenomena... If there was ever a mention of M—"

"Don't say his name!" Ana cried. "It's the same as an invitation. And he's been..."

"He hasn't... He's found you?" Arkhady paled.

"Tak, Ota. He came to me in a vision and said if I..." Ana trailed off, realizing Mortain hadn't tried to assail her mind since before she'd arrived at the cabin. His silence was as troubling as his presence though. "If I were to breed with the Ravenwoods, he would spare you. Niko. Tyreste. And he would put an end to Magda's hold on this family and village." She lowered her gaze to her lap. "And I accepted his terms. I thought I could outsmart him and find another way, once Magda was gone, but when I went to the observatory to warn Varradyn, he was dead. Magda had already taken his heart. And something inside of me, it snapped. I needed to warn the other Ravenwoods, to offer myself in atonement, and the sorcerer clung to that weakness and distorted it. He wanted me to lure another to replace Var. He almost won, but I was stronger, that time. And you know the rest, High Priestess. Ota, I assume you do as well."

Arkhady and Elyria nodded. Tyreste fixed his gaze on the fire.

"Tyreste, Ludya, and Grigor found me after. Saved me. Tyreste and I visited the kyschun, who told us about the wards, and we then split up, he to Books of All Things, and me to the library here at Fanghelm. I found nothing useful, but Tyreste and Adeline..." She turned toward Tyreste to give him a chance to speak.

He watched her, uncertain, before he started. "It was Adeline who found it. Using a cipher Ana sent, she translated a letter from Zofia Wynter, addressed to descendants searching for answers. She outlined the way she and her grandmother Imryll had joined together to place a ward over Witchwood Cross to keep... *him* out. And it worked. It's still working, because if it wasn't, he'd never have needed Magda. We can be sure he will send another in her place if... *when* Ana fails to deliver on his revolting ask. And our plan is to create a new ward, stronger than the last. More intentional than the last."

"We've tried wards," Elyria said with a dismissive scoff. "He's impervious to them. How can you be certain that's what has kept him from your village?"

"He is impervious to wards created by you," Tyreste replied. "He has Ravenwood blood, but you do not have Meduwyn blood. *Ana* does. All Wynters heirs do."

"He cannot hurt me, nor my family. Not directly," Ana said. "And unfortunately, this means we cannot harm him either. But we can keep his influence from our gates. From yours, High Priestess. We propose for the ward to surround the Rookery itself, protecting you from not only him but *us*. A ward that expels mal-intent, whether it comes from a Wynter or a Meduwyn or anyone doing the creature's bidding. An armistice isn't enough. There must be an assurance that future generations cannot choose to go backward. The sorcerer is already barred from these lands. So if *we* cannot fly to you, then no one can."

Arkhady shook his head. "How would that work, if you cannot..." He screwed his face into a wince. "If your flight was taken from you, Pjika?"

Elyria nodded to herself with a distant look. "I may be able to help with that."

The debate stretched for hours. The four of them traded ideas, objections, suggestions, and arguments. Supper came and went, food delivered but hardly touched, and by nightfall they had a plan.

When Elyria left to check on the other Ravenwoods, Ana leaned toward Tyreste and whispered, "Can I speak to my father alone for a few minutes?"

Tyreste nodded. He stretched and blinked his bleary eyes. "I should check on Addy anyway. But I'd like to speak with him when you're done."

Ana perked. "Speak with my father?"

He kissed her and stood. "Send for me when you're ready."

She listened to his footsteps fade down the hall. Already she missed him, felt less anchored in the absence of his soothing presence.

"Ana—" Arkhady said, but the screech of her chair cut him off. She raced down the length of the table and collapsed at his feet.

"Ota, say nothing. Pros." Ana rested her head sideways across his knees. His touch was tentative, his hands trembling as they brushed across her cheek and swept into her hair, as though he wasn't sure if she was real. "I know you tried to keep us safe."

"My darling." Arkhady's firm voice dissolved into a pained whimper. "How can so much hurt ever be healed? Your mother.

Stepan. All those Ravenwoods. What you... *you* have had to endure. Alone."

"The past isn't our concern," Ana said, channeling Tyreste's message from earlier. "All we can do is look to the future and refuse to let others take it from us." She wiped her eyes on his trousers and looked up from the floor. "Volemthe, Ota. Volemthe. I need you strong, not defeated. Will you try, for me?"

Arkhady's crestfallen face flushed with emotion, tears streaming down his cheeks. He stared down at her in wordless examination, his bloodshot eyes full of regret and devastation. "I owe you. I owe you the years she stole, the wounds that may never close. But since I cannot give those to you, I will never refuse you anything again, Pjika. I will never hold you from what you are meant to do. How could I? But must you really go up that mountain to solve this? What about your child... my grandchild..."

"The Ancestors are with me, Father. Imryll. Zofia. I *feel* them. Their love. Their wisdom. They will not leave me in my hour of need." She looked down again. "I thought I had to die to atone for my part in what happened to the Ravenwoods. But I see now there is no greater sacrifice I can make than the risk I must bear to protect them from the future Wynters. There will always be a Magda, a willing tool of a too-powerful creature. He will always find a way to infiltrate our family. But if we cut ourselves off from Midnight Crest forever, then no amount of temptation or control will provide him another way into the skies. We'll effectively be useless to him."

"I've never harbored the illusion anything I say will keep you from stubbornly doing what you want anyway," Arkhady said slowly. "But it doesn't mean I'm abiding losing my daughter either. I've only just got her back."

"You won't lose her," Ana said, even though it wasn't a promise she could reliably make. She and her child might die on the mountain. But if she couldn't gather the courage to go, she would eventually succumb to Mortain's torment, leaving her father and Niko vulnerable to his influence. And though she had always looked up to them in the past, she saw them so much differently after all she'd shouldered to keep them safe—after watching them easily succumb to the koldyna's thrall when she'd been strong enough to fight back, to not lose herself. If they were the ones tapped to travel up the mountain, they would crumble under the same pressure that had turned Ana's flesh to stone.

"A child..." Arkhady sighed with a soft laugh. "A husband should come first, Pjika. Have I taught you nothing?"

"I had my own lessons to learn, Ota." Ana stirred to her feet and bowed over him, gathering him in her arms. "And I love him. I've loved him for years. I should have told you before."

"How could you have, lost as I was?" Arkhady turned his sad face toward hers. "There is no recompense adequate for the neglect I've shown you. I thought by keeping Magda sated I was keeping you and Niko safe, but once she had her hold in me, there was nothing left to offer to you. That is *my* fault, not hers. I may be the patriarch of this family, but I have not acted like one."

"We're all getting a chance to set matters back to rights, Ota." Ana kissed him and pulled away, sensing that to stay, to linger in their shared remorse, would only delay the inevitable. "I'm going to find High Priestess Elyria and begin preparations. There's just one more thing I need to ask you first."

"Niko," Arkhady replied, guessing correctly. "Grigor found him. He's already on his way home to us, Pjika. And he'll be the first face you see when you come down from the mountain."

Tyr left Ana and Elyria to their plotting and made his way back to the dining hall. Arkhady was still at the table, quaking through another attempt to stand on his own. Tyr rushed over and helped the steward to his feet before the proud man could swat him away like he had Lenik earlier.

"Hvala. My veduhn says it will take time," Arkhady said with an abrupt, sour laugh. "It took years to make me this way. Would be stranger if I was back to my spry self overnight." He offered

Tyr a quick smile and returned to his seat. "You wanted to speak with me, Penhallow?"

Tyr warily chose the seat beside Ana's father. It was hard to look at him. He'd deteriorated so much from the last time Tyr had seen him in town that he wouldn't have recognized him at all. But unwell or not, Arkhady was the man whose daughter he'd impregnated, and nothing he'd ever done before had prepared him for how nervous he was. "Ana..." He reached for his throat and tried to grin. "She's... very dear to me, sir."

"Mhm." Arkhady flattened his back against his chair. He blinked, waiting.

"There's nothing I wouldn't..." Tyr coughed, dragging hard on his throat as he cleared it. "Do for her."

"Or to her, it seems." The man was unreadable.

Tyr pretended to comb his hair back to sneak in a brow mopping on his forearm. "I assure you, there was not... I have never... That is, she was always..."

"Don't hurt yourself, Penhallow. Speak plainly."

"I love her, sir," Tyr announced. He didn't fight the smile spreading across his face. Arkhady deserved to see how happy his daughter made him. "My family loves her. The child wasn't planned, but I would die for them, just as I would die for Ana. And since I don't know how tonight will go, sir, I feel compelled to assure you my intentions toward Anastazja are to ask her to be my wife, once the horrors are behind us." Tyr clutched the seat of his chair. "But first, I must ask you for *your* permission. I know I'm not of the same breeding as the Wynters, that I'm not a Vjestik or the caliber of man you wanted for your daughter, but I believe I make up for any deficits in passion and dedication and loyalty and—"

"Penhallow." Arkhady grimaced. "Stop. Please."

"Sir?"

"Wynters are... Vjestik first. Highborn second. You are neither, are you?"

Tyr shook his head. His heart deflated. "No. No, sir."

352

"And you suppose I am concerned about this?"

"I assume so, yes."

"Hmm." Arkhady stared down the length of the table. "I should be. My father was. Wynters were given the stewardship of Witchwood Cross from a matter of practicality. We weren't like our peers across the kingdom, and they knew it. When Niko weds a Dereham, it will be the highest we have risen in many years. But the Derehams, while good and just lords, have done nothing for us that we have not paid our share for. We have always relied on ourselves, our community, and though the Penhallows are neither Vjestik nor highborn, they have shown themselves to be of true quality and belong here as much as anyone. As much as *we*, once settlers ourselves, belong here."

Tyr bowed his head low. "I... thank you for that, sir. It means a lot to hear you say it, and I know it will mean a great deal to my family. Witchwood Cross is home to us."

Arkhady had a faraway look in his glossy eyes. "And this is what Anastazja wants?"

"I believe she does," Tyr said. He ran his sweaty palms down his trousers. "Though I'll respect whatever answer she gives."

"And this offer is not because you got her with child, is it?"

"No," Tyr started firmly. "No, sir. That was a surprise to both of us. She'd been so diligent with her grimizh—"

"*Not* another word!" Arkhady exclaimed, hands up in surrender. "You understand she's my child. My little bird. In my mind, she's still... still ten—eleven—running around with mischief and fire and all the potential in the world. Those days are not so far away for me."

"Right." Tyr winced and kicked himself mentally. "Right. Of course. Opros. My apologies."

"And you've considered what this would mean for you? Ana will take my place, sooner than she should have to. Are you prepared to accept the mantle of stewardship and all it comes with?"

Tyr hadn't considered it at all, and didn't want to. The prospect was as daunting as everything else ahead of them. But he would sail to Beyond if it was the path required, if Ana was waiting at the end. "I am."

Arkhady shakily stood. Tyr started forward in case he stumbled, but the steward found his own footing. "I told Ana I would never again deny her what she wants. If this... If *you* are what she wants, then you have my blessing."

Tyr gripped his chair with hard relief. "Hvala, sir. Hvala."

The steward hobbled to the broad, wheeled chair beside him and lowered into it. The agony on his face was palpable, but there was peace at the edges. "Gratitude is not something I will have earned again for many years. But I will accept yours as a promise. A promise to do better by Anastazja than I did. While I may not look the part of a formidable foe these days, Tyreste Penhallow, you'd be wise to remember the man I once was, for I fully intend to be him again." He gripped the wheels of his chair and nodded toward the door. "Let's rejoin the others and ready ourselves."

TWENTY-EIGHT
A HUNDRED RAVENS

The Ravenwoods met them outside the old abandoned hunting lodge north of the Wynter estate. They'd been there a while by the time Ana, Tyreste, Ludya, Grigor, and Addy showed up on foot. *You can fly ahead,* Ludya had said, but she didn't know if she could ever fly again. If she *wanted* to. If she even should.

"Ah, there you are." Elyria's feathered shoulders rose in an animated flutter. "Where's Arkhady?"

"His energy is spent," Ana said as she and her party gathered to fill out the other half of the semi-circle formed by the Ravenwoods. "He's been asleep for years and still has waking to do. He wanted to come, but I assured him my heart would feel less afflicted if I knew he was safe at home and not suffering up here in the foothills."

"It was the prudent choice," Elyria said. She examined Ana's companions with a scrutinizing frown. "Perhaps the others might have followed the same wisdom."

"Ludya is my vedhma," Ana said. "Tyreste is my partner. Addy is my sister."

Addy flushed deep, grinning.

"And Grigor is my..."

"Guardian," he said with a scowl. "And onk—uncle."

With one eye narrowed, Elyria nodded slowly at the man. Ana saw something else in her gaze though. In better circumstances, it would have been amusing witnessing Grigor's strange ability to charm women of all walks of life.

The other Ravenwoods watched their high priestess, awaiting direction. All except Raelyria, who was occupied with shooting glares at Ana.

Elyria stepped toward Ana and guided her away from the group. "Varradyn was her cousin, her friend and, though it would never have happened, the one she'd hoped would win the right to stand as her high priest in a couple of years." When Ana tried to look away, the high priestess gripped her by the chin and pinned her gaze forward. "I offer you forgiveness on behalf of our people, Anastazja Wynter. The others will forgive on their own time, Raelyria included. When we are again safe, the healing can begin."

Ana lifted her gaze to Icebolt. Midnight Crest could not be seen from any point on the ground, even on a clear day, but she knew the way. The outline of the spires and ramparts was etched upon her soul, a reminder of the past and a portend of a future not yet written. "I have not tried... to fly. Since..."

"Your lover healed you," Elyria said. "Whatever restrictions linger belong to fear."

"Fear is its own form of power. When I reflect back..." Ana shook her head at the ground. "That was Magda's greatest weapon against me." She met Elyria's eyes. "What if I cannot?"

Elyria pivoted, turning her attention to the skies. A cacophony of wings and cries followed, pulling Ana's focus there as well. "Never in all our history have we invited men to the Rookery. Never did I imagine we would." She closed her eyes and inhaled. "Even the wind has changed its song. We are not what we once were, and neither are you."

Ana shook her head. She tugged her furs tighter as the swarming ravens whipped the air into a fury. "I don't understand."

"You wouldn't," Elyria said curtly. "They have come for your lover."

Panic rose in Ana's chest. She stepped in front of the high priestess. "*What?*"

"To carry him where his legs cannot go. You risk your life to right a wrong that was never yours to own." Elyria looked down at her. "The child within you is equally his. He is entitled to the right to defend the lives of both of you."

Ana was thunderstruck. She watched the ravens descend in the same awe she saw written on the faces of her family. Elyria hadn't explained the logistics of how they would get Tyreste to the Rookery, but had she needed to? Was it not obvious what they intended?

"We can take you up the same way, Anastazja, but I don't believe it's necessary."

Ana shook her head, though she wouldn't know for sure if she could fly until she tried.

They returned to the group. Addy worked to catch Ana's focus and signed, *Never doubt what you are capable of. I believe in you.*

Tears burned as Ana signed back, *I aim to earn that belief tonight, Addy.*

Tyreste's palm nestled against her lower back, all the reminder she needed that he'd chosen to stand at her side.

The wings and caws turned to crunching boots and whispers as the last of the Ravenwoods landed.

"Silence," Elyria declared. She said it so softly, her words dissipated in the wind, but her presence was enough to quiet the clusters of conversation. "There will be no grand speeches. No debating the merits of the renewed alliance, which was *my* decision to make. Anastazja knows what she must do, is prepared to do it, and is fully aware of the inherent risk to herself and her child. *We* are here to remove all obstacles in her way until her work is done. To ensure safe passage to *and* from Midnight Crest. Is that understood?"

The Ravenwoods, both those who had been on the ground for hours and the newly arrived, nodded and verbalized their understanding. Some grumbled. Raelyria glowered. But none argued.

Elyria offered the moment to Ana with a nod.

Ana swallowed and stepped into the circle. A quick glance back at Tyreste gave her the last burst of strength needed. "I've never done this before. I have only the words and confidence of my Ancestors to guide me. Even now, I feel... I feel *him* within me, searching for a way in. When I create the ward, I'll be forced to shift my efforts from blocking him, and it will leave me vulnerable. I may fail. But if I do fail, I will because I tried. I will never again run and hide from what is right."

"Praise the gods," the Ravenwoods muttered.

Ana turned toward Tyreste. "They've offered to take you up, but, Tyr, you don't have to do it. It's utterly mad."

"I know," he said with a short smile. "But I've already accepted their offer."

Ana was taken aback. "And you know *how* they will take you?"

"If you mean riding on the backs of a hundred ravens, then yes, I'm fully apprised of the insanity awaiting me." He cupped her face and kissed her. "See you up there."

"But—"

"See you up there, love." He winked and disappeared into a sea of black leather.

Ludya stepped forward. Grigor hung back a step, hovering close to Addy. "We'll be here when you return. And you *will* return. Not on the backs of the ravens, as Tyreste must do, but by the strength of your *own* wings, Anastazja. Often bent, never broken. The kyschun showed you the path, and our Ancestors lit the way. There is only one thing left to do."

Ana wrapped Ludya in a hug, nodding. She sniffled and pulled back. "If the worst happens—"

The vedhma's eyes narrowed in disapproval. "We do not invite tragedy."

"But if it does, Ludya, I need to know... to know..."

"I will look after them all," Ludya vowed. "A promise that will prove wholly unnecessary."

"Thank you." Ana met Grigor's eyes behind Ludya.

He nodded once.

She returned it and blew a kiss to Addy.

From the corner of her eye she saw the ravens rise in perfect concert, a moving platform of black feathers. Tyreste lay in the middle, his pupils dilated with fear, but he was looking not at the ground but the skies. Ready. As she must be.

One by one, the other Ravenwoods shifted and took flight.

"Go," Elyria commanded. "I will be right behind you."

Ana folded her hands over her chest in silent prayer. Within her, Mortain knocked and rattled, demanding to be heard. But there were louder voices, and it was to those she paid heed.

The last words Ana heard as she launched into a sprint and turned her mind toward the most important shift of her life were *here I am*. They were not her own words, but they were the ones she needed.

Her arms elongated into wings, mouth forming into the arch of a beak. Her legs turned last, and she held her breath, expecting them to disappear altogether, but perfectly formed talons appeared.

Ana joined the throngs of Ravenwoods in the night sky, the lone warrior of orange and red among a sea of black, and aimed herself toward Midnight Crest.

When the melee subsided, Grigor nudged the Penhallow girl and nodded for her to follow him back to Fanghelm. He had half a mind to return her to her parents, but a hunch told him she'd just find her way back to him.

"Arkhady," he said when Ludya fell in beside him. The vedhma appeared to be somewhere else, lost to her thoughts, her worries... something. Her face was expressionless, her body moving on its own. "What can be done?"

"He'll recover, in time," she said in an even voice that matched her countenance. "There are vedhma and veduhn with him now."

"He should be there when his daughter returns home."

"We agree."

"So you will make this happen."

Ludya's eyes rolled upward, the first sign she was truly paying attention. "Focus on the girl. I'll do my part."

Grigor's lip curled. "What shall I do with her?"

Ludya judged him from the side. "Play with her?"

"Play?" Grigor's face contorted in befuddlement.

"You were a good onkel to Ana and her brothers," Ludya said with another scathing glance. "Once."

"Your estimation is unhelpful," he groused.

"There's an entire library she might enjoy. She does translations, like her brother. I understand she's keen to learn Vjestikaan."

"You want me to... *teach* her a language? In an evening?" Grigor asked. "Is there not a more useful task I could set her on?"

"What, like scrubbing the kitchens? Butchering a hog? Stitching the old standards?"

He scoffed. "That's not what I meant."

"Well, Grigor, I don't *want* you to do anything except allow me a bit of silence for the rest of the walk," Ludya said with a cool look and lifted her skirts, then pushed her pace ahead of his.

Addy turned back to look at Grigor. She signed something, but he no more knew her language than she knew his.

Grigor offered her a pained grin. She flashed a brighter one in return and looped her tiny arm through his. He stared down at the unasked-for union with a bland scowl.

"We'll figure something out," he muttered.

Tyreste used to dream of flying. It had started during his affair with Ana, when he had become fixated with trying to understand what it must feel like every time she broke and reformed her bones with magic. She once joked that if he were a touch lighter, he could hang from her talons and they could fly together, a bit prophetic in his present situation.

He'd expected to feel dread, terror, or even remorse as he climbed aboard the moving platform of ravens, but there were *so damn many* of them that all he could see was a blanket of midnight. Above was sky but below... There *was* no below. Only the concerted effort of a hundred Ravenwoods carrying him skyward.

What would my mother think? raced across his restless mind. He tried to crawl closer to the edge of the pack, to make the poor decision of looking over the edge to see how high they'd climbed, but several affronted caws sent him scooting back to the center.

He squinted through snow and sleet for any sign of Ana, but he couldn't find her.

Not in a hundred thousand years had Tyr ever imagined he'd be where he was in that moment, soaring above the clouds and preparing to be strength and shield for the woman he loved enough to risk everything for. Ana's greatest battle was an internal one, and he couldn't fight it for her, but he would stand at her side as she won it.

And when it was all over, when their child was safely born and their lives returned to some semblance of normalcy, he would travel back to Westerlands and tell the entire story to Asterin, Rhiain, and Sesto. He'd tell them he'd given the letters to the Wynters, with whom they belonged, so they could never fall into the wrong hands.

That they'd even fallen into *his* hands, as the same war waged beyond his walls, seemed an odd stroke of fate.

Everything, all of it, led back to one place for him.

Anastazja.

Love bade him climb aboard a flock of ravens and embark on the most ludicrous journey of his life.

Love would protect him.

Wisdom might claim love wasn't enough.

But for Tyreste Penhallow, his eyes wide against the onslaught of wind and storm—and his face pointed bravely west, toward Icebolt—love was more than enough.

Love would set them all free.

TWENTY-NINE
YOU DEVIOUS GIRL

Ana landed behind Elyria. The Courtyard of Regents was empty, as Ana imagined it was most of the time, a magnificent but lonely place where immortal goats milled about, munching on scattered patches of flora, and a frozen throne withered in solitude.

Though she'd seen and felt her talons, Ana didn't know if they'd work until she came screeching toward the icy shelf at the north end of the castle. But her landing was as smooth and graceful as ever.

"Where did…" Ana looked around, staggering as she regained her bearings.

"Raelyria will bring him here, to us," Elyria stated. "What do you need for this to… to work? What do you need from us?"

"I don't know," Ana confessed. The biting chill in the air took her breath away. "But I think I'll need… solitude."

"Should we find something else for your man to do?"

"Yes, please—" Ana stopped herself. "No. No, he has as much to lose as I do. He…" She couldn't help but laugh. "He *flew* here

363

to be with me. He put his trust in a hundred ravens with every reason to dump him into the Howling Sea, and came anyway. How could I ever turn him away?"

Elyria nodded and paced toward one of the giant trees holding court. "You're wondering why I brought you *here* and not elsewhere."

"I am," Ana replied. "I thought the Courtyard of Regents was sacred and off-limits to all but you and your heirs."

"So it is," Elyria called back, over her shoulder. "And that is part of why I chose *this* place and not another. Should it not be upon our most treasured land where we form the protective barrier that will keep my people safe for centuries onward?" She reached up into the tree and lovingly stroked the back of her hand across frozen leaves. "But that isn't the only reason, Anastazja. My people would never step foot upon this ice shelf unless they welcomed death. A hundred ravens, as you say, carried your love here. But there are a hundred more who would send you hurtling to your death."

Ana stiffened. "Tyreste..."

"Will be fine. They're ushering him here now and will not let harm come to him. Anyone who dares defy my order will find my reprisal swift and final."

"High Priestess, there is something..." Ana took a step on the ice. "When this is done, I have something for you. For your people."

Elyria snorted. "We do not place significance on gift giving here. And there is nothing you have that we need, save the reason I brought you here tonight—the *last* time you ever come here. You or any of your people."

"No. It's not a gift," Ana said, wondering if she'd ever get the chance to offer it. Grigor had assured her the task had been carried out with respect, and she trusted his word. Trusted he'd follow through if she didn't make it home. *All of them?* she'd asked hopefully. *Every last one,* he'd assured her.

"More of an offering of peace and closure," Ana stated. "And should I fail, my uncle will provide it in my stead."

"You will not fail unless you dwell on that outcome," Elyria snapped. She spun around, her expression broadening. "Ahh. And here he is."

Ana turned and saw a flush-faced, wide-eyed Tyreste standing underneath the trellis leading from the courtyard to the castle proper. He was flanked by several Ravenwoods, all of whom seemed afraid of taking another step. One regarded Tyreste with dark envy.

"They know better," Elyria muttered with a purposeful look at Ana. She marched to the trellis and snapped her fingers. "Come on then, boy."

Tyreste took one tentative step onto the ice, moving sideways. His eyes were on his feet, which he tapped on the frozen ground before each attempt.

"You won't slip," Elyria said, waving him in with impatience. "The ice never melts. It's as solid and reliable as stone. Come."

Tyreste looked up, his eyebrows knit in concentration. A small frown betrayed his distrust, which Ana understood because a part of her still expected Elyria to do what she claimed a hundred of her people were fantasizing about doing right at that moment.

"Tyr," she said, drawing his attention to her. "It's all right."

He wilted at the sight of her, then sprinted across the ice to envelop her in a ferocious hug. "Oh, Ana. Guardians deliver us. I can't believe..." He peeled back and kissed her forehead. "You flew on your own?"

Ana nodded, swallowing. "Thanks to you."

"You ready for this?"

"No." She laughed because it was better than crying. "Are *you*?"

"No," he said, sputtering into laughter as well. He rubbed his cold nose against hers and smiled. "But we're both here, and that's a start. And I'll be right here the whole time, no matter what happens. Even if a giant hand comes scooping out of the sky—"

"Tyreste." Ana shook her head. "What if I can't... What if it doesn't work?"

"It *will* work," he said, insistent. "You are every bit the warrior your ancestors were."

"You and Grigor with that cursed word," she said, practically spitting. Tension vibrated above and below her skin, threatening to explode. "Imryll was protecting her child. Then her grandchild." She gestured around. "But this is not my home. Our child will never live here. Will never walk these halls. They'll always be safe, won't they? For they have *his* blood, and he cannot harm them, even if he wanted to."

He slid a hand between them and palmed her belly. "There is more than one way to protect our children, Ana."

She looked up.

"Would you ever want your children, your grandchildren, to endure what you have? To be tricked into aiding murder, their own family dangled as threats?"

"Of course not," she answered. "How can you even ask me that?"

Tyreste pulled her closer. His breath, hot and urgent, warmed her cheek. "If your ancestors had seen the future waiting for you, they would have done it all differently. Imryll and Zofia would have laid the ward *here*, as you're going to, so none of their descendants would ever be put in the position you were. So no one, Wynter or otherwise, could return with the intention of doing harm. They would have *known* that there are some fates worse than death."

Ana nuzzled her face against his chest, one last bid for comfort and safety. Even breathing was a conscious act, her own body requiring specific commands simply to exist. And all the while, the sorcerer beat, beat upon her mind, demanding entry. Her defenses would soon crumble to make room for a level of focus that made holding an illusion feel like a child's game. Mortain would fight with everything he had to keep her from finishing.

She retreated and brushed away her remaining tears. "It feels like I'm going to war, but everything is so... quiet." She whipped her head around at the empty courtyard. Elyria had slipped away at some point, and there was no one but Ana, Tyreste, and the silvery, magical goats.

"Where do you want me?" Tyreste crossed his hands over his heart.

"I don't... I don't know. I have no idea." Ana sighed. "Ah, just not near the edge of the platform."

Tyreste gave her a quizzical look.

"It's a long way down if things go poorly."

"Right." He tightened his mouth. "I'm staying close to you, until you tell me otherwise."

Ana chewed the inside of her mouth. She could talk to him all night, discuss what would happen, what might go wrong, and what to expect. But all it would do was prolong what she *must* do. Ten years she'd been preparing for *this* moment. A Meduwyn had started this war, and only a Meduwyn could end it, and if she could not find it within her to see it done, she'd be sentencing her children to the same terrible fate.

Tyreste was right. There *were* some fates worse than death.

Ana closed her eyes and let her thoughts drift. She saw the frozen trees and strange goats disappear and the icy shelf fall away—all of it, everything, even her love—until she was alone in the void.

Drawing one final breath for strength, she released the bars of the cage suppressing Mortain.

You devious girl! Using my own power against me after the gift I've given you? The joy I returned to your cold, miserable life? What do you imagine will happen, going against me? What could you possibly be thinking right now that you would stand against me?

Ana held her place in the darkness, where fear couldn't breathe.

You think I cannot see what you are? What you aim to do?

I hope you can. Because it is your *magic I'm using to keep you from ever harming a Ravenwood ever again. Your daughter's wards persisted through death, and so will mine.*

You merely encourage more creative ways of achieving the same end!

No. For even if you sire more and more of your ilk, they will never reach these spires again. No Meduwyn will ever be allowed to fly these skies. No creature bearing ill intent, regardless of bloodline, will ever fly these skies. And good luck to you luring a Ravenwood south of Witchwood Cross, now that they know the depths of your resourcefulness.

A peal of thunder tore through the sky, rattling the courtyard. Ana staggered sideways, her arms out for balance. Tyreste yelped.

My resourcefulness is why you are even there, girl. I have waited thousands of years, and I can wait thousands more. You can outsmart me, but you'll never outlast me.

The ice cracked under her feet, splitting. With her eyes still squeezed shut, she used her senses to dance out of the danger, trusting Tyreste could handle himself. Elsewhere in the castle, she heard shouting.

You are done plaguing the Ravenwoods. And you are done plaguing the Wynters. My children will not even know your name, *sorcerer. We will strike you from—*

A boom split the sky above. Instinct alone pushed Ana from harm's way as she dodged the catastrophic thud that shattered part of the platform. Screams tore out, followed by more crashes, stone erupting and colliding with stone.

The castle was tearing itself apart.

"Ana! You're too close to the edge!" Tyreste cried. She sensed the panicked hesitation in his voice and silently begged him not to approach, to stay out of her reach, which was as treacherous as Mortain's.

Do you see now? It isn't me tearing their world down around them. It's you! How many more will you kill to save them?

You have no power over me. You never did.

You haven't thought this through at all, have you? Once you banish our blood from these walls, what will become of the phoenix and the little bird inside her?

Ana reached through the darkness for something to steady her, but she was alone. She'd *chosen* this, and there was nothing and no one but herself to call for aid.

Stupid girl. Foolish girl. What you're attempting to do will kill you and *your child.*

"Ana, it's all coming apart!" Tyreste. Somewhere.

Screaming. Crashing. Tearing. Splitting. It was all she could hear, feel, or sense, and her control was slipping, slipping with the castle and the Ravenwoods who had trusted her when they'd had no reason to. She *had* to find her concentration. *Had* to push him back into the shadows, into the nothingness he'd come from.

Your child will die, Anastazja, and you will be the one who murdered her.

"No, no one's daughters have to die for you ever again," Ana whispered into the maelstrom whipping her farther and farther away from the safety of solid ground. Tyreste screamed for her, but even if she'd wanted to find him, she was already gone. Lost. She grasped what was happening—that she had been building the ward from the moment she'd landed in the Courtyard of Regents, ripe with fresh doubts and a half-formed plan.

Ana's feet left the ground just as the last of the ice fell away, disappearing into the storm and clouds. She envisioned a little girl, hair like spun gold, running through the village without a care in the world. That same girl, her eyes pointed toward a part of the sky she could never reach, no matter how strong her wings. Though the girl would dream of the ravens, they would remain a beautiful myth, a fanciful story to excite her colorful imagination. Ana envisioned the stories she would tell her grandchildren of the haven in the sky, where ravens thrived without fear, without darkness.

Higher and higher Ana swirled, deep in the cocoon of a future not yet realized. A beautiful life wove together, a daughter who would become a woman, who would grow old and eventually spend her promise, but not before she'd created more life, more beauty. She saw the threads Ludya always spoke of, and somewhere inside of Ana, she was laughing in delight, for she at last—as her soul was seized by the storm and turned inside out—understood one of her vedhma's most perplexing riddles.

Ana breathed in the gale's violence, exalting in everything and nothing at once. She could no longer hear the screams or the desecration, not even her love. She'd gone somewhere no one could follow.

She held the air in her lungs, rising higher and higher. There was but one thing left to do: cut the thread.

By the wings of this life or the bones of the next, she sang in her mind as she tumbled through sky and stars. She turned her fingers to shears and ran them through every shimmering thread tethering her and her blood to a world that had never, ever belonged to them.

When Ana was done, she succumbed to the astonishing exaltation of complete and absolute release.

"She's awake." Tyr croaked the words, already half out of his chair. It fell backward and crashed to the floor of Ana's bedchamber.

Ana's eyes closed again, but her lips began to move.

"Ludya!"

Ludya approached leisurely, as though checking the dressing on a minor wound. She leaned down, pursed her mouth, and nodded. "So she is."

"And?" Tyr demanded, widening and blinking his eyes at her.

"And she's awake, as you said. I'll leave you two alone." She gathered her skirts and unceremoniously moved toward the door.

"Wait. *Wait.* What if she needs you?"

"It's not me she needs. There is nothing wrong with her. Take your moments as they are given, for as soon as I advise the steward his daughter has awakened, there will be no shortage of visitors." She nodded at him and left.

Tyr stared after her, dumbstruck. They'd found Ana, days later, huddled in a barn in a fugue. Ludya had said even before examining her that she would make a full recovery, that there was nothing left to fear except an overactive imagination spinning to life outcomes that wouldn't come to pass. But Ludya didn't understand the way Tyreste's heart had broken and reformed while waiting for Ana to come back to him.

"Come here," Ana beckoned, her voice cracking and distant. When he reached for the fallen chair, she grabbed his hand and tugged. "Nien. Lie with me."

Tyr carefully peeled back the layers of blankets and slipped in beside her.

She frowned at the space he'd left and he inched closer, but the moment he felt her warmth press against him, he burst into tears.

"I'm sorry. I'm sorry," he cried, burrowing his head into the pillow in shame. "I don't know what's wrong with me."

Ana lifted herself and nudged him closer.

He fell into her arms, still sobbing.

"Everything will be fine now, Tyreste," she said gently. Her whole body moved with the power of her nodding. Some of her golden hair—now streaked with silver, like those strange goats in the sky—brushed across his face. "Don't ask me to explain how I know, just trust I do."

"I trust you," he said. He ducked his head to wipe his eyes on the pillow. "I would never have let you go up that mountain if I didn't."

"Let me?" Some of the spirit had returned to her tone. "And just how do you think you would have stopped me?"

"I seem to remember a woman who could be brought to her knees with the right flick of my tongue." He smiled in her arms, grateful to be feeling something other than dread again.

"Are we speaking of me or you?" she asked, craning down to look at him with a mischief-filled grin. "Because *I* seem to remember a man who claimed to meet his so-called Guardians when his co—"

"You win!" he exclaimed, and they both laughed. "Aaand I'm hard as a rock. This is so inappropriate right now. Thank you for that."

"Victory is sweet," she said with a wistful sigh. "You had no problems getting down?"

"From the Rookery?"

Ana nodded.

"They delivered me as safely as they'd taken me," he said. "But you, how did you..."

Ana tilted her head, looking straight up. "I don't remember anything until you found me in the barn. And I would be surprised if I ever do. I'm not even sure I want to."

"But it worked?"

"I... felt myself being ripped away from that place, like cutting rot away from a festering wound. Piece by piece it excised me, and the last thing I remember is thinking, it's done. Never again will he haunt their spires." Ana closed her eyes. "How is the Rookery? Did it all..."

"Parts are gone, but it's mostly still intact."

Ana sighed in gratitude. She'd feared the cost of her ward had been the destruction of the very place she'd been trying to protect. "Has Elyria been down since?"

"She spent half a day with your father behind closed doors," Tyreste said. "I tried to speak to her, but she cut me off with that icy stare she's so good at."

"I know it." Ana's smile didn't reach her eyes. "I have something that belongs to her people, and I would like the chance to return it."

Tyr knew what she was talking about but didn't want to reignite her pain. "I'm sure she'll be back. Your father, when he visits you, speaks of alliances. Of the important role you'll play in the formation of a renewed agreement."

"He's been here?" Her eyes lit up, hopeful.

"He's so much better, Ana," Tyr replied with an exhalation of relief. It was good to be delivering joyous news, amid so much uncertainty. "He reminds me of the man I met when I moved here."

Ana's eyes welled with tears. She sucked her lower lip in. "You can't know the joy that brings me."

Tyr kissed the underside of her chin. "I think I do."

Ana's eyes fluttered closed. "Maybe you do." She yawned. "I know I've slept for a long time, but I feel like I could keep on sleeping forever."

"There's no reason to rush it," he said to assure her. "We have all the time in the world."

"No, we don't," she said, suddenly solemn. She turned her head on the pillow toward him. "Life is far too short not to claim the future we want. And now... now that the worst is behind us, I'm desperate to live, Tyreste. To really *live,* while I still can."

His mouth watered with the words on the tip of his tongue. He'd memorized them in different orders, enough that they'd all begun to blur. *Marry me. Be my wife. Allow me the honor of making you as happy as you've always made me.*

"That said, I love you, and I want to be your wife," she blurted, her eyes wide and searching. "If you'll have me."

Tyreste burrowed his face against her neck, pulling a string of giggles from her. "Dammit, woman! You stole my moment!" His racing heart pulsed behind his eyes, sending spots into his vision. All the time he'd spent worrying over the right words, when she'd managed them on a whim.

"What? You were going to ask *me?*"

Tyr balked. "You're really so surprised that I'd want to marry you?"

"Well... yes." Ana slid and propped herself up against the headboard. "I'm a mess. Any man who takes me on also takes on the stewardship of Witchwood Cross, which is no small responsibility. Our child, of course, sweetens the deal, but I don't particularly enjoy the idea of being chosen for that reason alone—"

Tyreste climbed up and silenced her with a hungered kiss. "Stop talking, Ana."

"But—"

"Love," he said, burying his tongue in her mouth and enjoying the little whimper that followed. "I've already spoken to your father. He gave his blessing."

Ana reared back in mock offense. "And you didn't tell me?"

"When was I going to tell you?"

She flopped back in a pout.

"Ana."

"So that's a yes?" she asked, staring ahead with her lips curling into a sulk.

"Would you look at me?"

Her feigned sourness dissolved, and a slow smile replaced it as she turned to face him.

The door opened and Arkhady Wynter stepped through, followed by Grigor, Addy, and a slew of others.

"Yes," Tyreste whispered, sneaking in one last kiss before breaking away to let others have their turn.

EPILOGUE

The air was still. Almost *too* still, considering the soft tufts of snow falling like ash and the giant flames turning black at the tips as they dwindled to smoke. Icebolt loomed large in the backdrop, unobscured by fog and clouds, though Midnight Crest, as always, remained invisible to those on the ground. Thanks to Ana, it would be invisible from the sky as well.

Dozens had come from across the village to watch the memorial. Some huddled at the perimeter, whispering in wonder at the forty or so Ravenwoods gathered. No one had ever seen so many in one place, and certainly not in their human forms.

Others drew closer, folding themselves into the funerary customs.

Ana clasped her hand in Tyreste's as they watched High Priestess Elyria, one by one, offer the hearts of her people to the flames. The other Ravenwoods—the ones who had come, who had risked disgust from the ones who had stayed—hummed what seemed more story than song, the verses climbing higher and deeper with each offering. They placed the hearts in the flames in the order they'd died. When Elyria was handed Varradyn's, Ana wiped her face on Tyreste's shoulder, but only briefly. She owed it to Varradyn and his people to face the flames and see him off to the gods of the Ravenwoods.

"Never again," Elyria sang, her voice carrying across the motionless crowd. "That is the foundation of the new armistice we create here, today, with men we once trusted. Trust is hard won, easily lost, and nearly impossible to regain. Many of you have come to me, prostrate with concern and fear, begging me not to sign this new pact. But it is not *trust* guiding us today, just as it was not *trust* guiding us before. Fear bade us sign an agreement the first time, but we go into this new era with both eyes open and the magic of the demon himself fortifying our walls. We go in knowing that it is no piece of paper that will keep us safe, nor the blood we stamp upon it, but the bravery of a young woman who risked everything to protect our future, when it would have been so much simpler for her to turn away." Elyria held out her hand and nodded at Ana.

"Go." Tyreste pecked a kiss on Ana's temple and nudged her.

"It should be my father," Ana whispered from the side of her mouth. She searched the crowd for signs of his movement, her eyes falling upon the Penhallows, Grigor, and others from Fanghelm before she found Arkhady. But he, too, was watching her. Waiting.

Ana moved along the edge of the fire to the other side. She stopped in front of Elyria and did something even she didn't expect; she bowed low.

Gasps and startled whispers sounded behind her. She couldn't see whether they were Ravenwood, men, or both. It didn't matter. A lack of respect had been at the heart of the prior agreement, and Ana would begin this one with the appropriate reverence.

"High Priestess," Ana said when she rose.

A smile softened Elyria's tight expression.

"The people of Witchwood Cross mourn with you. But those are words, and only through binding action can you and your people find peace. My ward will keep any with Meduwyn blood from flying your skies. The agreement we sign here today will keep your people safe on the ground as well."

Someone passed a heavy vellum from behind. She accepted it, unrolling it. "The words are simple because the agreement is simple. The punishment for fatally interfering with any of the Ravenwoods is death, the manner of which will be determined by the reigning high priestess. Likewise, Ravenwoods hold themselves to the same standard of peace, and any retaliation, now or in the future, renders them subject to the laws of the stewardship of Witchwood Cross. These laws are not necessary, however; they are mere words on paper. They are nothing when measured against the power of an agreement sealed in the blood of both races, binding all words and intentions through a joined magic that supersedes any law of any peoples."

Ana handed the vellum to the messenger and accepted a dagger in return. She closed her eyes, inhaled a steadying breath, and dragged the blade across her palm. The messenger rushed in to catch it on the page while Ana passed the bloody dagger to the high priestess.

Elyria's cut was longer and deeper, and as her blood spilled upon the page, mingling with Ana's, she led her people in a humming chant.

Arkhady stepped in beside Ana. He tilted his head down to nudge hers and smiled in approval. "Never again!" he cried and pumped his fist. He did it again, and the villagers slowly joined in as well.

"Never again!" they shouted, matching his passion and fervor as he marched around the circle of flames, beating his chest, his pitch and enthusiasm rising with every battle cry. "Never again!"

Ana made her way back to Tyreste, taking her time so she could survey the gathered. She prayed there were years left before the stewardship was hers, but her people would *know* her before that happened. Know her heart, her convictions... heart and convictions she would see passed to her own children, and theirs, so it was not only magic protecting the Ravenwoods but honor.

She slowed near the Penhallows, accepting their hugs and kisses with gladness. When she reached Tyreste, she joined his fevered "never again!" chanting, folding herself in under the protection of his strong arms.

"Niko will be here soon. They're bringing him straight to the tavern," Ludya said, appearing from behind. "When you're ready, Anastazja, I'll take you back to Fanghelm for preparations."

"Just a little while longer," Ana said, locking smiles with Elyria across the flames. "I want to remember this, so when I tell my descendants about the day, there won't be a single detail amiss."

"The Icebolt Accord," Tyreste said, musing. "History likes to name everything."

"I like it," Ana said, her eyes glossy as she swayed to the force of the chanting. "But this won't be written in *The Book of All Things*. We owe it to the Ravenwoods to keep their names from our histories. Better for the rest of the realm to be curious than to be knowledgeable."

Tyr craned his neck and waved at Addy, who was trying to catch his attention. "Looks like they're headed back. See you... soon?"

Ana kissed him. A great chill rippled through her, and when it finished, she felt weightless. "Soon."

"No one is more familiar with the precarious line between life and death than a man or woman of the Northerlands. Winter is what we know. It is in us, around us, a part of us. And in the direst, bleakest days and nights of midwinter, when the promise of springtide is but a myth beyond our reach, we are never closer to our beloved Guardians." Lenik lifted his gaze and passed it across the packed tavern from where he stood behind the bar. "And Ancestors, of course." He turned the page in the tome he had resting on the wood.

Tyr and Ana grinned at each other from the other side. He brushed his pinky along hers, biting back a giggle. He'd never wanted to touch her more than when he'd been ordered to be patient and wait.

His smile faded some when he realized everyone he knew was watching him try not to mount his soon-to-be wife.

"Our bones are ice," Lenik said, continuing. "Our flesh is snow. But our hearts are fire, the fire that kindles the spirit of the Northerlands, that coarsens us to any hardship, any suffering. The fire sets us apart. The fire is what gives life." The vodzhae folded his hands, lifted his chin, and inspected the crowd once more. "These are the Sacred Vows of the Northerlands, and we will say them as the tradition of our Reach decrees. Vjestik tradition is far simpler. We replace the customary marriage knot with a ritual of our own." He nodded at Arkhady.

Ana's father shuffled forward. He brandished a dagger, breaking into a tight, squeamish grin. Ana placed her bandaged hand on his arm with an encouraging smile to show him it was all right.

Rikard the Mouser snaked a deft, winding path through Tyreste's legs and then Ana's, purring hard enough to prompt comments on the strange cat someone forgot to shoo out.

Tyr dared anyone to touch his dearest friend.

Arkhady cradled Ana's injured hand in his palm and pricked the pad of her forefinger. A bead of blood rushed to the surface. He hurried to score the same mark on Tyr and then stepped back.

"You know what to do," Lenik said with a solemn head tip.

Ana pressed her finger into Tyr's mouth, and he slipped his into hers. The coppery taste of her blood flooded his tongue. He wasn't prepared for how sensual it would feel. His cock rebelliously stirred in his trousers as he silently pleaded for the damn thing to *be patient*.

Tyr withdrew his finger, swallowing as she swept her tongue along her bottom lip, showing him a flash of his blood before she closed her mouth and eyes and made a soft moaning sound only he could hear.

379

"Not fair," he muttered, groaning and shifting to hide the bulge straining his pants. "Not fair at all."

"More of that later," Ana purred, and he had to grip the back of Agnes's chair to keep from bowing over. His sister's disgusted scoff wasn't subtle.

"With Anastazja's blood on your tongue, Tyreste Penhallow, repeat after me," Lenik said and read from the weighty book. Apparently sensing Tyreste had only followed some of it, he turned the pages around and pointed at the spot.

Tyr cleared his throat, the taste of her still painfully intoxicating. "My flame is unique. There is only one of its kind. There is nothing I possess worth more." He shifted again, overcome with the terrible sense everyone gathered could see his cock hardening. "It is my light in the darkest months, my heat when the ice has forsaken us. I share it now with you, Anastazja. I join my flame to yours, creating a unified blaze. Though we have ahead of us the darkest of nights, the coldest of days, as long as we are me and thee, our fire will illuminate the stars in our immortal sky."

Lenik turned toward Ana. She tapped her foot in nervous excitement and pushed the book away.

"I know the words, Lenik. I've heard them many times before, though I never imagined saying them myself," she said. Only Tyr understood the full truth behind her words. No one else ever had to know that she'd lived the past decade of her life waiting to die. "My flame is unique. There is only one of its kind. There is nothing I possess worth more. It is my light in the darkest months, my heat when the ice has forsaken us. I share it now with you, Tyreste. I join my flame to yours, creating a unified blaze. Though we have ahead of us the darkest of nights, the coldest of days, as long as we are me and thee, our fire will illuminate the stars in our immortal sky."

Lenik pursed his mouth at her, impressed. "Your fires are now a blaze, a blaze that must be protected at any cost." He slammed the book closed. "You may codify this union with a kiss, a hug, or... whatever suits your, ahem, present disposition."

"Trust me, Lenik, you don't want me to indulge my present disposition," Tyr said and tugged Ana against him with a hard snap. Her eyes, wide and glazed, searched his, and he held her like this until he couldn't restrain his kiss any longer.

Cheers and applause rang out. Tyr sighed his relief into her mouth, and she angled herself forward, brushing his sensitive, swollen cock with her torso and laughing at his discomfort.

"You're *really* asking for it later," he said, clenching.

Ana swirled her tongue over his, mingling their blood. "I *really* hope so." She moaned and broke away with a devious grin. "Time to socialize."

"How in the bloody Guardians did *you* land a woman like her," Rikard said with a hard clap on Tyr's shoulder when Ana drifted into the crowd. "He's probably wondering the same, eh?" He nodded downward, at Tyr's little 'problem.' Tyr felt his cheeks grow even redder.

"I know *I'm* wondering," Agnes said, cradling her belly as Stojan helped her from her chair. "What is it with you and feisty, demanding women anyway, brother? Do you enjoy being ordered about?" When Stojan snorted, Agnes waved an affronted hand. "You dirty man. No, don't tell me, Tyr!"

"He knows what he wants," Olov said, joining them. He held his arm out for Fransiska, who was busy wiping her eyes on her sleeves. "He always has. But fate intervened and changed the course he was on, so he could find *this* one, leading him back to us. And her." He leaned in and swallowed Tyr in a broad hug. "We're happy for you, son."

"I can see the wheels turning in Father's mind as he tries to work poor Ana into the tavern schedule," Agnes quipped.

"I doubt she'd mind," Tyr said, watching his wife greet each of their guests with poise and kindness. "She likes to help."

"I'd be more worried about Tyr as a steward," Rikard said with a hard whistle. "We're all fucked, you know that, right? Better add Arkhady Wynter to your nightly beseeching now, Mother, get ahead of the devastation."

381

Tyr socked his arm amid good-natured laughter. "I wish I had a good retort for that, but I'm praying for his good health myself."

"One thing at a time," Fransiska declared. "Long before that day ever comes, we have a child to prepare for, don't we, Tyreste?"

"Hello, Mother? I'm right here. Your daughter. Days from popping." Agnes wiggled her fingers over her belly.

"As you were saying, Mother?" Rikard said with a wink at Agnes.

"Well, of course you are, dear. Who said you weren't?" Fransiska's head shook, her shoulders fluttering in annoyance. "But you *have* a mother, don't you? Our Anastazja..." She drifted off, searching the crowd.

Agnes followed their mother's gaze. "She has us now."

"Indeed." Fransiska's sadness turned to joy again. "And your daughter, Tyreste, will only be the first of many children, I'm sure."

Rikard cupped his mouth and leaned close to Stojan. "That's Mother's polite way of saying she knows how much her son likes to *fu*—"

Olov hushed him with a hard look all the Penhallow children were acquainted with.

Tyreste glanced down with an eyeroll and a chuckle. The others joined in.

It didn't quite feel real, as though there was something else they hadn't yet considered, some foe they hadn't yet vanquished.

In time, the feeling would fade, time he would be spending with *her*.

He was already planning their honeymoon to the Eesterlands. It would be a couple of years before they could leave, but they wouldn't want to leave until their daughter was old enough to make the trip. The timing would work out perfect for them to attend a wedding. Rhiain had written that her little brother Jesstin's betrothal season would begin in a year, when he turned nineteen. Tyr discerned what she didn't say—that something had caused them to move it up. It had to have been something serious enough for her to want to wed her brother off before he was ready to be a groom. No matter the reason, Tyr looked forward to sharing his wife with his old friends—to showing them what a *happy* Tyreste looked like.

He thought of the wedding gifts they'd sent. For Ana, Rhiain had chosen a beautiful gown in the style of Riverchapel. For Tyr, though, there'd been something unexpected in the crate. A stack of fresh paper and a box of charcoal. At the top of the stack was a drawing he'd made of Rhiain years ago, one she'd stolen before the tavern had burned. *I'd love to know how you see us now that we're all older, and wiser,* her note had said.

Would he pick up the charcoal and watch his hands dance upon the vellum? He wasn't sure. He didn't have to decide today or even tomorrow. As Ana had said, it was time to live.

Tyr's daze suddenly broke. "Where's Addy?"

Faustina stepped forward and pointed at a table in the corner. Addy sat on one side, Grigor the other, as she slowly signed to him. His return attempt was pitiful, and she let him know it, turning her head up with an exasperated look.

Tyr wiped a fresh tear from his eye and breathed deep. "I should follow Ana's lead and say hi to our guests."

"Of course," Olov said. He spread his arms wide. "But first..."

Rikard groaned. Agnes laughed. But they all moved in for one of their father's famous Penhallow hugs, Faustina and Stojan included.

Olov kissed the tops of each head and stepped back. "Home is where we make it," he said wistfully. "Family is who we choose."

As everyone broke away to mix with the crowd, Tyr met his father's eyes. He remembered all the times Olov had tried to steer him down another course.

Today, at least, he had his father's approval.

He didn't need it anymore.

But ah, he wanted it.

Thank you, Tyr mouthed. Olov nodded low, his eyes full of tears when he looked up.

Tyr went to join his wife.

"You look so beautiful today, Ana," Nikolaj said. He shook his head, sighing, the sound of a man, not a boy. Ana had watched him slowly shed the persona Magda had shaped him into, and as it fell away, so did her recognition of him. The last time she'd really *known* Nikolaj had been over a decade ago, when they had still been kids, playing games. She would need to get to know her twin brother all over again, a daunting prospect, but it was not a burden but a gift. Only when standing before her brother, recovered from his long spell, did she understand how incomplete she'd been without him.

"Doesn't she?" Arkhady pulled her in for a quick embrace. "Ksana is smiling beside the Ancestors. She'd never cared much for the pomp and ceremony of the broader realm. She was Vjestik, through and through. The moment she knew you'd given your heart to a publican would have been the moment she offered you her blessing. Wouldn't have asked after his pedigree or the coin in his bank."

"I appreciate you being willing to have the ceremony here," Ana said. She smiled up at her father. "It means a lot to Tyreste and me both."

"The keep has been in our family for many generations, but it's also a place of... sadness." Arkhady breathed in. "We have work to do before it can again be what it once was for us."

"We have time now," Ana said. She reached for his hand and squeezed it once, the way he used to do for her when she was a girl, scared and uncertain. "We—"

The air was knocked from her when Addy came barreling into her arms. Ana laughed and gave her a squeeze. She looked up and saw Grigor ambling over, a thin scowl darkening his always-serious expression.

"She's impossible," he said. "But when I'm in the village, I'll teach her."

Say it with your hands, you big oaf, Addy signed.

Ana snorted, but Grigor, Arkhady, and Niko eyed each other in confusion.

"Seems like she may be the one teaching you," Ana said. She signed the words as she said them.

Niko's mouth turned up playfully. "Am I witnessing our onkel going soft, Ana?"

Ana translated for Addy and then said, "Only Grigor can answer that."

"Never," the grumpy man said, and they all laughed. "Anastazja, a word alone?"

Ana glanced at her father and brother, who both nodded. There was so much to say, to do... so much time to make up for. But they *had* it now. Time. And she could walk away, knowing they'd be there when she returned.

Grigor guided her to the window. His eyes were pointed outside as he gathered himself to speak. "You know this isn't over. He'll find a way around it."

Ana sighed and leaned against the frosted panes. "Not today, Grigor."

"I'm leaving in the morning," he said. He rapped his knuckles on the wooden frame. "For the Reliquary."

"What? Why?"

"It's not enough to keep him from our walls. He must be ended."

Ana squeezed her eyes shut and shook her head in confusion. "But why the Reliquary?"

"They have their own secret scrolls."

Ana balked. Whatever was happening was happening too fast for her to understand it. "How do you know this?"

"I know." Grigor shifted. "There must be something written about the Meduwyn."

"Even if there is," she said. "What makes you think they'd ever let you see any of it?"

"I'm not looking for debate. I only wanted to explain my absence."

She eyed him strangely. "You've never explained your absences to me before."

Grigor stretched his hands at his sides. He closed his eyes with a bracing sigh and then met hers. "Our unwillingness to discuss things brought us here. I'll do my part." His mouth twitched. He seemed to debate with himself. With a defeated shrug, he hugged her and kissed the top of her head. "Be happy, Anastazja. Ksana would wish it so."

He broke away and disappeared into the crowd, leaving her dumbstruck.

"Everything all right?" Tyreste asked. He kissed her and pulled her gaze to his. "Ana?"

"Fine, actually. Grigor is... Well, he's going away for a while." Remembering her uncle's words about communication, she knew better than to leave it there. "To the Reliquary. To research our recent troubles and find a more permanent end."

"Good." Tyreste hardened in her arms. "I've sent a coded message to Asterin suggesting the same thing. I cautioned him to send anything relating to the Meduwyn my way, to do nothing except pass those items along. I won't risk their lives. They don't have the same protections we do, down in the Easterlands."

"When did you send it?"

"Earlier today, before the ceremony with the Ravenwoods. I didn't think it could wait. It's not enough to expel him from our lands and skies, Ana." Tyreste brought his hands to her face and cradled it, his thumbs caressing her cheeks. "Is it?"

Ana met his eyes and shook her head. "No. It's not."

"And maybe... Maybe it's not a trouble our generation will get the chance to solve," he said. "But we can start the conversation. Put words and ideas into momentum so that someone, one day, will succeed where we've failed."

She gazed up at her husband in awe. "When I met you, you were so determined to live a simple life. No complications. No troubles."

"An easy choice for a man who has no reason to fight." His throat jumped in a hard swallow. "Nothing to lose."

Ana started to rise, to kiss him, but commotion across the tavern floor drew both their attentions.

"What in the Guardians," Ana said on a heavy breath. "Is that..."

Tyreste clicked his tongue and crossed his arms. "Our fathers arm-wrestling on the bar? Yes, yes it is."

"My money is on Olov," Ana said, scrunching her nose in amusement.

"I wouldn't count out old Arkhady just yet," Tyreste replied. "But, eh... Maybe we take the opportunity, while everyone's attentions are fixed on this embarrassing competition..."

Ana responded by clasping her hand in his and tugging him into motion behind her.

Ana's wet hands slid along the edge of the basin, clamoring for grip. Her hips bucked over Tyreste's face as his hungered groans rattled her clit, pushing her too close, too fast. His tongue worked the length of her, dipping down to gather more of her wetness every few delectable strokes, making her clench with wanting.

His thumbs parted her ass, and he plunged them in and out, one by one, something she had never imagined she'd enjoy but couldn't get enough of. She pushed her ass down over him, needing more than his fingers, wet with her desire, could offer, knowing damn well what would come next. From the sounds reverberating from the back of his throat, he knew it too.

She shifted her weight to one side and chanced a reach for the table she'd pulled nearby. Had he even noticed her place the dagger there? Did he feel her reach for it then, to prick the same finger, in the same tender spot?

Ana lifted herself, enjoying the sound of his brief disappointment, which would make the pleasure so much stronger. She ran her bloody finger along her slit, wishing she could see his eyes light up. Instead she was rewarded with a low, throaty "fuck, *fuck*," right before he claimed her hips and slammed her down onto his face.

Stars exploded in her eyes as an orgasm came out of nowhere. Her ass splashed the water as she thrashed over him, dragging his tongue everywhere all at once and screaming in pleasure as he pushed more digits inside her ass.

Ana sagged, still gripping the basin. The water level dropped as Tyreste came up out of the bath behind her, giving her no chance to react before he had one arm looped around her neck, the crown of his cock pressed against her ass.

"Yes," she cried just as he shoved inside, filling her completely and transporting her to a new plane of pleasure, unlike any she'd known before. He thrust in long, painstaking strokes that had her feeling every last inch of him with every movement in... out.

"What you fucking do to me, Ana." He moaned and pumped faster. She'd never known pain could be so pleasurable, and she wanted more, more, which she showed him by slamming back against his cock to drive him deeper.

He pulled on her throat, tilting her head back to kiss him upside down right as he shuddered and exploded inside her. She tilted to receive everything he had to give, consumed by another wave of ecstasy as his fingers brought her over the edge.

Ana wilted against him. He caught her and spun her, sinking into the tub. She climbed over him and reached between his legs to clean his cock in the warm water.

"Was it..." His glistening belly clenched with every stroke she made, his mouth parted as he locked her gaze. "Did I hurt you?"

"I'm going to want that every night," she purred, rolling his cock up and down under the water. His eyes fluttered back. "But right now..." She lowered herself over him, his mouth widening with every inch of him she took in. "I want you to look me in the eye and give me everything you have."

"It will always be yours." He panted, breathless. He reached for her hips to direct her, but she swatted him away, planting her hands on his chest as she rode. "I love you so damn much, Ana. So much it hurts."

"Then hurt me. Love me," she whispered and lost herself to the safety of the life fate had stolen and then—beautifully, wonderfully, perfectly—given back.

The Book of All Things continues with a new story in *The Hand and the Heart*.

ALSO BY SARAH M. CRADIT

KINGDOM OF THE WHITE SEA
KINGDOM OF THE WHITE SEA TRILOGY
The Kingless Crown
The Broken Realm
The Hidden Kingdom

THE BOOK OF ALL THINGS
The Raven and the Rush
The Sylvan and the Sand
The Altruist and the Assassin
The Melody and the Master
The Claw and the Crowned
The Poison and the Paladin
The Belle and the Blackbird

THE SAGA OF CRIMSON & CLOVER
THE HOUSE OF CRIMSON AND CLOVER SERIES
The Storm and the Darkness
Shattered
The Illusions of Eventide
Bound
Midnight Dynasty
Asunder
Empire of Shadows
Myths of Midwinter
The Hinterland Veil
The Secrets Amongst the Cypress
Within the Garden of Twilight
House of Dusk, House of Dawn

For more information, and exciting bonus material,
visit www.sarahmcradit.com

ABOUT SARAH

Sarah is the *USA Today* and International Bestselling Author of over forty contemporary and epic fantasy stories, and the creator of the Kingdom of the White Sea and Saga of Crimson & Clover universes.

Born a geek, Sarah spends her time crafting rich and multilayered worlds, obsessing over history, playing her retribution paladin (and sometimes destruction warlock), and settling provocative Tolkien debates, such as why the Great Eagles are not Gandalf's personal taxi service. Passionate about travel, she's been to over twenty countries collecting sparks of inspiration, and is always planning her next adventure.

Sarah and her husband live in a beautiful corner of SE Pennsylvania with their three tiny benevolent pug dictators.

www.sarahmcradit.com

SARAH M CRADIT

WEAVER *of* WORLDS

Printed in the USA
CPSIA information can be obtained
at www.ICGtesting.com
LVHW072046190923
758698LV00024B/157/J